THERE WILL BE WAR

VOLUME X

CASTALIA HOUSE

MILITARY SCIENCE FICTION

Riding the Red Horse Volume 1 ed. Tom Kratman and Vox Day
Starship Liberator by David VanDyke and B.V. Larson
Battleship Indomitable by David VanDyke and B.V. Larson

SCIENCE FICTION

CTRL-ALT REVOLT! by Nick Cole
Soda Pop Soldier by Nick Cole
Pop Kult Warrior by Nick Cole
City Beyond Time by John C. Wright
Superluminary by John C. Wright
Back From the Dead by Rolf Nelson

FICTION

Turned Earth: a Jack Broccoli Novel by David the Good
The Missionaries by Owen Stanley
The Promethean by Owen Stanley
An Equation of Almost Infinite Complexity by J. Mulrooney
Six Expressions of Death by Mojo Mori
Loki's Child by Fenris Wulf
Hitler in Hell by Martin van Creveld

FANTASY

No Gods Only Daimons by Kai Wai Cheah
Iron Chamber of Memory by John C. Wright
The Green Knight's Squire by John C. Wright
The Dark Avenger's Sidekick by John C. Wright

NON-FICTION

Winning the War on Weeds by John Moody
Ship of Fools by C. R. Hallpike
The Last Closet by Moira Greyland
The Nine Laws by Ivan Throne
A History of Strategy by Martin van Creveld
Compost Everything by David the Good
Grow or Die by David the Good
Push the Zone by David the Good
Free Plants for Everyone by David the Good

THERE WILL BE WAR

VOLUME X

EDITED BY
JERRY POURNELLE

CASTALIA HOUSE

There Will Be War Vol. X
Edited by Jerry Pournelle

Published by Castalia House
Tampere, Finland
www.castaliahouse.com

Assistant Editor: Vox Day
Cover Art: Lars Braad Andersen

Contents

INTRODUCTION

When the *There Will Be War* series began, the Cold War was on with a vengeance. Twenty-six thousand nuclear warheads were aimed at the United States. Marxism had faded within the Communist Party, but Marxist/Leninist doctrine remained the official ruling principle; and it held that the worldwide establishment of the Dictatorship of the Proletariat—Communist rule—was inevitable. Détente was possible, but never peace; class war always continued. Most of the Nomenklatura—the inner ruling circle of the Communist Party—might be skeptical, but all of them had compulsorily taken many hours of Marxist theory in University, as well as the usual doctrines taught in grade and high school, and all claimed to believe in the scientific truth of Marxism.

The United States had endured the long and divisive Cold War. Korea, then Viet Nam, claimed American lives, but neither ended in victory parades or peace. The Cold War continued, and both sides kept ready-alert nuclear forces, with bomber crews ready to man their B-52's, and young men, then young men and women, spent much time deep underground, waiting for the sound of the klaxon and the dread words: "EWO. EWO. Emergency War Orders. Emergency War Orders. I have a message in five parts. Message begins. Tango. X-ray. Papa. Kilo...."

The protracted conflict came to an end in 1990, and then the Soviet Union itself dissolved. The series, *There Will Be War*, ended shortly thereafter, and the United States stood down in anticipation of a well-earned era of peace. The Strategic Air Command, the elite force which had existed to fight a world nuclear war, was disbanded, along with Systems Command, whose mission was to design and build the weapons of a future war that would never come. The blitzkrieg of the First Gulf War did little to dispel that illusion. There would be brush fires, world police activities, but the future was clear. The history of war had come to an end. One popular book even proclaimed "The End of History"; it would take time, but it was now inevitable that history would progress to its natural conclusion, a peaceful coalition of liberal democracies.

That belief vanished on the morning of September 11, 2001. Well before the rubble of what had once been the tallest buildings in America was cleared, the United States had already embarked on what has proven to be the longest war in her history. The armed forces responded splendidly. But what would have been glorious victory in another era became the prelude to endless nightmares as the civilian leadership tried vainly to build liberal democracy in lands that wanted no part of it; asymmetric war in the form of terror spread from Iraq to Syria to Paris to San Bernardino. A new power, dedicated to world peace through world submission, arose from the ashes of Iraq and continues to steadily grow.

History has not ended. The world has not united in peace and liberal democracy. This series has been revived to again offer stories and essays on the challenges of the future; in a time when *There Will Be War*. Herewith Volume Ten.

Jerry Pournelle
Studio City, 2015

The Man Who Wasn't There

Gregory Benford

Editor's Introduction

I have known Professor Greg Benford for a long time. He participated in the studies that generated the Strategic Defense Initiative, both in the Council I chaired to advise the incoming Reagan Administration in 1980 and many other venues, and he is well known for his non-fiction.

He is also a well-known science fiction writer. His latest works have been collaborations with Larry Niven on stories of the far future, but he has also paid attention to the news.

Given the events in Paris last month, this story is timely; but in fact it was one of the first chosen for this book and was accepted well before the Paris massacre. High tech versus low tech in defending the security of Western Civilization; another battle in a war that has gone on since before Charles Martel turned the tide at Tours in 732 A.D. But tides ebb and flow, and still the war continues.

The security 'bots zoomed around the looming mosque like supersonic butterflies in the cold air. Jean watched them with his infrared eyes as their tiny plumes darted over the bare zone, blazing high tech fireflies. They patrolled silently over the wide stone plaza, watching for movement up and down the spectral bands.

Sentinels of Islam in a suburb of Paris. Around the butterfly buzz hung a weekday midnight silence. Incense flavored the air with a pungent reek.

"*Merde du jour*," he muttered. The Islamic Front could afford the butterflies. They fed on endless money from the Saudis, part of the campaign to restore Islam to Europe after the regrettable Christian Era.

Not restored by the sword, of course—they were hopeless on a battlefield. But now, in softened consumerist Europe, their shopworn push-pull strategies of terror and political demand still worked. Islamic Front had plenty of followers in the immigrant masses. Their code of strict secrecy—talk and you die, unpleasantly—made them potent. Against them the French government deployed lawyers. Thinking of them, he spat on the floor of the apartment he had rented.

"Ready, Ajax?" He got a coded blip in answer—OK.

Time to move. Nobody knew where the Front would strike next with bombs, kidnappings, violent protests. Plus the usual rhetoric about being repressed. Very effective.

They had made such claims back in Lyon, after a street brawl on Montclair Boulevard. That was years ago, just as the Front started to use advanced technologies. All cameras, videos, and other recording systems near Montclair Boulevard had been blank, so the Front could claim that the fighting and the car bomb that followed were the work of others. So it had gone now for years, an arms race of technologies.

Unless, of course, the plans of the Islamic Front could be tapped. But that meant getting in fast, silent, deadly. Tonight.

Inside the shadowy compound ahead, the Head was at work. Under the shield of the looming mosque, he sent agents forth. He hid behind some holy name, but French Intelligence had pinpointed the Head's movements, and now was the time to strike. Remembering Montclair Boulevard.

Jean said softly, "Take out the microwaves."

Silently, the side teams did.

The details registered in his left eye, fed from his wearable computer. The Front was using the minarets at the square's corners to mount their detectors. Jean could see their snouts peeking out of the corbelled designs that wrapped around each artfully curved dome atop the minarets. The surveillance cameras were the usual IR motion-sensing type. But they were all connected to a central security center—the usual control-freak arrangement. They could be defeated by intersecting their microwave links, saturating them, blowing the electronics down the line.

Jean ordered the teams to open up. Soundless beams lanced instantly into the broad square of the compound. They were aimed at receivers, jamming the link back to the security center that squatted down on the mosque's roof.

Simple, really—flood them with a high-powered noise-spectrum signal. Their cameras looked in all directions, their sensors wide open in the winter dark—so they could be attacked from any direction, jammed from any angle. Thank God—whichever version you liked, Jean thought—the Front hadn't thought to use laser links—easier to find, but far harder to block or saturate.

"Their links are cut," came a whispered comm message from a nearby apartment, diagonally across the square.

"Now the security 'bots."

Microwave pulses transfixed each of the fireflies darting around the mosque square. Short bursts of microwaves flooded their diodes. The butterflies abruptly tumbled to the cobblestones.

He rasped in a short breath and beeped Ajax into action. "Send in the silver," Jean said. His buddy Ajax was in a silver suit, though why it got that name Jean never knew.

He switched to another spectrum, far beyond the visible, and searched for Ajax. Silver suits were layers of optical fibers and sensors, ever-watchful in all directions. There—

Ajax was a shifting blob of shimmering blue light in Jean's UV goggles, well beyond what ordinary cameras could capture. Each square centimeter of the silver suit took incoming light and routed it through chips, moving the image—say, of a wall—around the body, on its way to the directly opposite side of the suit. There another optical fiber emitted the same image in the same direction. It was as though the ray had passed through Ajax's body. Any guard looking toward the suit saw only the wall, as though nothing stood between them.

The silver suit gave Ajax invisibility. Jean watched as the blob flexed and moved across the Islamic Front's broad open plaza, toward the shadowy, looming mosque. He reached the first barrier, a cluster of concrete blocks, and just walked around them. Up in the minarets Jean could see shifting shadows. The guards had noticed that their gear was down.

"Here comes the glare," he sent on comm.

Searing light swept the compound. Spotlights on the minarets and the main mosque sent blaring beams into every corner.

Good coverage, Jean noted. Not that it would do them any good.

Because Ajax was inside by now. "I got it," Ajax's voice whispered in his ears.

Meaning that he had used the tap-and-read gear strapped to his wrist. It sent an electric charge wave through a lock and used the rebound signal to figure out the lock's codes. The information was buried in the door, so it had to be user-reachable. Almost like a dog waiting for the right signal from its master to go fetch a ball.

Well, Jean thought, the ball was in play now. "Follow on," he sent, and two more silver suits started across the compound's square. They came in from the sides. He could see them moving fast, wrinkled UV ghosts.

The guards up in the minarets had their hands full, scanning the square and seeing nothing. Not even their motion-sensing cameras could see anything through the smoky frequencies.

Shouts echoed across the square. Getting the reserve house guard up from their beds.

Time to get serious. "Blow their electrical."

Microwave bursts curled through the chill air. They were vectored in on the mosque's power source, where their standard external current hookup met their in-house generator. Throw the diodes there into confusion, blowing most of them with thirty kilowatts of bursty microwaves, and kiss your amperes goodbye.

The spotlight glare vanished. The minor mosque lamps went too. Louder shouts.

Jean was already running out of the apartment building. His IR took in the sputtering of random gunfire from the minarets. They were shooting blind, chunking rounds into the cobblestones. It was easy to avoid their sweeps.

But that gave his side all the excuse they needed. Snipers in nearby buildings took out the men in the minarets within seconds.

Halfway to the mosque, all fell silent. He could hear his own whooshing breath, it was that still.

The main gate was still locked but the side door yawned. He went through into utter blackness, dark even to him in IR.

In his left eye he received Ajax's map of the interior. It was made by a satellite, integrating the GPS feedback from Ajax and figuring out the implied mosque geometry.

Here—down a corridor and around a small high-roofed room like a chapel. Two men milled around in the room, shouting to each other. One fumbled to turn on a flashlight and Jean punched a button on his right wrist. It sent a skreeee he heard in the microwave spectrum. That caused flash-over of the filaments in flashlight bulbs. Sure enough, the tall, swarthy man could not get the flash to light up. Jean slipped by him.

They were saying something in French but Jean didn't bother to figure out their panicked sentences as they flung their arms about. He skirted around them and down a hallway. More men there, armed but blind. The place reeked of sour sweat and fear.

Ajax had left bootprints that showed up in crimson in his high-UV spectrum. He followed them through a room crammed with computers, all dead, and down a long corridor lined with AK-47s in steel wall racks.

Jean had his automatic out in his right hand but didn't intend to use it. The flash would give the enemy momentary light.

"Found the Head," Ajax sent.

"How is he?"

"Holed up in a safe room, looks like."

"Blow it."

"Already set up to. Punched a hole through at the top, wide enough for the percussion grenade."

"Go."

The boom rocked down the hallway and slapped Jean in the face. As he ran up to it he could see the massive door was skewed on its hinges. Ajax was a shimmer in Jean's goggles, planting a second charge. They wedged it into place at the top hinge.

Angry shouts came from behind them. Another silversuit came up, firing backward with a silenced pistol. The shouts stopped.

They all trotted down the corridor and Ajax hit his hand-held trigger. The blast was deafening. Fragments slammed into his carbon-fiber body armor.

Jean stepped through the yawning frame, a smell of something burnt curling up into his nostrils. Six bodies were slammed against the walls, clad in kaftans. Blood trickled from their ears. He had to check three before he was sure that they had the Head. The leathery face was contorted, gray foam oozed at the mouth, and Jean reflected that this did not look like someone who had ordered the deaths of thousands. Now it was just a shriveled little man.

The third silversuit was a surgeon, his ID patch glowing in the UV. Jean pointed and the surgeon knelt beside the Head.

"Pretty bad," the surgeon said.

"Dead?"

"Not yet, but he may have injected himself." Up came the sleeves of the kaftan and there was a plain needle mark. "Damn."

"How long have we got?" Jean asked.

"Maybe ten minutes."

Out came the tool kit and quick hands started to work.

It took only five minutes. Jean stared at the Head's face and thought about Montclair Boulevard. Then they started out, carrying the body in a sling.

There was fighting outside but it died down. He monitored the operation on a screen in his left eye lens, watching the support troops come in from all sides. Green motes circled and lit on the mosque grounds—choppers and ultralights. Some automatic weapons fire rose to greet them. The return fire lanced down, computer-directed by juddering robot guns in mini-aircraft.

It had been easy enough to take out the Islamic Front guards. Just attacking was simple, but experience showed that you got very little information that way. Jean had learned from their battles in Lyon, where the Front had many tendrils. Yet they had few ways to trace the Byzantine network that decades of immigrant communities had established.

A sour truth emerged from those years. The Front had learned that they could keep no database without risking its loss, so the only systematic memory was carried around in a few leaders' heads, encoded and rote-memorized. So there was only one way to get it.

They hauled the body out on a stretcher. Halfway out the one thing they could not defend against struck Ajax—low tech.

Ajax had the lead. A small bomb's sharp thump cut through him. It may have been triggered by his passage, armed sometime in the last few minutes. Acrid fumes filled the passageway.

Jean knelt in the iron scent of spilled blood. The charge had slammed down from the ceiling, punching in from above. The head was all blood and shattered white bone.

He could see Ajax was gone. A sour cough erupted from his throat, anguish throttled down. No time to rage, not now. *We came to kidnap a mind and Ajax lost his head for it.*

He used hand signs to get them moving again. He put Ajax out of his mind for the moment, a habit he had learned since his brother's death.

Army troops were securing the rest of the mosque, small arms rattling far down the hallways. There were still no lights and everyone was operating in the infrared, moving carefully.

The chopper waited just outside, squatting on the square with its ultra-rotors purring. Jean went with the surgeon. There was a lot of medical gear in the chopper bay and the specialists got the body into it while they lifted off. Jean looked out across the square at the maze of running men and bodies, the scene moving in an eerie hush except for the working machines.

Half an hour later he got to see the results. They had the entire top floor of a hospital. Jean went into the bare white clean room wearing whites and stood at the end of the operating theatre. They were all quiet here, too.

The Head was talking, in its way. The body lay spread out, heart machine chugging, the lungs heaving to the steady stroke of a breather-driver. The Head was certainly dead but the cowl of leads blossoming from his shaved skull was working. There were subtle ways to drive post-mortem synapses and force a memory to make its connections.

On the screens around the operating theatre the data flowed like syrup. Images, faces, cross-correlations like thickets of yellow-green vines. The entire Islamic Front was there, layered and bunched in cords and streams.

"This guy was a real savant," a specialist said nearby. "Look how his memory was organized—like a multi-layered filing cabinet."

"Too bad he used it to store such *merde*," Jean said. He saw flicker across the screen a scene retrieved from the Head's recollections, the farmer's market in Lyon. Off to the left were the maple trees of Montclair Boulevard, where Jean's brother had been torn to shreds by the car bomb.

Swimming up from cloudy, static-filled memory came the scene before the explosion, too, frozen in dead memory. The car, moving forward into the crowd, seconds before the detonation. The point of view swiveled and there in the room were the faces of the plotters, three bearded ones. Their lips were thin and pale with compressed anger, their eyes sharp.

Jean memorized them in a moment. He turned and walked out, getting ready for the next attack, knowing now who to look for and thinking again of Montclair Boulevard.

SEVEN KILL TIGER

Charles W. Shao

Editor's Introduction

Technology can be created on demand, as Stefan Possony and I showed in *The Strategy of Technology*. This does not mean that all technologies should be created, merely that once something is possible, it is only a matter of time before it becomes real. There will be war; there will also be technologies that can only be deterred, not defended against.

Zhang Zedong stared at his screen in disbelief. The monthly production numbers had fallen again, down from the previous quarter's low that had already led to one alarmingly polite video call from the Vice-Chairman of the Central Military Commission. General Xu was not technically in his formal chain of command, but as the largest individual shareholder in the China African Industries Group, the general's opinion was of considerably more concern to Zhang than that of his immediate superior, the Executive Vice-President for East Africa.

The damned *hei ren* were going to get him replaced, he thought bitterly. If he was fortunate. In the event General Xu decided that the growing gap between the region's quarterly objectives and the actual results achieved was the consequence of excessive greed rather than Zhang's inability to make the natives work, his family would be receiving a bill for the price of the bullet used to execute him before long.

But he hadn't diverted any significant resources into his own pockets, not any more than was expected of an executive in his position. He didn't have more than eleven or twelve million dollars safely stashed away in his American bank accounts, and if his son was studying at the University of California, Berkeley, so were fifty other children of high-ranking Party members. Still, it would be enough to see him shot if the general was looking for an excuse.

What he needed was more reliable workers. What he needed was more Han people. In Zambia alone, there were now 750,000 Chinese living in what amounted to a small colonial city, but they lived in walled enclaves almost under siege from the thieves, robbers, and rapists who preyed upon them daily despite the best efforts of CAIG's security forces to protect them. The police were useless, worse than useless, actually, as they were often among the worst thieves and sexual predators of all.

He sighed. Africa would be a glorious place were it not for the Africans. He'd been warned before coming to Lusaka that ninety percent of the *hei ren* were thieves, but he discounted that warning as the customary Han superiority complex. After seven years of futility in attempting to turn CAIG's $35 billion investment in the country into something resembling a reasonable return, he was beginning to wonder if that estimate had been on the low side.

Lusaka had always been known for its crime, but of late the criminal gangs were getting bolder. Just last week, ten young *hei ren* armed with AK-47s shot dead the two African security guards outside a gated Chinese complex, raped four young Chinese girls, and kidnapped two mining company executives. The company had paid the ransoms, which were trivial, and gotten its executives back, but the fear and outrage in the business community was palpable. Then, to make matters even worse, one of the girls committed suicide in shame at having been violated by *hóuzi*, and now the hunger for revenge in the expat community was threatening to get out of control.

To absolutely no one's surprise, the local police proved unable to identify the perpetrators, let alone arrest them. As far as Zhang could tell, they genuinely had no idea which of the eight gangs actively operating in the city might have been responsible.

If only the National People's Congress had followed through on its original plan to send 100 million colonists to Africa! But that plan had met with *intense* international criticism, and it wouldn't necessarily be enough anyhow; the problem wasn't limited to the dearth of Han labor. Bringing in more proper workers would solve the production problem, but it wouldn't solve the crime problem or the growing fraternization problem either. Far too many Chinese girls had fallen for the blandishments of persistent African suitors, failing to understand why the locals had so much time to pursue them or realize that the liaisons were unlikely to go anywhere in the long term. Even on the rare occasions a marriage did come to pass, what resulted was seldom what the average Chinese girl understood to be marriage.

African men thought of themselves as lions, and they lived like kings of beasts, entirely content to lounge about living off the labor of one or more of his lionesses. And the girls who succumbed to their exotic appeal could not return to China, not those who bore half-African bastards anyway. It was a growing problem, and even if it wasn't Zhang's responsibility, as CAIG's Senior Vice-President and Director for Zambia, Zimbabwe, Mozambique, and Tanzania, there were many looking to him to find a solution. But what was he supposed to do, ban interracial relations? Temporarily sterilize every Chinese woman between the ages of 10 and 40? Forbid Chinese firms to hire locals for even the most menial jobs? Any action that might make a substantive difference would generate a hailstorm of international protest that would focus very unwanted attention on him from General Xu, and perhaps even the Central Commission.

What he needed, he decided, was new ideas. Everything he had tried to date had failed. Positive incentives, negative incentives, threats, bribes, and shouting, everything had failed. The Americans had a curious phrase he'd heard once on a visit to California, the "Come to Jesus" meeting. He didn't quite grasp what it meant, exactly, but he decided it would serve as his inspiration for the staff meeting he intended to call tomorrow morning. Because if they didn't come up with something that at least had the *potential* to lead the way out of this utter debacle, he fully intended to rain fire and brimstone down upon them all.

He might not be able to avoid going down himself, but he could damn well ensure that he didn't go down alone.

* * *

Philip Thompson was reading a report of a small measles outbreak in Ecuador when a knock on the open door to his office disturbed him. He looked up and saw it was Scott Berens, one of his junior analysts, standing in the doorway.

"You heard about Ecuador, Dr. Thompson?" the younger man asked.

"Reading about it now. Looks as if the government has it under control."

"They caught it early enough. It's the Tungurahua province again. That's been a problem area for the Ministry of Health since 1996. The vaccination program misses too many of the indigenous children."

"Understandable." Thompson put the report down on his desk. "What's on your mind, Scott?"

"Do you remember that unknown outbreak in northern Zambia we started tracking six months ago?"

"I thought that was a false alarm."

"It was, insofar as we were able to determine that it wasn't Ebola, which was the initial concern. And there were only 142 cases and 26 deaths before it burned itself out, so we didn't even bother sending anyone over to investigate."

Thompson clicked his tongue against his lower lip, wondering where Berens was going with this. The young man was a bright young doctor and had graduated in the top ten percent of his class from Johns Hopkins, so he assumed Berens must have a good reason for bringing such an obscure incident to his attention.

"Are you saying we should have?"

"No, it's just that I was reading over the statistics, as part of a paper I was thinking about writing on east Africa, when I noticed an anomaly."

"What's that?"

"The population of the nearest town. It's mostly Chinese. I think they have a big mining camp up there."

Thompson shrugged and spread his hands. "It's hardly a secret that China has been moving into Africa in a big way for the last two decades. They have hundreds of such towns."

"True, but that only explains why the Chinese were there. It doesn't explain why most of the cases, and all of the deaths, were African. Only five Chinese were affected and all five recovered. Beyond the basic statistical odds involved, you would think the native population would be more *resistant* to whatever virus makes its way out of the jungle, not more susceptible to it."

Thompson frowned. Berens was right. It was an anomaly. And if there was one thing he had learned after 22 years at the Center for Disease Control, it was to pay particular attention to anomalies.

"Good catch, Scott. Dig into it and see if it's really just a mining town or if the PLA happens to have any laboratories or science facilities in the area. Not necessarily where the outbreak took place, but anywhere in the surrounding area. They went dark on the bio-war front a few years ago, and it may be that some of their test facilities were moved from Xi'an to Africa. This just might give us some insight as to where they went."

"Do you think someone got careless and a bio-weapon escaped the lab, Dr. Thompson?" There was an eager glint in the younger man's eyes that made Thompson smile despite himself. Such a discovery, even if it was never published in any of the public journals, could be the making of Berens's career, and both of them knew it.

"Let's not get ahead of ourselves, Scott. Go and see what you can find about this mining town, what is it called?"

"Mpolokoso."

"Right." He didn't even bother trying to pronounce it. "Look into what the Chinese are doing there and we'll see if it could have any connection to this mysterious outbreak. Write it up and email it to me; I'll call you when I've had a chance to read it and think it over."

"Will do, Dr. Thompson!" Berens made a mock salute with the paper and disappeared from the doorway.

Thompson leaned back in his chair, reflecting on the unwelcome news. Unlike his young subordinate, he already knew they weren't likely to find any evidence of laboratories, research facilities, an escaped bio-weapon, or even anything that was conventionally considered to be a bio-weapon. Conventional bio-weapons didn't discriminate between Asian and Sub-Saharan haplogroups. Genetic weapons, on the other hand, were designed to do just that. And he very much doubted that whatever it was had been released accidentally.

After consulting his contact list, he tapped in the number for Fort Detrick. A young enlisted woman answered the phone.

"US-AMRIID. How may I direct your call?"

"This is Dr. Phil Thompson of the CDC. Get me Colonel Hill, please."

"Right away, sir." She paused. "The CDC... is this urgent, sir?"

He smiled grimly. "That's exactly what I'm trying to determine."

* * *

It was the massacre that convinced Zhang to take action. After a Chinese entrepreneur's young daughter in Kapiri Mposhi was raped and killed by a pair of copper miners, the man took his vengeance by tracking the perpetrators down and shooting them dead at the New Kapira Mphoshi railway station. The shootings were caught on closed-circuit television, and before Zhang or anyone in Lusaka even knew about the incident, the images had spread all over Zambia and Tanzania, inflaming the African community, and in particular, the Nyanja-Chewa tribe to which the two miners belonged.

Within a week, all 87 Chinese residents of Kapiri Mposhi were dead. Some had been shot, some had been necklaced, but most had fallen to the knives of the *Nyau*, a masked secret society known for black magic and channeling the spirits of the dead. The pictures had been horrific. Zhang stared at them for a long time.

Black magic. I will show them black magic. I will show them their worst nightmares!

The Kapiri Mposhi massacre had been six months ago. Now the time to unleash the spirits of righteous vengeance had very nearly come, Zhang thought, as a tall young scientist entered his office. Gao Xing was humble and diffident. Despite his height, he could have walked down the street in Weinan or Xi'an without anyone taking notice of him. Only his eyes gave any sign that he might be unusual. They were coldly arrogant, and conveyed little in the way of warmth or humanity. He was in his middle twenties, and his pale skin indicated that he spent very little time outside under the Zambian sun.

The perfect scientist, Zhang thought wryly. The poor kid had probably never had a girlfriend. But the young girl in Kapiri Mposhi, the very first one to die, had been his cousin. He might not know how to love, but assuredly, he knew how to hate.

"They tell me your most recent test of *Huáng Hu* was successful."

"Yes, Director. The terminal rate is now in excess of 80 percent. Based on the most conservative spread models, the pseudo-epidemic will cross the Angolan border within two weeks. Within nine months, the continent is expected to be clear of all undesirable populations. The task of disposal will obviously be enormous, and will create considerable additional health hazards, but I would expect that it would be safe to begin the settlement programs within 18 months of zero day."

"Zero day?"

"The date upon which any opposing forces will be unable to stop the virus from going terminal in the target population. The estimates vary, but the average indicates zero day is D-day plus 28."

"Is there any way to reduce the time to zero day?"

"Increase the number of transmission vectors, preferably in a manner scattered widely across the continent."

Zhang nodded. "I will think on that."

"If I may offer a suggestion, Director?"

"Please do."

"There is an American foundation that has malaria vaccination campaigns running in every country in Africa. If a way could be found to substitute the substances injected, zero day could be reduced to a matter of two weeks or less."

"Wouldn't that increase the risk of detection?"

"Certainly." The young scientist's dark eyes were unperturbed. "But in light of how the vaccination campaigns are already regarded with a significant amount of local suspicion, detection would likely sow sufficient confusion to inhibit any effective response. Especially because the NGOs tasked with the response would be widely regarded as the guilty parties."

"And combined with cutting the potential response time in half, it's almost surely worth the risk as long as the substitutions can be made undetected."

"I cannot speak to that, Director. It is outside my competence."

Zhang thought a moment. "It's too risky to interfere with the Americans. We don't know their protocols. But Sinovac has a polio vaccine that's already been prequalified by the World Health Organization and the Global Polio Eradication Initiative has endorsed it as a substitute for their primary oral vaccine. It would be much easier to substitute that. We can even arrange to have the vaccines shipped in through Dar es Salaam."

"As you say, Director."

Zhang couldn't help but smile. The young scientist could not have made his indifference to anything but the technical aspects related to his specialty any more clear. "The potential consequences do not trouble you, Dr. Gao?"

"Not in the slightest, Director Zhang. To the contrary, you have my deepest admiration. What you propose to accomplish will make the Great Leap Forward appear little more than a precursor to the true advancement. What began as a Cultural Revolution has become a Scientific Revolution. Soon China will stand astride the globe as the master of two continents, and the nations of the world will bow before her!"

Zhang found himself mildly appalled by the young man's fanaticism. Did Mao ever feel similarly alarmed by the enthusiasm of his own Red Guards? But the sentiments Gao expressed were sound enough. Africa was wasted on the Africans. China had spent 50 million Chinese lives to become a 20th-century power, how could she hesitate to spend twenty times that many more African lives to assume her rightful place as the one true 21st-century superpower?

"Thank you, Dr. Gao."

"Director." The young man bowed and left his office.

Zhang reflected on Gao's words. A Scientific Revolution. A Greater Leap Forward! The young scientist's confidence in the project quelled any remaining doubts that it was time to move forward and let the Central Military Commission know about his plans for the Dark Continent. But one question still remained: to release *Huáng Hu* before or after General Xu's scheduled visit?

It would be a shame, after all, if he were to be executed before releasing the spirits to seek their revenge.

The World Health Organization (WHO) has announced the pre-qualification of a Chinese-made vaccine for polio. The new WHO pre-qualified vaccine is produced by Sinovac Biotech Ltd, and is an inactive-virus vaccine that is considered to be safer than the live-virus vaccines now widely used across Asia and Africa.

"WHO prequalification of the Sinovac vaccine is another feather in the cap of China's growing vaccine manufacturing industry," said Dr. Bernhard Schwartländer, WHO Representative in China.

"This is also very good news for the millions of children in low- and middle-income countries which cannot afford to manufacture or purchase their inactive-virus vaccines. WHO prequalification of Sinovac's vaccine will add to the worldwide arsenal of anti-polio vaccines, assisting the global campaign to eradicate the disease. In doing so, it will help to save lives," Dr Schwartländer said.

Sinovac's polio vaccine is the second vaccine made in China to achieve WHO prequalification, following prequalification of a Japanese-made encephalitis vaccine in 2013 and Hualan Biological's influenza vaccine in 2015.

Philip Thompson shook his head as he returned the printout to Scott Berens. "You don't seriously imagine that the Chinese would use a weaponized vaccine as a vehicle for genetic warfare, do you? They could maybe get one hot lot into the distribution system, two at most, and I can't imagine that could possibly be worth permanently trashing their ability to access the export markets!"

"No, of course not." His subordinate shrugged. "You told me to dig up anything that might be related to possible launch vectors. This is the only one I found that could conceivably be connected to Chinese corporate activity in the last two years."

"I'd use bird flu myself," Thompson mused.

"What's that?"

"If you're going to weaponize something, an aerosol vector is the most effective. And the world is accustomed to bird flu coming out of China every few years. That's what that vaccine from Hualan was, it was an H1N1 vaccine. You could even combine the two, put the bomb in the flu virus itself, then trigger it with the vaccine."

"Now who is imagining things, Doctor?"

Thompson smiled. "Well, perhaps it's nothing after all. There haven't been any further outbreaks in the last six months, so I suppose it was simply another unknown jungle disease. Here is hoping we've seen the last of it."

* * *

General Xu stood staring motionless at the image of the continent of Africa on the screen, his hands clasped behind his back, his square face impassive and unreadable. Zhang watched the man closely, looking for some sign of approval, of anger, of anything that would give him some indication of his fate. Finally, the general turned to face him, and something in the soldier's eyes seemed to indicate that he was feeling powerful emotion.

To Zhang's utter astonishment, the general bowed to him, so deeply that his torso was nearly parallel to the floor. Zhang didn't know what to do; he just stood there respectfully and hoped that the general's action was a good sign.

"You are a man of rare vision and a great tribute to our race," General Xu said hoarsely. "Not since *da duo shou* himself has China been blessed with a man of such insight! You have broken the power of the gun that has kept us chained since the *yingguo ren* arrived! You have abolished war with science!"

"The General is not displeased?"

The general indicated the screen. "Far from it. Your proposal is promising, extremely promising, Director. I will go to Beijing immediately and consult with the Chairman. How soon can you begin?"

"Three weeks. The next shipment from Sinovac will arrive in ten days. I am told it will take four days to replace the vaccines and reseal the vials. Then we will need to distribute them to the aid offices. We will start the flu-based vector in Mozambique two weeks prior to the first inoculations. Even if the Americans or the Europeans somehow manage to react quickly to one attack, the very effort required to do so will inhibit their ability to respond to the other."

"Remarkable!" The general shook his head admiringly. "Director, surely you were inspired by your ancestors! What led you to conceive such a vision?"

"Once all struggle is grasped, miracles are possible."

"Well said. What is the name of this miracle?"

"*Huáng Hu.*"

General Xu was an educated man. He smiled. "How very appropriate, Director. I shall inform you of the Chairman's decision before the end of the week. You will launch the initial phase on his command."

Zhang bowed, feeling both triumph and relief. It seemed he would survive the day. And the restless ghosts of Kapiri Mposhi would be avenged, a thousandfold and more. "Thank you, General."

* * *

As his Prius moved silently through the Georgia night, Philip Thompson thought about what he'd learned from his conversation earlier that day with Colonel Hill. He didn't know how to feel about the information he was trying to process. Far from being unthinkable, it was apparent to anyone capable of reading between the lines that the U.S. Army had already developed genetic weapons very similar to those he'd adduced the Chinese were developing. Moreover, the Russian Army and the IDF were well along the process of doing the same.

It was madness. Sheer madness. The world's militaries were quite literally preparing—prepared—to undo everything that Man's most dedicated warriors against the dread Rider on the White Horse had ever accomplished. The painstaking labor of decades could be undone in a matter of hours, and with a genocidal precision that had hitherto been literally unimaginable. Even though he'd known the United States could not permit itself to fall behind in such an important technological aspect of war, it was shattering to know, to actually have it confirmed beyond any shadow of a doubt, that his own government was preparing to exterminate entire populations. It was possible. There was no defense, as such. There was only deterrence. Or, perhaps, revenge.

How are we any better than them? The thought of warring genocides sickened him, all the more so knowing that he and all of his colleagues would be the first to be drafted and put on the front lines—the front labs—if any such genetic war should erupt. He was a doctor, he was a scientist, he was a *healer*. He had gone into medicine, and after that, science, in order to help people, not to kill them on an industrial scale!

And the worst thing was that he could not unburden his soul to anyone; the colonel had let him know, in no uncertain terms, that if he so much breathed a word of what he had learned to anyone else at the CDC, let alone the press, he would be prosecuted for violating national security.

The garage door recognized his license plate and opened automatically as he approached. He parked the car, took his briefcase from the passenger seat, and walked through the parking garage to the elevator. His apartment was on the fifth floor, and there was an audible snick as the door's face-scanner recognized him and unlocked the door. But he stopped in the doorway after opening the door: there was a soft glow from the living room indicating that one of the lights was on.

That was strange. He worked late so often that he was always careful to make sure the lights were all out before he left in the morning, so as not to waste electricity. Then he shrugged and closed the door behind him. He'd had a lot on his mind recently and must have forgotten to turn one of them off.

But when he walked down the hallway and turned the corner, he froze. An Asian man dressed all in black was sitting in his recliner, legs crossed, casually perusing the previous month's issue of *Nature*.

"Good evening. Have a seat, Dr. Thompson." The intruder indicated the couch to his right. He spoke perfect, unaccented English.

Dumbfounded and frightened, Philip obeyed. What are you doing here, he wanted to demand, but he was afraid that he already knew the answer. Did the man have a gun? He probably did. Was it worth trying to make a break for one of the knives in the kitchen? No, almost certainly not.

"You needn't be alarmed, Dr. Thompson. I realize this is unsettling, but please understand that I'm not here to harm you."

Philip swallowed hard, then couldn't help exhaling heavily with sudden relief. He hadn't even realized he was holding his breath.

"Why… why are you here?"

The intruder smiled, flashing straight white teeth. Probably not Japanese. Chinese-American? "I am here to encourage you to take that vacation in Hawaii. According to your calendar, it begins tomorrow. Fourteen days on Maui, at the Grand Wailea. It's about time you used up some of that vacation time you've been hoarding, after all."

"Hawaii? I don't have a vacation–"

"Ah, but you do!" The Asian man produced a folder and withdrew airplane tickets and an itinerary before sliding them across the coffee table to Philip. "If you check your emails, you'll see that you requested a vacation three months ago and it was approved by Deputy Director Sansom back in May."

"You hacked the CDC computers?"

"Dr. Thompson, with all due respect, we've been privy to all of your communications with Colonel Hill and everyone else at AMRIID for months. Making a few modifications to your email server is about as difficult as changing an undergraduate's grades at Georgia Tech."

"What do you expect me to do?"

"Take the vacation. And then, when they fly you to Frederick, do your job. Analyze the virus and tell them the truth about it."

"The truth. What is that?"

"The fact that the virus is no threat at all to 98 percent of the American population. Aside from some recent immigrants, most of whom are not American citizens anyway, your people will be entirely unaffected."

Philip sat back, his mind racing, rapidly putting together the various facts at his disposal. It was obvious that the man was a Chinese intelligence agent. Then he gasped. "Dear God! Is your government intending to murder the entire sub-Saharan population? That's over one billion people!"

"I have no idea, Dr. Thompson. We can speculate if you like, but I imagine you probably know more about it than I do. My part in this ends tonight, whereas you still have a very important role to play. In fact, one might go so far as to say the fate of the entire human race is in your hands. That's why I am here speaking to you now. It is possible that you will be all that stands in the way of a third world war."

Still reeling from the horrific conclusion he'd reached, Philip could only shake his head. Mass murder? The human race in his hands? World War III?

"When the news of the virus breaks, there will be widespread fear throughout your government hierarchy. Even panic. It is very important that someone with sufficient stature and the ability to understand exactly what is happening will be in a position to tell your President, and his generals, that there is no serious threat to America. My superiors do not wish to see a necessary evil transformed into an unnecessary apocalypse. Neither a genetic war nor a nuclear war between China and the United States will serve anyone's interests, as I'm sure you will admit."

"Retaliation," Philip murmured. "You want me to tell them not to retaliate."

"I expect you to tell them that retaliation would be tantamount to mutual suicide," the agent corrected. "As is, in fact, the case. As I said, we simply want you to enjoy your vacation, then do your job and tell them the truth. Nothing more than the truth. It is well within your competence."

"I assume that if I don't keep my mouth shut about what you are intending, you will kill me."

The agent smiled regretfully and gave a slight nod. "We are, of course, monitoring you very closely. If you attempt to communicate with anyone—anyone—then I fear it is very likely that a disgruntled former employee will return to the CDC with a pair of inexpensive handguns and kill a number of people there, yourself included, before committing suicide."

He withdrew another piece of paper from his folder and slid it across to Philip. It was a color printout with ten photographs, driver's licenses by the looks of them, and each one was familiar to Philip. Two former girlfriends, two more casual liaisons, and six of the nine other members of his fantasy football league. All of them were friends, all of them were people he cared about.

Philip snorted bitterly and shook his head. The ruthless bastards certainly did their homework. He'd all but forgotten about the weekend fling with Caitlin five years ago. She was married to a banker now, with a baby at home and another on the way.

"You cannot prevent what is about to happen, Dr. Thompson. But you can stop an even greater horror from taking place. You cannot save the Africans, but you can save the rest of the human race."

The Chinese agent extended the folder in his gloved hand. Philip took it, then returned the sheet with the pictures on it, but retained the tickets.

"Very wise, Dr. Thompson."

"Can I ask you one question?"

For the first time, the agent looked surprised, but he nodded.

"How on Earth do you people sleep at night?"

The agent laughed, genuinely amused.

"Soundly, in the knowledge that we are serving our nation, Doctor. We sleep very soundly indeed."

* * *

The message from the Chairman of the Central Military Commission was a short one that consisted of only four ideographs. It seemed the Chairman, too, was an educated man. Zhang nodded solemnly to Dr. Gao, who peered at the screen in confusion.

"This means we are to proceed? 'Heaven births ten thousand things'? I don't understand. What does it mean, Director?"

"It means we are ordered to release *Huáng Hu*," Zhang said calmly. "Dr. Gao, release the Yellow Tiger."

Heaven brings forth innumerable things to nurture man.
Man has nothing good with which to recompense Heaven.
Kill. Kill. Kill. Kill. Kill. Kill. Kill.

THE 4GW COUNTERFORCE

William S. Lind and LtCol Gregory A. Thiele, USMC

Editor's Introduction

In general, the most effective armies have been armies of combined arms, but there have been periods of ascendency for many different kinds of arms. Historically, the decisive arm has usually been heavy infantry, but the colorful feudal era was for a long time dominated by heavy cavalry—mailed, mounted knights armed with lances, swords, and banners. Infantry is called the Queen of Battles, but in truth, infantry and artillery contested the title of the battlefield's decisive arm for a century. Then came motorized forces, armor, armored cavalry, aircraft, and ballistic missiles.

We now live in an era of irregulars and special forces, and technological weapons of previously unimagined power.

But the following statement by a contributor to the second volume of *There Will Be War* remains true all the same:

> *You may fly over a land forever; you may bomb it, atomize it, and wipe it clean of life—but if you desire to defend it, protect it, and keep it for civilization, you must do this on the ground, the way the Roman Legions did—by putting your soldiers in the mud.*
>
> —T.R. Fehrenbach, *This Kind of War*

The History of Light Infantry

Due to different meanings of the word "light," light infantry has been understood in diverse ways around the world. These interpretations can be grouped into two different points of view. The present American concept of light infantry is related to weight, specifically weight of equipment, while Europeans understand "light" as relating to agility or operational versatility. They see light infantry as a flexible force capable of operating in austere conditions with few logistical requirements and employing tactics unlike those of line or mechanized infantry.

The distinction between regular or line infantry and light infantry goes back to ancient Greece. At that time, the regular infantry was the phalanx, a linear formation that based its power on mass and shock. Their tactics consisted of evolutions performed by the phalanx as a whole, in which each warrior adhered to carefully executed drills.

In contrast, classic light infantry did not fight in fixed formations, nor did it adhere to any type of prescribed methods. Its primary mission was to provide flank protection to the phalanx. Widely dispersed throughout a large area, its soldiers lacked the heavy bronze armor worn by hoplites. The survivability of the light infantry depended on speed and the use of bows, slings, and hand-thrown weapons. Light infantry tactics consisted mainly of individual actions or simple, loosely coordinated group maneuvers that were generally limited to advancing or withdrawing. The Romans applied the Greek concept to their legions, using light auxiliary infantry to support the heavily armored cohorts of their regular infantry.

After the medieval era, when cavalry ruled the battlefield, the Spanish tercios of the 16th and 17th centuries signaled the return of the infantry's dominance. The development of light infantry in Europe followed in the 18th century. The French chasseurs, the Prussian Jaegers, and the Austrian Grenzer regiments followed the ancient Greek concept; in contrast to the rigid maneuvers of their line infantries, the light units were fast, agile, and expected to adapt their tactics to the terrain and the situation.

Much as their predecessors had been in the past, the Napoleonic light infantry was employed in a decentralized manner to protect the flanks of larger forces, and to execute raids and ambushes in restricted terrain. As before, the light infantry was always careful to avoid frontal engagements with the enemy. When it was wisely employed, light infantry could sometimes prevail over the enemy's regular infantry thanks to its adaptability and reliance on creative tactics rather than drilled battlefield order. These capabilities were achieved by selecting high-quality troops to serve in the light infantry, often professional hunters or foresters.

In spite of the proven utility of light infantry units, they were not established as permanent formations in European militaries. Light infantry units only prospered during wartime, and they were usually dissolved when the conflict ended. The catastrophic defeat in 1755 in Pennsylvania of the British forces under General Edward Braddock by a small force of Indians and French light infantry that employed ambush tactics and took advantage of terrain, agility, and loose formations convinced the British to create Roger's Rangers and the Royal American Regiment, both of which eventually became famous light infantry units during the French and Indian War. Typically, both were dissolved when the war ended.

Light infantry reappeared in Europe during the wars surrounding the French Revolution. The light infantry ceased to be regarded as an "undisciplined group of irregulars" and were transformed into trained professional units, able to maneuver in a decentralized, but fast and organized manner. Between 1790 and 1815, light forces proliferated, even evolving into light artillery and light cavalry units. They also assumed a more significant role on the battlefield. Yet their basic role remained no different than that of their ancient Greek predecessors, as the European light infantrymen covered the regular infantry's advances and withdrawals, and harassed the enemy by executing ambushes deep in its rear.

The appearance of the breech-loading rifle and the machine gun gradually reshaped regular infantry tactics, which began to resemble more closely those of light infantry. However, true light infantry retained advantages in agility, operational versatility, capability for living off the land, and decentralized command and control. The Boers of the Transvaal Republic; the Jaeger battalions, mountain units and Sturmtruppen of the German army of World War I; General Wingate's Chindits; and the paratroop units of the Israeli Defense Forces and the British army are examples of true modern light infantry.

The Light Infantry Mentality

The appearance of semi-automatic and automatic weapons narrowed the tactical distance between light infantry and regular infantry. However, the essential difference between them remains. It is not easily observed because it is an intangible factor: the mentality of the light infantryman.

The light infantryman is characterized by his mental resourcefulness and physical toughness. Light infantry's inborn self-reliance, reinforced by hard training, convinces the light infantryman that he is capable of overcoming the most difficult situations that combat presents. Light infantrymen do not feel defeated when surrounded, isolated or confronted by superior forces. They are able to continue performing their duties and pursue their objectives for long periods of time without any type of comfort or logistical support, usually obtaining what they require from the land or the enemy. They are neither physically nor psychologically tied to the rear by a need to maintain open lines of communication. Their tactics do not depend on supporting arms. This attitude of self-confidence and self-reliance provides light infantry with a psychological advantage over its opponents.

Thanks to its decentralized command philosophy, light infantry operates at a high tempo. An ambush mentality, a preference for unpredictability, and a reluctance to follow rigidly specified methods are the essence of light infantry tactics. The ambush mentality generates other secondary light infantry characteristics. One is the speed with which light infantry adapts to the terrain. Far from resisting adverse environmental conditions, light infantry exploits them by turning rough terrain to its advantage, using the terrain as a shield, a weapon, and a source of supplies.

As a result, light infantry has an incomparable superiority in those terrains that restrict most regular infantry operations (especially mechanized forces), usually allowing the light infantry to face and defeat larger and better-equipped enemy forces whenever it encounters them. This advantage gives the light infantry its distinctive operational versatility, as it is able to operate alone in restricted terrain or in a symbiotic relationship with friendly units.

Light infantry is readily adaptable to a broad range of missions, and it faces the natural evolution of technology and tactics that always takes place in wartime with no need to substantially modify the way it operates. It should now be easy to see that the correct meaning for the term "light" is not the American notion of weight, but the European concept of agility and operational versatility.

Light Infantry Tactics

Light infantry tactics are offensive in character, even during defensive operations. Light infantrymen do not hold a line. Light infantry tactics follow the principles of maneuver warfare, attacking by infiltration and defending by ambush. It uses ambushes on the offensive as well, by ambushing withdrawing or reinforcing enemy units, sometimes deep in the enemy's rear. Light infantry applies an ambush mentality to both planning and execution.

A good way to understand light infantry tactics is to think of them as similar to those often used by "aggressors" or the "red team" during training exercises. Lacking the means to execute their missions in textbook fashion, they fight by deceiving, stalking, infiltrating, dispersing, looking for vulnerabilities, ambushing and raiding. They often prove highly effective against larger "blue" forces.

Light infantry operations often follow a cycle that can be divided into four steps: Dispersion, Orientation, Concentration, and Action (DOCA). Dispersion provides light infantry with its main tool for survivability. Units remain hidden, taking advantage of the terrain, using camouflage and fieldcraft to evade detection. Orientation includes shaping actions that "set up" the enemy and permit rapid concentration. This step requires an aggressive use of reconnaissance to identify enemy vulnerabilities the light infantry can exploit.

Concentration allows light infantry to transform the small combat power of many dispersed elements into one or more powerful thrusts. Action is led by reconnaissance elements, which focus available forces and target a specified enemy weakness. Finally, a new and rapid dispersion ends the cycle, protecting the light infantry from enemy counteraction.

Light infantry offensive tactics usually use infiltration to avoid casualties. Infiltration allows light forces to surprise the enemy and engage him at short distances. In close, light infantry can exploit its small arms skills while denying the enemy effective employment of his superior firepower. Light infantry hugs the enemy and forces him to fight at short ranges on its terms.

Defensive Tactics and "Force Protection"

Light infantry defenses are dispersed and granular, which prevents the enemy from determining the exact location of the defense's front, flank, or rear areas. This protects light infantry from concentrated firepower. The light infantry commander assigns sectors to each of his subordinates, areas where they plan and execute successive, independent ambushes on advancing enemy formations. The "baited ambush" is a common technique, where a unit will feign retreat or even rout to draw enemy units into a new ambush. Defenses run parallel to, not across, enemy thrust lines. Light infantry often focuses its efforts against follow-on enemy units rather than spearheads.

When threatened, light infantry units break contact and move to alternate positions, setting up a new array of interconnected ambushes. Light infantry never fights a defensive battle from fixed positions or strong points. From the light infantry perspective, a good defensive position is one that surprises the enemy from a short distance, but at the same time enables the defender to move fast and under cover to a new position unknown to the enemy.

Since light infantry lives mostly off the land, its success depends heavily on the support of the local population. This dependence on local support means light infantry operations always need to avoid a negative impact on the inhabitants and the local economy, as well as rigorously observe local customs and culture. This ties in directly with requirements for success in Fourth Generation wars.

Light Infantry vs. Fourth Generation Opponents

Most Fourth Generation forces are light infantry, some quite good, for example, Hezbollah and the Pashtuns. How does state light infantry defeat them? By being better light infantry than they are.

Fourth Generation war light infantry is likely to have some advantages over state light infantry. It will usually know the terrain better. It is likely to start out with stronger support among the local population, especially if the state forces on the other side are foreign. That support will mean a superior information network, among other benefits.

But at the tactical level, a state light infantry should usually be the more skillful force. State light infantrymen are full-time soldiers, while most Fourth Generation fighters will be part-time militiamen. State forces have more resources for training, better equipment, better logistics, and they can employ supporting arms when the opportunity arises, although they do not depend on them. State light infantry should be more skilled at techniques, including marksmanship and tactical employment of machine guns and mortars. Assuming they can at least match their Fourth Generation enemies in tactical creativity, the state light infantry's superiority in techniques should usually be decisive.

The superiority of state light infantry does depend on their being employed correctly. If they are compelled to defend static positions, given detailed, controlling orders, overburdened with weight (they should seldom if ever wear body armor or helmets; the soldier's load should not exceed 45 pounds), or tied to supporting arms or to communications "networks" that require constant input, they will lose the advantage they should have over non-state light infantry. Requiring cats to hunt like dogs will benefit only the mice.

For those interested in further reading on the subject of the use of light infantry in 4th Generation War, "The 4GW Counterforce" is a selection from The 4th Generation War Handbook, *Castalia House, 2015.*

Battle Station

Ben Bova

Editor's Introduction

Establishment of world government is an old theme in science fiction, and of course the first question is always the age-old question asked by Juvenal in the First Century AD: "*Quis custodiet ipsos custodes*?" Who will watch the watchers? And if no one does, what then?

In December 1980 I chaired a committee tasked with writing space policy for the transition team coming to Washington with Ronald Reagan. Part of that paper discussed missile defense. We advocated Strategic Defense and a policy of Assured Survival as opposed to the then-prevalent policy of Mutual Assured Destruction as the primary means for deterring a nuclear war with the Soviet Union. At that time the Soviet Union had some 20,000 nuclear weapons aimed at the United States. Mutual Assured Destruction—MAD—basically said, if you kill us, we will kill you back. To that end we hardened the ICBM force to assure the survival of missiles; "boomer" nuclear submarines were always on patrol; and manned bombers and their required tankers were on ready alert at Air Force bases in the U.S. and abroad. Looking Glass, a KC-135 with a general officer and staff aboard, was in the air 24 hours a day to provide command and control. Looking Glass didn't approach its landing field until another aircraft with a general officer was in the air and gone far enough that it would survive a nuclear attack on its base. We took MAD seriously.

The policy advocated to the Reagan Team was to add Strategic Defense to this mix; that the Constitution had as its purpose "to provide for the common defense", not for the common destruction. The policy was adopted by the Reagan administration. Senator Ted Kennedy called it "Star Wars" and the appellation stuck; but it became the Strategic Defense Initiative, and even if the Soviet missile force could have been revised to defeat some of the SDI proposals, the economic costs were prohibitive. The Cold War effectively ended in 1990, and the Soviet Union ceased to be shortly after.

After World War II there were numerous world government proposals. Herman Kahn thought that something of the sort would be inevitable after any nuclear exchange. The alternative was Cold War and MAD. A number of science fiction stories explored the concept. The problem was simple: to keep the world safe from nuclear weapons required someone to enforce that ban. Custodians.

But *quis custodiet ipsos custodes*?

Author's Introduction to "Battle Station"

"Where do you get your crazy ideas?"

Every science fiction writer has heard that question, over and over again. Sometimes the questioner is kind enough to leave out the word "crazy." But the question still is asked whenever I give a lecture to any audience that includes people who do not regularly read science fiction.

Some science fiction writers, bored by that same old question (and sometimes miffed at the implications behind that word "crazy"), have taken to answering: "Schenectady!" There's even a mythology about it that claims members of the Science Fiction Writers of America subscribe to the Crazy Idea Service of Schenectady, New York, and receive in the mail one crazy idea each month—wrapped in plain brown paper, of course.

Yet the question deserves an answer. People are obviously fascinated with the process of creativity. Nearly everyone has a deep curiosity about how a writer comes up with the ideas that generate fresh stories.

For most of the stories and novels I have written over the years, the ideation period is so long and complex that I could not begin to explain—even to myself—where the ideas originally came from.

With "Battle Station," happily, I can trace the evolution of the story from original idea to final draft.

"Battle Station" has its roots in actual scientific research and technological development. In the mid-1960s I was employed at the research laboratory where the first high-power laser was invented. I helped to arrange the first briefing in the Pentagon to inform the Department of Defense that lasers of virtually any power desired could now be developed.

That was the first step on the road to what came to be called the Strategic Defense Initiative.

My 1976 novel *Millennium* examined, as only science fiction can, the human and social consequences of using lasers in satellites to defend against nuclear missiles. By 1983 the real world had caught up to the idea and President Reagan initiated the "Star Wars" program. In 1984 I published a nonfiction book on the subject, *Assured Survival.* In 1986 a second edition of that book, retitled *Star Peace*, brought the swiftly-developing story up to date.

Meanwhile, from the mid-1960s to this present day, thinkers such as Maxwell W. Hunter have been studying the problems and possibilities of an orbital defense system. While most academic critics (and consequently, most of the media) have simply declared such a defense system impossible, undesirable, and too expensive, Max Hunter spent his time examining how such a system might work, and what it might mean for the world political situation.

I am indebted to Max Hunter for sharing his ideas with me; particularly for the concept of "active armor." I have done violence to his ideas, I know, shaping them to the needs of the story. Such is the way of fiction.

Another concept that is important to this story came from the often-stormy letters column of *Analog* magazine more than twenty years ago. Before the first astronauts and cosmonauts went into space, the readers of *Analog* debated, vigorously, who would make the best candidates for duty aboard orbiting space stations. One of the ideas they kicked around was that submariners—men accustomed to cramped quarters, high tensions, and long periods away from home base—would be ideal for crewing a military space station.

So I "built" a space battle station that controls laser-armed satellites, and placed at its helm Commander J. W. Hazard, U.S. Navy (ret.), a former submarine skipper.

I gave him an international crew, in keeping with the conclusions I arrived at in *Star Peace*: Assured Survival, that the new technology of strategic defense satellites will lead to an International Peacekeeping Force (IPF)—a global police power dedicated to preventing war.

Once these ideas were in place, the natural thing was to test them. Suppose someone tried to subvert the IPF and seize the satellite system for his own nefarious purposes? Okay, make that not merely a political problem, but a personal problem for the story's protagonist: Hazard's son is part of a cabal to overthrow the IPF and set up a world dictatorship.

Now I had a story. All I had to do was start writing and allow the characters to "do their thing."

The ideas were the easiest part of the task. As you can see, the ideas were all around me, for more than twenty years. There are millions of good ideas floating through the air all the time. Every day of your life brings a fresh supply of ideas. Every person you know is a walking novel. Every news event contains a dozen ideas for stories.

The really difficult part is turning those ideas into good stories. To bring together the ideas and the characters and let them weave a story—

that is the real work of the writer. Very few people ask about that, yet that is the actual process of creativity. It's not tough to find straw. Spinning straw into gold—that's the great magical trick!

We should avoid a dependence on satellites for wartime purposes that is out of proportion to our ability to protect them. If we make ourselves dependent upon vulnerable spacecraft for military support, we will have built an Achilles heel into our forces.

—Dr. Ashton Carter, Massachusetts Institute of Technology, April 1984

The key issue then becomes, is our defense capable of defending itself.

—Maxwell W. Hunter II, Lockheed Missiles and Space Co. Inc., February 26, 1979

The first laser beam caught them unaware, slicing through the station's thin aluminum skin exactly where the main power trunk and air lines fed into the bridge.

A sputtering fizz of sparks, a moment of heart-wrenching darkness, and then the emergency dims came on. The electronics consoles switched to their internal batteries with barely a microsecond's hesitation, but the air fans sighed to a stop and fell silent.

The four men and two women on duty in the bridge had about one second to realize they were under attack. Just enough time for the breath to catch in your throat, for the sudden terror to hollow out your guts.

The second laser hit was a high-energy pulse deliberately aimed at the bridge's observation port. It cracked the impact-resistant plastic as easily as a hammer smashes an egg; the air pressure inside the bridge blew the port open. The six men and women became six exploding bodies spewing blood. There was not even time enough to scream.

The station was named *Hunter,* although only a handful of its crew knew why. It was not one of the missile-killing satellites, nor one of the sensor-laden observation birds. It was a command-and-control station, manned by a crew of twenty, orbiting some one thousand kilometers high, below the densest radiation zone of the inner Van Allen belt. It circled the Earth in about 105 minutes. By design, the station was not hardened against laser attack. The attackers knew this perfectly well.

Commander Hazard was almost asleep when the bridge was destroyed. He had just finished his daily inspection of the battle station. Satisfied that the youngsters of his crew were reasonably sharp, he had returned to his coffin-sized personal cabin and wormed out of his sweaty fatigues. He was angry with himself.

Two months aboard the station and he still felt the nausea and unease of space adaptation syndrome. It was like the captain of an ocean vessel having seasickness all the time. Hazard fumed inwardly as he stuck another timed-release medication plaster on his neck, slightly behind his left ear. The old one had fallen off. Not that they did much good. His neck was faintly spotted with the rings left by the medication patches. Still his stomach felt fluttery, his palms slippery with perspiration.

Clinging grimly to a handgrip, he pushed his weightless body from the mirrored sink to the mesh sleep cocoon fastened against the opposite wall of his cubicle. He zipped himself into the bag and slipped the terry-cloth restraint across his forehead.

Hazard was a bulky, dour man with iron-gray hair still cropped Academy-close, a weather-beaten squarish face built around a thrusting spadelike nose, a thin slash of a mouth that seldom smiled, and eyes the color of a stormy sea. Those eyes seemed suspicious of everyone and everything, probing, inquisitory. A closer look showed that they were weary, disappointed with the world and the people in it. Disappointed most of all with himself.

He was just dozing off when the emergency klaxon started hooting. For a disoriented moment he thought he was back in a submarine and something had gone wrong with a dive. He felt his arms pinned by the mesh sleeping bag, as if he had been bound by unknown enemies. He almost panicked as he heard hatches slamming automatically and the terrifying wailing of the alarms. The communications unit on the wall added its urgent shrill to the clamor.

The comm unit's piercing whistle snapped him to full awareness. He stopped struggling against the mesh and unzippered it with a single swift motion, slipping out of the head restraint at the same time.

Hazard slapped at the wall comm's switch. "Commander here," he snapped. "Report."

"Varshni, sir. CIC. The bridge is out. Apparently destroyed."

"Destroyed?"

"All life-support functions down. Air pressure zero. No communications," replied the Indian in a rush. His slightly singsong Oxford accent was trembling with fear. "It exploded, sir. They are all dead in there."

Hazard felt the old terror clutching at his heart, the physical weakness, the giddiness of sudden fear. Forcing his voice to remain steady, he commanded, "Full alert status. Ask Mr. Feeney and Miss Yang to meet me at the CIC at once. I'll be down there in sixty seconds or less."

The *Hunter* was one of nine orbiting battle stations that made up the command-and-control function of the newly created International Peacekeeping Force's strategic defense network. In lower orbits, 135 unmanned ABM satellites armed with multimegawatt lasers and hypervelocity missiles crisscrossed the Earth's surface. In theory, these satellites could destroy thousands of ballistic missiles within five minutes of their launch, no matter where on Earth they rose from.

In theory, each battle station controlled fifteen of the ABM satellites, but never the same fifteen for very long. The battle stations' higher orbits were deliberately picked so that the unmanned satellites passed through their field of view as they hurried by in their lower orbits. At the insistence of the fearful politicians of a hundred nations, no ABM satellites were under the permanent control of any one particular battle station.

In theory, each battle station patrolled one ninth of the Earth's surface as it circled the globe. The sworn duty of its carefully chosen international crew was to make certain that any missiles launched from that part of the Earth would be swiftly and efficiently destroyed.

In theory.

The IPF was new, untried except for computerized simulations and war games. It had been created in the wake of the Middle East Holocaust, when the superpowers finally realized that there were people willing to use nuclear weapons. It had taken the destruction of four ancient cities and more than 3 million lives before the superpowers stepped in and forced peace on the belligerents.

To make certain that nuclear devastation would never threaten humankind again, the International Peacekeeping Force was created. The Peacekeepers had the power and the authority to prevent a nuclear strike from reaching its targets. Their authority extended completely across the Earth, even to the superpowers themselves.

In theory.

Pulling aside the privacy curtain of his cubicle, Hazard launched himself down the narrow passageway with a push of his meaty hands against the cool metal of the bulkheads. His stomach lurched at the sudden motion and he squeezed his eyes shut for a moment.

The Combat Information Center was buried deep in the middle of the station, protected by four levels of living and working areas plus the station's storage magazines for water, food, air, fuel for the maneuvering thrusters, power generators, and other equipment.

Hazard fought down the queasy fluttering of his stomach as he glided along the passageway toward the CIC. At least he did not suffer the claustrophobia that affected some of the station's younger crew members. To a man who had spent most of his career aboard nuclear submarines, the station was roomy, almost luxurious.

He had to yank open four airtight hatches along the short way. Each clanged shut automatically behind him.

At last Hazard floated into the dimly lit combat center. It was a tiny, womblike circular chamber, its walls studded with display screens that glowed a sickly green in the otherwise darkened compartment. No desks or chairs in zero gravity; the CIC's work surfaces were chest-high consoles, most of them covered with keyboards.

Varshni and the Norwegian woman, Stromsen, were on duty. The little Indian, slim and dark, was wide-eyed with anxiety. His face shone with perspiration and his fatigues were dark at the armpits and between his shoulders. In the greenish glow from the display screens he looked positively ill. Stromsen looked tense, her strong jaw clenched, her ice-blue eyes fastened on Hazard, waiting for him to tell her what to do.

"What happened?" Hazard demanded.

"It simply blew out," said Varshni. "I had just spoken with Michaels and D'Argencour when… when…"

His voice choked off.

"The screens went blank." Stromsen pointed to the status displays. "Everything suddenly zeroed out."

She was controlling herself carefully, Hazard saw, every nerve taut to the point of snapping.

"The rest of the station?" Hazard asked.

She gestured again toward the displays. "No other damage."

"Everybody on full alert?"

"Yes, sir."

Lieutenant Feeney ducked through the hatch, his eyes immediately drawn to the row of burning red malfunction lights where the bridge displays should have been.

"Mother of Mercy, what's happened?"

Before anyone could reply, Susan Yang, the chief communications officer, pushed through the hatch and almost bumped into Feeney. She saw the displays and immediately concluded, "We're under attack!"

"That is impossible!" Varshni blurted.

Hazard studied their faces for a swift moment. They all knew what had happened; only Yang had the guts to say it aloud. She seemed cool and in control of herself. Oriental inscrutability? Hazard wondered. He knew she was third-generation Californian. Feeney's pinched, narrow-eyed face failed to hide the fear that they all felt, but the Irishman held himself well and returned Hazard's gaze without a tremor.

The only sound in the CIC was the hum of the electrical equipment and the soft sighing of the air fans. Hazard felt uncomfortably warm with the five of them crowding the cramped little chamber. Perspiration trickled down his ribs. They were all staring at him, waiting for him to tell them what must be done, to bring order out of the numbing fear and uncertainty that swirled around them. Four youngsters from four different nations, wearing the blue-gray fatigues of the IPF, with colored patches denoting their technical specialties on their left shoulders and the flag of their national origin on their right shoulders.

Hazard said, "We'll have to control the station from here. Mr. Feeney, you are now my Number One; Michaels was on duty in the bridge. Mr. Varshni, get a damage-control party to the bridge. Full suits."

"No one's left alive in there," Varshni whispered.

"Yes, but their bodies must be recovered. We owe them that. And their families." He glanced toward Yang. "And we've got to determine what caused the blowout."

Varshni's face twisted unhappily at the thought of the mangled bodies.

"I want a status report from each section of the station," Hazard went on, knowing that activity was the key to maintaining discipline. "Start with…"

A beeping sound made all five of them turn toward the communications console. Its orange demand light blinked for attention in time with the angry beeps. Hazard reached for a handgrip to steady himself as he swung toward the comm console. He noted how easily the youngsters handled themselves in zero gee. For him it still took a conscious, gut-wrenching effort.

Stromsen touched the keyboard with a slender finger. A man's unsmiling face appeared on the screen: light brown hair clipped as close as Hazard's gray, lips pressed together in an uncompromising line. He wore the blue-gray of the IPF with a commander's silver star on his collar.

"This is Buckbee, commander of station *Graham.* I want to speak to Commander Hazard."

Sliding in front of the screen, Hazard grasped the console's edge with both white-knuckled hands. He knew Buckbee only by reputation, a former U.S. Air Force colonel, from the Space Command until it had been disbanded, but before that he had put in a dozen years with SAC.

"This is Hazard."

Buckbee's lips moved slightly in what might have been a smile, but his eyes remained cold. "Hazard, you've just lost your bridge."

"And six lives."

Unmoved, Buckbee continued as if reading from a prepared script, "We offer you a chance to save the lives of the rest of your crew. Surrender the *Hunter* to us."

"Us?"

Buckbee nodded, a small economical movement. "We will bring order and greatness out of this farce called the IPF."

A wave of loathing so intense that it almost made him vomit swept through Hazard. He realized that he had known all along, with a certainty that had not needed conscious verification, that his bridge had been destroyed by deliberate attack, not by accident.

"You killed six kids," he said, his voice so low that he barely heard it himself. It was not a whisper but a growl.

"We had to prove that we mean business, Hazard. Now surrender your station or we'll blow you all to hell. Any further deaths will be on your head, not ours."

Jonathan Wilson Hazard, captain, U.S. Navy (ret.). Marital status: divorced. Two children: Jonathan, Jr., twenty-six; Virginia Elizabeth, twenty. Served twenty-eight years in U.S. Navy, mostly in submarines. Commanded fleet ballistic-missile submarines Ohio, Corpus Christi, *and* Utah. *later served as technical advisor to the Joint Chiefs of Staff and as naval liaison to NATO headquarters in Brussels. Retired from the Navy after hostage crisis in Brussels. Joined the International Peacekeeping Force and appointed commander of orbital battle station* Hunter.

"I can't just hand this station over to a face on a screen," Hazard replied, stalling, desperately trying to think his way through the situation. "I don't know what you're up to, what your intentions are, who you really are."

"You're in no position to bargain, Hazard," said Buckbee, his voice flat and hard. "We want control of your station. Either you give it to us or we'll eliminate you completely."

"Who the Hell is 'we'?"

"That doesn't matter."

"The Hell it doesn't! I want to know who you are and what you're up to."

Buckbee frowned. His eyes shifted away slightly, as if looking to someone standing out of range of the video camera.

"We don't have time to go into that now," he said at last.

Hazard recognized the crack in Buckbee's armor. It was not much, but he pressed it. "Well, you goddamned well better make time, mister. I'm not handing this station over to you or anybody else until I know what in hell is going on."

Turning to Feeney, he ordered, "Sound general quarters. ABM satellites on full automatic. Miss Yang, contact IPF headquarters and give them a full report of our situation."

"We'll destroy your station before those idiots in Geneva can decide what to do!" Buckbee snapped.

"Maybe," said Hazard. "But that'll take time, won't it? And we won't go down easy, I guarantee you. Maybe we'll take you down with us." Buckbee's face went white with fury. His eyes glared angrily.

"Listen," Hazard said more reasonably, "you can't expect me to just turn this station over to a face on a screen. Six of my people have been killed. I want to know why, and who's behind all this. I won't deal until I know who I'm dealing with and what your intentions are."

Buckbee growled, "You've just signed the death warrant for yourself and your entire crew."

The comm screen went blank.

For a moment Hazard hung weightlessly before the dead screen, struggling to keep the fear inside him from showing. Putting a hand out to the edge of the console to steady himself, he turned slowly to his young officers. Their eyes were riveted on him, waiting for him to tell them what to do, waiting for him to decide between life and death.

Quietly, but with steel in his voice, Hazard commanded, "I said general quarters, Mr. Feeney. Now!"

Feeney flinched as if suddenly awakened from a dream. He pushed himself to the command console, unlatched the red cover over the "general quarters" button, and banged it eagerly with his fist. The action sent him recoiling upward and he had to put up a hand against the overhead to push himself back down to the deck. The alarm light began blinking red and they could hear its hooting even through the airtight hatches outside the CIC.

"Geneva, Miss Yang," Hazard said sternly, over the howl of the alarm. "Feeney, see that the crew is at their battle stations. I want the satellites under our control on full automatic, prepared to shoot down anything that moves if it isn't in our precleared data bank. And Mr. Varshni, has that damage-control party gotten underway yet?"

The two young men rushed toward the hatch, bumping each other in their eagerness to follow their commander's orders. Hazard almost smiled at the Laurel-and-Hardy aspect of it. Lieutenant Yang pushed herself to the comm console and anchored her softboots on the Velcro strip fastened to the deck there.

"Miss Stromsen, you are the duty officer. I am depending on you to keep me informed of the status of all systems."

"Yes, sir!"

Keep them busy, Hazard told himself. Make them concentrate on doing their jobs and they won't have time to be frightened.

"Encountering interference, sir," reported Yang, her eyes on the comm displays. "Switching to emergency frequency."

Jamming, thought Hazard.

"Main comm antenna overheating," Stromsen said. She glanced down at her console keyboard, then up at the displays again. "I think they're attacking the antennas with lasers, sir. Main antenna out. Secondaries…" She shrugged and gestured toward the baleful red lights strung across her keyboard. "They're all out, sir."

"Set up a laser link," Hazard commanded. "They can't jam that. We've got to let Geneva know what's happening."

"Sir," said Yang, "Geneva will not be within our horizon for another forty-three minutes."

"Try signaling the commsats. Topmost priority."

"Yes, sir."

Got to let Geneva know, Hazard repeated to himself. If anybody can help us, they can. If Buckbee's pals haven't put one of their own people into the comm center down there. Or staged a coup. Or already knocked out the commsats. They've been planning this for a long time. They've got it all timed down to the microsecond.

He remembered the dinner, a month earlier, the night before he left to take command of the *Hunter.* I've known about it since then, Hazard said to himself. Known about it but didn't want to believe it. Known about it and done nothing. Buckbee was right. I killed those six kids. I should have seen that the bastards would strike without warning.

It had been in the equatorial city of Belém, where the Brazilians had set up their space launching facility. The IPF was obligated to spread its launches among all its space-capable member nations, so Hazard had been ordered to assemble his crew at Belém for their lift into orbit.

The night before they left, Hazard had been invited to dinner by an old Navy acquaintance who had already put in three months of orbital duty with the Peacekeepers and was on Earthside leave.

His name was Cardillo. Hazard had known him, somewhat distantly, as a fellow submariner, commander of attack boats rather than the missile carriers Hazard himself had captained. Vincent Cardillo had a reputation for being a hard nose who ran an efficient boat, if not a particularly happy one. He had never been really close to Hazard: their chemistries were too different. But this specific sweltering evening in a poorly air-conditioned restaurant in downtown Belém, Cardillo acted as if they shared some old fraternal secret between them.

Hazard had worn his IPF summerweight uniform: pale blue with gold insignia bordered by space black. Cardillo came in casual civilian slacks and a beautifully tailored Italian silk jacket. Through drinks and the first part of the dinner their conversation was light, inconsequential. Mostly reminiscences by two gray-haired submariners about men they had known, women they had chased, sea tales that grew with each retelling. But then:

"Damn shame," Cardillo muttered, halfway through his entrée of grilled eel.

The restaurant, one of the hundreds that had sprung up in Belém since the Brazilians had made the city their major spaceport, was on the waterfront. Outside the floor-to-ceiling windows, the muddy Parã River widened into the huge bay that eventually fed into the Atlantic. Hazard had spent his last day on Earth touring around the tropical jungle on a riverboat.

The makeshift shanties that stood on stilts along the twisting mud-brown creeks were giving way to industrial parks and cinderblock housing developments. Air-conditioning was transforming the region from rubber plantations to computerized information services. The smell of cement dust blotted out the fragrance of tropical flowers.

Bulldozers clattered in raw clearings slashed from the forest where stark steel frameworks of new buildings rose above the jungle growth. Children who had splashed naked in the brown jungle streams were being rounded up and sent to air-conditioned schools.

"What's a shame?" Hazard asked. "Seems to me these people are starting to do all right for the first time in their lives. The space business is making a lot of jobs around here."

Cardillo took a forkful of eel from his plate. It never got to his mouth.

"I don't mean them, Johnny. I mean us. It's a damn shame about us."

Hazard had never liked being called "Johnny." His family had addressed him as "Jon." His Navy associates knew him as "Hazard" and nothing else. A few very close friends used "J.W."

"What do you mean?" he asked. His own plate was already wiped clean. The fish and its dark spicy sauce had been marvelous. So had the crisp-crusted bread.

"Don't you feel nervous about this whole IPF thing?" Cardillo asked, trying to look earnest. "I mean, I can see Washington deciding to put boomers like your boats in mothballs, and the silo missiles, too. But the attack subs? Decommission our conventional weapons systems? Leave us disarmed?"

Hazard had not been in command of a missile submarine in more than three years. He had been allowed, even encouraged, to resign his commission after the hostage mess in Brussels.

"If you're not in favor of what the American government is doing, then why did you agree to serve in the Peacekeepers?"

Cardillo shrugged and smiled slightly. It was not a pleasant smile. He had a thin, almost triangular face with a low, creased brow tapering down to a pointed chin. His once-dark hair, now peppered with gray, was thick and wavy. He had allowed it to grow down to his collar. His deep-brown eyes were always narrowed, crafty, focused so intently he seemed to be trying to penetrate through you. There was no joy in his face, even though he was smiling; no pleasure. It was the smile of a gambler, a con artist, a used-car salesman.

"Well," he said slowly, putting his fork back down on the plate and leaning back in his chair, "you know the old saying, 'If you can't beat 'em, join 'em.' "

Hazard nodded, although he felt puzzled. He groped for Cardillo's meaning. "Yeah, I guess playing space cadet up there will be better than rusting away on the beach."

"Playing?" Cardillo's dark brows rose slightly. "We're not playing, Johnny. We're in this for keeps."

"I didn't mean to imply that I don't take my duty to the IPF seriously," Hazard answered.

For an instant Cardillo seemed stunned with surprise. Then he threw his head back and burst into laughter. "Jesus Christ, Johnny," he gasped. "You're so straight-arrow it's hysterical."

Hazard frowned but said nothing. Cardillo guffawed and banged the table with one hand. Some of the diners glanced their way. They seemed to be mostly Americans or Europeans, a few Asians. Some Brazilians, too, Hazard noticed as he waited for Cardillo's amusement to subside. Probably from the capital or Rio.

"Let me in on the joke," Hazard said at last.

Cardillo wiped at his eyes. Then, leaning forward across the table, his grin fading into an intense, penetrating stare, he whispered harshly, "I already told you, Johnny. If we can't avoid being members of the IPF—if Washington's so fucking weak that we've got to disband practically all our defenses—then what we've got to do is take over the Peacekeepers ourselves."

"Take over the Peacekeepers?" Hazard felt stunned at the thought of it.

"Damn right! Men like you and me, Johnny. It's our duty to our country."

"Our country," Hazard reminded him, "has decided to join the International Peacekeeping Force and has encouraged its military officers to obtain commissions in it."

Cardillo shook his head. "That's our stupid goddamn government, Johnny. Not the country. Not the people who really want to defend America instead of selling her out to a bunch of fucking foreigners."

"That government," Hazard reminded him, "won a big majority last November."

Cardillo made a sour face. "Ahh, the people. What the fuck do they know?"

Hazard said nothing.

"I'm telling you, Johnny, the only way to do it is to take over the IPF."

"That's crazy."

"You mean if and when the time comes, you won't go along with us?"

"I mean," Hazard said, forcing his voice to remain calm, "that I took an oath to be loyal to the IPF. So did you."

"Yeah, yeah, sure. And what about the oath we took way back when—the one to preserve and protect the United States of America?"

"The United States of America wants us to serve in the Peacekeepers," Hazard insisted.

Cardillo shook his head again, mournfully. Not a trace of anger. Not even disappointment. As if he had expected this reaction from Hazard. His expression was that of a salesman who could not convince his stubborn customer of the bargain he was offering.

"Your son doesn't feel the same way you do," Cardillo said.

Hazard immediately clamped down on the rush of emotions that surged through him. Instead of reaching across the table and dragging Cardillo to his feet and punching in his smirking face, Hazard forced a thin smile and kept his fists clenched on his lap.

"Jon Jr. is a grown man. He has the right to make his own decisions."

"He's serving under me, you know." Cardillo's eyes searched Hazard's face intently, probing for weakness.

"Yes," Hazard said tightly. "He told me."

Which was an outright lie.

"Missiles approaching, sir!"

Stromsen's tense warning snapped Hazard out of his reverie. He riveted his attention to the main CIC display screen. Six angry red dots were working their way from the periphery of the screen toward the center, which marked the location of the Hunter.

"Now we'll see if the ABM satellites are working or not," Hazard muttered.

"Links with the ABM sats are still good, sir," Yang reported from her station, a shoulder's width away from Stromsen. "The integral antennas weren't knocked out when they hit the comm dishes."

Hazard gave her a nod of acknowledgment. The two young women could not have looked more different: Yang was small, wiry, dark, her straight black hair cut like a military helmet; Stromsen was willowy yet broad in the beam and deep in the bosom, as blonde as butter.

"Lasers on 324 and 325 firing," the Norwegian reported.

Hazard saw the display lights. On the main screen the six red dots flickered orange momentarily, then winked out altogether.

Stromsen pecked at her keyboard. Alphanumerics sprang up on a side screen. "Got them all while they were still in first-stage burn. They'll never reach us." She smiled with relief. "They're tumbling into the atmosphere. Burn-up within seven minutes."

Hazard allowed himself a small grin. "Don't break out the champagne yet. That's just their first salvo. They're testing to see if we actually have control of the lasers."

It's all a question of time, Hazard knew. But how much time? What are they planning? How long before they start slicing us up with laser beams? We don't have the shielding to protect against lasers. The stupid politicians wouldn't allow us to armor these stations. We're like a sitting duck up here.

"What are they trying to accomplish, sir?" asked Yang. "Why are they doing this?"

"They want to take over the whole defense network. They want to seize control of the entire IPF."

"That's impossible!" Stromsen blurted.

"The Russians won't allow them to do that," Yang said. "The Chinese and the other members of the IPF will stop them."

"Maybe," said Hazard. "Maybe." He felt a slight hint of nausea ripple in his stomach. Reaching up, he touched the slippery plastic of the medicine patch behind his ear.

"Do you think they could succeed?" Stromsen asked.

"What's important is, do they think they can succeed? There are still hundreds of ballistic missiles on Earth. Thousands of hydrogen warheads. Buckbee and his cohorts apparently believe that if they can take control of a portion of the ABM network, they can threaten a nuclear strike against the nations that don't go along with them."

"But the other nations will strike back and order their people in the IPF not to intercept their strikes," said Yang.

"It will be nuclear war," Stromsen said. "Just as if the IPF never existed."

"Worse," Yang pointed out, "because first there'll be a shoot-out on each one of these battle stations."

"That's madness!" said Stromsen.

"That's what we've got to prevent," Hazard said grimly.

The orange light began to blink again on the comm console. Yang snapped her attention to it. "Incoming message from the *Graham*, sir."

Hazard nodded. "Put it on the main screen."

Cardillo's crafty features appeared on the screen. He should have been still on leave back on Earth, but instead he was smiling crookedly at Hazard.

"Well, Johnny, I guess by now you've figured out that we mean business."

"And so do we. Give it up, Vince. It's not going to work."

With a small shake of his head Cardillo answered, "It's already working, Johnny boy. Two of the Russian battle stations are with us. So's the *Wood*. The Chinks and Indians are holding out but the European station is going along with us."

Hazard said, "So you've got six of the nine stations."

"So far."

"Then you don't really need *Hunter*. You can leave us alone."

Pursing his lips for a moment, Cardillo replied, "I'm afraid it doesn't work that way, Johnny. We want *Hunter*. We can't afford to have you rolling around like a loose cannon. You're either with us or against us."

"I'm not with you," Hazard said flatly.

Cardillo sighed theatrically. "John, there are twenty other officers and crew on your station…"

"Fourteen now," Hazard corrected.

"Don't you think you ought to give them a chance to make a decision about their own lives?"

Despite himself, Hazard broke into a malicious grin. "Am I hearing you straight, Vince? You're asking the commander of a vessel to take a vote?"

Grinning back at him, Cardillo admitted, "I guess that was kind of dumb. But you do have their lives in your hands, Johnny."

"We're not knuckling under, Vince. And you've got twenty-some lives aboard the *Graham*, you know. Including your own. Better think about that."

"We already have, Johnny. One of those lives is Jonathan Hazard, Jr. He's right here on the bridge with me. A fine officer, Johnny. You should be proud of him."

A hostage, Hazard realized. They're using Jon Jr. as a hostage.

"Do you want to talk with him?" Cardillo asked.

Hazard nodded.

Cardillo slid out of view and a younger man's face appeared on the screen. Jon Jr. looked tense, strained. This isn't any easier for him than it is for me, Hazard thought. He studied his son's face. Youthful, clear-eyed, a square-jawed honest face. Hazard was startled to realize that he had seen that face before, in his own Academy graduation photo.

"How are you, son?"

"I'm fine, Dad. And you?"

"Are we really on opposite sides of this?"

Jon Jr.'s eyes flicked away for a moment, then turned back to look squarely at his father's. "I'm afraid so, Dad."

"But why?" Hazard felt genuinely bewildered that his son did not see things the way he did.

"The IPF is dangerous," Jon Jr. said. "It's the first step toward a world government. The Third World nations want to bleed the industrialized nations dry. They want to grab all our wealth for themselves. The first step is to disarm us, under the pretense of preventing nuclear war. Then, once we're disarmed, they're going to take over everything—using the IPF as their armed forces."

"That's what they've told you," Hazard said.

"That's what I know, Dad. It's true. I know it is."

"And your answer is to take over the IPF and use it as your armed forces to control the rest of the world, is that it?"

"Better us than them."

Hazard shook his head. "They're using you, son. Cardillo and Buckbee and the rest of those maniacs; you're in with a bunch of would-be Napoleons."

Jon Jr. smiled pityingly at his father. "I knew you'd say something like that."

Hazard put up a beefy hand. "I don't want to argue with you, son. But I can't go along with you."

"You're going to force us to attack your station."

"I'll fight back."

His son's smile turned sardonic. "Like you did in Brussels?"

Hazard felt it like a punch in his gut. He grunted with the pain of it. Wordlessly he reached out and clicked off the comm screen.

Brussels.

They had thought it was just another one of those endless Easter Sunday demonstrations. A peace march. The Greens, the Nuclear Winter freaks, the Neutralists, peaceniks of one stripe or another. Swarms of little old ladies in their Easter frocks, limping old war veterans, kids of all ages. Teenagers, lots of them. In blue jeans and denim jackets. Young women in shorts and tight T-shirts.

The guards in front of NATO's headquarters complex took no particular note of the older youths and women mixed in with the teens. They failed to detect the hard, calculating eyes and the snub-nosed guns and grenades hidden under jackets and sweaters.

Suddenly the peaceful parade dissolved into a mass of screaming wild people. The guards were cut down mercilessly and the cadre of terrorists fought their way into the main building of NATO headquarters. They forced dozens of peaceful marchers to go in with them, as shields and hostages.

Captain J. W. Hazard, USN, was not on duty that Sunday, but he was in his office nevertheless, attending to some paperwork that he wanted out of the way before the start of business on Monday morning.

Unarmed, he was swiftly captured by the terrorists, beaten bloody for the fun of it, and then locked in a toilet. When the terrorists realized that he was the highest-ranking officer in the building, Hazard was dragged out and commanded to open the security vault where the most sensitive NATO documents were stored.

Hazard refused. The terrorists began shooting hostages. After the second murder Hazard opened the vault for them. Top-secret battle plans, maps showing locations of nuclear weapons, and hundreds of other documents were taken by the terrorists and never found, even after an American-led strike force retook the building in a bloody battle that killed all but four of the hostages.

Hazard stood before the blank comm screen for a moment, his softbooted feet not quite touching the deck, his mind racing.

They've even figured that angle, he said to himself. They know I caved in at Brussels and they expect me to cave in here. Some sonofabitch has grabbed my psych records and come to the conclusion that I'll react the same way now as I did then. Some sonofabitch. And they got my son to stick the knife in me.

The sound of the hatch clattering open stirred Hazard. Feeney floated through the hatch and grabbed an overhead handgrip.

"The crew's at battle stations, sir," he said, slightly breathless. "Standing by for further orders."

It struck Hazard that only a few minutes had passed since he himself had entered the CIC.

"Very good. Mr. Feeney," he said. "With the bridge out, we're going to have to control the station from here. Feeney, take the con. Miss Stromsen, how much time before we can make direct contact with Geneva?"

"Forty minutes, sir," she sang out, then corrected, "Actually, thirty-nine fifty."

Feeney was worming his softboots against the Velcro strip in front of the propulsion-and-control console.

"Take her down, Mr. Feeney."

The Irishman's eyes widened with surprise. "Down, sir?"

Hazard made himself smile. "Down. To the altitude of the ABM satellites. Now."

"Yes, sir." Feeney began carefully pecking out commands on the keyboard before him.

"I'm not just reacting like an old submariner," Hazard reassured his young officers. "I want to get us to a lower altitude so we won't be such a good target for so many of their lasers. Shrink our horizon. We're a sitting duck up here."

Yang grinned back at him. "I didn't think you expected to outmaneuver a laser beam, sir."

"No, but we can take ourselves out of range of most of their satellites."

Most, Hazard knew, but not all.

"Miss Stromsen, will you set up a simulation for me? I want to know how many unfriendly satellites can attack us at various altitudes, and what their positions would be compared to our own. I want a solution that tells me where we'll be safest."

"Right away, sir," Stromsen said. "What minimum altitude shall I plug in?"

"Go right down to the deck," Hazard said. "Low enough to boil the paint off."

"The station isn't built for reentry into the atmosphere, sir!"

"I know. But see how low we can get."

The old submariner's instinct: run silent, run deep. So the bastards think I'll fold up, just like I did at Brussels, Hazard fumed inwardly. Two big differences, Cardillo and friends. Two very big differences. In Brussels the hostages were civilians, not military men and women. And in Brussels I didn't have any weapons to fight back with.

He knew the micropuffs of thrust from the maneuvering rockets were hardly strong enough to be felt, yet Hazard's stomach lurched and heaved suddenly.

"We have retro burn," Feeney said. "Altitude decreasing."

My damned stomach's more sensitive than his instruments, Hazard grumbled to himself.

"Incoming message from *Graham*, sir," said Yang.

"Ignore it."

"Sir," Yang said, turning slightly toward him, "I've been thinking about the minimum altitude we can achieve. Although the station is not equipped for atmospheric reentry, we do carry the four emergency evacuation spacecraft and they do have heat shields."

"Are you suggesting we abandon the station?"

"Oh, no, sir! But perhaps we could move the spacecraft to a position where they would be between us and the atmosphere. Let their heat shields protect us—sort of like riding a surfboard."

Feeney laughed. "Trust a California girl to come up with a solution like that!"

"It might be a workable idea," Hazard said. "I'll keep it in mind."

"We're being illuminated by a laser beam," Stromsen said tensely. "Low power—so far."

"They're tracking us."

Hazard ordered, "Yang, take over the simulation problem. Stromsen, give me a wide radar sweep. I want to see if they're moving any of their ABM satellites to counter our maneuver."

"I have been sweeping, sir. No satellite activity yet."

Hazard grunted. Yet. She knows that all they have to do is maneuver a few of their satellites to higher orbits and they'll have us in their sights.

To Yang he called, "Any response from the commsats?"

"No, sir," she replied immediately. "Either their laser receptors are not functioning or the satellites themselves are inoperative."

They couldn't have knocked out the commsats altogether, Hazard told himself. How would they communicate with one another? Cardillo claims the *Wood* and two of the Soviet stations are on their side. And the Europeans. He put a finger to his lips unconsciously, trying to remember Cardillo's exact words. The Europeans are going along with us. That's what he said. Maybe they're not actively involved in this. Maybe they're playing a wait-and-see game.

Either way, we're alone. They've got four, maybe five, out of the nine battle stations. We can't contact the Chinese or Indians. We don't know which Russian satellite hasn't joined in with them. It'll be more than a half hour before we can contact Geneva, and even then what the hell can they do?

Alone. Well, it won't be for the first time. Submariners are accustomed to being on their own.

"Sir," Yang reported, the *Graham* is still trying to reach us. Very urgent, they're saying.

"Tell them I'm not available but you will record their message and personally give it to me." Turning to the Norwegian lieutenant, "Miss Stromsen, I want all crew members in their pressure suits. And levels one and two of the station are to be abandoned. No one above level three except the damage-control team. We're going to take some hits and I want everyone protected as much as possible."

She nodded and glanced at the others. All three of them looked tense, but not afraid. The fear was there, of course, underneath. But they were in control of themselves. Their eyes were clear, their hands steady.

"Should I have the air pumped out of levels one and two—after they're cleared of personnel?"

"No," Hazard said. "Let them outgas when they're hit. Might fool the bastards into thinking they're doing more damage than they really are."

Feeney smiled weakly. "Sounds like the boxer who threatened to bleed all over his opponent."

Hazard glared at him. Stromsen took up the headset from her console and began issuing orders into the pin-sized microphone.

"The computer simulation is finished, sir," said Yang.

"Put it on my screen here."

He studied the graphics for a moment, sensing Feeney peering over his shoulder. Their safest altitude was the lowest, where only six ABM satellites could "see" them. The fifteen laser-armed satellites under their own control would surround them like a cavalry escort.

"There it is, Mr. Feeney. Plug that into your navigation program. That's where we want to be."

"Aye, sir."

The CIC shuddered. The screens dimmed for a moment, then came back to their full brightness.

"We've been hit!" Stromsen called out.

"Where? How bad?"

"Just aft of the main power generator. Outer hull ruptured. Storage area eight—medical, dental, and food-supplement supplies."

"So they got the Band-Aids and vitamin pills," Yang joked shakily.

"But they're going after the power generator," said Hazard. "Any casualties?"

"No, sir," reported Stromsen. "No personnel stationed there during general quarters."

He grasped Feeney's thin shoulder. "Turn us over, man. Get that generator away from their beams!"

Feeney nodded hurriedly and flicked his stubby fingers across his keyboard. Hazard knew it was all in his imagination, but his stomach rolled sickeningly as the station rotated.

Hanging grimly to a handgrip, he said, "I want each of you to get into your pressure suits, starting with you, Miss Stromsen. Yang, take over her console until she…"

The chamber shook again. Another hit.

"Can't we strike back at them?" Stromsen cried.

Hazard asked, "How many satellites are firing at us?"

She glanced at her display screens. "It seems to be only one—so far."

"Hit it."

Her lips curled slightly in a Valkyrie's smile. She tapped out commands on her console and then leaned on the final button hard enough to lift her boots off the Velcro.

"Got him!" Stromsen exulted. "That's one laser that won't bother us again."

Yang and Feeney were grinning. Hazard asked the communications officer, "Let me hear what the *Graham* has been saying."

It was Buckbee's voice on the recording. "Hazard, you are not to attempt to change your orbital altitude. If you don't return to your original altitude immediately, we will fire on you."

"Well, they know by now that we're not paying attention to them," Hazard said to his three young officers. "If I know them, they're going to take a few minutes to think things over, especially now that we've shown them we're ready to hit back. Stromsen, get into your suit. Feeney, you're next, then Yang. Move!"

It took fifteen minutes before the three of them were back in the CIC inside the bulky space suits, flexing gloved fingers, glancing about from inside the helmets. They all kept their visors up, and Hazard said nothing about it. Difficult enough to work inside the damned suits, he thought. They can snap the visors down fast enough if it comes to that.

The compact CIC became even more crowded. Despite decades of research and development, the space suits still bulked nearly twice as large as an unsuited person.

Suddenly Hazard felt an overpowering urge to get away from the CIC, away from the tension he saw in their young faces, away from the sweaty odor of fear, away from the responsibility for their lives.

"I'm going for my suit," he said, "and then a fast inspection tour of the station. Think you three can handle things on your own for a few minutes?"

Three heads bobbed inside their helmets. Three voices chorused, "Yes, sir."

"Fire on any satellite that fires at us," he commanded. "Tape all incoming messages. If there's any change in their tune, call me on the intercom."

"Yes, sir."

"Feeney, how long until we reach our final altitude?"

"More than an hour, sir."

"No way to move her faster?"

"I could get outside and push, I suppose."

Hazard grinned at him. "That won't be necessary, Mr. Feeney." Not yet, he added silently.

Pushing through the hatch into the passageway, Hazard saw that there was one pressure suit hanging on its rack in the locker just outside the CIC hatch. He passed it and went to his personal locker and his own suit. It's good to leave them on their own for a while, he told himself. Build up their confidence. But he knew that he had to get away from them, even if only for a few minutes.

His personal space suit smelled of untainted plastic and fresh rubber, like a new car. As Hazard squirmed into it, its joints felt stiff—or maybe it's me, he thought. The helmet slipped from his gloved hands and went spinning away from him, floating off like a severed head. Hazard retrieved it and pulled it on. Like the youngsters, he kept the visor open.

His first stop was the bridge. Varshni was hovering in the companionway just outside the airtight hatch that sealed off the devastated area. Two other space-suited men were zippering an unrecognizably mangled body into a long black-plastic bag. Three other bags floated alongside them, already filled and sealed.

Even inside a pressure suit, the Indian seemed small, frail, like a skinny child. He was huddled next to the body bags, bent over almost into a fetal position. There were tears in his eyes. "These are all we could find. The two others must have been blown out of the station completely."

Hazard put a gloved hand on the shoulder of his suit.

"They were my friends," Varshni said.

"It must have been painless," Hazard heard himself say. It sounded stupid.

"I wish I could believe that."

"There's more damage to inspect, over by the power generator area. Is your team nearly finished here?"

"Another few minutes, I think. We must make certain that all the wiring and air lines have been properly sealed off."

"They can handle that themselves. Come on, you and I will check it out together."

"Yes, sir," Varshni spoke into his helmet microphone briefly, then straightened up and tried to smile. "I am ready, sir."

The two men glided up a passageway that led to the outermost level of the station, Hazard wondering what would happen if a laser attack hit the area while they were in it. Takes a second or two to slice the hull open, he thought. Enough time to flip your visor down and grab on to something before the air blowout sucks you out of the station.

Still, he slid his visor down and ordered Varshni to do the same. He was only mildly surprised when the Indian replied that he already had.

Wish the station were shielded. Wish they had designed it to withstand attack. Then he grumbled inwardly, wishes are for losers; winners use what they have. But the thought nagged at him. What genius put the power generator next to the unarmored hull? Damned politicians wouldn't allow shielding; they *wanted* the stations to be vulnerable. A sign of goodwill, as far as they're concerned. They thought nobody would attack an unshielded station because the attacker's station is also unshielded. We're all in this together, try to hurt me and I'll hurt you. A hangover from the old mutual-destruction kind of dogma. Absolute bullshit.

There ought to be some way to protect ourselves from lasers. They shouldn't put people up here like sacrificial lambs.

Hazard glanced at Varshni, whose face was hidden behind his helmet visor. He thought of his son. Sheila had ten years to poison his mind against me. Ten years. He wanted to hate her for that, but he found that he could not. He had been a poor husband and a worse father. Jon Jr. had every right to loathe his father. But dammit, this is more important than family arguments! Why can't the boy see what's at stake here? Just because he's sore at his father doesn't mean he has to take total leave of his senses.

They approached a hatch where the red warning light was blinking balefully. They checked the hatch behind them, made certain it was airtight, then used the wall-mounted keyboard to start the pumps that would evacuate that section of the passageway, turning it into an elongated air lock.

Finally they could open the farther hatch and glide into the wrecked storage magazine.

Hazard grabbed a handhold. "Better use tethers here," he said.

Varshni had already unwound the tether from his waist and clipped it to a hold.

It was a small magazine, little more than a closet. In the light from their helmet lamps, they saw cartons of pharmaceuticals securely anchored to the shelves with toothed plastic straps. A gash had been torn in the hull, and through it Hazard could see the darkness of space. The laser beam had penetrated into the cartons and shelving, slicing a neat burned-edge slash through everything it touched.

Varshni floated upward toward the rent. It was as smooth as a surgeon's incision, and curled back slightly where the air pressure had pushed the thin metal outward in its rush to escape to vacuum.

"No wiring here," Varshni's voice said in Hazard's helmet earphones. "No plumbing either. We were fortunate."

"They were aiming for the power generator."

The Indian pushed himself back down toward Hazard. His face was hidden behind the visor. "Ah, yes, that is an important target. We were very fortunate that they missed."

"They'll try again," Hazard said.

"Yes, of course."

"Commander Hazard!" Yang's voice sounded urgent. "I think you should hear the latest message from *Graham,* sir."

Nodding unconsciously inside his helmet, Hazard said, "Patch it through."

He heard a click, then Buckbee's voice. "Hazard, we've been very patient with you. We're finished playing games. You bring the *Hunter* back to its normal altitude and surrender the station to us or we'll slice you to pieces. You've got five minutes to answer."

The voice shut off so abruptly that Hazard could picture Buckbee slamming his fist against the Off key.

"How long ago did this come through?"

"Transmission terminated thirty seconds ago, sir," said Yang.

Hazard looked down at Varshni's slight form. He knew that Varshni had heard the ultimatum just as he had. He could not see the Indian's face, but the slump of his shoulders told him how Varshni felt.

Yang asked, "Sir, do you want me to set up a link with *Graham*?"

"No," said Hazard.

"I don't think they intend to call again, sir," Yang said. "They expect you to call them."

"Not yet," he said. He turned to the wavering form beside him. "Better straighten up, Mr. Varshni. There's going to be a lot of work for you and your damage-control team to do. We're in for a rough time."

Ordering Varshni back to his team at the ruins of the bridge, Hazard made his way toward the CIC. He spoke into his helmet mike as he pulled himself along the passageways, hand over hand, as fast as he could go:

"Mr. Feeney, you are to fire at any satellites that fire on us. And at any ABM satellites that begin maneuvering to gain altitude so they can look down on us. Understand?"

"Understood, sir!"

"Miss Stromsen, I believe the fire-control panel is part of your responsibility. You will take your orders from Mr. Feeney."

"Yes, sir."

"Miss Yang, I want that simulation of our position and altitude updated to show exactly which ABM satellites under hostile control are in a position to fire upon us."

"I already have that in the program, sir."

"Good. I want our four lifeboats detached from the station and placed in positions where their heat shields can intercept incoming laser beams."

For the first time, Yang's voice sounded uncertain. "I'm not sure I understand what you mean, sir."

Hazard was sweating and panting with the exertion of hauling himself along the passageway. This suit won't smell new anymore, he thought.

To Yang he explained, "We can use the lifeboats' heat shields as armor to absorb or deflect incoming laser beams. Not just shielding, but *active* armor. We can move the boats to protect the most likely areas for laser beams to come from."

"Like the goalie in a hockey game!" Feeney chirped. "Cutting down the angles."

"Exactly."

By the time he reached the CIC they were already working the problems. Hazard saw that Stromsen had the heaviest work load: all the station systems' status displays, fire control for the laser-armed ABM satellites, and control of the lifeboats now hovering dozens of meters away from the station.

"Miss Stromsen, please transfer the fire-control responsibility to Mr. Feeney."

The expression on her strong-jawed face, half hidden inside her helmet, was pure stubborn indignation.

Jabbing a gloved thumb toward the lightning-slash insignia on the shoulder of Feeney's suit, Hazard said, "He *is* a weapons specialist, after all."

Stromsen's lips twitched slightly and she tapped at the keyboard to her left; the fire-control displays disappeared from the screens above it, only to spring up on screens in front of Feeney's position.

Hazard nodded as he lifted his own visor. "Okay, now. Feeney, you're the offense. Stromsen, you're the defense. Miss Yang, your job is to keep Miss Stromsen continuously advised as to where the best placement of the lifeboats will be."

Yang nodded, her dark eyes sparkling with the challenge. "Sir, you can't possibly expect us to predict all the possible paths a beam might take and get a lifeboat's heat shield in place soon enough..."

"I expect—as Lord Nelson once said—each of you to do your best. Now get Buckbee or Cardillo or whoever on the horn. I'm ready to talk to them."

It took a few moments for the communications laser to lock onto the distant *Graham,* but when Buckbee's face finally appeared on the screen, he was smiling—almost gloating.

"You've still got a minute and a half, Hazard. I'm glad you've come to your senses before we had to open fire on you."

"I'm only calling to warn you: any satellite that fires on us will be destroyed. Any satellite that maneuvers to put its lasers in a better position to hit us will also be destroyed."

Buckbee's jaw dropped open. His eyes widened.

"I've got fifteen ABM satellites under my control," Hazard continued, "and I'm going to use them."

"You can't threaten us!" Buckbee sputtered. "We'll wipe you out!"

"Maybe. Maybe not. I intend to fight until the very last breath."

"You're crazy, Hazard!"

"Am I? Your game is to take over the whole defense system and threaten a nuclear missile strike against any nation that doesn't go along with you. Well, if your satellites are exhausted or destroyed, you won't be much of a threat to anybody, will you? Try impressing the Chinese with a beat-up network. They've got enough missiles to wipe out Europe and North America, and they'll use them. If you don't have enough left to stop those missiles, then who's threatening whom?"

"You can't…"

"Listen!" Hazard snapped. "How many of your satellites will be left by the time you overcome us? How much of a hole will we rip in your plans? Geneva will be able to blow you out of the sky with ground-launched missiles by the time you're finished with us."

"They'd never do such a thing."

"Are you sure?"

Buckbee looked away from Hazard, toward someone off-camera. He moved off, and Cardillo slid into view. He was no longer smiling.

"Nice try, Johnny, but you're bluffing and we both know it. Give up now or we're going to have to wipe you out."

"You can try, Vince. But you won't win."

"If we go, your son goes with us," Cardillo said.

Hazard forced his voice to remain level. "There's nothing I can do about that. He's a grown man. He's made his choice."

Cardillo huffed out a long, impatient sigh. "All right, Johnny. It was nice knowing you."

Hazard grimaced. Another lie, he thought. The man must be categorically unable to speak the truth.

The comm screen blanked.

"Are the lifeboats in place?" he asked.

"As good as we can get them," Yang said, her voice doubtful. "Not too far from the station," Hazard warned. "I don't want them to show up as separate blips on their radar."

"Yes, sir, we know."

He nodded at them. Good kids, he thought. Ready to fight it out on my say-so. How far will they go before they crack? How much damage can we take before they scream to surrender?

They waited. Not a sound in the womb-shaped chamber, except for the hum of the electrical equipment and the whisper of air circulation. Hazard glided to a position slightly behind the two women. Feeney can handle the counterattack, he said to himself. That's simple enough. It's the defense that's going to win or lose for us.

On the display screens he saw the positions of the station and the hostile ABM satellites. Eleven of them in range. Eleven lines straight as laser beams converged on the station. Small orange blips representing the four lifeboats hovered around the central pulsing yellow dot that represented the station. The orange blips blocked nine of the converging lines. Two others passed between the lifeboat positions and reached the station itself.

"Miss Stromsen," Hazard said softly.

She jerked as if a hot needle had been stuck into her flesh.

"Easy now," Hazard said. "All I want to tell you is that you should be prepared to move the lifeboats to intercept any beams that are getting through."

"Yes, sir, I know."

Speaking as soothingly as he could, Hazard went on, "I doubt that they'll fire all eleven lasers at us at once. And as our altitude decreases, there will be fewer and fewer of their satellites in range of us. We have a good chance of getting through this without too much damage."

Stromsen turned her whole space-suited body so that she could look at him from inside her helmet. "It's good of you to say so, sir. I know you're trying to cheer us up, and I'm certain we all appreciate it. But you are taking my attention away from the screens."

Yang giggled, whether out of tension or actual humor at Stromsen's retort, Hazard could not tell.

Feeney sang out, "I've got a satellite climbing on us!"

Before Hazard could speak, Feeney's hands were moving on his console keyboard. "Our beasties are now programmed for automatic, but I'm tapping in a backup manually, just in– ah! Got her! Scratch one enemy."

Smiles all around. But behind his grin, Hazard wondered, Can they gin up decoys? Something that gives the same radar signature as an ABM satellite but really isn't? I don't think so—but I don't know for sure.

"Laser beam… two of them," called Stromsen.

Hazard saw the display screen light up. Both beams were hitting the same lifeboat. Then a third beam from the opposite direction lanced out.

The station shuddered momentarily as Stromsen's fingers flew over her keyboard and one of the orange dots shifted slightly to block the third beam.

"Where'd it hit?" he asked the Norwegian as the beams winked off.

"Just aft of the emergency oxygen tanks, sir."

Christ, Hazard thought, if they hit the tanks, enough oxygen will blow out of here to start us spinning like a top.

"Vent the emergency oxygen."

"Vent it, sir?"

"Now!"

Stromsen pecked angrily at the keyboard to her left. "Venting. Sir."

"I don't want that gas spurting out and acting like a rocket thruster," Hazard explained to her back. "Besides, it's an old submariner's trick to let the attacker think he's caused real damage by jettisoning junk."

If any of them had reservations about getting rid of their emergency oxygen, they kept them quiet.

There was plenty of junk to jettison, over the next quarter of an hour. Laser beams struck the station repeatedly, although Stromsen was able to block most of the beams with the heat-shielded lifeboats. Still, despite the mobile shields, the station was being slashed apart, bit by bit. Chunks of the outer hull ripped away, clouds of air blowing out of the upper level to form a brief fog around the station before dissipating into the vacuum of space. Cartons of supplies, pieces of equipment, even spare space suits, went spiraling out, pushed by air pressure as the compartments in which they had been housed were ripped apart by the probing incessant beams of energy.

Feeney struck back at the ABM satellites, but for every one he hit, another maneuvered into range to replace it.

"I'm running low on fuel for the lasers," he reported.

"So must they," said Hazard, trying to sound calm. "Aye, but they've got a few more than fifteen to play with."

"Stay with it, Mr. Feeney. You're doing fine." Hazard patted the shoulder of the Irishman's bulky suit. Glancing at Stromsen's status displays, he saw rows of red lights glowering like accusing eyes. *They're taking the station apart, piece by piece. It's only a matter of time before we're finished.*

Aloud, he announced, "I'm going to check with the damage-control party. Call me if anything unusual happens."

Yang quipped, "How do you define 'unusual,' sir?" Stromsen and Feeney laughed. Hazard wished he could, too. He made do with flashing a brief grin the Chinese-American, thinking, *at least their morale hasn't cracked. Not yet.*

The damage-control party was working on level three, reconnecting a secondary power line that ran along the overhead through the main passageway. A laser beam had burned through the deck of the second level and severed the line, cutting power to the station's main computer.

A shaft of brilliant sunlight lanced down from the outer hull through two levels of the station and onto the deck of level three.

One space-suited figure was dangling upside-down halfway through the hole in the overhead, splicing cable carefully with gloved hands, while a second hovered nearby with a small welding torch. Two more were working farther down the passageway, where a larger hole had been burned halfway down the bulkhead.

Through that jagged rip Hazard could see clear out to space and the rim of the Earth, glaring bright with swirls of white clouds.

He recognized Varshni by his small size even before he could see the Indian flag on his shoulder or read the name stenciled on the front of his suit.

"Mr. Varshni, I want you and your crew to leave level three. It's getting too dangerous here."

"But, sir," Varshni protested, "our duty is to repair damage."

"There'll be damage on level four soon enough."

"But the computer requires power."

"It can run on its internal batteries."

"But for how long?"

"Long enough," said Hazard grimly.

Varshni refused to be placated. "I am not risking lives unnecessarily, sir."

"I didn't say you were."

"I am operating on sound principles," the Indian insisted, "exactly as required in the book of regulations."

"I'm not faulting you, man. You and your crew have done a fine job."

The others had stopped their work. They were watching the exchange between their superior and the station commander.

"I have operated on the principle that lightning does not strike twice in the same place. In old-fashioned naval parlance this is referred to, I believe, as 'chasing salvos.' "

Hazard stared at the diminutive Indian. Even inside the visored space suit, Varshni appeared stiff with anger. Chasing salvos—that's what a little ship does when it's under attack by a bigger ship: run to where the last shells splashed, because it's pretty certain that the next salvo won't hit there. I've insulted his abilities, Hazard realized. And in front of his team. Damned fool!

"Mr. Varshni," Hazard explained slowly, "this battle will be decided, one way or the other, in the next twenty minutes or so. You and your team have done an excellent job of keeping damage to a minimum. Without you, we would have been forced to surrender."

Varshni seemed to relax a little. Hazard could sense his chin rising a notch inside his helmet.

"But the battle is entering a new phase," Hazard went on. "Level three is now vulnerable to direct laser damage. I can't afford to lose you and your team at this critical stage. Moreover, the computer and the rest of the most sensitive equipment are on level four and in the Combat Information Center. Those are the areas that need our protection and those are the areas where I want you to operate. Is that understood?"

A heartbeat's hesitation. Then Varshni said, "Yes, of course, sir. I understand. Thank you for explaining it to me."

"Okay. Now finish your work here and then get down to level four."

"Yes, sir."

Shaking his head inside his helmet, Hazard turned and pushed himself toward the ladderway that led down to level four and the CIC.

A blinding glare lit the passageway and he heard screams of agony behind him. Blinking against the burning afterimage, Hazard turned to see Varshni's figure almost sliced in half. A dark burn line slashed diagonally across the torso of his space suit. Tiny globules of blood floated out from it. The metal overhead was blackened and curled now. A woman was screaming. She was up by the overhead, thrashing wildly with pain, her backpack ablaze. The other technician was nowhere to be seen.

Hazard rushed to the Indian while the other two members of the damage-control team raced to their partner and sprayed extinguisher foam on her backpack.

Over the woman's screams he heard Varshni's gagging whisper. "It's no use, sir… no use…"

"You did fine, son." Hazard held the dying little man in his arms. "You did fine."

He felt the life slip away. Lightning does strike in the same place twice, Hazard thought. You've chased your last salvo, son.

Both the man and the woman who had been working on the power cable had been wounded by the laser beam. The man's right arm had been sliced off at the elbow, the woman badly burned on her back when her life-support pack exploded. Hazard and the two remaining damage-control men carried them to the sick bay, where the station's one doctor was already working over three other casualties.

The sick bay was on the third level. Hazard realized how vulnerable that was. He made his way down to the CIC, at the heart of the station, knowing that it was protected not only by layers of metal but by human flesh as well. The station rocked again and Hazard heard the ominous groaning of tortured metal as he pushed weightlessly along the ladderway.

He felt bone-weary as he opened the hatch and floated into the CIC. One look at the haggard faces of his three young officers told him that they were on the edge of defeat as well. Stromsen's status display board was studded with glowering red lights.

"This station is starting to resemble a piece of Swiss cheese," Hazard quipped lamely as he lifted the visor of his helmet.

No one laughed. Or even smiled.

"Varshni bought it," he said, taking up his post between Stromsen and Feeney.

"We heard it," said Yang.

Hazard looked around the CIC. It felt stifling hot, dank with the smell of fear.

"Mr. Feeney," he said, "discontinue all offensive operations."

"Sir?" The Irishman's voice squeaked with surprise.

"Don't fire back at the sonsofbitches," Hazard snapped. "Is that clear enough?"

Feeney raised his hands up above his shoulders, like a croupier showing that he was not influencing the roulette wheel.

"Miss Stromsen, when the next laser beam is fired at us, shut down the main power generator. Miss Yang, issue instructions over the intercom that all personnel are to place themselves on level four—except for the sick bay. No one is to use the intercom. That is an order."

Stromsen asked, "The power generator?"

"We'll run on the backup fuel cells and batteries. They don't make so much heat."

There were more questions in Stromsen's eyes, but she turned back to her consoles silently.

Hazard explained, "We are going to run silent. Buckbee, Cardillo, and company have been pounding the hell out of us for about half an hour. They have inflicted considerable damage. However, they don't know that we've been able to shield ourselves with the lifeboats. They think they've hurt us much more than they actually have."

"You want them to think that they've finished us off, then?" asked Feeney.

"That's right. But, Mr. Feeney, let me ask you a hypothetical question..."

The chamber shook again and the screens dimmed, then came back to their normal brightness.

Stromsen punched a key on her console. "Main generator shut down, sir."

Hazard knew it was his imagination, but the screens seemed to become slightly dimmer.

"Miss Yang?" he asked.

"All personnel have been instructed to move down to level four and stay off the intercom."

Hazard nodded, satisfied. Turning back to Feeney, he resumed, "Suppose, Mr. Feeney, that you are in command of *Graham*. How would you know that you've knocked out *Hunter*?"

Feeney absently started to stroke his chin and bumped his fingertips against the rim of his helmet instead. "I suppose… if *Hunter* stopped shooting back, and I couldn't detect any radio emissions from her…"

"And infrared!" Yang added. "With the power generator out, our infrared signature goes way down."

"We appear to be dead in the water," said Stromsen.

"Right."

"But what does it gain us?" Yang asked.

"Time," answered Stromsen. "In another ten minutes or so we'll be within contact range of Geneva."

Hazard patted the top of her helmet. "Exactly. But more than that. We get them to stop shooting at us. We save the wounded up in the sick bay."

"And ourselves," said Feeney.

"Yes," Hazard admitted. "And ourselves." For long moments they hung weightlessly, silent, waiting, hoping.

"Sir," said Yang, "a query from *Graham,* asking if we surrender."

"No reply," Hazard ordered. "Maintain complete silence."

The minutes stretched. Hazard glided to Yang's comm console and taped a message for Geneva, swiftly outlining what had happened.

"I want that tape compressed into a couple of milliseconds and burped by the tightest laser beam we have down to Geneva."

Yang nodded. "I suppose the energy surge for a low-power communications laser won't be enough for them to detect."

"Probably not, but it's a chance we'll have to take. Beam it at irregular intervals as long as Geneva is in view."

"Yes, sir."

"Sir!" Feeney called out. "Looks like *Graham*'s detached a lifeboat."

"Trajectory analysis?"

Feeney tapped at his navigation console. "Heading for us," he reported.

Hazard smiled grimly.

"They're coming over to make sure. Cardillo's an old submariner; he knows all about running silent. They're sending over an armed party to make sure we're finished."

"And to take control of our satellites," Yang suggested.

Hazard brightened. "Right! There're only two ways to control the ABM satellites—either from the station on patrol or from Geneva." He spread his arms happily. "That means they're not in control of Geneva! We've got a good chance to pull their cork!"

But there was no response from Geneva when they beamed their data-compressed message to IPF headquarters. *Hunter* glided past in its unusually low orbit, a tattered wreck desperately calling for help. No answer reached them.

And the lifeboat from *Graham* moved inexorably closer.

The gloom in the CIC was thick enough to stuff a mattress as Geneva disappeared over the horizon and the boat from *Graham* came toward them. Hazard watched the boat on one of Stromsen's screens: it was bright and shining in the sunlight, not blackened by scorching laser beams, unsullied by splashes of human blood.

We could zap it into dust, he thought. One word from me and Feeney could focus half a dozen lasers on it. The men aboard her must be volunteers, willing to risk their necks to make certain that we're finished. He felt a grim admiration for them. Then he wondered, is Jon on board with them?

"Mr. Feeney, what kind of weapons do you think they're carrying?"

Feeney's brows rose toward his scalp. "Weapons, sir? You mean, like sidearms?"

Hazard nodded.

"Personal weapons are not allowed aboard station, sir. Regulations forbid it."

"I know. But what do you bet they've got pistols, at least. Maybe some submachine guns."

"Damned dangerous stuff for a space station," said Feeney.

Hazard smiled tightly at the Irishman. "Are you afraid they'll put a few more holes in our hull?"

Yang saw what he was driving at. "Sir, there are no weapons aboard *Hunter*—unless you want to count kitchen knives."

"They'll be coming aboard with guns, just to make sure," Hazard said. "I want to capture them alive and use them as hostages. That's our last remaining card. If we can't do that, we've got to surrender."

"They'll be in full suits." said Stromsen. "Each on his own individual life-support system."

"How can we capture them? Or even fight them?" Yang wondered aloud.

Hazard detected no hint of defeat in their voices. The despair of a half hour earlier was gone now. A new excitement had hold of them. He was holding a glimmer of hope for them, and they were reaching for it.

"There can't be more than six of them aboard that boat," Feeney mused.

I wonder if Cardillo has the guts to lead the boarding party in person, Hazard asked himself.

"We don't have any useful weapons," said Yang.

"But we have some tools," Stromsen pointed out. "Maybe..."

"What do the lifeboat engines use for propellant?" Hazard asked rhetorically.

"Methane and oh-eff-two," Feeney replied, looking puzzled.

Hazard nodded. "Miss Stromsen, which of our supply magazines are still intact—if any?"

It took them several minutes to understand what he was driving at, but when they finally saw the light, the three young officers went speedily to work. Together with the four unwounded members of the crew, they prepared a welcome for the boarders from *Graham*.

Finally, Hazard watched on Stromsen's display screens as the *Graham*'s boat sniffed around the battered station. Strict silence was in force aboard *Hunter*. Even in the CIC, deep at the heart of the battle station, they spoke in tense whispers.

"I hope the bastards like what they see," Hazard muttered.

"They know that we used the lifeboats for shields," said Yang.

"Active armor," Hazard said. "Did you know the idea was invented by the man this station's named after?"

"They're looking for a docking port," Stromsen pointed out.

"Only one left," said Feeney.

They could hang their boat almost anywhere and walk in through the holes they've put in us, Hazard said to himself. But they won't. They'll go by the book and find an intact docking port. They've got to! Everything depends on that.

He felt his palms getting slippery with nervous perspiration as the lifeboat slowly, slowly moved around *Hunter* toward the Earth-facing side, where the only usable port was located. Hazard had seen to it that all the other ports had been disabled.

"They're buying it!" Stromsen's whisper held a note of triumph.

"Sir!" Yang hissed urgently. "A message just came in—laser beam, ultracompressed."

"From where?"

"Computer's decrypting," she replied, her snub-nosed face wrinkled with concentration. "Coming up on my center screen, sir."

Hazard slid over toward her. The words on the screen read:

From: IPF Regional HQ, Lagos.

To: Commander, battle station *Hunter*.

Message begins. Coup attempt in Geneva a failure, thanks in large part to your refusal to surrender your command. Situation still unclear, however. Imperative you retain control of *Hunter*, at all costs. Message ends.

He read it aloud, in a guttural whisper, so that Feeney and Stromsen understood what was at stake.

"We're not alone," Hazard told them. "They know what's happening, and help is on the way."

That was stretching the facts, he knew. And he knew they knew. But it was reassuring to think that someone, somewhere, was preparing to help them.

Hazard watched them grinning to one another. In his mind, though, he kept repeating the phrase, "Imperative you retain control of *Hunter*, at all costs."

At all costs, Hazard said to himself, closing his eyes wearily, seeing Varshni dying in his arms and the others maimed. At all costs.

The bastards, Hazard seethed inwardly. The dirty, power-grabbing, murdering bastards. Once they set foot inside my station, I'll kill them like the poisonous snakes they are. I'll squash them flat. I'll cut them open just like they've slashed my kids.

He stopped abruptly and forced himself to take a deep breath. Yeah, sure. Go for personal revenge. That'll make the world a better place to live in, won't it?

"Sir, are you all right?"

Hazard opened his eyes and saw Stromsen staring at him. "Yes, I'm fine. Thank you."

"They've docked, sir," said the Norwegian.

"They're debarking and coming up passageway C, just as you planned."

Looking past her to the screens, Hazard saw that there were six of them, all in space suits, visors down. And pistols in their gloved hands.

"Nothing bigger than pistols?"

"No, sir. Not that we can see, at least."

Turning to Feeney. "Ready with the aerosols?"

"Yes, sir."

"All crew members evacuated from the area?"

"They're all back on level four, except for the sick bay."

Hazard never took his eyes from the screens. The six space-suited boarders were floating down the passageway that led to the lower levels of the station, which were still pressurized and held breathable air. They stopped at the air lock, saw that it was functional. The leader of their group started working the wall unit that controlled the lock.

"Can we hear them?" he asked Yang.

Wordlessly, she touched a stud on her keyboard.

"…use the next section of the passageway as an air lock," someone was saying. "Standard procedure. Then we'll pump the air back into it once we're inside."

"But we stay in the suits until we check out the whole station. That's an order," said another voice.

Buckbee? Hazard's spirits soared. Buckbee will make a nice hostage, he thought. Not as good as Cardillo, but good enough.

Just as he had hoped, the six boarders went through the airtight hatch, closed it behind them, and started the pump that filled the next section of passageway with air once again.

"Something funny here, sir," said one of the space-suited figures.

"Yeah, the air's kind of misty."

"Never saw anything like this before. Christ, it's like Mexico City air."

"Stay in your suits!" It was Buckbee's voice, Hazard was certain of it. "Their life-support systems must have been damaged in our bombardment. They're probably all dead."

You wish, Hazard thought. He gave the order to Feeney. "Seal that hatch."

Feeney pecked at a button on his console.

"And the next one."

"Already done, sir."

Hazard waited, watching Stromsen's main screen as the six boarders shuffled weightlessly to the next hatch and found that it would not respond to the control unit on the bulkhead.

"Damn! We'll have to double back and find another route."

"Miss Yang, I'm ready to hold converse with our guests," said Hazard.

She flashed a brilliant smile and touched the appropriate keys, then pointed at him. "You're on the air!"

"Buckbee, this is Hazard."

All six of the boarders froze for an instant, then spun weightlessly in midair, trying to locate the source of the new voice.

"You are trapped in that section of corridor," Hazard said. "The mist that you see in the air is diluted oxygen difluoride from our lifeboat propellant tanks. Very volatile stuff. Don't strike any matches."

"What the hell are you saying, Hazard?"

"You're locked in that passageway, Buckbee. If you try to fire those popguns you're carrying, you'll blow yourselves to pieces."

"And you too!"

"We're already dead, you prick. Taking you with us is the only joy I'm going to get out of this."

"You're bluffing!"

Hazard snapped, "Then show me how brave you are, Buckbee. Take a shot at the hatch."

The six boarders hovered in the misty passageway like figures in a surrealistic painting. Seconds ticked by, each one stretching excruciatingly. Hazard felt a pain in his jaws and realized he was clenching his teeth hard enough to chip them.

He took his eyes from the screen momentarily to glance at his three youngsters. They were just as tense as he was. They knew how long the odds of their gamble were. The passageway was filled with nothing more than aerosol mists from every spray can the crew could locate in the supply magazines.

"What do you want, Hazard?" Buckbee said at last, his voice sullen, like a spoiled little boy who had been denied a cookie.

Hazard let out his breath. Then, as cheerfully as he could manage, "I've got what I want. Six hostages. How much air do your suits carry? Twelve hours?"

"What do you mean?"

"You've got twelve hours to convince Cardillo and the rest of your pals to surrender."

"You're crazy, Hazard."

"I've had a tough day, Buckbee. I don't need your insults. Call me when you're ready to deal."

"You'll be killing your son!"

Hazard had half expected it, but still it hit him like a blow. "Jonnie, are you there?"

"Yes I am, Dad."

Hazard strained forward, peering hard at the display screen, trying to determine which one of the space-suited figures was his son.

"Well, this is a helluva fix, isn't it?" he said softly.

"Dad, you don't have to wait twelve hours."

"Shut your mouth!" Buckbee snapped.

"Fuck you," snarled Jon Jr. "I'm not going to get myself killed for nothing."

"I'll shoot you!" Hazard saw Buckbee level his gun at Jon Jr.

"And kill yourself? You haven't got the guts," Jonnie sneered. Hazard almost smiled. How many times had his son used that tone on him.

Buckbee's hand wavered. He let the gun slip from his gloved fingers. It drifted slowly, weightlessly, away from him.

Hazard swallowed. Hard.

"Dad, in another hour or two the game will be over. Cardillo lied to you. The Russians never came in with us. Half a dozen ships full of troops are lifting off from IPF centers all over the globe."

"Is that the truth, son?"

"Yes, sir, it is. Our only hope was to grab control of your satellites. Once the coup attempt in Geneva flopped, Cardillo knew that if he could control three or four sets of ABM satellites, he could at least force a stalemate. But all he's got is *Graham* and *Wood.* Nobody else."

"You damned little traitor!" Buckbee screeched.

Jon Jr. laughed. "Yeah, you're right. But I'm going to be a *live* traitor. I'm not dying for the likes of you."

Hazard thought swiftly. Jon Jr. might defy his father, might argue with him, even revile him, but he had never known the lad to lie to him.

"Buckbee, the game's over," he said slowly. "You'd better get the word to Cardillo before there's more bloodshed."

* * *

It took another six hours before it was all sorted out. A shuttle filled with armed troops and an entire replacement crew finally arrived at the battered hulk of *Hunter.* The relieving commander, a stubby, compactly built black man from New Jersey who had been a U.S. Air Force fighter pilot, made a grim tour of inspection with Hazard.

From inside his space suit he whistled in amazement at the battle damage.

"Shee-it, you don't need a new crew, you need a new station!"

"It's still functional," Hazard said quietly, then added proudly, "and so is my crew, or what's left of them. They ran this station and kept control of the satellites."

"The stuff legends are made of, my man," said the new commander.

Hazard and his crew filed tiredly into the waiting shuttle, thirteen grimy, exhausted men and women in the pale-blue fatigues of the IPF. Three of them were wrapped in mesh cocoons and attended by medical personnel. Two others were bandaged but ambulatory.

He shook hands with each and every one of them as they stepped from the station's only functional air lock into the shuttle's passenger compartment. Hovering there weightlessly, his creased, craggy face unsmiling, to each of his crew members he said, "Thank you. We couldn't have succeeded without your effort."

The last three through the hatch were Feeney, Stromsen, and Yang. The Irishman looked embarrassed as Hazard shook his hand.

"I'm recommending you for promotion. You were damned cool under fire."

"Frozen stiff with fear, you mean."

To Stromsen, "You, too, Miss Stromsen. You've earned a promotion."

"Thank you, sir," was all she could say.

"And you, little lady," he said to Yang. "You were outstanding."

She started to say something, then flung her arms around Hazard's neck and squeezed tight. "I was so frightened!" she whispered in his ear. "You kept me from cracking up."

Hazard held her around the waist for a moment. As they disengaged he felt his face turning flame red. He turned away from the hatch, not wanting to see the expressions on the rest of his crew members.

Buckbee was coming through the air lock. Behind him were his five men. Including Jon Jr.

They passed Hazard in absolute silence, Buckbee's face as cold and angry as an Antarctic storm.

Jon Jr. was the last in line. None of the would-be boarders was in handcuffs, but they all had the hangdog look of prisoners. All except Hazard's son.

He stopped before his father and met the older man's gaze. Jon Jr.'s gray eyes were level with his father's, unswerving, unafraid.

He made a bitter little smile. "I still don't agree with you," he said without preamble. "I don't think the IPF is workable—and it's certainly not in the best interests of the United States."

"But you threw your lot in with us when it counted," Hazard said.

"The hell I did!" Jon Jr. looked genuinely aggrieved. "I just didn't see any sense in dying for a lost cause."

"Really?"

"Cardillo and Buckbee and the rest of them were a bunch of idiots. If I had known how stupid they are I wouldn't…"

He stopped himself, grinned ruefully, and shrugged his shoulders. "This isn't over, you know. You won the battle, but the war's not ended yet."

"I'll do what I can to get them to lighten your sentence," Hazard said.

"Don't stick your neck out for me! I'm still dead-set against you on this."

Hazard smiled wanly at the youngster. "And you're still my son."

Jon Jr. blinked, looked away, then ducked through the hatch and made for a seat in the shuttle.

Hazard formally turned the station over to its new commander, saluted one last time, then went into the shuttle's passenger compartment. He hung there weightlessly a moment as the hatch behind him was swung shut and sealed.

Most of the seats were already filled. There was an empty one beside Yang, but after their little scene at the hatch Hazard was hesitant about sitting next to her. He glided down the aisle and picked a seat that had no one next to it. Not one of his crew. Not Jon Jr.

There's a certain amount of loneliness involved in command, he told himself. It's not wise to get too familiar with people you have to order into battle.

He felt, rather than heard, a thump as the shuttle disengaged from the station's air lock. He sensed the winged hypersonic spaceplane turning and angling its nose for reentry into the atmosphere.

Back to… Hazard realized that *home,* for him, was no longer on Earth. For almost all of his adult life, home had been where his command was. Now his home was in space. The time he spent on Earth would be merely waiting time, suspended animation until his new command was ready.

"Sir, may I intrude?"

He looked up and saw Stromsen floating in the aisle by his seat.

"What is it, Miss Stromsen?"

She pulled herself down into the seat next to him but did not bother to latch the safety harness. From a breast pocket in her sweat-stained fatigues she pulled a tiny flat tin. It was marked with a red cross and some printing, hidden by her thumb.

Stromsen opened the tin. "You lost your medication patch," she said. "I thought you might want a fresh one." She was smiling at him, shyly, almost like a daughter might.

Hazard reached up and felt behind his left ear. She was right, the patch was gone.

"I wonder how long ago..."

"It's been hours, at least," said Stromsen.

"Never noticed."

Her smile brightened. "Perhaps you don't need it anymore."

He smiled back at her. "Miss Stromsen, I think you're absolutely right. My stomach feels fine. I believe I have finally become adapted to weightlessness."

"It's rather a shame that we're on our way back to Earth. You'll have to adapt all over again the next time out."

Hazard nodded. "Somehow I don't think that's going to be much of a problem for me anymore."

He let his head sink back into the seat cushion and closed his eyes, enjoying for the first time the exhilarating floating sensation of weightlessness.

The War Memorial

Allen M. Steele

Editor's Introduction

"IT IS WELL that war is so terrible! Otherwise we should grow too fond of it!" Robert E. Lee is said to have told General James Longstreet as he watched the Union forces, banners waving, advance to engage Lee's well-prepared army in the Union disaster at Fredericksburg. Allen Steele tells us of another battle that emphasizes the lesson.

The first-wave assault is jinxed from the very beginning.

Even before the dropship touches down, its pilot shouts over the comlink that a Pax missile battery seven klicks away has locked in on their position, despite the ECM buffer set up by the lunarsats. So it's going to be a dust-off; the pilot has done his job by getting the men down to the surface, and he doesn't want to be splattered across Mare Tranquillitatis.

It doesn't matter anyway. Baker Company has been deployed for less than two minutes before the Pax heatseekers pummel the ground around them and take out the dropship even as it begins its ascent.

Giordano hears the pilot scream one last obscenity before his ugly spacecraft is reduced to metal rain, then something slams against his back and everything within the suit goes black. For an instant he believes he's dead, that he's been nailed by one of the heatseekers, but it's just debris from the dropship. The half-ton ceramic-polymer shell of the Mark III Valkyrie Combat Armor Suit has absorbed the brunt of the impact.

When the lights flicker back on within his soft cocoon and the flatscreen directly in front of his face stops fuzzing, he sees that not everyone has been so lucky. A few dozen meters away at three o'clock, there's a new crater that used to be Robinson. The only thing left of Baker Company's resident card cheat is the severed rifle arm of his CAS.

He doesn't have time to contemplate Robinson's fate. He's in the midst of battle. Sgt. Boyle's voice comes through the comlink, shouting orders. Traveling overwatch, due west, head for Marker One-Eight-Five. Kemp, take Robinson's position. Cortez, you're point. Stop staring, Giordano (yes sir). Move, move, move…

So they move, seven soldiers in semi-robotic heavy armor, bounding across the flat silver-gray landscape. Tin men trying to outrun the missiles plummeting down around them, the soundless explosions they make when they hit. For several kilometers around them, everywhere they look, there are scores of other tin men doing the same, each trying to survive a silent hell called the Sea of Tranquillity.

Giordano is sweating hard, his breath coming in ragged gasps. He tells himself that if he can just make Marker One-Eight-Five—crater Arago, or so the map overlay tells him—then everything will be okay. The crater walls will protect them. Once Baker Company sets up its guns and erects a new ECM buffer, they can dig in nice and tight and wait it out; the beachhead will have been established by then and the hard part of Operation Monkey Wrench will be over.

But the crater is five-and-a-half klicks away, across plains as flat and wide-open as Missouri pasture, and between here and there a lot of shitfire is coming down. The Pax Astra guns in the foothills of the lunar highlands due west of their position can see them coming; the enemy has the high ground, and they're throwing everything they can at the invading force.

Sgt. Boyle knows his platoon is in trouble. He orders everyone to use their jumpjets. Screw formation; it's time to run like hell.

Giordano couldn't agree more whole-heartedly. He tells the Valkyrie to engage the twin miniature rockets mounted on the back of his carapace.

Nothing happens.

Once again, he tells the voice-activated computer mounted against the back of his neck to fire the jumpjets. When there's still no response, he goes to manual, using the tiny controls nestled within the palm of his right hand inside the suit's artificial arm.

At that instant, everything goes dark again, just like it did when the shrapnel from the dropship hit the back of his suit.

This time, though, it stays dark.

A red LCD lights above his forehead, telling him that there's been a total system crash.

Cursing, he finds the manual override button and stabs it with his little finger. As anticipated, it causes the computer to completely reboot itself; he hears servomotors grind within the carapace as its limbs move into neutral position, until his boots are planted firmly on the ground and his arms are next to his sides, his rifle pointed uselessly at the ground.

There is a dull click from somewhere deep within the armor, then silence.

Except for the red LCD, everything remains dark.

He stabs frantically at the palm buttons, but there's no power to any of the suit's major subsystems. He tries to move his arms and legs, but finds them frozen in place.

Limbs, jumpjets, weapons, ECM, comlink… nothing works.

Now he's sweating more than ever. The impact of that little bit of debris from the dropship must have been worse than he thought. Something must have shorted out, badly, within the Valkyrie's onboard computer.

He twists his head to the left so he can gaze through the eyepiece of the optical periscope, the only instrument within the suit that isn't dependent upon computer control. What he sees, terrifies him: the rest of his platoon jumpjetting for the security of the distant crater, while missiles continue to explode all around him.

Abandoning him. Leaving him behind.

He screams at the top of his lungs, yelling for Boyle and Kemp and Cortez and the rest, calling them foul names, demanding that they wait or come back for them, knowing that it's futile. They can't hear him. For whatever reason, they've already determined that he's out of action; they cannot afford to risk their lives by coming back to lug an inert CAS across a battlefield.

He tries again to move his legs, but it's pointless. Without direct interface from the main computer, the limbs of his suit are immobile. He might as well be wearing a concrete block.

The suit contains three hours of oxygen, fed through pumps controlled by another computer tucked against his belly, along with rest of its life-support systems. So at least he won't suffocate or fry...

For the next three hours, at any rate.

Probably less. The digital chronometer and life-support gauge are dead, so there's no way of knowing for sure.

As he watches, even the red coal of the LCD warning lamp grows dim until it finally goes cold, leaving him in the dark.

He has become a living statue. Fully erect, boots firmly placed upon the dusty regolith, arms held rigid at his sides, he is in absolute stasis.

For three hours. Certainly less.

For all intents and purposes, he is dead.

In the smothering darkness of his suit, Giordano prays to a god in which he has never really believed. Then, for lack of anything else to do, he raises his eyes to the periscope eyepiece and watches as the battle rages on around him.

He fully expects—and, after a time, even hopes—for a Pax missile to relieve him of his ordeal, but this small mercy never occurs. Without an active infrared or electromagnetic target to lock in upon, the heat-seekers miss the small spot of ground he occupies, instead decimating everything around him.

Giordano becomes a mute witness to the horror of the worst conflict of the Moon War, what historians will later call the Battle of Mare Tranquillitatis. Loyalty, duty, honor, patriotism… all the things in which he once believed are soon rendered null and void as he watches countless lives being lost.

Dropships touch down near and distant, depositing soldiers in suits similar to his own. Some don't even make it to the ground before they become miniature supernovas.

Bodies fly apart, blown to pieces even as they charge across the wasteland for the deceptive security of distant craters and rills.

An assault rover bearing three lightsuited soldiers rushes past him, only to be hit by fire from the hills. It is thrown upside down, crushing two of the soldiers beneath it. The third man, his legs broken and his suit punctured, manages to crawl from the wreckage. He dies at Giordano's feet, his arms reaching out to him.

He has no idea whether Baker Company has survived, but he suspects it hasn't, since he soon sees a bright flash from the general direction of the crater it was supposed to occupy and hold.

In the confines of his suit, he weeps and screams and howls against the madness erupting around him. In the end, he goes mad himself, cursing the same god to whom he prayed earlier for the role to which he has been damned.

If God cares, it doesn't matter. By then, the last of Giordano's oxygen reserves have been exhausted; he asphyxiates long before his three hours are up, his body still held upright by the Mark III Valkyrie Combat Armor Suit.

When he is finally found, sixty-eight hours later, by a patrol from the victorious Pax Astra Free Militia, they are astonished that anything was left standing on the killing ground. This sole combat suit, damaged only by a small steel pipe wedged into its CPU housing, with a dead man inexplicably sealed inside, is the only thing left intact. All else has been reduced to scorched dust and shredded metal.

So they leave him standing.

They do not remove the CAS from its place, nor do they attempt to pry the man from his armor. Instead, they erect a circle of stones around the Valkyrie. Later, when peace has been negotiated and lunar independence has been achieved, a small plaque is placed at his feet.

The marker bears no name. Because so many lives were lost during the battle, no one can be certain of who was wearing that particular CAS on that particular day.

An eternal flame might have been placed at his feet, but it wasn't. Nothing burns on the Moon.

Rules of Engagement

Michael Flynn

Editor's Introduction

Mike Flynn is a polymath. He is known as a hard science SF writer who is also a storyteller, but he is also a quality control engineer who uses advanced probability theory in his work, a medieval history expert, and an accomplished writer on the history and philosophy of science. He is co-author, with Larry Niven and Jerry Pournelle, of *Fallen Angels*.

When veterans get together they often tell war stories. Here we have war stories told with a decided twist.

Winter having locked the passes with snow and ice, the brass parceled out long-deferred leaves and junior officers scattered across the country. Some descended on their hometowns to rest in the bosoms of their families. Some came to the City to rest in other sorts of bosoms. That was the last winter before the big offensive, when I still had the flat in Chelsea. Jimmy Topeka dropped in to see me, all somber as always. He seemed to have something on his mind, but he talked around it six ways from Sunday the way he always does and hadn't gotten to the nub of it before Angel Osborne clumped his way up the stairs. I hadn't seen Angel in almost three years, though he and Jimmy had crossed paths during the Red River campaign. I thought how we lacked only Lyle "the Style" Guzman to make the old gang complete; and the Angel ups and beeps him over the Lynx and, wouldn't you know it, Lyle was in the City, too. So before long we were all together, just like old times, drinking and shooting the shit and waiting for the sun to come up. Those were wild years, and we were still young enough to be immortal.

I hadn't much in the way of furniture; and once Angel had occupied two-thirds of the sofa, there was less of it to go around. Lyle, being slightly built, perched himself on the table, while Jimmy raided my kitchen and passed out bottles of Skull Mountain before squatting cross-legged on the floor. We all said what a coincidence and long time no see and what've you been up to.

It wasn't quite like old times. A few years had gone by between us. They were long years; it didn't seem possible they'd held only three-hundred-odd days each. The four of us had been different places, seen different sights; and so we had become different men than the ones who had known each other at camp. But also there was a curtain between me and the three of them. Every now and then, in the midst of some tale or other, they would share a look; or they would fall silent and they'd say, well, you had to be there. You see, they'd been Inside and I hadn't, and that marks a man.

Angel had served with the 82nd against the Snakes; and Lyle had seen action against both the Crips and the Yoopers. Jimmy allowed as he'd tangoed in the high country, where the bandits had secret refuges among the twisting canyons; but he said very little else. Only he drank two beers for every one the others put down, and Jimmy had never been a drinking man.

They asked politely what I'd been up to and pretended great interest in my stories and news dispatches. They swore they read all of my pieces on the ©-Net, and maybe they did.

They didn't blame me for it. They knew I'd as soon be Inside with them, suited-up and popping Joeys. The four of us had been commissioned power suit lieutenants together; had gone through the grueling training side by side. I still had the bars. I still looked at them some nights when the hurt wasn't so bad, when I could think about what might have been.

Talk detoured through the winter crop of Hollywood morphies and whether American could take Congress from Liberty next year and how the Air Cav had collared El Muerte down in the panhandle and have you seen Chica Domosan's latest virtcheo. Angel and Lyle practically drooled when I told them I had the uncensored seedy; and they insisted on viewing it right then and there. I only had the one virtch hat, so they had to take turns watching. With the stereo earphones and the wrap-around goggs enclosing your head it was just like she was dancing and singing and peeling right there in front of you.

Afterwards, we talked Grand Strategy, shifting troops all over the continent, free of all political constraints and certain we would never hash it the way the Pentagon had. Doubt flowers from seeds that spend decades germinating; confidence is a weed that springs up overnight. And so youth gains in certitude what it lacks in prudence. It was no different back then; only, the stakes were higher.

Eventually, we spoke of our own personal plans. Lyle went how he was angling for an assignment down in the Frontera—"because that's where the next big yee-haw's going to be"—and Angel wanted nothing more than to hunt Joeys up in the Nations. White teeth split his broad, dark face. The rest of us counted the Nations a nest of traitors and secessionists; but with Angel it was personal. Then Jimmy said, in that quiet voice of his, that he'd put in for a hoofer. We grinned and waited for the punch line and when it didn't come our smiles slowly faded. "I'm serious," he said. "I won't go Inside again."

Angel looked shocked and Lyle's face stiffened in disapproval; but I was the one who spoke up. "How can you say that, Jimmy? After what we went through together in camp? You're a suit lieutenant, God damn it!" Dismay pried me from the chair behind my cluttered workstation; or rather, it tried to. My legs betrayed me and I nearly cracked my head on the edge of the desk as I toppled.

The others were all around me. I swatted Jimmy's hand away and let the Angel bear me up and set me back in my accustomed place. "Why'd you do that, man?" Lyle asked as he fussed the blanket around my waist. "You shouldn't oughta do that." Jimmy wouldn't meet my eyes. We'd just gotten our bars, we were celebrating, and that hog of Jimmy's looked phatter and stoopider the more I drank. Jimmy always blamed himself, but it was my idea; so what the hell. That was then.

"I get around all right," I said to excuse myself. I could function. Most days, I could even walk. "Sometimes, the spasms—You know."

They all said they knew; but how could they? You dream and you train for months and months and then in one drunken moment you throw it all away for a God-damned motorcycle ride. Power suits amplify the suit louie's every move. A man can't wear it if he suffers unpredictable seizures. As if to underscore my thoughts, my left leg began to twitch. If I'd been suited up, my walker would have toppled. Stress, the doctors all said. It was stress that brought it on; but what did they know?

I was barred by circumstance; but Jimmy planned to walk away. That made no sense. Who would give up a power suit if he didn't have to? Angel was puzzled, too; and Lyle said, "Sometimes a guy gets syndrome and he just can't take being Inside no more." He was so damned understanding that Jimmy flushed and said how it wasn't that at all; or at least, not exactly.

"You know how things stand up in the mountains," Jimmy said. "I don't suppose it's much different with the Yoopers or the others, except maybe the terrain's rougher. Straight up or down as often as not, and canyons pinched as tight as a preacher's wife on Sunday. Officially, the whole area's pacified; only someone forgot to tell the militias."

"They are not 'militias,' suit lieutenant," said Angel in a mock-official voice. "They are 'bandits'."

"I know that," Jimmy told him. "We only *call* 'em 'militias.' Like you say 'gangs' when you pull urban duty." He swigged his Skull and sat with the bottle dangling by its neck between his knees while he scowled at nothing. "The war's platoon-size up there," he said at last. "The regiment's scattered in firebases all across God's Country—only God ain't home. The only time I ever saw my colonel was over the Lynx. We got our orders—when we got any orders at all—from the twenty-four. Otherwise, we were on our own." He shook his head. "Pacified..."

"Who was your colonel," Lyle asked.

"Mandlebrot. He was a sumbitch. Worried more about the cost of patrolling than whether Joey walked the line. When I took the platoon out, I used to sling the word off the twenty-four, then put my dish tech on arrest so I could say I never got the bounceback telling me to stay put."

Angel laughed. "That's good. That's bean. Wish I'd thought of that."

That was the sort of hack Jimmy used to pull. Always by the book, but sometimes he wrote notes in the margins. "How long did you fool him?" I asked.

"Oh, not long," Jimmy admitted. "I said he was a sumbitch. Never said he was stupid. So sometimes I would go out unofficial-like with the reg'lar militia—the sheriff's posse. They had their own ATVs. Horses, too. Some places hooves'll take you where tires won't go. They were locals, and knew the country just as well as the bandits. I mean they knew it close up, like you know your girl-friend, not just from the up-and-down."

"You were too far north for the twenty-fours?" asked Angel.

Jimmy shrugged. "Nah, but the twenty-fours can't give you terrain detail the way an up-and-down in LEO can. Sometimes a little sliver between canyon walls was all the sky we could dish. There's always *something* up there but you have to code dance, depending on what sat' your dish can catch. Well, that sheriff was a clever pud. Didn't need an eye in the sky, because he had eyes and ears all over ground level—and kept his county in pretty good law 'n' order, considering. But he knew when he needed extra weenie, so he was happy enough when I tagged along. Not *happy*, you understand; but happy enough. The irregulars don't much like us; but they hate the bandits worse—'cause it's their brothers and cousins and all getting kneecapped and necklaced."

"An' half the time," said Angel, "it's their brothers and cousins and all that're doing the kneecaps and necklaces."

"Word up," said Lyle. "Neighbors huntin' neighbors. No wonder they ain't happy campers."

"Folks back here don't always draw a line between bandits and friendlies," I said, thinking about my ©-Net story, "The Loyalist." "So your possemen feel they have to prove their loyalty."

"Righteous beans," said Angel. "Hey. You hear what happened to the 7th down in the live oak country? 'Rooster' McGregor—you ever meet 'im? Skinny guy with teeth out to here?—he was doing just what you were, Jimmy. Riding with the posse when he couldn't take his platoon out. Only it turns out the possemen *were* the bandits. Deputy Dawgs by day; camos and piano wire by night. Rooster, he got his ticket stripped over it, but he accidentally hung the sheriff before the court martial took his bars."

Jimmy hadn't been listening. "They don't respect us," he said. "Never understood that 'til the last time I was Inside. Now…" He voice trailed off and his eyes took on a distant look. I traded glances with Lyle and Angel, and waited.

"We called him 'Wild Bob'," Jimmy said finally. "I suppose he had his own name for himself and some mumbo-jumbo, self-important rank. Generalissimo. Grand Kleagle. Lord High Naff-naff. Maybe he called himself The Bald Eagle, cause he sure as shit had no hair; but he could've called himself Winnie the Pooh, for all I cared. 'Cause what he was was a murderer and a rapist and an armed robber, and he probably picked his nose in public. What he'd do every now and then—just to let us know he was still around—he'd send a body floating down the river from the high country. One of our agents or a friendly or maybe just someone looked at him cross-eyed. Or he'd throw a roadblock up and collect 'tolls' from everybody passing through. Or he'd yee-haw a firebase and pick off a freshie or two.

"Yeah, he was a piece of work, all right," Jimmy said. "And he knew to the corpse just how far he could push it before the higher-ups would scratch their balls and wonder how 'pacified' the area really was. So Badger Stoltz—that was the sheriff—he developed a keen interest in learning Wild Bob's whereabouts.

"One day, word came in that Bob was holed up in an old mining town, name of Spruce Creek. The silver gave out way back when, but no one had the heart to close it up. I seen the place, and I can't say I blame 'em. It's a spot worth stayin' in, just to open your eyes to it in the morning. It sets in a high, isolated meadow, with peaks on every side and four passes leading out. A spruce forest surrounds it and climbs halfway up the mountain flanks before giving way to krummholz and bare, gray rocks. The state road follows the creek through the center of town; but the Joeys have watchtowers on both east and west passes and it wouldn't take 'em more'n ten minutes to turn either one into a deathtrap if anybody tried to come in that way. The townies either support Wild Bob or they're too scared not to. Or both. Hell, like I said, even the friendlies don't much like us. And I can't say they weren't given cause in the old days."

"Don't mean nothin'," Angel said. "Don't excuse what they done. Don't excuse collaborating, neither."

Jimmy just shook his head. "It's a damn shame what things have come to. Gimme another Skull, would you."

Lyle handed him the bottle. "So what about this Wild Bob?"

"I'm comin' to it." He popped the cap and tipped the neck toward us in salute. "In and Out," he said.

"Yeah." That was Lyle. "Except you want Out."

Jimmy darkened. "I said I was comin' to that. I just gotta give you the topo. There's another road. A county road. Packed dirt and gravel, mostly. Comes in from the south, gives the townies something they can call an intersection, and meanders out over the north pass. At that point whoever put the road in, must've figgered out there wasn't any place to go over on the other side; so it just fizzles out in the rocks and tundra. The Joeys keep an eye on the south pass, but don't pay much mind to the north."

Angel spoke. "I sense a plan," he said clapping his hands together. "A strategy!"

"Four suit louies," I said. "Two to keep 'em interested in the state road; one to block their retreat over the south pass; and one to sneak in through the bathroom window."

"Sure," said Jimmy, "except I didn't have no four suit louies at the firebase. Just me and Maria Serena—and one of us had to stay Out if the other went In, in case Joey yee-hawed the firebase. Wild Bob had maybe twenty, twenty-five bandits with him—he ran the town like a damn safe house, and every terrorist in three states could put up there for a week or two. I had the sheriff's posse—Badger Stoltz and ten whipcord guys who took their tin stars serious—and I had my power suit. So I figured the odds at better'n even. Plan was, the sheriff would waltz with our boy on the county road, draw 'em south a ways, while I took the walker in from the north."

"Couldn't use a floater, then?" Angel asked.

Jimmy shook his head. "Too steep. Ground effect don't work too good when the ground is vertical. I'd have to do finger-and-toe climbing the last stretch. There's a reason that road don't go nowhere. Sheriff sent one of his guys with me—a cute little bit named Natalie who just happened to be his daughter—to show me the way. I had the photos from the up-and-down, but like I said, things can look real different on the ground. Me and Stoltz worked it out and didn't say beans to nobody until the day I went In—'cause, you know, someone might have a cousin or talk in his sleep or something. So the day comes and Stoltz rides his ten guys south—they got the most ground to cover before they get in position—and Natalie waits while I go into the teep room and wriggle into my power suit–"

"Duck into a phone booth!" said Lyle. "Put on your cape and Spandex!"

"Superman!" said Angel. "Ta da-daah!"

"–fiber ops and hydros hooked up–"

"–leap tall buildings–"

"–set my virtch hat–"

"–faster than a speeding bullet–"

"–power up the suit and–"

"Oh, man, I *know* that feeling–"

"–ain't nothing like it–"

They bubbled, their words tumbling one atop the other, a glow spreading across their faces. I remained quiet and stared into my beer. I could remember what it felt like. Infinite power. You could dribble the world and shoot hoops. My fingers cramped into a sudden ball and I hid the rebellious limb under the desk.

"I took the walker out to the firebase perimeter and leaped over the wall right beside Natalie."

"Yee-haw!" said Lyle.

"It scared her. She hadn't been expecting it, and her horse reared up and near threw her. I told her I was ready-Freddy; and she just looks in my optics and says, let's not waste any more time, and she yanks on her bridle and heads off toward Spruce Creek." Jimmy drained his bottle and tossed it to Angel, who placed it carefully in the growing architectural wonder our empties were creating.

"The town wasn't too far, as the bullet flies; but you couldn't rightly get there going straight. Still, her dad and the others needed time to get in position, so Natalie set off at an easy canter with me loping along beside her. You know what it's like in those walkers. You want to leap and soar. And of course it's scaled about twice the human body, so you have to get used to the difference in stride and reach and squeeze. So I'd stretch my arms and the walker's manipulators would reach out and tear a limb off a cottonwood. Or I'd take a couple giant steps, just for the hell of it; then wait for Natalie to catch up. Third or fourth time I did that, she told me I was scaring her horse and please stop; so I had to plod the rest of the way. It was like being hamstrung."

"Hang a handicap sign on your back," Lyle agreed. "Get prime parking."

"Tell it, Brother Lyle!" said Angel. They tossed the thoughtless jape from one to the other.

"Satellite recon is a wonderful thing; but even the up-and-down can't see through trees or overhangs or pick fine details from a shadow-black canyon. Natalie led me the last part of the way. Took me down game paths, along a creek bed, through stands of Douglas fir that looked like they'd been there since God spread his tarp. She knew her horses, that Natalie. Couldn't have been more'n nineteen, twenty; but she sat in the saddle like she'd been born there. Well, in that country, maybe she had. She never said more'n two dozen words to me the whole trip; and those were mostly 'this way' or 'over there.'

"Finally, we come to the base of a sheer cliff. There was three canyons cut into it. No, not even canyons. More like cracks. Recon barely showed 'em, but Badger Stoltz and his daughter swore there was one of 'em led to the top. Natalie rode along the base of the mountain and ducked a little ways into each. Then she come out and said, 'The right one. It slopes up real sharp, then goes vertical into a chimney that opens out on the high tundra. From there, your GPS should show you the way.' "

"Wasn't she going with you?" asked Angel.

I snorted. "Weren't you listening? Take a horse up a fissure like that?"

Jimmy rubbed his palms together. "I said, 'Wish me luck?' and she just yanked on her horse's reins. 'You don't need luck when you've got that,' she said. I knew she meant the walker, so I come back and said, 'I ain't no Imperial Storm Trooper and Wild Bob ain't the Rebel Alliance. I'm on *your* side. We're the *good* guys.'

" 'The good guys,' she said. And, oh, she was pissed. Angry and afraid all at once. 'Was your government ragged on folks until bandits like your Wild Bob could play the hero. And now my daddy has to ride out and maybe take a splash of fléchettes in his belly, 'steada ticketing speeders along the state road.'

" 'He ain't my Wild Bob,' I said. 'I come to take him down.'

"Her lips curled. Full, soft lips. Oh, they were lips for kissing. And here I was a young suit louie going off to do battle. I deserved a kiss. But I was suited up, teeping a walker, and there was more than telemetry and digital screens between us. Instead of a kiss, I got a kiss off. 'You come to take him down?' she said, and she leaned forward over her horse's head and pointed a finger into my optics. 'You listen to me, mister "suit louie." If my daddy even gets wounded bad, you'll have one more militia in the high country to worry about, and that'll be me!'

"Hoo!" said Angel. "And she'd be a bad 'un, too."

"She was just worried about her Pa," I suggested. Jimmy looked at me, then shrugged.

"Maybe. I couldn't let it bother me, though. I had a job to do; and if I didn't get up that cut, her daddy probably would take a slug. Without me, the possemen were outnumbered and outgunned."

"So how'd you do it?" Lyle asked. "Sounds like you'd be out of line o' sight in that fissure."

"Oh, I had an aerostat hovering at the relay point, and Lieutenant Serena kept it on station. But you're right. Inside that chimney, the microwave beam would be blocked. So I asked Natalie to handle the little dish. You know, stake a repeater at the entrance, then crawl after me with the parabolic until I got up to where I could bounce sky again."

"Helluva thing to ask a girl," said Angel.

"Did you trust her?" I asked.

"You don't get it, Angel," Jimmy said. "She was a posseman, not just the Badger's daughter. She packed a nine and a railgun and there was a street sweeper in her saddle scabbard. Oh, *mano a mano*, any one of us could have taken her down; but we'd be walking funny for a long time after.

"Well, I took that walker into the cleft and it was like someone drew a window shade, you know what I mean? All the I/O was juiced into the walker's receptors by that little, hand-held parabolic that Natalie Stoltz held. All she had to do was toss it aside, or even drop it accidentally, and that walker would be nothing but a pile of armor and circuitry stuck inside some rocks.

"I can't say I didn't think about that while I climbed that chimney; and what the colonel would say if I got stuck while I was on an unofficial outing. What I didn't think about until later was Natalie. My walker depended on the power beam she was aiming, and the farther up the cleft I climbed, the harder it was to keep the beam targeted. She had to stand right underneath the walker and aim straight up. So if anything happened, that'd be a couple tons of composite armor and metalocene plastic come tumbling down on her head."

"Takes balls," Angel agreed. "I wouldn't care to do it."

"Almost made me wish the walker was self-powered."

Lyle hooted. "Yeah, right. Carry a honking fuel cell around."

"Said 'almost'," Jimmy told him. "The climb was the sort of work-around any good suit louie could pull off. Maybe a little closer to the edge, is all. Took me maybe half an hour to reach the top. I looked down over the edge to maybe wave Natalie my thanks, but all I seen was her riding off a-horseback without so much as a glance back."

"Not very grateful for your help, was she?" Angel said.

"Found out later she went 'round the long way to hook up with her dad. Can't fault her—her place was with him. Got there too late for the action, but then old Badger might've had that in mind when he assigned her to guide me."

"That must have been some climb," I said, "teep shadow, and all." I tried to keep my voice professional; but some of the envy must have come through, because Jimmy winced and wouldn't meet my eyes.

"Yeah, some climb," he said, and gave no more details.

Lyle leaned forward. "But once you were out of the cleft, you could bounce..."

"Yeah. Got my bearings from the GPS, shook hands again with the aerostat, checked in with Serena and Stoltz. Gauged the distance and told Stoltz I'd call him when it was time to open the dance. Serena said there was no movement on the up-and-down; but hell, those bandits know how to get around without smiling for the sat'-cams. Anything worth noticing would have been under trees or camo overhangs or down in the bunkers. You know how it is."

Lyle and Angel said they knew how it was. I chimed in, too; but for me it was a theoretical knowledge, cadged from recon photos, official briefings, or picking the brains of Insiders. I'd written about it in "The Ambush." People tell me how my stories make everything come alive for them—a funny expression to use about stories of combat—but only I knew how dead the words felt under my fingertips.

"There was this one building, though, seemed to have a lot of in-and-out. The Artificial Stupid thought it was either a headquarters, an entrance to the bunker system, a whorehouse, or a public library."

Angel shook his head. "Jesus. No wonder they call 'em Stupids–"

"You put up any bumblebees?" asked Lyle.

"About two hives, all slaved into the aerostat relay. Gave me a good, close-in aerial of the town, so I knew right where the action was. I figured folks'd come pouring out of that building when the Badger opened the dance, and I wanted to know if they came out waving Kalashnikovs or library cards."

"Shoot 'em if they have the cards," said Lyle. "It's the shit they read drives 'em to it."

"You don't believe that, Lyle," I said.

He stuck his chin out. "You're the writer," he said. "Either you move people or you don't. And if you don't, why bother writing? Maybe there'd be fewer murdering rebel scumbags if we'd put some of those books and websites off-limits."

"No," said Jimmy. "I'd rather shoot a man dead because he's a murdering rebel scumbag than treat him and everyone else like children who're told what they can read or listen to."

Lyle was unconvinced. "Yeah? What do you owe Joey Sixpack?"

Jimmy said, "I'm coming to that part." He leaned forward and rubbed his palms against his lap. We had run out of beer already—not unusual when the four of us gathered in those days—but no one volunteered to make a run, which was unusual.

"I walked my machine to a low ridge overlooking the town and scanned the target with my high-rezz 'nocs. It was just like the Badger figured. No one was watching the north. Just to be on the safe side, though, I turned on my pixelflage."

"Me," said Angel, "I just boogie right on up."

I didn't think there was any imputation of cowardice in what Angel said, but I pointed out that pixelflage could help the suit louie round up more Joeys because the bandits wouldn't know how close he actually was. "Yeah, I read that story," Angel said. " 'Invisible Avenger.' Pretty good, 'cept it's not like you're really invisible."

And there it was again. That curtain. "I know that," I growled. "I juice it a little for the civilians, is all."

"All it does is duplicate the landscape on your pixel array, so–"

My right arm twitched and knocked over an empty bottle. "I said, I *know* that. I went through the training with you. Got higher scores, too. If it hadn't been for the accident–"

Lyle looked at me. "An' we know that. Sure, you woulda been good. You woulda been hell on wheels. You woulda been the next Lieutenant Bellcampo, with medals down to your crotch, if you hadn't spilled on Jimmy's bike that night. But you did; so you're not; and it's over. We love you, man. You know that. We're the 'Fantastic Four,' right? But you can't change what happened. You just got to go on from where you are."

Jimmy reached out and touched me on the arm. "It's over for me, too," he said, but I jerked my arm away. Blame it on a spasm.

"I still don't understand that," I said.

Jimmy and I locked eyes for a moment. "I don't know if I can explain," he told me quietly, "if you never been Inside." I looked away and he touched my arm again. This time, I did not pull back. "No diss, man," he said. "Just word. I really don't know if I can make you feel what I felt." He looked at the others. "Don't know if I can make them feel it, either."

"Try us," said Lyle. "But the beer's gone; so–"

Jimmy shrugged. "Yeah. We're just swapping Inside stories, right? No big deal." He made a fist of his right hand and rubbed it with his left. "Okay, so it goes down like this.

"I get as far as the spruce on the north edge of town, just where it gives way to open meadow around the creek. That puts me three jumps from the center of town and one jump from a herd of cows. There's a cowboy out with them. Don't know if he was a bandit or one of the regular townfolk. Never did find out, and it didn't matter in the end. You lie down with dogs; you wake up with fleas.

"I put the walker on stand-by, so nothing moves. The pixels is all green and brown and black, so I blend into the forest behind me. The cowboy looks my way once or twice, puzzled-like, like he ain't sure he's seen something or not. Me, I got my 'nocs locked in on the big building, waiting for Badger to call the dance.

"I didn't have long to wait before I hear gunshots over my channel to Stoltz. Maybe they were loud enough to carry by air, because my cowboy, he frowns and peers south. Wild Bob's pickets call in for help and my Artificial Stupid locks in on their freq. Can't make heads or tails of the traffic, though, because it's all black..."

"Shoulda kept that kind of encryption illegal," Lyle said.

"Oh, yeah," I said. "Illegal. That would have stopped the likes of Wild Bob. Codes don't make conspiracies; conspirators do. Besides, PGE and other black codes were all over the Net. Might as well've made the wind illegal."

"And besides," Angel said, "the big corporations didn't like the idea of the government holding keys to all their codes. And they're the ones that call the shots."

Jimmy looked at him. "Yeah? That's what Wild Bob always said. Big corporations, Wall Street, the Jews. Besides, what do I care what Joey's saying, coded or not? It wasn't more'n fifteen seconds after Badger started the music that they come pouring out of that big building. They all have 'sault rifles and bags full of bananas. Two of 'em are lugging a mortar and some shells. I give Badger a heads-up over the aerostat relay and tell him what's coming his way.

"The cowboy decides either to join the fun or to head for home. He spurs his horse and goes galloping across the meadow. I take that as my cue and go into leaper mode. Anyone hears a noise, they look over and see that cowboy easier than they can see me. That gives me maybe another jump or two before the balloon goes up. Last jump put me right in front of the main building. The bandits usually don't post guards—they own the town's soul—but all the shooting has got them nervous. So there's a Joey standing around the front door with one thumb on his rifle's safety and the other'n up his ass. When I come down on the street behind him, he jumps like Old Shaq' in his glory days, and I chop him up before he even hits ground."

"What'd you use," Lyle asked. "Finger gun?"

Jimmy ignored him. "I bust through the front door and bounce from office to office, leaving little calling cards in each. The radio was in the third room. Some old bat was on the horn, hollering. When she sees me, she reaches in her desk drawer and pulls a .38. I don't have time for that crap, so I give her a spray and then shred the radio set."

"Think she got the warning out?"

"I know she did. But a suit louie never figures to go unnoticed when he's Inside. I work my way through the building—and pop a few more Joeys who want to field-test their ammo. By the time I bust out the back wall, my little presents start going off and pretty soon the whole building's in flames. So you see, what did I care about the radio? I was the one sending the message. If she hadn't gone for the gun, she could've run with the others."

"Generous," said Lyle.

"Those were the Rules of Engagement, Style. Remember, the area was officially 'pacified.' I could shoot whoever came at me armed; but anyone else, I had to tranq, smoke, strobe, or leave alone."

"And decide which is which on a moment's notice," Angel commented bitterly. "All Joey has to do is not go for his gun and he's a peaceable citizen."

"So I guess I lucked out, because I don't think there were more'n two dozen folks there who weren't potting at me. Some heavy rounds. Armor piercing. One cholo had ramjet rounds. You know, with the discarding sabot and the jet core through its middle? They hit with a couple of Mach. My walker took some damage; and the blowback..."

"Oh, yeah," said Lyle, rubbing his arm. "The blowback."

"I had bruises for a week where the walker got knocked around. I mean, I know you gotta have feedback through your suit pads, otherwise you got no 'touch,' but I wish the dampers would react faster than the blowback from impacts."

"Better'n being hit by a round direct," I said.

Angel went, "Word up. Sprained my wrist one time when a mortar shell wrenched the manipulator arm on my floater."

"It's like having a spasm." Lyle looked at me. "You remember what it was like during live-round training. Must be a lot like what you got now, right?"

I went "right" and didn't try to fine-tune his opinion. He wouldn't have believed me anyway. People have a need to reduce things to what they think they understand.

"I wiped that town's butt good," Jimmy went on. "Pretty soon, though, Wild Bob figures out that the possemen were just a decoy so's I could yee-haw, and the 'away team' come streaming back from the south pass on their ATVs and dirt bikes. Well, I'd already gotten the range for a couple of landmarks along the county road, and my submunitions were already in place. I watch my heads-up until the column reaches the right point, then I trigger my subs and let loose. Ducks in a barrel. I couldn't have done better if they'd all held still and said 'cheese'."

Angel pumped his fist and went yee-haw.

"Pretty," said Lyle. Jimmy shook his head.

"It's never pretty. I went in to break them; so of course that's what I did. But it was a dirty business and I hate those sumbitches for making me do it. Wild Bob himself, he was still functional. He'd been bringing up the rear, in case Badger tried following him to town, and he hadn't taken a hit. My sensors spotted his bald dome flashing in the afternoon sun and I high-leaped right over to him. I bet that was one day in his life when he wished he had all his hair back. He sees me land and his face twists into a sneer. He's got a grenade launcher in his hands and the devil in his eyes.

"Now, he knows the Rules of Engagement like he wrote 'em his own self. And who knows? They way they tie us in knots, maybe he did have a hand in the drafting. So he knows if he drops the grenade launcher, I got to switch to non-lethal."

Angel shrugged. "Me, I got slow reflexes."

"Yeah, well, it didn't matter, 'cause he didn't drop nothing except another grenade in the chamber. I opened a channel and give him his chance, saying, 'Bob, I come to take you in.' But he just curls his lip and goes how I ain't come anywhere and lobs a grenade at my optics."

"Hell," said Lyle, "that ain't nothing to swat away. Artificial Stupid can handle it on automatic."

"Sure, but the arm swing puts you off balance for a second because it's automatic; and that's the second when Wild Bob melts into the rocks. That forces me to run the instant replay so I can see where he went and follow him.

"We played peek-a-boo all across those rocks. He'd pop up and try another round, always going for the optics or the ee-em arrays. Oh, he knew power suits and where the weak points were. Then he'd scurry off to some new position." Jimmy shook his head and he looked at the wall, except he wasn't seeing the wall. "I'll give old Bob this much. He had sand. Not many folks'd buck a suit louie that way. Deep down, he believed in his cause. Had to, to do the things he did. He knew all along this day would come and he sort of looked forward to it, if you know what I mean. Maybe he even welcomed it. I thought about saving the county the expense of a trial—I had some HE in reserve and could have made some mighty fine rubble out of those rocks; but, strictly speaking, this was a police action, not military, and Badger hankered for a trial. He wanted the public to know how Bob wasn't some damned Robin Hood, but a murdering, thieving traitor. Last thing he wanted was a martyr and a folk-song.

"So Bob and me, we play cat and banjo for maybe fifteen, twenty minutes; and the more Bob backs away from me, the closer he gets to Badger and his posse. I thought maybe he didn't realize that because a firefight concentrates your attention, you know what I mean? But he knew exactly what he was doing. I call on him once more to surrender, and he goes, 'not to the likes of you.' And then, I swear, he hollered for Badger.

" 'What do you want, Bob?' Badger asks him from behind the next rim; and he says, 'I want it to be you, not him,' and Badger goes, 'You sure you want it that way?' and Bob said he was sure. 'If a man gotta go down, it oughta be to another man. And Badger, you may suck the gummint tit; but you are, by God, man enough to come for me your own self.'

"So Badger he tells Bob to step out where he can be seen and hold his hands up. Maybe ten, fifteen seconds go by; then Wild Bob steps out from behind a finger of rock—which surprised me, because I had him pegged a couple meters the other way. He's still holding that grenade launcher. Badger—I can see him now, skylined on the rimrock twenty meters past Bob—he's got the high ground and a 'sault rifle. He says, 'Bob, throw down the launcher,' and Bob says, 'Now, Badger, you know I can't do that,' and the sheriff goes, 'Throw it down *now*, Bob!'

and Bob doesn't say anything except he works the pump to chamber another round. Badger goes, 'I don't want it to end this way,' and Bob goes, 'Only way it could. Tell Ma and Natalie good-bye.' Then he raises the launcher to his shoulder and Badger sprays him with a cloud of fléchettes, which rip him up something bad, so I think he was dead before he knew it."

Lyle the Style shook his head and said, "Jesus." Angel crossed himself. Jimmy ground his fist into his palm, like a mortar and pestle, and didn't say anything for a long time. Finally, I spoke.

"They were brothers, Wild Bob and the Badger?" Oh, what a story that would make! If I could only find the right words to tell it. Duty versus fanaticism—with love ground to powder in the middle.

"I leaped on over," Jimmy said, "and grounded next to Badger where he stooped over Wild Bob. Badger looks up at me and says, 'It was empty.' "

"What was?" asked Angel.

"The grenade launcher," I said. "That's right, Jimmy, isn't it? Bob's weapon was empty."

Jimmy nodded. "I told Badger I'd carry the body back to town if he wanted. You know those walkers; they can carry a lot in their cradles. A single body wouldn't be much. But Badger just gives me a look and says if I want so bad to carry the body, I could damn well come up to Spruce Creek and pick it up my own self."

"Oh, man," said Angel. "Diss."

"What did you say to him?" I asked.

Jimmy shook his head. "I didn't say nothing. I yanked off my virtch hat and threw it to the floor. Lieutenant Serena asked me what I was doing, but I didn't pay her no mind. I just stared at the walls of the teep room, thinking."

"Thinking," said Lyle. "That's always a mistake."

Jimmy gave him a look, as if he were a stranger. "I left the teep room and checked an ATV from the motor pool. I know I left the walker out there untended—and the colonel chewed me a new asshole over that later on—but I had to go to Spruce Creek. Not just be telepresent. You understand? I had to be there myself."

"Dumb move," said Angel. "It's telepresent fighting waldoes helps keep down body-bag expenses."

"*Our* body bags," I pointed out.

Lyle shrugged. "Those are the only ones that matter to me."

Jimmy shook his head. "You're right, Angel. It was a dumb move. By the time I reached Spruce Creek, they were all gone. Badger and his posse. The bandits. Most of the townfolk. Shit, most of the town was gone. Even the walker. Lt. Serena had teeped it after I went Outside. So I got out of the ATV and retraced the path of the firefight, walking from rock to rim. I had cornered Wild Bob there. He fired his last grenade there. Badger shot him there. The rocks were all splashed red; there were shell casings and sabots all over. I don't know how long I crouched where Badger had crouched. If any of Wild Bob's friends had still been around, I would've been easy pickings. Finally, a squall blew up and I hiked back to my vehicle and pulled up the clamshell. I sat there for a while listening to the high country wind. After a while, I drove back down to the firebase."

"And after that," I said, "you put in your papers."

Jimmy nodded.

"For the ATV/horse cavalry."

Another nod.

Angel said, "I still don't get why."

I leaned forward in my chair. My arms on the armrests barely trembled. "It's because it wasn't a fair fight."

Lyle grunted. "It wasn't supposed to be."

Jimmy raised his head and looked at me. "It's not that."

"Then what?" I asked.

Lyle laughed. "It's because he wants the respect of that hick sheriff. Or his daughter."

Jimmy rose from the floor. "I didn't think you'd understand." He looked at me. "Though I hoped you would."

We locked eyes for a moment. Then he turned to go. When he got to the door, I blurted out. "Oh, Jesus. It's Wild Bob's respect you want."

Angel scowled. "That hemorrhoid? What's his respect worth?"

Jimmy paused with his hand over the doorplate. "What he believed in was all wrong and twisted," he said. "But he was willing to die for it. If what we're fighting for is right, shouldn't we be willing to risk something besides equipment damage and feedback bruises?"

When he had gone, there was silence in the room. Lyle and Angel and I looked at one another. Finally, Angel said, "He's nuts. You don't fight snakes by wriggling in the dirt and trying to bite 'em first. That doesn't make you brave, just stupid. You stand back and blow 'em away with a sweeper. Only one way to end this fighting: Stomp hard and stomp fast."

Lyle shook his head and said, "He'll get over it. It's just syndrome."

"Well," said Angel, "he'll find out there's a hell of a difference between teep fighting and fighting in person."

"Maybe," I said, "he already found that out."

* * *

That was the last I saw any of them until after the big offensive. Angel and I shared a platform at a bond rally, but that was near the end, when Angel was the Hero of Boise. We'd both heard how Lyle—and half his firebase—got scragged by the Sacramento car bomb and after the ceremonies we emptied a couple of Skull Mountains for him. That's when Angel told me that Jimmy Topeka lost an arm in a firefight in the Bitterroots. He's married now and living in the high country.

I managed to etch a half-dozen stories out of that one day's bull session. "The Brothers." "Rules of Engagement." You've read them. They were compiled on ©-Net at <The Insiders> website.

The funny thing—and it must be just a coincidence—is that ever since then my seizures haven't bothered me so much.

War and Migration

Martin van Creveld

Editor's Introduction

Martin van Creveld is arguably the world's most pre-eminent military historian. Here he presents us with an analysis of war and migration, and reaches the inevitable conclusion: war is often indistinguishable from migration, although sometimes it takes longer. The Governor of Louisiana, Bobby Jindal, himself an assimilated child of immigrants, says that migration without the intent of assimilation is invasion; an act of war.

It is often said that the United States is a nation of immigrants. This is true enough, but it is a nation created by "the Melting Pot", by assimilated immigrants, who entered legally and came to be Americans, or at least were not openly opposed to the idea. As Bill Buckley said, one could study to become an American in a way that one could not become Swiss, or a Swede. Assimilation was not always easy, and for freed slaves it was difficult; but it was generally the goal. The story of America and migration is as old as America.

The more recent migrants do not all accept assimilation as a goal; they seek to preserve their diversity. *E Pluribus Unum* is not the goal of the Caliphate; open rejection of toleration without dhimmitude is proclaimed.

The United States faces numerous decisions about migration, immigration, and assimilation. Dr. Van Creveld gives us crucial information on the history of migration, from the times before the Trojan War to the present.

War and migration have always been closely related. The relationship was recorded as early as 1300 BC, when we are informed the Israelites followed Moses out of Egypt to embark upon the enterprise that ultimately led them to the Promised Land of Canaan. As you will no doubt recall, they promptly conquered it. And since that time, for over 3,315 years, the link between war and the large-scale movement of people from one place to another has never been broken. Yet despite the way these mass movements of peoples have had a profound effect on human history, there has never been a systematic effort to explore the ways in which the two great phenomena, war and migration, interact. This essay is a preliminary attempt to rectify the situation.

1. From the Exodus to the Great Trek

The Old Testament tells the famous story of the Israelites, which begins sometime around 1800 BC when Canaan was visited by famine. This caused the patriarch Jacob and his extended family to travel to Egypt, where they and their offspring were initially welcomed, but later enslaved.

Four centuries later, having multiplied considerably, a leader by the name of Moses arose. Under his divinely-inspired command, they left Egypt. After crossing the Red Sea, they marched into the Sinai Desert where God, who was waiting for them, gave them the Pentateuch. From the desert they proceeded, very slowly, to what is known today as the Kingdom of Jordan. It is said that Moses must have been the first general staff officer, for who else would have required forty years to cross what is actually a very small desert? And after finally arriving on the threshold of the holy land four decades later, he died. His successor Joshua, who subsequently proved to be a formidable military commander, buried Moses, then led the Israelites across the river and into Canaan proper. These intrepid immigrants swiftly conquered the land and settled it after killing or enslaving most of the inhabitants.

Whether or not the tale of the Conquest of Canaan is historical has been debated for generations. In particular, scholars have questioned whether the Israelites could realistically have fielded a 600,000-man army, not counting the women and children. Israel's first Prime Minister, David Ben Gurion, fancied himself a Biblical scholar and considered 6,000 to be a more acceptable figure. His view brought him into immediate conflict with Israel's orthodox rabbis, who consider literally every word in the Old Testament to be Gospel truth.

But for our purposes, it does not really matter whether the story is historical or symbolic. Still less do the details concern us. What is important is that after all these years, this story of geographic relocation and conquest is still commemorated by all Jews around the world.

In other words, migration *was* war. In fact, insofar as ancient war frequently involved not only soldiers and armies, but entire nations who left their homeland "*mit man und Ross und wagen*" (with man and horse and wagon), as the Germans say, war *was* migration. The Exodus was far from the only episode of its kind. For example, the Dorians are believed to have entered Greece from the north in the years around 1100 BC. As with the Conquest of Canaan, the question of whether the Dorian migration really took place or not has been much disputed. Thucydides has the following to say about the topic in the introduction to his book on the Peloponnesian War:

> *The country now called Hellas had no settled population in ancient times; instead there was a series of migrations, as the various tribes, being under the constant pressure of invaders who were stronger than they were, were always prepared to abandon their own territory... In the belief that the day-to-day necessities of life could be secured just as well in one place as in another, they showed no reluctance in*

moving from their homes, and therefore built no cities of any size or strength, nor acquired any important resources. Where the soil was most fertile there were the most frequent changes of population, as in what is now called Thessaly, in Boeotia, in most of the Peloponnese (except Arcadia), and in others of the richest parts of Hellas. For in these fertile districts it was easier for individuals to secure greater powers than their neighbors: this led to disunity, which often caused the collapse of these states, which in any case were more likely than others to attract the attention of foreign invaders. It is interesting to observe that Attica, which, because of the poverty of her soil, was remarkably free from political disunity, has always been inhabited by the same race of people. Indeed, this is an important example of my theory that it was because of migrations that there was uneven development elsewhere; for when people were driven out from other parts of Greece by war or by disturbances, the most powerful of them took refuge in Athens, as being a stable society; they then became citizens, and soon made the city even more populous than it had been before, with the result that later Attica became too small for her inhabitants and colonies were sent forth to Ionia.

There are other examples besides the Israelites and the Dorians. The Etruscans migrated from Armenia to central Italy, around 850 BC according to a recent study. The Gaels launched numerous attacks on the Hellenistic kingdoms in the Balkans and Asia Minor in the third and second centuries BC, although they were ultimately repulsed. And in 58 BC, as Caesar tells us, the Helvetii wished to migrate from their homeland in southern Germany to southeastern Gaul and asked him, the newly-established pro-consul of Gaul, for permission to cross Roman-occupied territory on the way. After he refused to grant it, they fought him, were badly beaten, and were forced to turn back. That failed migration triggered a whole series of wars which ended in the Roman conquest of the entirety of Gaul within six years.

The nomadic Arabs who occupied much of the territory of the Byzantine Empire in the seventh and eighth centuries provide another informative example. So do the Magyars, whose original home was in the southern Ukraine and who reached what is Hungary today in the tenth century AD. Their westward migration was halted in 955, when they were defeated at the Battle of Lechfeld, near present-day Augsburg. The Mongol and Manchurian conquests of China (1205–79 and 1618–44 respectively) also led to large-scale migrations as various peoples retreated to the west, displacing other nations in turn.

The largest and most famous migratory episode, if that is the correct label for a process that stretched out over several centuries, was the so-called *Völkerwanderung*, "the migration of peoples." It entirely transformed Europe from about the middle of the second century AD to the middle of the sixth century, destroying countless old polities and creating an equally large number of new ones. Driven out of the east by their more formidable neighbors, wave after wave of barbarian tribes crashed into Central and Western Europe. Some bypassed the Roman Empire to the north, whereas others crossed its frontiers and entered its territory to wage war on the inhabitants. The Saxons reached England, the Visigoths southwestern France, Spain and Portugal. The Vandals invaded North Africa, the Burgundians (whose original home was in Poland) traveled to the land that is now named after them, Burgundy. The Huns, whose original habitat was the Caucasus and Central Asia, traveled west, slaying and conquering everyone and everything on their way until a coalition of Romans and Visigoths finally stopped them at Chalon in 451. But the defeat of Attila did not by any means put an end to the series of migrations. The Huns were followed by the Lombards, the Lombards by the Bulgars, and between them they changed the maps, and the very placenames, of Europe.

All these migrating peoples, as well as many others that could be mentioned, were relatively simple tribal societies. In terms of organization, technology, material civilization, literature, the arts, and the like, they could not match the settled, more civilized, societies they encountered and often conquered. The book of *Joshua* describes Canaan as a land bristling with fortified cities, and yet they were quickly defeated by the nomadic Israelites. At a time when Roman power, encompassing practically all the lands around the Mediterranean, was approaching its zenith, Rome's enemies in Germany and Gaul consisted of endlessly shifting tribes who lived in wooden huts. Four centuries later, the Germanic Visigoths sacked Rome.

The Huns, Ammianus Marcellinus says, were "a race savage beyond all parallel." He describes them in distinctly unfavorable terms:

> *They are certainly in the shape of men, however uncouth, and are so hardy that they require neither fire nor well-flavored food, but live on the roots of such herbs as they get in the fields, or on the half-raw flesh of any animal, which they merely warm rapidly by placing it between their own thighs and the backs of their horses. They never shelter themselves under roofed houses... Nor is there even to be found among them a cabin thatched with reeds; but they wander about, roaming over the mountains and the woods, and accustom themselves to bear frost and hunger and thirst from their very cradles....*

The anonymous Roman author of *de rebus bellicis*, writing early in the fifth century AD, speaks of other migratory tribes as "baying barbarians." Baying may have been all these barbarians were capable of, but they did so with sword in hand. Although the process might take time, such as the 514 years that separated the Cimbrian War from the Sack of Rome, very often the barbarians eventually managed to defeat their more developed opponents and take over their lands. There are two cardinal factors that explain the frequent victory of the simple and less civilized migrants over their more sophisticated stationary opponents. First, while the settled societies enjoyed technological superiority in terms of joules of energy available per capita, the primary sources of mechanical energy were stationary devices such as windmills and water-mills. When it came to war and battle, which are intrinsically mobile, both the civilized soldiers and their barbarian enemies depended entirely upon the muscles of men and beasts. As a result, most of the technological advantage enjoyed by the civilized societies was irrelevant because it could not be brought to bear on the battlefield.

Second, the migrations were usually long, drawn-out processes. Though armed invasions and battles were frequent, there were also long periods of peace. Therefore, there was plenty of time for both sides to take each other's measure and to learn from each other. Renegades and captives taken in war often played a large role. This exchange of information almost invariably worked to the benefit of the less civilized parties. For example, the Mongol armies which conquered China and came close to overrunning Europe in the mid-thirteenth century included many specialists who utilized technologies learned from the Chinese, including various types of siege engines. Two hundred years later, the Ottoman Turks did the same in their westward drive towards Constantinople and beyond.

The migratory phenomenon was not solely a Eurasian one. Africa also abounds with stories of armed migrations, some historical, others mythological. 3,000 years are said to have passed since the Bantu tribes began expanding out of their original homelands in what are today Cameroon and Nigeria, and now they can be found all over the central and southern parts of the continent. The Zulu established KwaZulu-Natal, in South Africa, after migrating southward along Africa's east coast. Many of these migrations bear strong resemblances to the Exodus described in the Pentateuch. In every case, the movement was said to have been initiated by one or more gods. On their way, the migrants witnessed many different miracles which confirmed that they were, in fact, doing the right thing. One of the best-known African migration tales is that of the Ashanti, a martial tribe that migrated westward from Ghana into the Ivory Coast, who on their way received *Sika 'dwa*, the

Golden Stool, a royal and divine throne believed to house the spirit of the Ashanti people.

One of the last, and most peculiar, African migrations was the Great Trek of the Boers. The Boers were European settlers, of Dutch and Huguenot descent, who left Cape Province in order to remain independent in the face of a growing British presence there. The Trek lasted from 1835 to 1846 and was unusual in the sense that the Boers set out to settle in lands inhabited by less civilized and less technologically advanced "kaffirs," mostly Bantu and Hottentot tribes, thus reversing the usual pattern of migratory conflict. But like their less-civilized antecedents, the Boers never hesitated to use their superior arms against anyone who stood in their way. The Trek also resembled other previous migrations in the sense that the migrants were strict Calvinists who believed they acted under divine guidance. Visiting the region around Pretoria back in late 1994, I saw the famous monument to the *Voortrekkers*. It must be said, to the credit of the African National Congress who took over South Africa after apartheid, the region's new rulers have not demolished it. Yet.

So migration was war and war was migration. Aside from relatively equal situations in Africa and North America when tribal societies fought each other, militarized migrations were chiefly a matter of less developed mobile societies attacking more developed, settled civilizations. That likely explains why, in the more technologically advanced parts of the world, migration-wars came to an end in the fifteenth century. As the history of the American West illustrates, once tribal warriors were able to lay their hands on modern weapons—particularly firearms—they quickly learned to use them just as well as their opponents. But what they could not do was produce the weapons and required ammunition for themselves. The development of firearms was a decisive shift in the balance of power towards more technologically advanced societies, particularly those of the West. How long this advantage will last is an open question, but there are indications that it is already on the wane.

2. *Ethnic Cleansing*

Thucydides illustrated how the process works in both directions: migration usually leads to war, but war can also lead to migration. For after war takes place, one of the common consequences is the forced migration that is currently known as ethnic cleansing. Some of the earliest migrations of this kind are recorded in the Old Testament. The Assyrian kings had an established policy of exiling half the population from the lands they conquered, one they followed after conquering the kingdom of Israel. A century later the Babylonians sent part of the population of Judea into exile after subjugating that kingdom. The small quasi-Jewish communities in Kurdistan, as well as the larger, pre-1948 ones in Iraq, are said to consist of the descendants of the Israelites forced to leave Israel by the Assyrians. Both empires made a habit of bringing in other peoples to take the place of those they had exiled. Thus the Samaritans, a small community of under a thousand people who currently live in Israel and the West Bank, are believed to be descended from settlers brought to the region by its Assyrian conquerors during the seventh and sixth centuries BC.

The spectacular reliefs at the British Museum that originally decorated the palace of the Assyrian king Sennacherib (reigned 705–681 BC) at Nineveh provide us with some idea of what an Assyrian ethnic cleansing operation may have looked like. The subject of the reliefs is the siege of Lachish, a city in the Judean Plain, in 701 BC. In addition to the military operations, they also show us what happened to the prisoners and deserters who left the city. Men were decapitated—there are lots of headless corpses lying around—or impaled. Women and children were left more or less unharmed and were taken away by the victors, accompanied by wagons laden with loot. Since Lachish was never rebuilt, the captives presumably went to places from whence they never returned. This suggests that women and children represented the majority of those who went into exile, although accounts from the Old

Testament suggest that on at least some occasions, men were spared to share their fate.

The Romans preferred not to exile those they defeated, but to subjugate, rule, and levy taxes on them. Cicero calls such taxes "a perpetual penalty for defeat". However, during the period between 200 BC and 120 AD, they regularly took enormous numbers of prisoners. These prisoners, men, women and children, were then transported to the slave markets, especially the famous ones of Rhodes and Delos, and sold there. Entire communities, including great cities such as Corinth and Carthage, were left almost devoid of inhabitants. This conquest-based slave trade brought a wide variety of different tribes, cultures and religions together and transformed Rome, the greatest slave market of all, into a new Babylon. The men who followed Spartacus, the Thracian gladiator who led the great slave revolt against Rome in 73–71 BC, came from many different lands. Spartacus's goal was for them to all return to their countries of origin, but his men refused, preferring to stay in Italy where they could kill, pillage and rape. They were eventually defeated at Brundisium by eight legions led by Marcus Licinius Crassus, and hundreds were crucified along the Appian Way. Spartacus himself is believed to have been killed in the battle, but his body was never found.

In 66–70 AD, and again in 135–37 AD, the Jews of Palestine rose against their Roman conquerors. The Romans suppressed both rebellions and responded by engaging in extensive ethnic cleansing. Hundreds of thousands of people were driven out, and to use an expression coined nearly two thousand years later, Jerusalem was made *Judenfrei*. Jews were prohibited from living in the city or even entering it. Such episodes are by no means rare in history; the reason so many Jewish examples exist is that despite the forced migrations they experienced, they managed to preserve their religion and their ethnic identity. Other peoples forced to leave their homelands were either less fortunate or less determined. That does not necessarily mean that the Jews kept their race pure, however, for as modern genetic studies show, Jews settled in different countries tend to genetically resemble the host populations more than they do each other.

Not all forced migrations were the result of war. For example, throughout the Middle Ages and the early modern period Jews were regularly expelled from many countries but this had little to do with war. During the century and a half after the Reformation, there were reciprocal expulsions of Catholics by Protestants and of Protestants by Catholics throughout Europe. The most famous example of these forced migrations was Louis XIV's decision to revoke the Edict of Nantes in 1685, which resulted in 400,000 Huguenots being exiled from France. Even in Switzerland, the cantons were divided on the basis of being Catholic or Protestant and much smaller forced migrations took place.

Large-scale ethnic cleansing again raised its ugly head during the early years of the twentieth century. The Balkan Wars led to the expulsions of Muslims from the Balkan states that broke free of the Ottoman Empire. Soon after the outbreak of World War I, the Turks, fearing lest the Christian Armenians might aid and abet the Russian enemy, enacted the first modern genocide. Hundreds of thousands of Armenian men were massacred; the rest of the population was expelled and driven to the Syrian Desert where they were left to die. The Turks also expelled the Jews of southern Palestine and drove them north, although some were taken to Alexandria, Egypt, by American ships. No sooner had the Great War ended than the Turks again initiated a massive ethnic cleansing campaign, this time against the Greeks of Western Anatolia. This region had been home to important Greek communities for over three millennia, but barely 5,000 Greeks remain there today.

The period 1919–21 also witnessed the expulsion of Hungarians from Romania, and of Germans from what had been West Prussia and Silesia, but was claimed by Poland after the war. Twenty years later, the jackboot was on the other foot. Having defeated the Poles, Hitler expelled masses of them from Western Poland and replaced them with

Germans. He also expelled the Jews of Alsace-Lorraine, driving them into France, after which they were subsequently re-expelled to the gas chambers in Eastern Europe.

As these events touch upon one of history's most infamous crimes, it is important to note that the series of complicated campaigns of expulsion, directed primarily against Europe's Jews, Gypsies, and Slavs, that ended in the murder of millions, could never have taken place had it not been for the cover provided by war. In Hitler's mind, the war and the *Endlösung der Judenfrage*, or Final Solution of the Jewish Question were linked. Speaking to intimates in August 1941, the Führer of the Third Reich claimed the fact that so many Germans had lost their homes after World War I justified the "humane" expulsion of Germany's Jews. Five months later, at the Wannsee Conference, the policies that lay the foundation for the Holocaust were worked out in detail.

There were more forced migrations to the east. After being unexpectedly attacked by his ally Hitler in violation of the 1939 Molotov-Ribbentrop Pact, Stalin ordered the evacuation of the Tatars from the Crimea. His rationale was the same as many others before him; he feared the Tatars might join the advancing Germans. But the expulsion of the Tatars was nothing compared to the huge migrations that took place from 1944 to 1946. As the Soviet Red Army marched west towards Berlin, it was often joined by local militias in the Eastern European countries it occupied. 12 million Germans were driven out of their homelands in Romania, Hungary, Yugoslavia (Slovenia and Croatia), Czechoslovakia, Poland, West Prussia, East Prussia, and Silesia, and about one-sixth of them died in the process. As the war came to an end, tens of millions of people were on the move across the continent. Refugees, slave workers, former concentration-camp prisoners, prisoners of war… almost all had nothing but rags to their name and were trying to either escape the advancing Russians or simply return home.

The forced migrations and ethnic cleansing did not end in 1945. The 1947 Indo-Pakistani War divided British India into two different countries and caused millions of people, terrified by the interreligious violence, to cross the newly established frontier between India and Paksistan in both directions. Triggered by the flight of ten million Bengali refugees from what was then known as East Pakistan, the Third Indo-Pakistani War, which broke out in 1971, brought about the creation of an independent Bangladesh. After the Pakistani surrender, the refugees returned and a smaller, though still considerable, number of Pakistanis were driven out of Bangladesh into West Pakistan. The end of the Vietnam War led to the expulsion of 250,000 ethnic Chinese Hoa from that country, as well as the migration of the two million Vietnamese "boat people", over half of whom ultimately settled in the United States. The 1980 Russian invasion of Afghanistan caused as many as a million Afghanis to cross the border into Pakistan's north-western provinces. Despite being settled in refugee camps there, they eventually came to jeopardize their hosts' control over the region—a problem, that may very well present itself in other parts of the world in the future.

Some of the wars that have taken place in Africa since the 1970s, particularly those in the Sudan, Eritrea, Somalia, Uganda, Rawanda-Burundi, the Congo, Liberia, Angola, and Mozambique also led to enforced migration on a massive scale.

And after a forty-two year hiatus, ethnic cleansing returned to Europe when, following the death of longtime dictator Tito, Yugoslavia broke up. When Bosnia-Herzegovina, whose population is predominantly Muslim, declared independence from Belgrade, the Serb minority in the province embarked on an all-out effort to avoid coming under Muslim rule. Their efforts were supported by the Serbian government under Slobodan Milosevič, which provided its kinsmen with men, weapons, and money.

The Bosnian war, which lasted from 1992 to 1995, witnessed widespread ethnic cleansing. The war was brought to an end by NATO aircraft launching airstrikes at the stronger Serbian forces. It later turned out that there was little difference between the two sides, both of whom committed atrocities, including mass executions. The number of people who were displaced by the war has been estimated at 2.2 million, including 250,000 Serbs who were driven out of the Krajina. That fact did not prevent the world, with President Clinton at its head, from pointing to the Serbs as the culprits and condemning them by every available means.

The current wars in Syria, Iraq, Afghanistan, and several other countries in Asia and Africa are also creating large numbers of migrants. Often they are prepared to do almost anything to escape the fighting even though life as a refugee is a perilous endeavor. Women are in particular danger, as they run the risk of being kidnapped and sold as prostitutes. According to the *New York Times*, there are currently 60 million people who have been forced to leave their homes. That represents just under one percent of the entire global population. Of the 60 million homeless, one-third are refugees who are presently living abroad. The remaining 40 million have been displaced by civil war but remain inside their own countries. Since the figures include millions of children who were born to refugees—even second generation refugees—or displaced people after they fled, it is possible that they are inflated. That is especially true in the case of the Palestinians, whose number the Palestinian Authority puts at a literally incredible six million. However, there is every sign that the number of displaced people is only going to grow and increase the size of the global mass migration in coming years.

For example, Israel's War of Independence, which the Palestinians call the *naqba* (catastrophe), actually led to the expulsion of about 600,000 people. The June 1967 War created, at most, another 300,000 refugees. Nevertheless, the refugee camps near Jericho have become ghost towns and have largely remained so to the present day. As of 2015 large numbers of Palestinian refugees are scattered in the Gaza Strip, the West Bank, Jordan, Syria, and Lebanon, while others have joined the ongoing Muslim migration to Europe and the United States.

Because Israel's Arab neighbors find it useful and have no intention of permitting it to go away, the plight of the displaced Palestinians is both the most persistent refugee situation as well as the one that has attracted the most sustained international attention. Unfortunately, the future does not bode well, since the possibility that Jordan will eventually fall to Daesh (ISIS) is all too real. Should that come to pass, it is not inconceivable that the government in Jerusalem would deem it necessary, for reasons of national security, to drive out the two million Palestinians remaining in the West Bank as well.

3. Voluntary War-Related Migration

Though the use of force is war's outstanding characteristic, not all war-related migrations are carried out by force. Very often, people decide to leave a war-torn region out of their own free will. One reason for doing so, which played an important role during the nineteenth century, is the desire to avoid conscription. In the decades following the development of the French Revolutionary Army, conscription became common throughout Europe and was rigidly enforced. Many of those wishing to evade forced military service went to the U.S.A., the British colonies, and Latin America.

Today, Eritrea is the country that produces the largest number of refugees trying to avoid national service, military or other. The country is governed by a despot named Isaias Afwerki. Freedom and human rights are unknown. Men and unmarried women are conscripted, often for life. This has caused thousands of Eritreans, particularly young men, to flee to Ethiopia. From there they usually continue on towards any other country they can enter, legally or illegally.

War also leads to migration in another way. From the earliest days of war, victorious soldiers have been besieged by the women of the defeated in search of safety, food, and, not least, sheer masculine force. That still remains the case. Armies often prohibit fraternization, as the Allied ones did in Germany after World War II. Some states even forbade marriages between their troops and women from the occupied population. Usually these efforts are to no avail. In World War II, American soldiers, "overpaid, oversexed, and over here," as their British allies described them, often had the time of their lives after the war's end. Most of them eventually returned home alone. But an estimated 60,000 American soldiers brought back a *signorina* or a *Fräulein* as a wartime souvenir. The Korean War is known to have produced an even larger migration, most likely because the ban on marrying Japanese women—Japan served as the principal U.S. base during the Korean war—was lifted. From 1942 to 1952, the number of GIs who married foreign women was around one million.

The wars in Southeast Asia from 1965 to 1975 that involved about 2.5 million American troops generated another crop of war brides. But although the phenomenon is not entirely unknown in Afghanistan and Iraq, it is much less common. The difference is that Muslims are extremely jealous of their women and segregate them as much as possible. Hence the U.S. military, in the hope of not further inflaming the occupied populations, has done its best to discourage the troops from fraternizing with the local women.

Much more important than either of these forms of post-war migration is the kind which is driven by the hope of a safer, more orderly, and more prosperous life abroad. This describes the majority of modern migrations. Their destinations are primarily the rich countries of the West, as well as Australia. Migrants with a Christian background are normally absorbed without too many problems, especially if they are white, as refugees from the former Yugoslavia are. However, the Lebanese Christian diaspora has shown that even those from Arab backgrounds can adapt to the West. Hindus and Buddhists also tend to do well.

By contrast, most Muslim migrants are fanatically opposed to any kind of cultural assimilation. Using their mosques as community centers and accepting religious imams as their leaders, they actively resist any attempt to integrate them. Some even begin proselytizing for their way of life, as they have every right to do in a democratic country. Their objective is to spread their views on what the late Samuel Huntington used to call identity. Identity, as Huntington describes it, includes "the relations between God and man, the individual and the group, the citizen and the state, parents and children, husband and wife, as well as differing views of the relative importance of rights and responsibilities, liberty and authority, equality and hierarchy." It also includes general relations between the sexes as well as the rights of homosexuals, as well as many of the rights many Westerners hold dear in both their private lives and in the socio-political arena.

As of 2015, Muslims form about eight percent of the population of the European Union. In large cities, especially wealthy ones situated on important communication lines or featuring seaports, the percentage of Muslims tends to be much higher. In some cities, entire neighborhoods have been taken over and reshaped in accordance with the migrants' preferences. These neighborhoods, such as Tower Hamlets in east London and the Kuregem district of Brussels, have assumed a decidedly Mohammedan character, complete with mosques, veiled women, and muezzins calling the faithful to prayer. Most of these neighborhoods are slums where the inhabitants tend to be unskilled, under-educated, and unemployed. Many of the residents cannot even speak the language of their hosts. Further complicating the situation, the newcomers lose their accustomed control over wives and children who tend to be more amenable to integration; this ongoing intra-family conflict not infrequently leads to domestic violence. Muslim immigrants often feel underprivileged and discriminated against, even though they are living off the largesse—one might even say the tribute—of the people whose lands they are occupying.

It is true that only a small percentage of the immigrants in question turn to violence, let alone politically motivated violence. But it is also true that in all the countries to which they have immigrated, Muslim immigrants are committing crimes at a rate that far exceeds the native population. A portion of this crime represents the continuation of politics that is indistinguishable from terrorism and will inevitably lead to harsh countermeasures, and eventually, reprisals. The present situation is more than a little reminescent of past migration-inspired wars and bodes ill for the future; it is estimated that as many as 5 million of France's Muslims already live in *zones urbaines sensibles* where the French police and government have relatively little control.

The modern form of economic migration is not caused by war but it is threatening to turn into a cause of war, as has happened many times before. An informative example of how a minority-majority conflict can lead to violence can be seen in sixteenth-century France. For thirty years following John Calvin's break from the Roman Church in 1530, Catholics and Huguenots looked at each other with increasing mistrust. This mistrust occasionally sparked sporadic violence, and over time, the violence gradually escalated. In 1562, with the Huguenots numbering 12.5 percent of the French population, full-scale war finally broke out. The religious issues were intertwined with political differences, and foreign powers, such as England, Spain, the Low Countries, various German princes, and even the Papacy, were drawn into the struggle. By the time Henry IV was finally able to put an end to the eight Wars of Religion in 1598 by issuing the Edict of Nantes, more Frenchmen had been killed than in any other conflict prior to World War I, including the French Revolution and the Napoleonic wars.

4. Conclusions

War is far from the only cause of migration. Other reasons, primarily economic, have always played an important role in encouraging people to leave their native lands. As the examples of the Puritans and the Huguenots show, religious motives can also be a factor. Yet even when these other reasons were the cause, war and migration have been closely linked in various and complex ways.

At some times, war and migration were essentially the same, as in the great migration of peoples during the first few centuries after Christ, the Arab expansion after 632 AD, the Magyar invasion of Europe, the Mongol invasions of China, and the movements of many African tribes from one part of the continent to another. At other times, the relationships between the two phenomena were more complicated, such as ethnic cleansings that rendered war unnecessary or took place after war's end, mass avoidance of conscription, or soldiers bringing home concubines and war brides. All these various forms have often intermingled, all appear regularly in the annals of human history, and all will doubtless continue to do so in the future. The only thing that changes is their relative importance at any given point in time.

As far as the West is concerned, the most significant migration today is the massive influx of Muslims. The reason is that, unlike the people of the secularized West, Muslims take their religion, and the way of life it prescribes, seriously. As a consequence, they are much harder to integrate than other, more malleable immigrants.

For the present, it would be going too far to say that the refugees, as well as those who are responsible for their plight back in their homelands, are actively waging war against the West. They lack the leadership and organization required for the effective, large-scale violence that war entails. However, it must be recognized that more than a few in their midst are not averse to using violence in order to achieve their aims. They have, after all, invaded numerous countries without regard for the will of the people of those countries, and their presence is no less likely to spark resistance than the armed invasions of the past. Since war, as Clausewitz teaches, has a built-in tendency to escalate, the resistance can be expected to graduate into all-out armed conflict over time. Especially, as seems likely, if the influx continues and all the valiant efforts at integration prove futile.

From Berlin to Jerusalem, let those with ears to listen, listen!

THE LAST SHOW

Matthew Joseph Harrington

Editor's Introduction

It is often said of the Society for Creative Anachronism, it isn't the way it was, but it's the way it ought to have been. The same could be said of this story.

The 700-odd prisoners were moved to the new compound at the Sagan POW camp on April 1st, 1943. As was often the case during such a large operation, there was an amount of confusion among the Germans guarding them, and some escapes were attempted. They failed. The X Committee was subsequently established to improve their chances the next time.

"X", of course, stood for "escape".

More prisoners kept showing up as flyers were captured. One of the earliest additions was an American named Eric White, who'd joined the RAF at the end of '39 and was a squadron leader by the time he was finally shot down. He was a short fellow who shaved his head, wore a thick handlebar mustache worthy of a melodrama villain, and kept his body hard as brick. He'd arrived on April 2nd, and spent a couple of days ambling around the camp sightseeing.

Early on the morning of the 5th, he went to the X headquarters hut and asked to speak with the head of the escape committee.

The very existence of the X committee was being kept secret from most of the prisoners. He was hustled inside, where Squadron Leader Bushell—big X—demanded, "Who the devil's been talking out of turn?" He could be intimidating as Hell when he chose, and he chose.

"I wouldn't know," White replied mildly. "I've been watching movements. Every time an escape attempt fails, one of six men makes a beeline for this hut."

"Oh, Hell," said Junior Clark, who was in charge of security.

"The goons haven't noticed yet," said White. "I've been watching them too."

"Ill wind," Bushell remarked, relieved. "Here about a plan, then, are you?"

"Yes, but it needs a lot of help. And I don't see how to get everybody out before the end of September."

Interested, Bushell said, "Just how many men do you mean to get out?"

White gave him a blank look. "I just said. Everybody."

There was a long moment of silence.

It was never certain just how many men broke it with the words, "Mad as a hatter," but it was at least three.

Bushell was not among them. He waved for silence, gradually got it, and said, "There's more than seven hundred men here."

"I figure by then it'll be closer to nine hundred," White said, nodding. "We'll need some kind of printing press for forged documents. I can carve blanks for casting type. Oh, and here." He got out and passed over a small camera. "I'm afraid about half the film is used up, I was taking pictures of the route here from Saarbrücken. You'll need to get more from the guards when you bribe them for developer."

"You just *happened* to have brought along a camera?" Clark said.

"No, of course not, it would have been confiscated. I stole it when they photographed me. Oh, and you'll need these." He held out a child's balloon, uninflated, that seemed to have fine gravel tied in the end. "Diamonds. To bribe the guards."

"How in the *world*–" said Clark, who stopped and looked at the balloon in his palm with visible misgivings.

"It's all right, that's a clean one. I started with twelve, one outside the next. Washed the outer one off and threw it away whenever I got them back. Good thing they don't feed prisoners much, they took their time getting me here. There's only three layers left. The texture was starting to be noticeable."

Bushell broke the ensuing silence with, "Where did you get so many diamonds?"

"Bought 'em in '27 when the German banks crashed. Had a bad accident the year before, made me start thinking hard about the future. Turned out handy later."

Clark looked him over suspiciously. "Just how old are you?"

White grinned. "As old as my tongue and a little bit older than my teeth. I beat the physical by shaving my head and using misdirection. I'm good at misdirection. Do you want to hear my plan?"

"I think we do," said Bushell.

White told them. It took several minutes.

There followed another minute or so of dead silence. Clark finally said, "It's impossible."

"I hope the Germans think so," said White.

"Do you have any idea how much of that damned yellow sand we'd have to hide?" Clark demanded.

"Something close to a thousand tons," White said, and smiled. "I doubt anyone will be looking at much of it too closely."

And there was the heart of the matter. Slowly, smiles appeared on faces to match his own.

White had brought with him a remarkable collection of seeds in cellophane bags, along with a couple of books on gardening and nutrition, respectively. He had been permitted to keep these, possibly due to his practice of avidly proselytizing any German who couldn't get away quickly enough on the subject of vegetarianism. (Hitler being a vegetarian, they could hardly just tell him to shut up.) White spoke German quite badly, at least when there were Germans about. This was ostensibly the reason it was left to Group Captain Massey, who was senior British officer, to make an appointment to see the camp commandant with some odd but fairly reasonable requests.

Colonel Von Lindeiner, who was an old-school Prussian and considered himself a fair man, was deeply suspicious of the idea of letting prisoners collect firewood in the surrounding forest, but had to acknowledge that without it most of the rest of the requests would be pointless. Besides, no RAF prisoner had ever broken his parole once given; and the huge vegetable gardens that were being planned would keep a lot of prisoners very busy indeed.

It completely overshadowed any suspicions he might have had about increasing the size of the theater to allow the whole camp to attend.

The tunnel between the camp theater and hut 119 was being started even as the requests were being approved. The conspicuous yellow sand that underlay the feeble gray topsoil of the compound was packed into the generous space under the sloping floor of the original theater. Boards were taken from hut bunks to provide shoring for the sides and roof of the tunnel.

White said that was temporary. The work of expansion covered the constant movement back and forth between the theater and all the huts nicely. An avid watch was kept on tools and lumber, but White had offered to flense the calluses off the feet of any man who stole so much as a nail. Nobody ever took him up on it.

The goons were less than pleased to learn the purpose of all the buckets. However, human sewage couldn't be safely used as fertilizer without being sterilized, and that could hardly be done indoors. There wasn't time or room to compost it, so it had to be brought to a boil to sterilize it, mixed with dirt, and buried in the garden plots. The resulting soil was acidic, which meant that a good deal of chalk was needed to neutralize it. Since that cut the stink, the Germans were more than pleased to supply it.

It was exceedingly fertile, and the amount of weeds that came up with the first vegetable shoots was not to be believed. The gardens took even more tending than the commandant had imagined. Some of the chalk was burned to make whitewash, which was applied to the sides of each hut, to reflect sunlight onto the gardens. Linseed oil was painted over the whitewash to keep it from being rinsed away in the rain. Nets of string were strung over the gardens to trap birds, most of which were killed and cleaned to make pots of soup. Trapped pigeons were kept alive in cages of wire netting to fatten and eat. Low fences were put around the gardens to block rodents, and gaps were left in the fences to keep them from simply gnawing through. The gaps held snares of string and wire, killing rats, mice, and even an occasional rabbit. These were skinned, cleaned, and stewed to feed the pigeons. Once all the cages were full, which was soon, fattened pigeons were roasted and replaced as fast as new ones were caught. After the sunflowers began to blossom, a couple of pigeons a day per hut wasn't unusual.

It never once occurred to any of the Germans to wonder what happened to the skins and feathers. White was a pilferer of extraordinary talent, and had acquired considerable equipment from various parts of the camp. This included far more wire than anyone had supposed was available. The proteins of the feathers were broken down by electrolysis in brine, then the lye was neutralized with the acid that had been produced, leaving a brackish slush that was rendered into gelatin for a mimeograph. Once there was more gelatin than was needed by the forgers, the acid was used to break down potatoes into slush, which was dried and saved, as was the alkaline gel. White demonstrated that it was possible to live on about a pound of the combined powders a day, which when added to a quart or so of water made a nourishing if salty self-heating soup. However, not even he claimed to like the stuff.

The skins were scraped clean and cured by boiling in distilled vinegar—all the plant matter that wasn't eaten was more than happy to participate in the production of vinegar on its own, let alone with encouragement—and stitched together into undergarments. The clothing situation being what it was, this was a Godsend even if nothing else came of it.

Meanwhile most of the chalk was being put to a much better use than gardening.

A shaft had been started straight down in every hut. These were shored with bed slats at first, and the yellow sand went under the theater. More sand was rinsed, dried, and put into cans with a little chalk, to about a third full. Men were assigned to shake cans of the mix until it stopped rattling, which meant the sand had ground up the chalk. The mix was roasted inside the stoves every hut had, then cooled and shaken up again. When wetted and pushed into rectangular casting frames it dried to a pretty good cement brick.

The tunnel from 104 out into the forest was twenty-five feet deep at its ceiling, and big enough for two men to work side by side, standing up, at the tunnel face. An arched framework made from bed slats would be pounded in at the start of each shift, and sand dug out around it to insert bricks to make a cement archway. Then the sand within the framework was dug out and moved, and the framework would be driven forward again. It was ridiculously fast.

Men in each hut tunneled sideways from the shafts to connect to adjacent huts. The wooden shaft liners were replaced with bricks, and the wood used to shore the tunnels until bricks could be moved in. Once the tunnels were finished, the wood was used to smoke pigeon meat for carrying later.

Escape attempts were made throughout the whole procedure, giving the Germans something to pay attention to. That was in addition to the extra attention they were paying to the gardens, trying to find yellow sand. None was going in—it all went under the theater. Bushell took White aside after a while and asked him, "Not that I object to the extra food, but what was the purpose of all the gardens if not to put the sand there?"

"Misdirection, for one thing," said White.

"Misdirected us too, you think there's an informer?" Bushell wasn't sure whether to be offended or worried.

"Hardly, but the best actor is one who really believes in the part. Also, the men are putting on some weight and getting more sun. They're not going to look so much like prisoners once they get out. More misdirection, later on."

"They're still not going to be out for long. We won't be able to provide documents for more than a quarter of them."

"They may be out longer than you think," White said.

"Why d'you say that?"

White looked at him over that walrus mustache. "How good an actor are you?"

"Pretty bloody good."

"Good enough to hide being in a ridiculously good mood for six more weeks?"

Bushell studied him for a long moment, then said, "Maybe not."

White wasn't spending all his time walking about and doing his ferocious course of exercise. (He'd offered to hold wrestling matches for entertainment, but nobody ever took him up on it twice.) In addition to being the best scrounger and all-around thief in the prisoner population, he turned out to be an excellent forger, a superlative tailor, and an extraordinary toolmaker. Just for example, he came up with a method of magnetizing compass needles that was far better than anybody could have reasonably hoped: bunch steel needles together, wrap them in a steel strap (hammered out of a bullybeef tin and baked with soot to add carbon to the wrought-iron), heat them red-hot with a torch (he made town gas for it by blowing steam over charcoal heated in a tin, and anybody who had to do welding or soldering blessed him daily), slip a densely-wrapped coil of electrical wire around it, and run current through until the metal had cooled. You had to be terribly careful undoing the strap, because the needles would fly apart at the first opportunity. They were a sight more powerful than Wehrmacht field-issue.

He also consulted on other escape attempts. More misdirection, yes, but some of them worked. The most wildly successful involved two dozen men escorted out the gate in a delousing party by two other prisoners dressed as guards. Six of them made it all the way to Spain, where they arrived from their separate routes at the British Consulate on the same day.

White was also in charge of the language classes. He spoke German and French himself, both with a hilarious New York accent; his inspiration was to get all the men in each hut to learn the same language, *and to speak nothing else while in the hut*, a la Berlitz, but with more homework—they were learning to read and write it too. Men who were planning to use a different language for their escape identities were required to swap with someone else learning the hut language. There were a few who were hopeless cases, and they were sent to fill up spare bunks in any hut that didn't have a full set of students, and partnered with men who were quick studies, to cover for them.

Traffic back and forth to the theater didn't let up much, since White had also organized rehearsals and set production for half a dozen plays he'd learned off by heart. Von Lindeiner was conspicuously magnanimous about using the office mimeograph to make multiple copies of the scripts White had laboriously done in large print. It came to an awful lot of pages for each one. White produced bleach with the feather-dissolving works and took the lettering off about half the scripts. (Massey had asked for just as many as they needed, and then kept coming back with damaged scripts for replacements, until von Lindeiner printed up far more than necessary, on better paper. From then on the forger team had all the material to work with that they wanted.)

Of course the goons watched the theater traffic, but of course nobody was getting rid of sand above ground anymore.

The forgers, tailors, and tinkers worked down in the main tunnel, which White dubbed "Philip Morris," on the grounds that the use of those words would arouse absolutely no suspicion among the goons. He gave Tim Walenn Hell for calling the forging operation "Dean and Dawson," after the travel agency; he said it gave the show away the instant any German who'd done any traveling abroad heard it, and before the War a lot of them had done. White renamed it "Betty Grable," and Massey was able to talk von Lindeiner into having a lot of copies of a rather famous picture of her printed up. These were posted in every room in every hut. Any reference to "Betty Grable" was instantly covered. (They did something for morale, too.)

The diamonds traded to the guards—no more than one each, and they certainly didn't compare notes about the subject—paid for all manner of useful little trinkets, including equipment to develop film, more film, and an extraordinary selection of pens, indelible inks, and document-quality paper. It also got them quite a lot of razor blades, which would see a lot of use on the night of the breakout.

Light for the work was provided by batteries White had worked out. They were just iron tins with brine in them, with copper wire wrapped in blotting paper stuck into one and leading to the outside of the next. A man could get a bad jolt from several put together in a row, and they produced enough power to keep the work well-lit. He arranged to recharge them at night, when the electricity was on.

Walenn kept training more forgers, giving the new ones basic stuff to do while his experts did the precision work, until it was getting to be quite a factory below ground. Other men were kept going back and forth between huts from time to time on a scheduled, irregular basis, so the goons wouldn't notice any reduction in the population or get suspicious of a pattern. There wasn't one to notice.

They ended up putting together thousands of the little bits of paper that Germans and their subjects had to have about their persons at all times. They also mimeographed maps, with compass roses and directions on them.

Massey was able to talk von Lindeiner into giving the camp material for patching and for making clothes to replace ruined uniforms. It was bright red, indelibly dyed, making it useless for putting together a disguise for an escaped prisoner. It never occurred to von Lindeiner to wonder about what happened to the clothing it replaced, but every man in camp learned to sew a good seam, very quickly.

The main drag of the tunnel was finished September 20th, with a roofed ramp leading up to about five feet from the surface. There were sturdy ladders in place, and the end was calculated to be about fifty yards into the woods—White wasn't satisfied with its length until they'd had to cut through the taproot of at least one tree. Breakout was scheduled for the 28th, 29th, or 30th of September. They were days in the middle of the week, so the train timetables were regular, and there would be plenty of passengers for the escapees to mix with.

Some men weren't informed until the evening of the 28th. There was a mad scramble all round to get dressed after lights-out, then get down into each hut's tunnel to the main shaft. A lot of men had had no idea of the scope of the digging, but herders had been appointed for each hut to keep the gaping and astounded moving along.

The tunnel was well-lighted, light bulbs being top priority on the list of things to steal. Men were assembled in it in a column, two by two, and had a certain amount of room at that. Muller and Macintosh had hand-wound little motors, each one different according to what scraps they'd had on hand at the moment, and they were attached to fan blades that were now mounted in each hut. These were used to draw air out of the branches of a cement pipe that ran parallel to the electric wire along the tunnel roof. When they were all running, there was a faint but noticeable breeze running down the shaft toward the exit.

Massey took Bushell aside and said White ought to be the first man out. Bushell said he would be staying behind.

"For Christ's sake, why?" Massey demanded in a voice of almost normal volume.

Bushell told him.

"Mother of God," Massey said softly. "I never noticed."

"You weren't supposed to," Bushell said. "I didn't until he told me. Why do you imagine he worked so hard not to let von Lindeiner get a good look at him? The Kommandant has done some traveling, and White's done a sight more."

"Jesus," Massey said, and it was reverent. "Jesus," he repeated.

When the signal was given to open the end, the men on the ladders pulled boards out of the roof, then backed off and threaded together the handles Travis had made for their scoops and started digging the roof out. There was a lot of sand from that, then a sudden cave-in, then a breeze from above. They were through. Men passed buckets down the line to scoop out the sand, and as they were passed back each man took out a little handful and dropped it by the wall. There was plenty of room for it, and when a man got an empty bucket he handed it to the man next to him to pass forward again. The men with the scoops widened the hole and smoothed the sides to prevent another big fall, and when they were done clearing the sand they passed their scoops back. Longer ladders were passed forward, they set them up, and Wally Floody, master tunneler, was the first to poke his head out. "It's clear," he said quietly. "I can barely see the lights from the far towers, and I don't see the road at all."

"Well get out of the way, then," said Johnny Dodge, and Floody got.

They were all out in an hour, scattering like rats dumped out of a sack, with Bushell being the last to go. He shook White's hand and said, "I hope it bloody works the way you expect. If not you're probably going to be skinned alive."

"No worries," said White, who had been housed with Aussies for the past six months. "I've seen pictures. Amazing it hasn't happened already. Now get going."

Bushell nodded, then gave one of his rare grins. "I almost want to stay to see their faces."

" 'Almost'," said White, and grinned back. "Now if you'll excuse me, I have to go shave."

With that, he strolled back up the tunnel, took the branch to his hut, went to his room, shaved off his mustache, and went to bed.

At Appell the next morning, he showed up without a shirt.

Alone.

The goons charged into all the huts and found all the tunnel openings, unclosed, right away. *Oberfeldwebel* Glemnitz, chief of camp security, screamed abuse at White in German until von Lindeiner arrived, having been informed by a hysterical guard that the prisoners had left through fifteen separate tunnels. Glemnitz shut up then, and von Lindeiner came up to White and asked him where the prisoners had gone.

"Everywhere," said White, and smiled as von Lindeiner studied his face, frowning.

"I know you," von Lindeiner said presently.

"I get around," said White, nodding.

Guards kept coming over and delivering deeply impassioned reports about the tunnels, and finally one shouted something lengthy and almost inarticulate from outside the fence. Von Lindeiner went gray and said, "You realize that this will create a hysterical response. Possibly the only thing I can do to salvage my own career is to shoot you at once."

"You might wait until you get word from Berlin," White suggested. "By all means, do mention my name."

Von Lindeiner studied him again, then put a hand to his chest. "*Mein Gott*."

White was taken to von Lindeiner's office. When Glemnitz asked if he should be put in irons, von Lindeiner laughed so long his men began looking concerned. "No," said the *Kommandant* at last, "I see no point in that."

"Are you all right?" White said.

"As well as a man can be who expects to be shot," said von Lindeiner.

"Don't make any hasty assumptions about that right now," White said.

"What do you mean?"

"I doubt I can explain and be believed right away. I'm afraid I didn't get breakfast," White said.

"Feed him," said von Lindeiner. "Plenty. He has been working very hard for this."

Word was sent to Berlin at once, of course. A series of conflicting instructions was sent back for about an hour. They ended with a notice that the *Fuehrer* was indisposed at present, and further instructions would be forthcoming shortly.

When the sole remaining prisoner heard this, he said, "I don't expect to hear from him again. Apoplexy. Between his rages and the signs of illness I've seen in pictures, he's probably already dead, and the dispute over the succession will take up everyone's attention. Whoever wins is going to be ready to talk terms about ending this war. You know," he added thoughtfully, "if someone had thought of breaking off relations with Japan after Pearl Harbor, stopping all advance, and using the *Kriegsmarine* to escort neutral ships, you might not have brought America into the European conflict for a couple more years. Maybe ever."

"You got yourself captured deliberately, didn't you?" von Lindeiner realized aloud. "It was to do this. Nothing else."

"You suspect me of deception? I'm shocked! As you can see, I ain't got nothing up my sleeves," said Houdini.

This story is respectfully dedicated to Paul Brickhill; to the Fifty; and to the incomparable Erich Weiss.

FLASHPOINT: TITAN

Cheah Kai Wai

Editor's Introduction

Arthur C. Clarke said that if the human race is to survive, for most of its history the word ship will mean space ship. I will add to that the obvious implication that *Navy* will soon mean *Space Navy*. The Space Navy will certainly keep many of the traditions and practices of the wet navies, for the same reasons that they developed in the first place.

Navy stories are as old as going to sea in ships. The heroines of those stories are often ships as well as their crews. Here a story of a heroic ship and her crew.

Something was wrong. Somewhere in the sea of data before him, there was a shark swimming amidst a school of fish. Commander Hoshi Tenzen of the Japanese Space Self Defense Force narrowed his eyes, studying his ship's combined sensor take on his console.

The console displayed the data as a three-dimensional hologram. In the center of the display, *Takao* was a blue triangle pointing towards a bright yellow mass. That was Titan, the largest moon in the Saturnian system, ten thousand kilometers away. Other yellow dots indicated satellites, orbital structures and shuttles with Titanian registration. White tracks indicated civilian space traffic. A number of small green dots orbited Titan, each representing American orbital patrol ships. Each contact carried a unique tag, displaying vector, velocity, name and other critical information.

There was too much data. He was drowning in it. Leaning back, he studied the big picture, looking for patterns of activity. Ships came to Titan, dropped off cargo, picked up other cargo, and left. It was their purpose in coming here.

But there were ships that did *not* fit this pattern.

Four of them. Their beacons claimed they were merchant ships registered to Clementine Space Transport Services, headquartered in Ceres. They were burning at five milligees, their vectors pointed at deep space.

But there was nothing of interest beyond Titan. The only other significant human activity past the moon was the gas mines at Uranus, which were almost completely automated.

So why were these ships *accelerating*?

Hoshi opened a new window, studying the radar track history. For the past week, the quartet had plodded steadily towards Titan on deceleration burns. They arrived three hours ago, entering the ten thousand kilometer orbit at a velocity of two klicks per second. An hour later, they flipped around and burned their engines. And they hadn't stopped since.

His console chirped. Prometheus, the largest colony on Titan, was hailing *Takao* on the laser communications array. They had a message for *Takao*'s ears only.

He accepted the hail on his implants. A broad Midwestern accent flooded his skull. "*Takao*, this is Prometheus Control. Welcome to Titan. I wish I could greet you under more auspicious circumstances, but we need your help."

"Copy, Prometheus Control," Hoshi replied in English. "What kind of help do you need?"

"*Takao*, I want to draw your attention to *Cloud Nine, Summer Squall, Autumn Lightning* and *Blue Jasper*. They just pinged the laser launch array, the space elevator and the colony with lidar. They claim they are testing their instruments, but I've never heard of merchies that need military-grade lidar. We think they're up to something."

Hoshi looked for the ships. They were the same four ships he had flagged. *Takao* had designated them S-547 through S-550. They had formed a box, each ship separated by two hundred and fifty kilometers. He'd never known civilian freighters to take up such a formation in orbit.

But he knew warships did prior to a bombing run.

"Prometheus Control, understood. If these are Q-ships, we are ready to provide assistance. Be advised, we are carrying a full war load."

Q-ships were warships disguised as merchant vessels. They couldn't match the performance of real warships, but they could remain concealed until they released their weapons, making them the favorite of pirates and terrorists.

"Thank you kindly, *Takao.* We're going to run an emergency drill, clear the airspace, and launch the alert squadron. Our plan is to lock down the ships and board 'em for surprise inspections. Give us a half hour and we'll be in place."

"Roger, Prometheus Control. If the suspect ships attempt to resist or escape, we will provide fire support."

"Much obliged, *Takao.* Let's do this."

Hoshi typed a command on his console. Throughout the ship, a klaxon sounded. He keyed the ship-wide intercom and said, "All hands, *sentou youii.* All hands, *sentou youii.*"

The crew rushed to assume their battle stations. Around him, the duty personnel in the Combat Information Center tensed. Other spacers streamed in, taking their places.

Hoshi buckled himself into his seat and summoned a window that tracked the ship's status. One by one, the boxes representing each deck and department turned green. He patted down his blue skinsuit, checking for holes. Two minutes later, the ship was at maximum readiness.

Lieutenant Kamishiro Takeshi, whose place as Executive Officer was in the astrogation deck above Hoshi, called him. "Sir, the ship is battle ready."

"Thank you, Lieutenant." Hoshi turned off the klaxon, brought his officers into a conference call, and briefed them.

"Gentlemen, this is no longer a shakedown cruise," he concluded. "Remember: everyone back home is watching. Do not screw up."

Only Kamishiro had the courage to snicker over the line. "*Ryoukai!*" *Roger!* "We won't let you down."

No one was watching him, so Hoshi allowed himself a momentary smile. "Sensors, extend telescopes and track the bogies. If they pull in their radiators, inform us immediately. Intelligence, assume the bogies are Q-ships and develop a threat profile. Weapons, create a solution for long-range engagement. Astrogation, plot an interdiction vector at full thrust."

Hoshi and his Astrogation head, Lieutenant Sato Koichi, went back and forth until they were satisfied. Then Ensign Tanaka Michi, the Engineering officer, got on the intercom.

"All hands, accelerating, accelerating."

The Japanese Space Self Defense Force called *Takao* a multimission patrol ship, the first of her class. But that was a misleading misnomer. *Takao* was truly a *torch* ship.

Mobilizing her gyroscopes, *Takao* rotated in place. Once vector-aligned, the fusion drive roared, accelerating the ship at one-third gravity, faster than any warship ever built. As *Takao* ate up the distance to Titan, Ensign Subaru Ryuto, the Weapons chief, hailed Hoshi.

"Sir, I have a solution."

Subaru's solution called for engaging the threats with *Takao*'s main laser from standoff range, then finishing them with missiles. Her point defense lasers and railguns would handle counterfire.

"Very good, Subaru. But while use of the laser is as per doctrine, there are Chinese forces a week out from Titan, and the Americans don't need to know our capabilities. Set the lasers to ultraviolet-A.

Then launch two sunrays and program them for the same frequency. Boost the sunrays to a deep space vector that enables us to make broadside shots against the bogies."

Lieutenant Junior Grade Nakamura Makoto was next in line, ready with the threat profile. "Captain, the ships are registered as independent merchant vessels, displacement of twelve hundred tons each. They have deuterium-tritium drives, maximum acceleration of five milligees. They have a payload of five hundred tons each, mounted on external cargo pods. They claim to be carrying a shipment of ice from Ceres. Assuming these are Q-ships, I expect the pods to be filled with missiles and possibly drones."

"Nakamura, did you say *five* milligees?"

"Yes sir. The reactor is either pretty small or pretty underpowered." Nakamura hesitated. "Or they are concealing their actual acceleration profile."

"Let's assume the latter," Hoshi said. "If they are Q-ships, they must suspect something by now. Titanian airspace is being cleared, the orbital patrol is converging on them, and our drive capabilities are as plain as day. Why haven't they attacked yet?"

Nakamura took a moment to think it through. "Sir, they must be waiting for all their targets to enter their engagement envelope. That means the orbital patrol squadron, the laser launch array… and us."

Hoshi's blood chilled. Maybe they pinged the colony and pulled a burn so that everybody would come running into their sights. If *Takao* closed with an enemy too fast, she would be setting herself up for a point-blank missile swarm—one even she could not dodge in time.

"Thank you, Nakamura. Tanaka, halt acceleration."

The drive cut off. Hoshi contacted Prometheus Control and passed on his men's thoughts.

"Thank you very much, *Takao*," Control said. "We're moving slow too. We don't want to spook them into doing something stupid. Way I figure, they will want to wait until we launch the alert squadron before striking."

"Roger. What's the plan for Q-ships?"

"Our priority will be to protect the Elevator, the colony, and the laser launch array, in that order. We will aim for impactors first, drones second, missiles third, and the Q-ships last."

"Copy. We will target the Q-ships, drones and missiles in order of decreasing importance. We will also try to trash enemy weapons, but we don't want to splash you by mistake."

"Much obliged, *Takao*. If you don't mind, let us handle impactors. That should prevent friendly fire. Also, let us know if you have to fire kinetics and I'll get my birds out of your way."

"Roger that, Prometheus Control."

Subaru contacted Hoshi as soon as he closed the connection. "Sir, sunrays are good to go."

Hoshi checked the solution and nodded. "Thank you, Subaru. Stand by."

Hoshi brought up the radio controls, tuning it to the guard channel. "Attention all stations, attention all stations. This is JS *Takao*. We will be launching laser-propelled probes shortly. Please maintain separation of one hundred kilometers from my vector."

Space warships launched probes so often that nobody would think twice about the announcement. Hoshi repeated the announcement three times, then said, "Launch sunrays."

Powerful gas generators kicked the two Type 99 missiles into space. *Takao* trained a point defense laser bank on the nozzles of both missiles. Each of her lasers housed two independent turrets. The turrets picked a sunray each, and ignited the solid propellant in the missiles' nozzles. Subaru's solution would place the sunrays just over a thousand kilometers from the suspect ships when the operation was slated to begin.

Hoshi called up the telescope feed. Ensign Mori Arata, the Sensors officer sharing the CIC with Hoshi, was tracking the four-ship formation with his telescopes. The ships were still making steady burns, barely deviating from their predicted paths.

White dots bloomed from Titan's surface. The Americans were launching on schedule. The rest of the orbital patrol closed in on the bogies.

Hoshi tapped his fingers against the console. If the bogies continued to behave themselves, all would be well. Yes, Hoshi would have to explain expending two Type 99 mirrors, but they were replaceable. On the other hand, if the bogies…

"Sir, Sierras 547 to 550 are retracting their radiators!" Mori called.

Radiators, being the primary means of shedding heat in space, were the most vulnerable and critical component of a ship. Ships only ever retracted them to prevent them from being harmed—or shot off. Over a colonized world, pulling in radiators was tantamount to a declaration of war.

He hailed the ships on the guard channel. "Attention, attention. This is JS *Takao.* You are in orbit over an inhabited surface. Retracting your radiators is against international law. Extend your radiators or you will be fired upon. This is your only warning."

"Sir, we're being pinged by multiple lidar sources," Mori said. "They're from the bogies."

"Subaru, what's the status of the main laser?"

"Captain, the capacitors are fully charged and the firing solution is ready."

Clusters of cylindrical objects decoupled from each of the spaceships and fired tiny chemical rockets, burning towards the moon.

"Sir, bogies have ejected cargo pods," Mori reported. "They are increasing acceleration to fifty milligees and are taking an escape vector."

With fifty milligees of acceleration they could outrun most ships. But to *Takao*, they were slower than slugs.

"Subaru, initiate solution."

"Initiating solution, *ryoukai.*"

Takao sent an encoded laser pulse to the sunrays. Their boosters kicked out their payloads, and the smaller projectiles inflated their smart-matter mirrors. The mirror modules discharged their onboard capacitors, energizing the lenses to alter their shape and molecular structure to reflect UV-A beams. *Takao* unshuttered her main laser, situated in her nose, and unleashed a stream of pulses. Bouncing off the mirror, the invisible pulses drilled into Sierra 547.

The two main laser turrets alternated their fire, pausing just long enough to recharge their ultracapacitors. The lasers burned through the Q-ship's engine. A ball of hot plasma erupted from the target's rear. Secondary explosions followed, then *tertiary* explosions, and the ship broke apart.

Hoshi blinked. Ships do not blow up like that, not unless the laser punched all the way into the reactor. *Takao*'s laser couldn't do that, not at this angle of attack.

But that didn't matter now. He had a fight to win.

Prometheus Control sent lasers snapping skywards, destroying as many pods as they could. The orbital patrol ships launched volleys of missiles, then closed into laser range. But there were too many pods and they could not get them all. The pods split open, dispersing their payloads.

In Hoshi's display, huge numbers of red triangles popped into existence around the Q-ships, clustered so thick they formed a scarlet blanket. An alarm sounded.

"Captain, threat radar!" Mori called. "Ninety-eight strikers and twenty buzzards are locked on to us!"

"*Chikusho*!" Hoshi swore. "All hands, full guard, full guard!"

At the call, the entire crew snapped into action, following pre-established protocols. All non-essential systems and compartments shut down. Sato plotted the safest vector. Subaru directed his men to activate the point defenses. Nakamura activated the electronic warfare suite. Mori fed data to everybody as needed.

Powered by miniature nuclear reactor engines, ninety-eight missiles sped in at a quarter gravity. As they closed in, Tanaka yelled, "All hands, side kick! Side kick!"

Takao spun her gyroscopes, pointing her skywards. Her chemical maneuvering rockets fired, adding velocity to the turn, then fired again to cancel her momentum. The ship accelerated, burning for a higher orbit.

The missiles turned, trying to keep up. But the real threat was the twenty incoming drones. Fitted with nuclear gas-core rockets, they screamed in at one gravity, turning faster than *Takao* could, and fired barrages of smaller missiles from their coilguns.

"Sir!" Nakamura called. "Buzzards match profile of *Tiannu* drones!"

The *Tiannu* drone was an armed drone employed by the Chinese Space Forces. It was also obsoleted a few years ago, and its sensors were vulnerable to modern electronic warfare.

Some of the drones went berserk, firing blindly into empty space and chasing phantom targets. The point defense lasers burned down the rest. *Takao* continued spinning, giving her lasers a chance to cool off and recharge. The lasers fired low-powered pulses, melting sensors, electronics and payloads, sacrificing power for rate of fire. Many of the struck missiles detonated prematurely. More missiles spiraled away, confounded by the white noise in the air.

But dozens of threats survived to enter *Takao*'s kinetic engagement envelope.

"Subaru! Snap shot bursters, snap shot guns! Tanaka, retract radiators!"

The ship rumbled. Twenty-four Type 82 missiles leapt from her missile banks. Scorching towards the threats, the warheads detonated into sprays of tungsten cubes, each striking with the force of a small bomb.

Then *Takao*'s 60mm railguns fired. The guns churned out a barrage of fragmentation shells, placing an ocean of steel between *Takao* and the threats. The unguided flechettes disintegrated. The missiles tried to dodge. At this range, if the shells forced the missiles off a threat vector, it was as good as a kill.

But it was not enough. There were still too many missiles.

Takao still had reserves. If he launched them Hoshi was certain *Takao* would survive. Unscathed, even. But he had his orders, and his duty was absolute. The weapons could only be fired under exceptional circumstances, and a counter-piracy mission was, by definition, not exceptional. He could not use them, even if it meant the death of his ship and his crew.

He would not use them even to save his own life.

"Sir!" Subaru called. "Lasers have overheated!"

"Tanaka, divert all available coolant to point defense! All hands, brace for impact!"

Even as he spoke, twelve missiles survived to engagement range and detonated.

The lasers shut down completely. The railguns continued firing. They drew power from explosively pumped generators and had a separate coolant store, but were far less accurate than the lasers. Hoshi clenched his fists, watching tens of arrows close in on his ship.

Long seconds later, the lasers returned to life. Together with the railguns, they plucked the darts from the sky. Tanaka pulled one last trick, firing the engine and maneuvering rockets. The superheated exhaust consumed every flechette that entered the plumes.

But it was not enough.

The lasers dropped their shutters. The guns got off a final barrage. Then dozens of flechettes crashed into the ship. Tortured metal screamed. The blasts slammed Hoshi into his seat. Sirens went off. Alerts popped up on his console.

"Kamishiro," Hoshi said, "damage report."

The XO took a moment to check his boards. "Whipple shields compromised, no hull breaches. Forward missile cells damaged. Point

Defense Laser Two reports damaged shutters, but not the turrets. No crew casualties."

Hoshi heaved a sigh of relief. The enemy had loaded up with general-purpose flechettes. Hundreds could fit inside a warhead, but they lacked the punch to penetrate *Takao*'s armor.

He checked the display. The red blanket was rapidly dispersing. At some point, Sierra 549 had died in the hail of fire; she was now little more than debris and plasma. But the orbital patrol had been obliterated too, and so had the sunrays. And Sierra 548 and 550 were about to leave Titan orbit.

Hoshi wanted answers. At this angle, *Takao*'s lasers could punch through the enemies' engines and into their reactors. But even civilian-grade compartment bulkheads would stop hypervelocity munitions.

"Tanaka, extend radiators. Subaru, target the enemy ships' engines with muskets."

Takao launched eight Type 83 missiles. These were fitted with anti-ship warheads, not the light flechettes *Takao* had endured. Her point defense lasers sent them soaring at the threats at three-quarters of a gravity.

The Q-ships couldn't hope to outrun the missiles. But they had one last surprise. Hidden panels retracted, revealing automatic railguns. Two per ship.

"*Nani?*" Hoshi muttered. *What?*

Even as he spoke, the leading ship rained heavy metal down on the colony, while the other blasted at *Takao* and her missiles.

"Tanaka, evasive maneuvers. Subaru, snipe the railguns with lasers," Hoshi said. "Prioritize the ones firing on Prometheus."

Takao's main laser discharged. Four shots later, the railguns blew apart. Then the point defense lasers kicked in, destroying the shells threatening *Takao*.

Prometheus didn't take the insult lightly either. A lance of light carved through the heart of Sierra 548. Another speared Sierra 550.

Shortly after, the four surviving muskets fired their payloads, spewing clusters of segmented-rod penetrators optimized for defeating armor.

The threats tried to turn their drives on the incoming flechettes, but they were too slow. The darts slammed into their engines, blowing them out.

Mori said, "Sir, bandits have ceased acceleration. No escape pods. No further targets. We have a grand–"

The telescopes blanked out.

"–slam?" Mori finished. "What the hell?"

The telescopes cleared. Sierras 548 and 550 were now rapidly expanding balls of plasma.

"Nakamura? What the hell happened?" Hoshi demanded.

"Looks like a reactor failure, sir. Mori, what's in the vapor?"

"Lieutenant, laser spectroscope is picking up deuterium, tritium and heavy metals. Definitely a catastrophic reactor failure."

"How likely is that to be from combat damage?" Hoshi asked.

"Our penetrators shouldn't have damaged the reactor deck," Subaru said. "Maybe the Americans?"

"Negative," Mori said. "Spectroscope did not pick up fusion fuels following the laser strikes."

"Suicide trigger then?" Nakamura wondered. "But that doesn't make sense. Pirates aren't suicidal. Even most terrorists aren't that crazy these days. They'd rather surrender if they can't maneuver."

Hoshi thought again of Sierra 547. The secondary explosions were plausible, if the laser had struck a capacitor bank. But tertiaries? Ships were compartmented to prevent just that. It shouldn't be possible, unless someone, or *something*, deliberately induced a reactor failure.

But now wasn't the time and place to ponder such things.

"Gentlemen," Hoshi said, "I'm sure we have plenty of questions. For now, we will secure from battle stations and clean up the skies."

He had a very strong suspicion that this was not over. Not by a long shot.

* * *

Takao spent the next two days trawling Titan orbit, recovering expended missile boosters and sweeping up orbital debris. Each piece of debris could smash other objects in orbit and create even *more* debris. Known as Kessler Syndrome, a collision cascade could deny the orbits, and with them access to space. Having created the mess, the responsibility fell to *Takao* to clean up after herself.

Now she was berthed at the space port attached to the Titan Space Elevator, undergoing resupply and repair. Most of Hoshi's men were enjoying surface liberty, with a skeleton crew to look after *Takao* and oversee the civilian workers. Hoshi had other business to attend to.

Inside the port's habitat module, he made his way to the Last Call, some strange combination of bar, restaurant and cafe. A Westerner waited at the entrance, wearing the khaki skinsuit of the US Space Force.

"Commander Hoshi?" he asked. "Major Robert O'Neil. Glad to meet'cha."

Hoshi shook hands, trying to place the man's voice. "Were you on the radio during the attack?"

"Yup. Soon as the radar crew picked up the acceleration I decided to run things myself."

"A wise choice."

"Thank you. Good thing you were carrying a full combat load during your shakedown cruise, huh?"

Japan had announced that *Takao*'s maiden cruise would take her to Titan and beyond. If *Takao* could reach the outer solar system in weeks, it would usher in a second golden age of space travel. Tokyo wasn't lying; they just weren't telling the whole truth.

All Hoshi could do was shrug lamely at the American's obvious skepticism. "Standard operating procedure," he replied.

"Welp, your SOP certainly saved our asses. That makes you a good guy in our books."

O'Neil led Hoshi into the cafe. There was a private room in a corner. Inside, the American pulled out his terminal, waving it around. Hoshi realized the modular pad had been fitted with a bug detector.

"I believe we are not simply having a cup of coffee," Hoshi said.

"Got that right. But first, drinks."

O'Neil ordered a cup of coffee from the desktop assembler. Hoshi selected a green tea. The American insisted on paying, so Hoshi accepted, reluctantly.

"Good thing the bastards missed the Elevator," O'Neil said, sipping at his cup.

"Indeed. Striking the Elevator would be unthinkable."

"Exactly. And you know something? I think they deliberately avoided targeting the Elevator."

"Oh?"

"They aimed their weapons at you, the orbital patrol and the laser array. None of them could have hit the Elevator or the colony. And the array is so remote, a miss wouldn't hit anything important."

"Did they issue demands?"

"No. They never said a word."

"A terrorist bombing, then?"

"Terrorists would have targeted the Elevator. With so many impactors, they could have overwhelmed the lasers, wiped out the Elevator, and let the debris kill the colony."

"*Masaka…*" *It can't be.* "It doesn't make sense to spend so much ordnance to destroy the lasers alone. Maybe they wanted to take out your defenses and force you to pay a ransom."

"My Espatiers boarded the wrecks. The enemy had expended all of their munitions. They wouldn't do that if they couldn't back up a threat."

Laser launch arrays were composed of hundreds of smaller lasers arranged in a grid. Individual lasers could be rapidly repaired or replaced, even under fire. A pirate who threatened to bombard a world but did not follow through would soon be blown out of the sky.

"They didn't have anti-ship missiles. Maybe they..." Hoshi shook his head. "No. If they thought they had to expend their entire payload to kill *Takao* they wouldn't have initiated."

"Exactly. It seems they were just trying to knock out our defenses. Damn near did, too. Lasers are down to fifty percent. Without you, well, we wouldn't be here."

"No problem. I think they would only have attacked if they were expecting a second wave."

"Yup. I've declared a no-fly zone around Titan. Only military and medical ships are allowed around our orbits. Everybody else is being rerouted to Saturn. But I can't maintain the no-fly zone forever. My boss is gonna bitch."

Hoshi sympathized. Most civilian spaceships operated under the assumption that they could resupply regularly. They carried just enough fuel, supplies and propellant to reach their destinations. They simply did not have enough delta-vee, the impulse needed to perform a maneuver, for anything but the gravest of emergencies.

"I mean, he's complaining about all the billions of dollars a no-fly zone is gonna cost," O'Neil continued. "Since this morning he's been yapping about how Titan is the heart of the interplanetary economy."

Titan had seas of hydrocarbons hundreds of times greater than Earth's oil and gas reserves. Prometheus also provided a base for industrial-scale helium-three gas mining at Saturn and Uranus. With helium-three the primary driver of fusion power, Prometheus was practically the cornerstone of modern civilization.

"Can people stay at Saturn?"

O'Neil sighed, shaking his head. "There're only robots and resupply depots over there. Not much in the way of consumables for humans. The ships' owners will be losing money for every second they're not on the move to Titan, and some of 'em won't have the delta-vee to turn around and go home. No-fly zone or no, they can't stay there for long."

"What's your plan?"

"I'll keep 'em there for a week. It'll take that long to bring what's left of my lasers back online. Then I'll re-open the skies, but we'll inspect all ships before they so much as stick their noses into my orbits."

"You're going to need help with that."

"The Chinese said they'll arrive at Titan in five days and are eager to help."

"How very fortunate that their nearest task element just happens to have two assault carriers filled with Space Marines. On exercises. Or so they say."

"They have three guard ships as escorts as well."

"Such a task element would be perfect for invading Titan. But it would be the height of paranoia to suggest that, yes?"

"'Course not. After all, they just wanna 'assist local forces to secure Titan in the wake of this tragedy'." O'Neil shook his head. "The Chinese Space Forces are conducting their largest-ever fleetwide 'exercise' across the Solar system, and suddenly everyone else just *happens* to be 'exercising' right alongside them. Mars, Mercury, Venus, practically everywhere in the Solar system. The smallest provocation's gonna lead to an interplanetary war, and that would be a disaster for everyone."

"You don't sound convinced that the Chinese have our best interests at heart."

"We've recovered bodies from *Cloud Nine*, the one ship that didn't blow up. They were all Chinese in their twenties. Fit, strong, even for spacers. Two or three were older, in their thirties or forties. It was a skeleton crew barely large enough to man a vessel of that size. Looked to me like they were military spacers flyin' incognito."

"Any survivors?"

"None. Not that it would have mattered. They were all sterile."

Hoshi wasn't familiar with the Americanism. "Sterile?"

"They had nothing that could ID them. No personal effects, nothing that could be traced. All they had were passports, but we're drawing a blank on 'em."

"They sound like special forces. Or intelligence."

"Either way, it doesn't matter. Point is somebody didn't want anyone to find out who they were. Pirates are never sterile; they usually carry multiple IDs. You noticed the other ships self-destructed?"

"Yes. And they blew up too quickly for humans to have manually engaged the self-destruct. Perhaps their computers would automatically trigger the self-destruct if, say, the ship suffered irreparable engine damage."

"And that, my friend, is something only a space military is paranoid enough to implement."

"Do you think the CSF has something to do with this?"

"Damned if I know. Won't be surprised if they were. All the same, the US Space Force has eight ships trailing the Chinese formation by a week. The Chinese have five days to try something."

"You sound confident that the Chinese want to take Titan."

"Among the major space powers, China is ranked near the bottom. In the past decade they've been embarking on modernization programs, but they've been consistently over-budget. Their premier isn't pleased, but the hawks in the CSF insist that the programs are vital, even if they are taking money that could go into, say, education or healthcare."

"And so, to secure their place in the hierarchy, the hawks must present a triumph. Like Titan."

"Yup. You could say they've had their sights set on Titan for a long time."

"He who controls Titan controls the gas giants. He who controls the gas giants controls the Solar system." Hoshi smiled gently. "I imagine the hawks would also prefer not to see you Americans control Titan."

"Hey, buddy, we're all about spreading the wealth. That's why Prometheus is an international colony, ya?"

The Americans might have founded the colony along with several other anchor nations, but only they had a permanent garrison on Titan. It would also be impolite to point that out. Instead, Hoshi simply nodded and sipped at his tea.

"How do you think the Chinese will invade Titan?" Hoshi asked.

"They'll launch a coordinated space and ground offensive. They'll land troops beyond the horizon, where the lasers can't reach 'em, and execute a ground assault against the laser array. The guard ships will provide fire support and secure the orbits. With the lasers out of the way, and ships dominating the sky, nothing can touch them."

"How many forces do you have?"

"Groundside, just a company of Espatiers. Only way they can fight the Chinese with those numbers is to force a battle inside Prometheus proper. And so long as the Chinese can put ships in orbit, they can simply blow the hell out of the colony. I mean, they don't even *need* Prometheus, you know? If things get too troublesome they'll just drop rocks on us from orbit, then build their own colony later."

"That's a war crime."

"When did the Chinese care about war crimes? And, more importantly, who's going to punish *them?*"

Hoshi couldn't reply. Throughout human history, war criminals only had to fear a victor's justice. Even today, it was simply too expensive to enforce international law against nation-states across interplanetary distances.

"Aside from the lasers, what do you have for orbital defense?" Hoshi asked.

O'Neil exhaled sharply. "I've got a wing of orbital patrol ships left, but… look, they are meant to fight pirates, smugglers and the odd bit of space junk. Warships outrange and outgun them any day of the week. There's no point sending them up there. It'll be a slaughter."

"*Takao* can defend Titan."

"Against five ships? That's suicide."

Hoshi thought of the secret payload sleeping in *Takao*'s hull. No, it probably wasn't suicide, but the American didn't need to know. Yet.

"There is no one else."

"There is. Buddy, we've got an eight-ship task element behind the Chinese, remember? They won't be stupid enough to attack Titan now. Not unless they want boots up their asses. The hawks might have plans to capture Titan someday, but it won't be anytime soon."

"*Sou ka?*" Then a thought struck Hoshi. "They might invade us anyway."

"They can't be stupid enough to–"

"Yes they can. Think about it. They cannot capture Titan by subterfuge now. But if they do so by force, they can present it as a... a... fate..."

"*Fait accompli*?"

"Yes. Either the nations of Earth accept that the Chinese own Titan, or they will be forced to fight over every inhabited world. No matter who wins, a war *will* cause Kessler Syndrome across the Solar system, and shut off humanity from space forever."

"C'mon, man, the Space Force element I told you about can blow 'em to kingdom come."

"Yes, but they will need days to catch up. In that time, Beijing could order their fleet to keep destroying interplanetary infrastructure everywhere else until your ships turn around. It may start a war the Chinese can't win, but they can make sure nobody else does."

O'Neil paled. "My God. Who would be crazy enough to do that?"

"Are the hawks madmen?"

"No. But... I think they're gambling that nobody would risk Kessler Syndrome on that scale. The threat alone would make anyone blink."

"The interplanetary economy is dependent on helium-three. The gas must flow." Hoshi shook his head. "My government would rather give in than risk the helium-three shipping. And yours?"

O'Neil looked away, his face contorted in frustration. "Same. If they can reach a settlement without spending months and billions of dollars to mount a military expedition, they will. And everybody else... I don't think they care who sells 'em helium-three, so long as it keeps flowing." He sighed. "Goddammit."

"What can we do?"

"We can send our suspicions back home, but we both know nobody's gonna act without proof. The stakes are just too high."

"We must probe the Chinese into revealing their intentions without starting a space war ourselves."

"How?"

Hoshi finished his tea and straightened his back.

"If they attack *Takao*, even the most hardheaded bureaucrat back on Earth must listen to you."

"My God… Are you crazy?"

"Do we have any other choice?"

"No. I don't see that we do."

* * *

Hoshi proposed taking *Takao* to patrol the orbits of Saturn, claiming that the Americans had asked him to watch over the civilian spacecraft there. Wonder of wonders, Tokyo approved.

The spaceport patched up *Takao*'s wounds and topped off her fuel, propellant, ice and other consumables. Without charge.

The orbital patrol was equally generous. The Japanese munitions were license-produced versions of American designs. The Americans replaced the damaged missile cells and reloaded her magazines, the Japanese changed the language settings and ran compatibility tests, and *Takao* was pronounced fit for service.

Thus rearmed and resupplied, on the sixth day after the attack on Titan, *Takao* burned for Saturn.

And the Chinese followed.

"Captain, the Chinese have altered their vector," Kamishiro reported. "They are making an emergency burn towards Saturn at six hundred milligees. They have not stated the reason for doing so."

The Chinese were going all out, augmenting their main engines with chemical maneuvering rockets. A six hundred-milligee burn was not sustainable. It was used only to make a sudden vector change in the direst of circumstances: racing to a resupply depot before life support failed, scrambling to aid a stranded spacer, clearing out of a no-fly zone before the orbital patrol arrived.

Or intercepting a target.

"Interesting," Hoshi said. "Nakamura, do you think they will make it to Saturn?"

"They could, *if* they expend their chemical propellant reserves. They are committed to the vector and there is no turning back."

Spaceships do not simply alter course mid-mission. Every vector change imposed a delta-vee cost above and beyond existing propellant expenditure, and there was only so much propellant a ship could store before losing performance. It was especially important for military spaceships: the more propellant a ship carried, the fewer weapons, ammo and supplies she could carry.

Military spaceships usually budgeted just enough delta-vee for their missions, with a reserve for engagements. The Chinese in particular exercised strict control of their fleet from Earth. A Chinese spaceship commander who wanted to make a course correction during a mission had to seek permission from Beijing. This far away, it would take at least three hours to receive a response. The only thing that could have prompted the Chinese to alter course so suddenly was *Takao*'s own flight.

Which meant the Chinese were after *Takao*.

Hoshi composed a report for his superiors, then summoned his officers to an unused compartment in the crew deck. As the men tethered themselves to safety moorings, Hoshi discussed the situation and dispensed intelligence files. If the Chinese were truly friendly, it would make good practice for combat. If the Chinese had designs on *Takao*, they would be ready. Probably.

"Nakamura, what do we know about the Chinese ships?" he asked.

Nakamura cleared his throat. "Captain, the task element is composed of two assault carriers and three guard ships. The assault carriers are named *Zhejiang* and *Guangdong.* The escorts are *Shanghai, Nanjing* and *Chongqing.* The escorts are in the lead, forming a triangle with a separation of eight hundred kilometers. The assault carriers are trailing them by five hundred kilometers, and are arranged side-by-side with a separation of four hundred kilometers.

"The assault carriers have a displacement of forty thousand tons. They have helium-three-deuterium drives, combat acceleration of twenty milligees. Cargo capacity of ten thousand tons each. That's enough for a battalion of Space Marines, landing craft, and twenty drones. Eight point defense lasers, effective range of one thousand kilometers.

"The guard ships have a displacement of ten thousand tons. They also have helium-three-deuterium engines, combat acceleration of fifty milligees. Weapons payload of five thousand tons each. Main weapon is a three-hundred-millimeter spinal railgun. Secondary armament are multiple missile banks, two hundred and eighty missiles total. Six point defense lasers, effective range of one thousand kilometers."

"Thank you," Hoshi said. "We are presently eleven hours from Saturn orbit, and the Chinese will arrive a day later. Our mission is to draw out the Chinese intentions without starting a war. Suggestions?"

"Captain, if the Chinese have any more Q-ships, they'll deploy them against us," Kamishiro said. "If the Q-ships defeat us the Chinese have an excuse to take over the Saturnian system. If the Q-ships lose, the Chinese will have an excuse to approach us to assist with 'law enforcement' and put us within their railguns' engagement envelope."

"Excellent thought," Hoshi said. "Now, how do we solve this?"

"Let's take an orbit that would put us in standoff range of civilian traffic," Sato said.

"Lieutenant Sato, Saturn's orbits are cluttered," Mori said. "We've got civilian traffic intermixed with robot miners. There's no one entity performing global traffic control at Saturn. We should take up station in high orbit and direct the civilians to the lower orbits."

"And that is when a Q-ship would strike to cause maximum havoc," Subaru said. "I suggest we put mirrors parallel to our vectors to let us control the orbits."

Kamishiro nodded. "Let's take up orbit at an altitude of twenty thousand kilometers, and have the civilians form a convoy at an altitude of fifteen thousand klicks and fifteen hundred klicks forward relative to our position. If anyone starts trouble, we can shoot down at their engines, radiators and reactors."

"I foresee the civilians complaining about it," Sato remarked.

"If they are willing to eat our exhaust, they are very welcome," Tanaka said.

The men shared a chuckle.

"I'm more concerned about the Chinese complaining," Hoshi said. "They will accuse us of 'unlawfully seizing control of Saturn orbit'."

"Or they may praise us for our initiative and volunteer to help out," Kamishiro said.

"If they do the latter, I will tell them that we have the situation under control, and they should move on to Titan," Hoshi said. "If their intentions are benign, they will be needed there to inspect the ships already in Titan orbit."

"What if they are *not* benign? Captain, what do you think they will do?"

"They will make excuses to maintain their current vector. I am confident they will not make a burn for Titan. They won't want to risk being shot in the back."

"And if they want to give battle around Saturn?"

"We give them all the fight they want."

"Captain, may I express the general sentiment of the crew?" Kamishiro said formally.

"Carry on," Hoshi said.

"Captain, the Chinese have *twenty-two* times our mass. If we have to fight..." Kamishiro sucked in air between his teeth. "I must strongly recommend against a prolonged engagement."

Hoshi nodded. The crew were neither cowards nor mutineers. But they were as cognizant as he was of the odds against *Takao.*

He thought of his family. Hana understood a spacer's life, recognized that the iron laws of duty dictated that he had to be absent from home for months at a time, and return home for visits that sometimes lasted mere weeks. But Kikyo was only three years old, and she was not old enough to understand. He desperately wanted to make it home to them.

But not at the price of an Earth dominated by a Chinese space empire.

"What if we have no choice, Kamishiro?"

"We will do our duty, Captain."

"Yes, we shall."

* * *

The Chinese exhausted their chemical rocket propellant the moment they had locked in a vector for Saturn. When Hoshi arrived, the Chinese were 2.4 light seconds from the planet.

Takao restocked fuel and propellant from an orbital depot. Then, Subaru boosted four sunrays into Saturn orbit, while Kamishiro had the unenviable task of herding the civilians into a single large convoy. The civilians complained, whined and argued, but *Takao* had the biggest guns—actually, the *only* guns—around the planet.

Over the space of hours, the civilians formed a long ragged line orbiting the planet. No Q-ships emerged to wreak havoc, for which Hoshi was grateful. When the Chinese closed to one light-second, Hoshi hailed them on the radio in English.

"Attention CSF formation, this is JS *Takao.* Welcome to Saturn. May I speak to your commander, please?"

"*Takao*, this is *Guangdong*. Thank you for your greeting. Please identify yourself and state the nature of your business."

"*Guangdong*, as mentioned, this is JS *Takao*. We are conducting civilian escort mission until Titan lifts no-fly zone."

Hoshi was deliberately being obtuse. He was also tempted to confuse his 'l's and 'r's, but that would be going overboard.

"*Takao*, *Guangdong*. I meant to say, please state your rank and name. We are on a patrol to the Saturnian system. We saw your engagement with the pirates at Titan and are willing to assist."

"*Takao* copies. Pirates beaten. Local authorities say no need of assistance. Thanks for offer. Also, what you need rank and name for, over?"

"I'd like to know who I'm talking to."

"You first, please."

It took a full minute before he replied. "This is Captain Huang Wei. Now your rank and name, please."

"Nakamura, look up a Captain Huang Wei," Hoshi ordered. Returning to the radio, he said, "Thank you, Captain Huang. I'm Commander Kano Makoto. Please to meet you."

"The pleasure is mine, Commander. We are glad to learn that the pirates have been beaten, but we still need to resupply at Saturn."

"Roger that. We are taking up patrol at angels twenty. When you arrive at Saturn, please maintain separation of five thousand kilometers from my ship."

"Acknowledged, Commander Kano. I look forward to meeting you."

Hoshi cycled out of his duty shift and retreated to his cabin to catch up on paperwork. Nothing would happen for hours. *Takao* had to keep watching the Chinese, and pounce when they revealed their intent.

Four hours after his request, Nakamura called him.

"Commander, response from Earth. No records of a Captain Huang Wei in known personnel records of the Chinese Space Forces."

Japanese knowledge of Chinese records was incomplete. The captain could simply be a nobody, and utterly expendable if he failed. Or else he had lied.

No matter. Hoshi needed to be fresh to face the Chinese. He exercised with his men, took a shower, had a meal, sent mail back home, and took a nap.

Kamishiro shook him awake.

"Sir, the Chinese want to speak with you."

Hoshi dragged himself to the CIC and took stock of the situation. The Chinese had now closed to seventy thousand kilometers. Both carriers were discharging smaller craft. Sensors identified the latter as *Houyi* drones, the current-generation Chinese military drone.

"Commander Kano," Huang said. "I have received new orders. Our mission is to assist the local forces in securing Saturn. The Titanian authorities have agreed to lift the no-fly zone for ships that have been inspected. We have two battalions of space marines ready for inspection duties. We would like to work with you to assist the Titanian authorities."

It sounded reasonable, but there were the matter of the drones. Also, the Chinese were using laser communications. They didn't want the civilians listening in.

"Captain Huang, I look forward to working with you. I see you have launched *Houyi* drones. Please to explain this launch?"

"There are a large number of ships in Saturn orbit. The drones will help monitor the situation and provide assistance where necessary."

"Very well, Captain Huang. Please to put them on vector ahead of my ship to prevent collision."

"Commander Kano, roger that. We will do so at the soonest possible moment."

Hoshi could not accuse the Chinese commander of perfidy, not openly, but they had launched way outside typical Chinese engagement ranges. Why?

Hoshi typed up his observation report and sent it off to Earth.

When he looked back up, the drones were burning in at *three* gravities, adopting an attack vector aimed at *Takao*.

Hoshi briefed his intelligence officer and asked, "Nakamura, what do you think about Captain Huang's explanation?"

"Captain, it is bullshit. Saturn's escape velocity is thirty-five and a half klicks per second. The drones are making *fifty*, and they are burning straight at us. If they are headed for orbital injection they should be decelerating by now."

"Unless they are setting up kinetic shots at our flanks."

"Yes sir. We cannot let them cross five thousand klicks. Past that and their missiles will be flying faster than our point defenses can track them."

The textbook insisted that he should pull in his radiators and call home. But home was one and a half hours away. By the time a response arrived, the situation would be over—and *Takao* would have cooked in her juices. Also, the Chinese would see it as a hostile act, and would be justified in firing first.

At the same time, if he kept his radiators out, the Chinese drones would have a clean line of fire at them. If they fired first, they could end *Takao*.

He needed to buy time.

"Captain Huang, we are pleased to see you are sending drones to help us," he radioed on the guard channel. "However, they are flying too fast for orbital injection and are still on a collision course with us. We advise to decelerate and adjust vector."

"Commander Kano, roger that and thank you for your concern. Our *Houyi*s have expanded propellant tanks. They will be able to make the trip. They will also adjust their vector at the appropriate time."

"Please to adjust vectors to avoid collision, or we will take necessary actions."

"Rest assured, Commander, we are simply taking the fastest vector possible. We will endeavor to avoid a collision."

Bullshit. Hoshi typed up his observations, attached recordings of the exchange, and sent them on to Tokyo. It would arrive too late, but he needed to keep a paper trail.

"Subaru, launch four sunrays. Boost them to angels twenty-five."

When the sunrays reached an orbital altitude of twenty-five thousand kilometers, Hoshi placed them on a track parallel to *Takao*'s. Then he ordered, "Mori, ping the drones with lidar."

In military terms, this was the equivalent of saying, *What the hell are you doing?* And sure enough, *Guangdong* hailed *Takao* on the guard channel.

"Commander Kano, please refrain from pinging our drones with active sensors. Our drones are loaded with live ammunition and are on AI control. They may fire upon ships that paint them without warning. We would like to avoid misunderstandings."

"Captain Huang, your drones are still on an intercept vector with my ship."

"We have no hostile intentions towards your ship, but we cannot prevent our AIs from following their programming."

The game had to end here.

"Be advised, Captain, my lasers are on automated point defense mode. If your drones close to within five thousand kilometers, they will be assumed hostile and fired upon."

"Roger, Commander. Do not fret. We wish you no harm."

Hoshi muttered darkly under his breath and hit the ship-wide intercom.

"All hands, *sentou youii.* All hands, *sentou youii.*"

Klaxons sounded. The crew rushed to their places with alacrity. Moments later, Kamishiro announced, "Sir, the ship is battle ready."

"Very good." Addressing his officers, Hoshi said, "We will draw our line in the sand here. The moment the drones cross six thousand klicks, prepare targeting solutions with passive sensors only. If they cross the five thousand kilometer mark, or if they fire, retract radiators and destroy the drones."

"Sir, won't this start a war?" Sato asked.

"Drones are expendable," Hoshi said. "Destroying drones is not as severe as destroying ships. I believe they mean to intimidate us out of the system. Before the drones reach their engagement envelope, I think Huang will claim that he has received orders from Beijing and 'request' that we leave, or he will be forced to shoot."

"It's unlikely they want to be seen as the bad guys, sir," Tanaka said. "If they fire first, they risk starting a war."

"Not if they use drones," Kamishiro said. "They accused us on the guard channel of targeting their drones, and said their drones' artificial intelligence allows them to fire without men in the loop. If their drones fire, they can simply claim self-defense."

"Thank you, gentlemen. Keep an eye out for suspicious Chinese activity, and be prepared to broadcast our side of the story over the radio. The Chinese will use deception, so we will use the truth. We must have witnesses on our side."

The minutes sped past. Hoshi grew restless. The ship was turning, trying to present as small a target to the drones as possible. The Chinese drones had finally cut their acceleration, but showed no signs of altering their course.

At sixty-five hundred kilometers out, Mori yelled, "Threat lidar!"

Arrows streaked from the drones. Eight of them.

"Tanaka, defensive maneuvers! Subaru–"

A string of flashes played across the feed.

"*Nani?!*"

"Side kick! Side kick!" Tanaka yelled belatedly.

Her maneuvering rockets fired. *Takao* turned faster, bringing her nose to face the threats. Hoshi glanced at the display.

The ship reported no damage.

But the sunrays were destroyed.

"Commander Kano, this is Captain Huang. Our drones reported being pinged by active sensors, and fired upon your mirrors. As a sign of good faith we prevented them from targeting your ship directly. Please exit the Saturnian system to avoid further misunderstandings."

The maneuvering thrusters fired again, canceling the ship's momentum. Hoshi ignored the Chinese officer, instead addressing his officers.

"Tanaka, retract radiators. Nakamura, Mori, what the hell was that?"

"Sir, flashes were consistent with nuclear weapon initiations," Mori replied. "Estimated yield of five hundred kilotons."

"A nuke couldn't harm anything at this range. What the hell did they use?"

"Mori," Nakamura said, "Did we pick up anything from the flashes?"

"Negative. But the fireball took the shape of a cone. Indicative of a directed nuclear charge."

"*Sa...*" Nakamura said. "Captain, I think it's a *Tianlei.* It's a bomb-pumped x-ray laser. It's a classified experimental project. We have no data on it. But Chinese doctrine encourages the use of lasers the moment a target enters their maximum effective range. Perhaps the *Tianlei* has a max *known* effective range of sixty-five hundred klicks."

Hoshi shook his head. This was a show of force, one step away from outright aggression. But they didn't know what *Takao* had.

"Thank you, gentlemen. Designate the Chinese ships as hostile and prepare for immediate action."

On the display, the Chinese ships turned red. Hoshi returned to the radio and broadcast his reply on the guard frequency. "Captain Huang, you fired upon us with nuclear bomb-pumped lasers. We will not tolerate this act of aggression. You are in violation of international law. Withdraw your drones immediately."

On his display, four red columns, five deep, marched towards *Takao.*

"Negative, *Takao*. They are committed. They do not have the delta-vee to withdraw."

All of humanity could see that the drones were on an intercept vector with *Takao,* and that the drones could accelerate much faster than *Takao* could. And the Chinese did not deny using nuclear weapons.

He was now free to act.

"Subaru, initiate defensive solution! Dial lasers to UV-C!"

"Initiate defensive solution, dial lasers to UV-C, *ryoukai!*"

The eight laser turrets facing the threats fired at will, taking one target each. A quarter of the enemy formation vaporized. Five more blew apart, then the survivors began launching missiles. But before the missiles reached minimum standoff distance every last threat flashed into rapidly-expanding plasma. In the space of a breath, everything that could pose a threat to *Takao* was gone.

"Sir, we have a grand slam," Mori reported.

This was *Takao*'s first secret. A UV-C beam would remain coherent far beyond a UV-A laser's effective range. *Takao* could deliver more megawatts per square centimeter than any vessel smaller than a capital ship.

Hoshi returned to the radio. "Captain Huang, we were fired upon by your drones and acted in self-defense. Take an exit vector immediately, or we will take every necessary action to safeguard our ship and the Saturnian system."

The Chinese could not depart, of course. They did not have the acceleration to make such a radical vector change, not without making an orbital injection and turning slowly, very, very slowly, with their gyroscopes to align the vector. Hoshi was simply covering his ass.

"*Takao*, we do not have the delta-vee and acceleration regime to do so. We recommend *you* leave the system to avoid future mishaps."

"*Guangdong*, we cannot. The civil authorities have requested us to ensure the security of the Saturnian system. We have every right to be here, but we have not received confirmation that the civil authorities have requested your presence. Depart the system immediately or we will carry out our orders."

The next response came on a laser narrowcast.

"Commander *Hoshi*, today is not a good day to die. You are outnumbered, outmassed and outgunned. Fighting us is suicide. Your crew have families. *You* have a family. Please, think of Hana and Kikyo. They are waiting for you in Osaka. Please don't throw your life away. Just make a burn for Earth and you can see them again."

Hoshi was unsurprised to learn that Huang had known who he had been all along. But indignant fury exploded in his chest all the same. How dare they try to use his family against him!

"Kamishiro. Rebroadcast that last message to Titan, Tokyo, and the civilians around us. Let them know that the Chinese have fired upon us with nuclear weapons and are now personally threatening our families. Tanaka, extend radiators. Sato, plot an attack vector towards *Chongqing*. Subaru, boost four sunrays."

As the sunrays blasted off on beams of black light, the Chinese ships cut acceleration and skewed around to aim their weapons. They, too, were on an attack vector, and they were committed. There was no turning back, no diverting, nothing but death or glory.

"Commander Hoshi, that was a mistake. We will send flowers to your family at the funeral."

Hoshi knew his next words would be recorded for posterity. And he knew he should be very, very careful with them. Instead, he threw caution to the winds.

"You do not threaten me, Captain. You do not threaten my crew. You do not threaten my family. *Kusokute shine, Chankoro! Kuroso zo!*"

Eat shit and die, Chink! I will kill you!

Takao could run. She had the delta-vee to exit Saturn and avoid this fight, or head to Titan and make a last stand there with the Americans.

But he would not shirk this battle. Unlike *Takao*, Titan could not dodge. The Chinese could bombard Prometheus with their railguns even as they lined up for an approach. Hoshi wasn't afraid of a hit; he was afraid of a *miss*, of a stray shot striking the space elevator. At least here the civilians could evade stray kinetics. If he had to fight, it had to be around Saturn.

Also, he had promised to kill Huang, and he always kept his promises.

Kamishiro called Hoshi. "Captain, we have been attacked by Chinese nuclear weapons. I believe this fulfills the special conditions in our rules of engagement."

"The Chinese destroyed our mirrors. They could argue they didn't attack us directly."

"They can't. Those drones were launching missiles at us. They had to be *Tianlei*s too. If those had gone off, we'd all be dead. We have to release our special weapons."

"I..." Hoshi shook his head. This was not a time to hesitate. For the third time in history, Japan had been attacked by a nuclear power. But this time, Japan could strike back. This time, Japan *would* strike back!

"Ensign Mori," he said. "In your professional opinion, have we been attacked by nuclear weapons?"

"*Hai!* The enemy drones launched missiles on attack vectors. Laser spectroscope shows significant amounts of fusion material in the vapor and debris clouds."

"The Chinese drones use nuclear gas-core engines. Is there any possibility of contamination?"

When this was over, the court-martial would pore over the ship's black box. He needed Mori to state what he had seen on the record.

"No sir. Nuclear gas-core rockets use uranium hexafluoride fuel. The debris clouds contain concentrated amounts of deuterium, tritium and lithium. This is consistent with materials used in Chinese nuclear fusion warheads."

"Very well." Clearing his throat, Hoshi hit the intercom. "Attention all hands. We have been attacked by nuclear weapons. As per our rules of engagement, we will now release our special munitions."

"Release special munitions, *ryoukai*," Kamishiro acknowledged.

Hoshi pressed his palm against a sensor-embedded corner of his desk. A green light lit up, and a translucent guard box sprung open, exposing a keyhole. He opened a breast pocket and produced a tiny key.

"Insert keys," Hoshi ordered.

"Insert keys," Kamishiro echoed.

Hoshi inserted the key.

"On my mark, rotate key," Hoshi said.

"On your mark, rotate key."

"Three. Two. One. Mark."

Hoshi turned the key.

A new window popped up, displaying *Takao*'s secret arsenal: sixteen Type 82 missiles. Visually indistinguishable from the other Type 82s in the missile banks, they were the reason *Takao* carried a full war load.

They were also experimental weapons, originally slated for testing at the edges of the Solar system. Hoshi hoped they worked as designed.

"Nakamura, how will the Chinese fight us?"

"Sir, they know what our lasers can do. They will deploy drones and laser-propelled missiles to overwhelm our lasers and destroy us at stand-off range. They will also use their railguns to shape the battlespace."

Hoshi smiled. "No, Nakamura, they only *think* they know what our lasers can do. Subaru, charge the ultracapacitors."

The Chinese continued to turn. Their hulls were long and vulnerable, but still too far away for *Takao* to target accurately. When the guard ships stopped turning, they fired their railguns. Projectiles sped towards *Takao* at twenty klicks per second relative to her velocity. They were guided shells, firing rockets to take them on an intercept course with *Takao*.

"It's harassing fire," Nakamura said. "They want us to expend delta-vee to dodge them, maybe even force us out of the Saturnian system. At this range, those have got to be flechette shells."

"Very good. Nakamura, Sato, Tanaka, Subaru: develop a vector that will take us towards *Chongqing* and minimize acceleration and delta-vee expenditure. Priority is to set up a laser solution at standoff range. What flechettes we can't dodge, we trash."

The Chinese shells approached. *Takao* adjusted her vector just so, occasionally firing her maneuvering thrusters to jink sideways. The shells followed, but their fuel reserves were limited, and when they burst into flechettes, Subaru only needed to destroy four darts to ensure *Takao*'s safety.

The following waves of shells weren't aimed at *Takao*. They went for the mirrors. Hoshi ordered the shells destroyed before they could wreck the mirrors. It told the Chinese how Hoshi intended to strike them, but not where or when.

The Chinese kept their formation tight, staying within each other's point defense envelopes. The guard ships were specialized in counter-missile and counter-drone defense. Hoshi needed to blow a hole in their formation before he could employ his special weapons. He glued his eyes to the display. The opportunity would come soon enough. Either *Takao* would get close enough or…

At the forty-thousand-kilometer mark, the guard ships separated. *Shanghai* and *Nanjing* made tight turns, as tight as their gyroscopes would allow. *Chongqing* swept through a massive arc. The assault carriers hung back. They would coordinate their drone launches with the guard ships.

The Chinese guard ships were setting up velocity-augmented shots. They would burn in on an attack vector, then turn and fire their weapons, using their own velocity to further accelerate their projectiles. *Shanghai* and *Nanjing* would deploy their railguns, *Chongqing* her missiles. The Chinese were gambling that they could overwhelm *Takao* and form up again before she could respond.

But there was something the Chinese did *not* know.

"Subaru, snipe *Chongqing*'s radiators."

Chongqing's liquid droplet radiators were tiny targets at this distance, but with the sunrays extending their effective range the UV-C lasers only needed one good hit to blow off a radiator. *Takao* wove a massive buckshot pattern of black light. Flashes erupted around the ship, spewing streaks of rapidly-freezing coolant.

"Hit!" Mori called. "Radiators have broken off. *Chongqing* is heat-killed."

Hoshi nodded. "Good work, Subaru."

The other Chinese ships pulled in their radiators. Against the perfect cold of space, only *Takao*'s radiators still blazed. That would stress the Chinese commanders, showing everyone that *Takao* could shoot but not them. Also, spinal railguns generated huge amounts of heat. Hoshi figured the guard ships would save their coolant for their point defense lasers and missiles instead.

As for *Chongqing*, she would melt—

"Sir! *Chongqing* is launching an alpha strike!" Mori called.

Hoshi swore. *Chongqing* was dead already, but her artificial intelligence sought to take *Takao* with her.

Hundreds of missiles burst out into the void. Railgun shells followed. The surviving guard ships launched their own missiles and altered their vectors, trying to close the hole in their flank.

"Full guard!" Hoshi ordered. "Tanaka, keep radiators extended until strikers cross seven thousand kilometers. Subaru, deploy bursters and starbursts against incoming strikers."

The officers snapped into action. Railguns and lasers unleashed a torrent of fire. *Takao* launched every burster in her arsenal. Hoshi's console chimed, and one by one, all eight starbursts left their cells.

With the last of the missiles away, Subaru said, "Sir, I have an engagement solution for *Guangdong*. I can bounce beams into her reactors."

That was tempting. But if he killed *Guangdong* now, the lasers would have to cool down and recharge, giving the enemy missiles time to close the distance.

"Save the solution. For now, engage incoming threats. Tanaka, orient ship to face the strikers. Employ side kick."

Hoshi braced himself and rode out the chemical impulses. As she turned, *Takao* lashed the swarm with beams of black light. The drones died first, but got off a volley of missiles. As the Chinese missiles melted down, *Takao*'s electronic warfare suite forced a few more off course.

Chongqing disintegrated in a flash of actinic light. She was *finally* dead. But her missiles were still coming.

Takao's bursters arrived, finding a target-rich environment. Exploding amongst the threat missiles, they eliminated thirty-eight. The Chinese had employed bursters of their own among the swarm, and as they went off their shrapnel scored own goals.

The starbursts arrived next. Spreading out into a gigantic net, they closed in the swarm. Three hundred kilometers out from the threats, the starbursts split open. Ten warheads jetted forth from each missile. All eighty warheads fired chemical thrusters, dispersing themselves for optimum coverage. And exploded.

These were nuclear warheads. *Shaped* nuclear warheads. Each blast converted a giant alloy plate into millions of pellets, and every pellet had a velocity of five hundred kilometers per second. On the display, the pellets spread out in dense cones thousands of kilometers long, each cloud engulfing dozens of missiles at once.

But there weren't enough starbursts. The shrapnel fog dissipated, and enemy missiles sneaked through. Ten, twenty, thirty, more. *Takao*'s lasers went back online and picked off more missiles. Then the railgun shells arrived, picking off a few threats, and the point defense lasers fired again, bouncing off the mirrors and taking out more missiles.

At eight thousand kilometers away, four missiles remained on threat vectors.

And separated into sixteen warheads.

Hoshi exhaled. "*Kuso.*"

They exploded.

Explosions rocked *Takao.* Hoshi slammed against his harness, driving the breath out of him. The lights went out. Secondary blasts went off, deafening Hoshi. Holes opened in the CIC. Hot metal sprayed through, slashing through the compartment. Air rushed out.

The hull breach alarm sounded.

Hoshi exhaled sharply and reached under his seat, pulling out his helmet. As his vision faded, he mated the helmet to his suit's seals, checked that the emergency air bottle was in place, and twisted the valve open. Breathing mix flooded the helmet. He took a few energizing breaths and took stock of the situation.

He was alive, apparently unscathed, and his skinsuit was intact. But a few of his CIC team were slumped over their seats, bleeding. Moments later, the damage-control party entered the compartment. Two crewmen rushed to patch the holes. The others administered what aid they could and carried the casualties out. Hoshi's console had shut down in the chaos, and he switched it back on.

The lights went back on. Life support resumed. Detecting fresh air outside, the helmet opened its breathing port and politely informed Hoshi to turn off the gas valve. He did so, then massaged his battered chest. When he felt he could speak again, and the ringing in his ears subsided, he returned to the conference call.

"Kamishiro, damage report."

No response.

"Kamishiro? Are you still alive?"

Silence.

Hoshi's console rebooted. He called up the damage report and beheld the butcher's bill.

Kamishiro was dead. So were Sato, Nakamura, and half of *Takao*'s crew. Entire decks were open to space. Railguns Two and Three were ruined. The gyroscopes were destroyed. Point Defense Lasers One and Two were knocked out. The main laser had lost a turret. The forward missile banks were shattered, multiple ultracapacitors and laser engines had blown, and even the fuel tank was holed.

And the radiators were gone.

Hoshi sighed. The Chinese had outplayed him. They had detonated their small *Tianlei* missiles at sixty-five hundred kilometers, letting him think that that was their maximum effective range. He also hadn't considered the possibility that multiple *Tianlei* warheads could also be mated to a conventional missile chassis. And *Takao* had paid the price.

"All hands, initiate Ohka Protocol," Hoshi said.

"Engineering. Overriding heat and reactor safety limits."

"Weapons. Solutions ready."

"Sensors. Targets locked."

"*Minna, domo arigato gozaimasu.*" *Everyone, thank you very much.* "It has been an honor serving with you. All non-essential personnel, abandon ship."

The damage-control party evacuated the CIC with the rest of the wounded. Hacking and coughing, Hoshi checked his special munitions window. Four special weapons had survived. He needed at least one per guard ship, two per assault carrier. He was short of two.

There was only one solution.

"Subaru."

"Sir?"

"Kill *Guangdong* with lasers."

"Kill *Guangdong* with lasers, ryoukai."

Takao launched her two remaining sunrays and dedicated every last watt she had to the remaining lasers. They pounded *Guangdong,* smashing through her defenses and biting into her hull. The ship rotated, spreading out the damage, but she was too slow. The guard ships launched more missiles, but they were too slow. Spears of black light drilled into the *Guangdong*'s core, blowing out pillars of vapor, generating secondary explosions.

"Sir!" Tanaka called. "Heat load has reached critical levels!"

Hoshi was *sweating.* The air grew thick and stale. But he didn't care. *Guangdong* had to die.

"Acknowledged. Subaru, keep firing."

The lasers kept firing, pounding the reactor deck. The ship *bulged.* Plumes of white-hot plasma roared through the holes in the hull.

Molten metal sprayed in all directions. The blast broke the back of the ship, reducing her to scrap.

"Sir!" Mori called. "*Guangdong* is evacuating!"

Escape pods broke away from *Guangdong*. Dropships punched out of the mass driver. There would be hundreds of survivors, but they would not have the delta-vee to reach Titan. Not before the Americans arrived.

"And that was for Hana and Kikyo," Hoshi muttered.

Minor eruptions rocked *Takao*. The ultracapacitors melted. Circuits blew.

"Sir, heat sinks are boiling!" Tanaka reported. "Recommend we abandon ship!"

"In a moment, Tanaka. Subaru, alpha strike. Launch all meteors, anti-ship configuration."

Takao rumbled. Her four meteors surged into the void, turning for the flanks of the Chinese ships.

"Captain, reactor failure imminent!" Tanaka warned. "We must evacuate *now!*"

Hoshi wanted dearly to watch the Chinese die, but he wanted to see Hana and Kikyo more. He keyed the intercom and said, "All remaining personnel, abandon ship."

Hoshi followed his crew down the ladders to the escape pods, avoiding sprays of sparks, jets of steam, and holes into space. By tradition, Hoshi was the last to board the final pod, and forced himself in next to Mori. Moments later, the crowded pod blasted off.

When they were safely clear of the dying ship, Hoshi keyed the pod's radio. "All crew of the JS *Takao*, this is Commander Hoshi. You did your duty today. I commend you all. We will regroup in Saturn orbit. Make for angels fifteen and activate your SOS beacons. Also, be informed you may have been exposed to ionizing radiation. As a precaution, everyone will take one dose of anti-radiation medicine."

As Mori worked the pod's controls, a crewman opened the first-aid box and distributed syringes of anti-radiation drugs. Hoshi injected himself with one, then pulled up the feed from the pod's sensors on the pod's holographic display.

The meteors closed. The Chinese turned to face their threats, but their gyroscopes were too sluggish. They fired more missiles instead, but it was too late, and the ones they had in flight were still too far away.

The missiles separated, deploying fifteen warheads each. They maneuvered to form a loose net, bracketing their targets. And then they initiated.

In the fury of a nuclear blast, each meteor forged a penetrator with a velocity that reached one percent of the speed of light. The penetrators flew so fast the Chinese could not track them. Anti-missiles were fired uselessly into the dark. Point defense lasers, those that were lucky or fast enough, emitted a single pulse each, far from enough to break the assault.

The penetrators struck. Set to anti-ship mode, they arrived in threes. The first cratered a section of the target's armor. The second passed through the hole and wrecked the compartment beyond. The third punched into the heart of the ship.

Zhejiang was the first to go, breaking apart in a storm of superheated plasma. *Shanghai*'s engine disappeared in a great cloud of gas and twisted metal. And *Nanjing*… it was as though an *oni* had carved her up with a serrated knife. Escape pods blossomed from the ships, but very few before explosions rendered escape impossible.

At last came the inevitable. Like a lightbulb popping, *Takao* vanished in an ephemeral star as bright as a thousand suns.

Mori cleared his throat. He did not wipe away the tears streaking his face. "*Takao* is the finest ship in the fleet, *na?*"

"*So yo*," Hoshi said firmly. "The finest."

War at the Speed of Light

Col Douglas Beason, USAF, ret.

Editor's Introduction

Doug Beason is an old friend. I first met him when he was on the faculty at the Air Force Academy at Colorado Springs, but for most of his career he has been a scientist of war. He is the former Chief Scientist of Space Command, and has commanded many of the Air Force's weapons laboratories. He also writes science fact and fiction. *The Cadet* tells the story of the formation of the U.S. Air Force Academy.

"War at the Speed of Light" looks at the future weapons of war from the view of one of their creators.

The date is late fall, 2027, and a cacophony of sound reverberates through the city—sounds of cars honking, animals braying, police whistles blowing. The air is dense, humid and heavy with the smell of dung, car fumes and urine. Beggars crowd the street, fighting for rupees given in embarrassed sorrow by widows, visiting dignitaries and students who now stare agape at the world's most extreme poverty.

The place is New Delhi, India, home of the world's largest democracy and unwavering friend to the United States. Until now.

An unruly crowd surges through the trash-laden streets, picking up stragglers as the mob grows in frenzy. Women and children slip around corners and cover their faces, trying to hide, but they are swept along with the roiling crowd. Shouts erupt, rocks are thrown. Within minutes, the growing riot approaches the iron gates of the American Embassy.

A glass bottle filled with gasoline and stuffed with a burning rag is hurled over the gate. Burning liquid from the Molotov cocktail splatters across the ground. Someone shoots a gun. In a panic, with the unpredictable mentality of a mob, the crowd surges forward.

Stoic U.S. Marines guarding the entry points fall back into position, drawing their automatic weapons. Having learned from the debacle of the Iranian hostage situation 50 years before, the Marines are under unwavering orders not to give up the Embassy, no matter what.

Their orders are 'shoot to kill'.

Their actions could set back diplomatic relations with India for decades.

Behind them, hundreds of American and Indian Embassy staff members are hastily ushered into basement 'safe' areas. The situation is rapidly escalating out of control.

Women and children in the crowd are roughly grabbed, to be used as human shields to prevent the Americans from stopping them. The rioters know the Marines won't kill innocent women and children, and they use their hostages to advance toward the embassy. The insurgents boldly shove their innocent shields in front of them as they advance.

The crowd surges forward. The guards must act.

The political balance with one of America's greatest democratic allies now hinges on the split-second decisions made by the gun-toting Marines, young men who are brave, but barely out of high school. They are well-trained, but they are soldiers, not diplomats. Visions of their predecessors being overrun at Fallujah and Mogadishu swirl through their heads. They are all too aware of what happened in Tehran and at Benghazi.

These young warriors are faced with immense pressure to react, to defend this small vestige of American soil… but they also know their commander has provided them with an ace in the hole.

Their predecessors only had options: to shout at the insurgents, ordering them to stop—or to shoot them. A simple binary decision: shout or shoot.

Today, however, there is a third option.

As the Marines raise their rifles, a deep humming sound envelops the compound. Without warning, the rioters feel intense heat, as if a giant, invisible oven has suddenly opened in front of them. Within seconds the pain is unbearable. They cannot think, they cannot reason—they can only react.

They turn and flee, trying to escape as far as they can from the invisible heat. Screaming in pain, the rioters drop their weapons as they sprint away. No one looks back as they scramble to flee.

Curiously, none of the women or children in the mob are affected. As if divided by a Maxwellian Devil who can distinguish between hostile intent and innocence, only those people who had been carrying weapons had felt the intense, excruciating pain—a heat like that from a supercharged oven. The mysterious weapon defending the embassy is that accurate, that precise.

In less than a minute the streets are clear, the compound is eerily quiet. Warily, the women and children disperse, unharmed.

As the Marines lower their weapons, the only noise in the Embassy is the low mechanical thrumming that comes from a geodesic sphere, inconspicuously located on top of the sprawling building. Inside the sphere is a phased-array dipole antenna that directed the millimetre waves from the world's first non-lethal Directed Energy Weapon: Active Denial.

Science Fiction? No... Active Denial is being tested today. And if funding had not been cut at the turn of the century, it could have been used to quell the urban warfare in Baghdad, in Fallujah and in other cities where allied warfighters have been stationed.

And countless lives might have been saved.

Technology Wins Wars

The size of the army matters, but it's the technology that wins wars. At the height of the Roman Empire, Roman legions armed with arrows, longstaffs and shields used precise, steadfast formations to devastate the more numerous, but ill-equipped, barbarian hordes.

The invention of the stirrup in the sixth century gave horsemen the ability to use their mount as a lethal weapon for the first time—an astonishing transformation from the centuries-old use of transportation or ploughing, allowing warriors to combine their horse's mass and speed with their devastating thrust of a spear.

In 1232 during the battle of Kai-Keng, the Chinese repelled Mongol invaders with the first known use of rudimentary rockets powered by gunpowder, called 'arrows of flying fire'.

On 9 August 1945, a lone B-29 bomber flew over Nagasaki, Japan, and dropped a single atomic bomb that ended World War Two.

And in February 1991, precision-guided 'smart' bombs, ground-hugging cruise missiles and invisible stealth fighters forced the massively equipped and much more numerous Iraqi army to its knees.

In 2003, the war in Iraq just missed seeing the introduction of a new generation of sophisticated weaponry, a new type of weapon based not on missiles, bombs or bullets… nor on anything you can hold in your hands. This weapon is made of ordinary light utilizing the same spectrum of energy found in your microwave, your light bulb or in your TV remote control. It's called Directed Energy (DE).

Science Fiction?

The date is just before the end of the decade. The place is Osan Air Force Base, home of 7th Air Force and the 51st Fighter Wing, located just 48 miles south of the Demilitarized Zone, the DMZ. Negotiations have broken down again and the tensions between North and South Korea have never been higher.

45,000 American troops are still stationed on the 55-year-old DMZ, along the 38th parallel. They are on highest alert as 500,000 South Korean soldiers back them up. But facing them across the border are over 1.5 million North Korean regulars... armed with an unknown number of Taepodong-3 ballistic missiles, now believed to be tipped with nuclear warheads.

And all can reach the western United States within 45 minutes of launch.

Home to the last oppressive, totalitarian government in the world, little is known about the North Korean capabilities, or its motivations. All that is certain is that the world sits at the brink of war.

Suddenly, seven sleek missiles roar from silos deep in the valleys of North Korea. Three rockets streak to the south, arrowing toward Seoul and its five million inhabitants. The other four missiles veer east; they are heading towards San Francisco, Los Angeles, Seattle and San Diego.

Within seconds the missiles break through the cloud layer. In another two minutes they will exhaust the fuel in their upper stages and will soar unfettered to their targets in an arcing, parabolic trajectory. Officials estimate that 10 to 50 million deaths will occur over the next few days. Nothing can be done. Most observers believe the situation is hopeless.

But that is far from the case.

Orbiting at 65,000 feet above ground in a 'racetrack' pattern, 100km south of the DMZ, two high-altitude UAVs fly safely well away from enemy fire. Infrared seekers onboard the UAVs pick up the bright rocket plumes as the Taepodong-3 missiles break through the cloud layer.

In milliseconds—mere thousandths of a second—low-power targeting and tracking lasers lock onto the missiles. On-board computers calculate trajectories and, in the nose of the UAVs, concave mirrors five feet across swing toward the still-rising missiles. Inside each giant drone, a megawatt-class electric laser is activated. At the front of the UAV, deformable mirrors shaped by hundreds of actuators, embedded behind each mirror's highly-polished surface, change the mirror's surface hundreds of times a second.

This is adaptive optics, invented by the military and now used by every major astronomical telescope in the world. Adaptive optics make a perfect laser beam as the deformities in the atmosphere are taken out of the laser, even before the beam leaves the vehicle.

Thirty seconds after the Taepodong-3 missiles break cloud layer, nearly a million watts of invisible laser energy streak from each of the UAVs at the speed of light. The UAVs hold their beams with ruthless precision against the missiles, heating their metal skin with enough power to cause the missile's fuel tanks to explode from internal pressure within seconds.

One by one, like shotguns shattering clay pigeons at a skeet-shooting range, infrared beams from the two AirBorne Lasers target and destroy one missile after another. Exploding debris falls on enemy territory, leaving both South Korea and the United States unharmed.

Is this science fiction? No. The Boeing YAL-1 Airborne Laser Testbed was first test-fired in flight at an airborne target in 2007. In February 2010, it successfully destroyed two test missiles. While the program was canceled and YAL-1A was grounded in 2012, the Missile Defense Agency began working on deploying lasers on high-altitude UAVs in 2015.

New Technology, New Thinking

Directed Energy (DE) weapons such as lasers and high-power microwaves have come of age. Over the past two decades, DE power has increased by nine orders of magnitude—over a billion times—from milliwatt to megawatt. This is like supercharging your laser pointer used for highlighting PowerPoint slides to shoot down ballistic missiles a hundred kilometres away.

DE is making revolutionary, world-changing advances in warfighting and battling terrorism. And it's doing so today. It's happening so fast, it's the equivalent of a military *Future Shock*. The first DE weapons have already been developed, their successors are being refined, and in the next decades, when they are deployed on the battlefield, they may prove to be more revolutionary than the longbow, machine guns, stealth airplanes, cruise missiles, nuclear submarines, or even the atomic bomb.

The wars in Ukraine and Syria may be among the last to not make use of DE weapons.

The reason Directed Energy is likely to prove so revolutionary is that national leaders will soon have the ability to respond to threats anywhere in the world and instantly deter them with infinite precision at the speed of light.

The profound change these capabilities will make to international relations will reverberate throughout society. It will transform our way of life. This is because Directed Energy is not just about winning wars; it's more than just a new weapon in the warrior's arsenal. It is the basis for a completely new way of thinking, a new way of employing force from the strategic to the non-lethal levels and interacting with the international community.

The large, industrial allied defence establishment that served so well throughout the Cold War will be transformed into a lighter, more agile, and information-centric force, which will shift hundreds of thousands of people and billions of dollars from the government to the commercial marketplace.

Over the next decade, this shift will result in the most profound change to the U.S. Defense Department since World War II. Just as tourism was revolutionised by the jet engine, and communication was forever changed by the transistor, the next societal change will be fueled by Directed Energy in the form of DE weapons.

The Next Big Thing

But does everyone share this view? And if DEWs are so revolutionary, then why aren't they being championed as 'the next big thing'?

DEWs have many critics, and societies such as the world's premier organisation of physicists, the American Physical Society (APS), have sponsored several politically-charged studies as the critics are skeptical of the benefits and capabilities of DE's military applications. The first APS study was conducted in 1986 in response to President Reagan's Strategic Defense Initiative.

The criticism is not limited to strategic uses of laser weapons; High Power Microwaves have their foes as well. Human rights advocates are up in arms both about the unknown long-term effects of Active Denial, as well as the possibility of civilians receiving eye damage from airborne lasers as the light glints off ballistic missiles.

Other criticisms face DEWs as they make their way to the battlefield: what happens when they proliferate? What will happen when, not if, gangs and criminals who could disrupt our way of life manage to obtain them? Or even worse, what if terrorists obtain DEWs? And are there any long-term effects that might occur when exposed to DE? How many remember American soldiers marching and flying into atomic fallout clouds in the 1950s, or US citizens being used as unsuspecting LSD and bio-warfare test subjects?

Apart from its potential, Directed Energy's future is ridden with political and societal uncertainty. So the question is: will politicians ever allow it to be used under fear of these possible long-term effects? Well, they'd better decide fast, because DE is not science fiction. DEWs are real weapons being tested in real scenarios, today. DE is maturing on a daily basis, and advances in technology are accelerating its use.

The only reason these major DEW systems were not used in the last war with Iraq is that they were still being tested, and were not yet ready for the battlefield. Largely shrouded in a highly classified environment, DEW research is conducted by a cadre of closed-mouthed technical wizards. The government labs that worked on revolutions of military affairs in the past—nuclear weapons, stealth airplanes and precision-guided weapons—have now turned their talents toward what they hope is their next ace in the hole: DEW. And they're on a path to move them to the battlefield. What they're betting on is that before the world knows it, DEW will break into the headlines as it provides an overwhelming, asymmetrical advantage in war.

And those nations that are not prepared to exploit Directed Energy will stagnate… or, even better for us, lose by clinging to outmoded, traditional forms of warfare. They will fall behind in the same manner as civilisations that clung to the bow-and-arrow lost to the rifle… just as bullets and bombs will fall to DEW.

Cheaper, Faster, Better

When the laser was invented on 6 July 1960, everyone from military strategists to science fiction writers predicted that DE would soon be used as weapons. But people were quickly disappointed when lasers didn't cause a 'Buck Rogers' blow-it-up effect, like you'd see in a Star Wars movie. Tests showed that the most sophisticated lasers in the early sixties only produced a low-power, although intensely brilliant, point of light. The reason was that the technology for producing the laser was relatively immature.

In the early 1960s, laser power levels were measured in thousandths of a watt. Typical laser pointers today, available for a few dollars at any office store, produce unwavering low-power beams on the order of 5 milliwatts (or 5 thousandths of a watt), a hundred thousand times less power than the light bulb shining in your hallway.

Laser weapons require a billion times more power. But, because of investments in science and technology over the last 40 years, DEWs are now poised to be a cheaper, faster and better method of winning wars and saving lives.

Despite DE's obvious advantages, what about good old 'bombs and bullets', the stuff that won wars for years? One problem with them is that bullets and bombs have reached the limits of their capabilities. Military authorities state that in World War II it took approximately 5000 bombs to destroy one target. In Vietnam, the addition of laser-guided technology dropped that number to around 500, an increase of a factor of 10. Precision-aiming technology advanced, and by 1991 in the Iraq war it took approximately 15 bombs to destroy a target; in Kosovo, then Afghanistan, that number dropped from 10 to five bombs. Even more precise weapons were used in the 2003 war with Iraq, and ratios began to approach one target killed for every weapon dispensed.

However, with the ultimate limit of one bomb being used to destroy one target, warriors can't do any better: they will be limited by the number of bombs they can carry, even if they use a weapon system such as the B-2, which can hit dozens of targets per flight.

Another drawback is that bombs and bullets reach their target by following the law of gravity. This means that they travel in trajectories constrained by ballistics, and thus take a finite time, sometimes measured in minutes, to reach their target. This is where DEWs can radically change the nature of warfare, and why national and military leaders are so excited about its use: not only because it ignores the law of gravity or because it is incredibly precise, but because it can engage a target *near-instantaneously*, thousands of times faster than any conventional weapon.

Speed of Engagement

Directed Energy travels at the speed of light—186,000 miles a second. This velocity may be incomprehensible to anyone who is used to the normal world where people jog at 3 miles an hour, cars zip down the Interstate at 65 miles an hour, and the fastest airliners traverse the

Atlantic at speeds approaching 600 miles an hour. Even the world's absolute speed record, held by astronaut General Tom Stafford, commander of Apollo X, when his spacecraft returned from orbiting the Moon, stands at only 28,547 miles per hour, 8 miles a second, or 0.002 percent the speed of light, which marks the world's all-time speed record for a human being.

Light, be it produced from the sun or from a light bulb hanging in your hallway, travels fast enough to circle the Earth over 7 times in a second. That means that DE—light that is in the form of lasers or microwaves—can reach its target in less than the blink of an eye.

Another way to view this is by comparing the equivalent muzzle velocities as a way of measuring military effectiveness. A bullet's muzzle velocity may be as high as 6,000 feet a second, but DE's 'muzzle velocity' is greater than 982,000,000 feet a second, which is over 160,000 times faster than a typical bullet.

Another advantage to DE is that it can flood areas, allowing one DEW to defeat hundreds or even thousands of targets, as opposed to the best, absolute limit of one bomb killing one target. This gives the military the ability to carry a 'deep magazine', and thus shorten the so-called 'logistics tail' of ferrying a crate of bullets or bombs from the factory to the war zone to the fighter.

The Impetus for the Next Revolution

World-changing events are fuelled by revolutions in military affairs, and they are brought about by inventions of disruptive technologies so profound that they forever change the nature of society. DEWs are so different from traditional weapons that they will be the impetus for the next revolution. As such, DE will change strategy, national policy and ultimately, affect billions of dollars in funding for the military services.

Despite the dissimilarities of lasers and HPM, both are DEWs and their similarities far outweigh their perceived differences. That's because lasers and HPMs both:

- Exploit different parts of the electromagnetic spectrum.
- Travel at the speed of light.
- Are impervious to the effects of gravity or ballistic motion.
- Are ultra-precise, allowing for enormous amounts of energy to be applied exactly where the warfighter wants. This is in contrast with precision weapons using kinetic energy, which, although accurate, have devastating unintended collateral effects due to blast and fragments.

Such an ultra-precise weapon, capable of striking around the globe near-instantaneously, provides the technological advantage needed to defeat the next generation of adversaries. And that advantage is only provided by DEWs capable of engaging the enemy at the speed of light, exploiting the electromagnetic spectrum.

Boomer

John DeChancie

Editor's Introduction

John DeChancie is a versatile writer, as his science fiction *Skyway* series and the *Castle Perilous* fantasy series bear witness. He is currently collaborating with me on a near future novel about asteroid mining and artificial intelligence.

He knew he had led his platoon into a classic L-shaped ambush when a Soviet RPD opened up with the sound of a jackhammer on a New York street, 7.62x54R rounds splintering trees all around him, chipping through eight-inch trunks like they were toothpicks, powerful slugs, and one of them had torn through his side, he was sure, when his hand brought away wetness and a warm, funny feeling started crawling up his ribs, a feeling he'd never felt before, and he knew something was terribly wrong; he'd been hit maybe with the first round as they entered the woods, where the bastards were waiting, NVA all lined up classically alongside the trail with the goddamned machine gun on the trail wedged between two trees just off to the side, angled to rake the whole area, and wham, they opened up, not even a chance to yell, not even to draw his damn .45, shit, shit....

Funny colors in the trees, what the hell kind of trees... no pain yet... funny no pain... just that creepy feeling creeping... wet... I don't want to look at my hand...

Jackhammers, that's what the fucking thing sounds like, jackhammers, whacking away at the pavement, half a dozen guys hammering, tearing the shit out of the street for no goddamn good reason; they used to do that a lot, those street guys in NY, always ripping up the place and you'd think why did they have to do it here, blocking the bus route, now I'll have to take the subway and I'll be late for the piano lesson—maybe someday I'll have a show on Broadway, which they'll probably tear up next week, to the sound of hammers blasting away…

His mind suddenly focused and he wondered about Ramirez, the radio man, and he thought Ramirez had probably taken a slug, too, right off the bat, just like him, because Ramirez wasn't anywhere around.

"Ramirez!"

No answer, just the jackhammer.

"Ramirez! Radio man! Where the fuck are you?"

Ramirez wasn't answering and things were getting worse by the second because he didn't hear any answering fire, didn't hear any crack of M-16s to answer the braying chatter of the Soviet weapon and he knew it was a heavy machine gun, not an SKS or AK, but he couldn't help but wonder why he wasn't hearing the sharp ear-piercing *thwack* of M-16s so he knew his platoon was at least shooting back at the fuckers, popping away with rifles, if not the—

"McCluskey, where's your grenade-thrower?" he yelled toward the rear where he thought McCluskey, the M79 carrier, would be. But no word from McCluskey.

"Harrison! Harrison?"

Christ, no grenade launcher, no M-60 fire to answer the RPD. Could they both have been taken out, first thing? That would be the way to take out a whole platoon. Start with the heavy fire power first. And the radio man.

"Ramirez!"

He knew it wasn't any good. Ramirez was probably dead.

Funny-colors in the leaves. What? Odd green, funny-looking trees.

He looked at his hand.

No blood! Right! OK, something had hit him, but he didn't know what. Or was he hit someplace other than his side. Must've grazed his noggin, must be some reason he wasn't thinking straight.

Sun blazing through the trees, harsh sun, hot sun, and a hot breeze passed over his body as he lay in the undergrowth. He had trouble moving, joints were achy… he could barely move.

Gotta call Battalion. Gotta find Ramirez or the radio, and he inched to the side thinking to discover Ramirez's body but all he found was more funny grass, and the spotted sunlight was molten on his back as it came through the thin, funny trees, trees that hid the enemy but didn't provide cover, and you'd think what was sauce for the goose… Shit. He wasn't thinking straight.

"Ramirez?"

Forget him. He was gone, off the side of the trail, lying there, dead.

Why was he hearing Bob Dylan in his head? Used to lie in bed and listen to Dylan records with many a girlfriend… OK, not many, not bragging, come on, give me a break, but he loved Dylan and his music, not the folksy stuff all that much but when he started playing with The Band, and the floodgates opened and all the Sixties shit bubbled up while he tried to find Ramirez, because he must've taken a damn slug to the head and something was screwy because he just wasn't thinking straight, why the hell couldn't he think, find Ramirez, find that radio, call in air support; he had seen at least three Cobras in the area, and they were there to back up the operation, at his beck and call, even if he couldn't reach battalion headquarters, he could always throw a smoke marker and call in that Cobra to spray the area with 20mm cannon, and that ought to take care of the son of a bitch NVA bastards, but he couldn't find Ramirez or the radio and he wasn't feeling very good, maybe he was hit, but goddamn no pain, no pain yet, so he didn't know what was wrong, but something was terribly wrong…

WHUP WHUP WHUP WHUP WHUP WHUP WHUP WHUP WHUP…

Helicopters! Not firing yet. Maybe they could see the machine gun position, but no, they couldn't, he'd have to lob a yellow smoke grenade to show them where to fire. He looked up through the trees.

All he saw were birds. Big, skinny, funny-looking birds, what was with that? Abstract expressionist birds, nothing was looking normal, not the vegetation, not the birds, not anything that looked normal for the Central Highlands, but what did he know about local fauna, they didn't teach you that at OCS, they just make you into a 90-day wonder leader of men, men like Corporal Ramirez, who was dead because the Second Lieutenant platoon leader wasn't a very goddamn good leader of men, were you, Lieutenant, sir, you asshole, sir?

"Ramirez?"

He just wanted an answer now, he didn't expect Ramirez to do anything. Maybe Ramirez had been hit by mortar. But there was no explosions, just *boom boom* coming from all around, but not near. Other battles nearby? Other units pinned down? The whole operation was a snafu, maybe he wasn't to blame.

"Ramirez, if you can hear me, call battalion headquarters, call in air cover."

Ramirez wasn't around. Maybe Ramirez never existed, and all of a sudden strange things got into his head, like the time he put on his mother's nylon stockings, but that didn't mean anything, didn't mean he was queer or anything, just meant he was curious about feminine things, because he liked girls, always had. But he had these strange feminine memories. He felt guilty about holding back with the Army psychiatrist. Routine exam, he'd kept his mouth shut, the doc didn't press, and that was that. Who would know?

What the hell is going on? Now he was hearing the thump of mortars hitting somewhere off in the distance.

He rolled over onto his stomach and there still was no pain, only pain in his ears from the incessant roar of the machine gun, and sweat stinging his eyes. Otherwise, he was all right. But he couldn't move. He tried to get to his knees and could not.

Smoke grenade. He needed one. He rifled his pants pockets. No smoke grenade. He wasn't carrying any. Jesus Christ, had he forgotten to take any? What was the Lieutenant thinking, sir? You shithead.

Splinters were still flying, slugs cutting into wood like it was cheese.

Well, he was checking out. He was out of the battle. It could rage, he was somewhere else, back in the early 60s in high school watching Dick van Dyke and his lovely Laura in her capris pants and flip hairdo, and the Beaver and Eddie Haskell—there was a Haskell Avenue in LA when he lived out there, in the Valley somewhere.

He reached for his service .45, Colt 1911 A-1, and brought it up to look at. It looked strange. What the hell had happened to it? It didn't look right.

His eyes dimmed, everything dimmed, he was blacking out… and back in the Fifties there was Milton Berle and Martin and Lewis and Sid Caesar, *Your Show of Shows,* and God was that funny, and even when he didn't understand the sketches, they were still funny, like when they parodied Japanese films, Kirosawa, *The Seven Samurai*, you were a kid and didn't even know the Japanese made movies, for God's sake, you still laughed at Howie Morris wrapping a kimono or whatever around Sid Caesar, prancing around him and chattering doubletalk Japanese, was that racist, I guess it was racist, but it was hilarious and you laughed, and then there was *The Twilight Zone*, with cigarette-puffing Rod Serling standing there with a one-way ticket to infinity, submitted for your approval.

Ramirez! McCluskey?

"Where's that M-60?" he screamed. "Somebody shoot the fuck back!"

Why wasn't anybody firing? Where was the answering fire. Don't tell me they're all hit, for Christ's sake, don't tell me that! All thirty of them? Can't be!

Darkness visible again, dimming light through the trees in waning shafts, spots of blue-green through the rustling leaves, funny leaves, and back we go to the Fifties, Saturday morning lineup of kiddie shows, spending all morning in front of the TV watching cartoons, live action, *Fury, Sky King, Johnny Jupiter, Kookla, Fran, and Ollie, Lassie, Space Patrol... Tom Corbett, Space Cadet!* Documentary footage of V-2s lifting off, rocketships, space cadets, rays guns, blasters, robots, aliens...

He was hearing more mortar fire now, *boom... boom... boom...* maybe it was a cannon. No, it had to be mortar fire.

Mighty Mouse, Tom Corbett, Space Cadet, Rocky Jones, Space Ranger...! Disney on Sunday nights, old Walt... and on weekend afternoons, *Mickey Mouse Club*—forever let us hold our banners high...

Something had hit his side. It was getting numb. There was something, but all he could bring away with his hand was sweat. He was soaked in sweat. He angled his head and looked down at his body. What the fuck. He was going out of his head. What he saw didn't make sense.

No, don't look. You're screwy. You got hit, you're bleeding to death... God, I'm bleeding to *death* here, and he was woozy and not really there, he was elsewhere, somewhere back in his childhood in the nineteen-fifties decoding Captain Midnight's messages on the Secret Decoder Ring—what was that you said, Captain? Drink Ovaltine, that's what the captain sent encrypted. Drink Ovaltine he did, every morning and sometimes before his mom tucked him into bed.

Oh, his favorites were the space shows. Always liked *Space Patrol*, and *Tom Corbett* and *Captain Video*—done live from New York, pretty sure, that must've been something. He didn't remember any plots, any stories, just the doc footage of World War II German vengeance-weapons lifting off their pads, doubling for rockets into space. Space travel was simpler then, no fussing with Delta V or... Delta V? Or quantum fluctuation. Or...? TV kid shows? Quantum fluctuation? String-theory spatiometrics? Stray memories, bits of dialogue from those shows. Decoder rings. Space cadets, silly crap. But he remembered he loved those shows and now they were really going to the moon, the Apollo guys.

String-theory spatiometrics? Where did that come from?

"Lieutenant Ramirez, are you there?"

A voice, somewhere off to the left. Ramirez! Maybe.

"Lieutenant? Come in, this is Rescue Three."

What the hell was "Rescue Three"? We need a Cobra gunship, buddy. Where was the voice coming from? It sounded like someone was speaking right next to him, not like a field radio, but like high-end audio on a classical channel. Clear fidelity. What?

Inching in the direction of the voice, parting the odd-colored grasses off the trail while the Soviet gun still hammered away, spreading deadly fire at the edge of the woods, and still that booming and the *whup whup whup* of helicopters, strange sounds, filtered and changed through whatever was happening to him inside his head, something screwy, something that was the result of getting hit, but he can't figure out where he was hit. He chances to sit up, like a fool, and hunches over, but he must be out of the line of fire because no slugs find him, and he pulls his shirt out of his uniform pants and looks at his bare side.

His side has a swelling of some sort, a lump topped with a tiny red dot. Not big enough to be an entry wound. He doesn't know what it is.

And he doesn't know what *those* swellings are on his chest. Something is definitely screwy.

"Lieutenant? Rescue Three to Lieutenant Ramirez. We lost you, there. Are you all right?"

He stretched out again and lay his head near where he thought the voice was coming from. Then he found it. But it wasn't the PRC-25 field radio. It was some tiny little hand-held thing, black, with no antenna, and it was squawking.

"Lieutenant Ramirez? Are you there? You were just talking to us a while ago. Did something happen?"

He grabbed the unfamiliar object and spoke into the tiny metal mesh grate. "What is this thing? Are you a Cobra, come in? This is McElroy, Joshua T., Second Lieutenant commanding Third Platoon,

Alpha Company. Need a Cobra for air support, any Cobra in the area, will mark target with yellow smoke. Can you read, over?"

A short silence.

"Lieutenant Ramirez? Is that you?"

"Ramirez is dead! This is Lieutenant McElroy! NVA unit pinning down my platoon! Need air support! Can you assist?"

Another silence preceding: "Lieutenant, I think you are in need of medical assistance. Don't worry, we will be down to take you out of there very shortly. Stand by." It was a calm voice, authoritative, soothing.

What in the hell are they talking about? "No! No, no, no! Need air support *before* medical evacuation! We are pinned down by heavy NVA machine gun fire! Need air support, any helicopter gunship in the vicinity. Come in! Do you read me?"

No answer.

"Don't send the Huey. Need a Cobra, now! Need concentrated fire on my marker."

But he had no marker! What was he going to do? Nobody was answering. Was he completely alone? Did they all vamoose back to the clearing as soon as the RPD had opened up? Maybe Hueys were coming to take them out and here he was, still on his back in the woods, being shot at.

But it got dark again and he was in Saigon at Lee's and the bar girls were sidling up to him and the sound system was blaring the Doors and he was sipping a beer watching the busy thoroughfare through the window, people in dark pajamas pedaling bicycles up and down the street; he really hates it here, hates the war, but he got drafted and he is no peacenik and wanted to do the right thing but he has doubts, he thinks the war may be a mistake, but he has no say in the matter, so he takes the Officer Qualifying Test and scores big, because he has his BA and Army tests are a snap for any college grad, and lo and behold, he is an officer leading men into battle...

The machine gun stops. What is going on? He still hears the thud and boom of mortar explosions. But the machine gun has stopped chattering. He hears something humming.

Two figures, shadows at the edge of the woods now, backlighted by sun, and why aren't they getting hit? Silence now. Strange silence. As if…

"Lieutenant Ramirez?"

They are standing over him, looking at him through goggles.

"*Who's the leader of the club that's made for you and me?*"

"He's crazy."

"Take another look, Corporal."

"Oh. *She's* crazy. The hair fooled me."

"Cadet Lieutenant Patricia Ramirez, meet Planetary Guardsman Anselm Reilly. 'Ansy' is what he's called, usually. Right, Ansy?"

"Who *are* you guys?"

"We're here to help. Cadet Ramirez, you have passed your Survival Training Field Exam. I see something has bitten you, here on the side. Puncture mark, swelling. You're pretty well envenomed, but I recognize the single puncture. I have the appropriate antivenin right here, but we'll have to get you up to the cruiser pronto."

"Don't you guys realize there's this huge unit of North Vietnamese regulars around here? This is a big operation. What the hell are you doing in those space suits?"

"Take it easy, Lieutenant. Lie back down. I want to give you an injection. Never mind about the North Vietnamese. What we have to worry about is an anaphylactic reaction to the critter that bit you."

Reilly edged closer. "And she passed the exam?"

"Sure, she stayed alive well past the pick-up time. Then a pesky little local poisonous slug bit her, and there's obviously been some hallucinating."

"What was she chattering about? North who?"

"Tom Corbett! Are you guys space cadets?"

"No, but you are, Cadet Lieutenant. I have no idea, Corporal. Sounds like twentieth-century historical and cultural references. You familiar with the period?"

"Me? Hell, sir, I don't know anything about Earth. Who cares?"

"Right. I've seen this before. Rare, but it happens. It's those historical war simulations, and the deep social and cultural immersion cadet gamers undergo. It's very specialized neuralware to give an extra dimension to the simulation. They take on historical personae complete with life histories, memories, the whole panoply of cultural baggage, so as to better understand how the war in question was fought."

"And when she got bit, she starts hallucinating the last simulation she was in?"

"They do quite a lot of military gaming at the Academy."

"Didn't she say she was some guy named McElroy and that Ramirez was dead?"

"One of her avatars, most likely. I don't think women took part in actual combat in that historical period. But she obviously remembered that 'Ramirez' was around here somewhere. She'll come around as soon as this stuff gets working. There. Cadet, can you walk?"

"She doesn't look like it."

"Get the gurney, Corporal."

"Yes, sir."

"I'm a space cadet!"

"Whoa, is she going to be all right?"

"Perfectly. After all, that's what she is. Ancient term for it, but she is one."

"What the *hell* are those noises, if you don't mind my asking, sir?"

"I know this planet. That chattering sounds like an Uzi bird."

"Bird?"

"Actually, a tree-dwelling reptile."

"Sounds like an automatic weapon! And what's that booming sound?"

"The locals call them 'boomers.' "

“Huh. And those birds up there. Sounds like a war zone.”

“I don’t know what they’re called. Maybe all this racket triggered the hallucinations.”

“I’m sure you’re correct, sir. I’ll be right back.”

“*Who’s the leader of the club that’s made for you and me*?”

“Uh-oh, that antivenin might take a little longer than I thought.”

The ship lifts and the jungle rolls below. It’s not a helicopter, hardly makes a sound. Could it be one of ours, or are these guys little green men? Where are they taking me?

My breasts seem part of me now. I am a woman. I’ve got my commission! I’m Patricia Ramirez, Second Lieutenant, Terran High Guard. And she closes her eyes and her head lolls toward the window and the ship hums and throbs around her.

As she opens her eyes again, the jungle falls away. Why is the horizon curving like that?

...Forever let us hold our banners high—High! High! High!

The Deadly Future of Littoral Sea Control

Commander Phillip E. Pournelle, U.S. Navy

Editor's Introduction

The United States has always been a maritime power, and freedom of the seas has been our policy since the founding of the Republic. We have known since President Thomas Jefferson refused to pay tribute to the Barbary Coast pirates that blockade might not be enough. Sometime you must control the coastal areas and send the Marines to the shores of Tripoli.

The control of littoral areas generates different fleet requirements than controlling the high seas. Commander Phillip Pournelle has been involved with the future of naval requirements, including fleet structure, for years. This article was recently published by the United States Naval Institute and is reprinted here by permission of the institute. The opinions in the article are, of course, his own. There is a lively debate about the future of the Navy, and how the Fleet should be structured, in Naval circles. Those interested in it should consult the Naval Institute *Proceedings*, where the various features of the force, including submarines, carriers, surface vessels, information warfare, and the Marines, are discussed. This essay concentrates on an important part of the debate.

When I was in the aerospace industry, I used to say that "the opinions expressed here are my own, and not necessarily those of the

Aerospace Corporation or the United States Air Force, and I think that's a damn shame." The opinions expressed here are those of Commander Pournelle, and not necessarily those of the United States Navy.

And I think that's a damn shame.

Reprinted with the permission of the United States Naval Institute

In an age of precision-strike weapon proliferation, a big-ship navy equals a brittle fleet. What is needed is a revamped force structure based on smaller surface combatants.

The U.S. Navy is building a fleet that is not adapted to either the future mission set or rising threats. It is being built centered around aircraft carriers and submarines. Surface ships are being constructed either as escorts for the carriers or as ballistic-missile-defense platforms. While the littoral combat ship (LCS) was originally intended for sea-control operations in the littoral environment, its current design is best employed as a mother ship for other platforms to enter the littorals. The result of all this is a brittle—and thus risk-adverse—fleet that will not give us influence, may increase the likelihood of conflict, and will reduce the range of mission options available to the national command authority.

This trend is not unique to the Navy. Like other services, it has been operating since the end of the Cold War in unchallenged environments. For the last 12 years in particular, the United States has been operating against opponents who do not have the means to seriously challenge it in multiple arenas such as the air, sea, cyber, space, and other domains. However, due to the proliferation of precision-strike-regime (PSR) weapons and sensors, these domains are increasingly being contested, and the sea, particularly in the littorals, may become one of the most threatened of all these domains.

Sea control is the *raison d'être* for a navy. The littorals have become, and will increasingly be, critical to the global economy and joint operations. To be relevant a fleet must have the ability to secure the littorals, dispute them, or just as importantly, exercise in them, in the face of an enemy who will contest them. Different platforms perform each of these tasks, some more effectively than others, which should drive fleet architectures. As the proliferation of weapons changes the littoral environment, the U.S. Navy will be forced to reexamine fleet architectures and make some significant changes to remain viable. This is due to the poor staying power of surface vessels in relation to their signature in the face of these rising threats. This new deadly environment will have tactical, operational, and strategic implications for the fleet, and will require significant changes if the fleet wishes to remain effective.

Sir Julian's Three Elements

What is sea control? As the Royal Navy puts it, it is "the condition in which one has freedom of action to use the sea for one's own purposes in specified areas and for specified periods of time and, where necessary, to deny or limit its use to the enemy. Sea control includes the airspace above the surface and the water volume and seabed below."[1]

Without sea control, all other attributions and capabilities for a fleet are irrelevant. As noted by the classic naval strategist Sir Julian Corbett, control (he used the word "command") of the sea is fleeting and "the only positive value which the high seas have for national life is as a means of communication."[2] Given the fleeting status of command/control then, accomplishing it must be in support of further goals. Corbett breaks down his concept of control of the sea into three distinct areas: securing command, disputing command, and exercising command. Where securing enables exercising command, disputing may deny, or at least reduce, the ability of an opponent to use the sea for his own purposes.[3]

So it would appear a navy unable to accomplish Corbett's three elements is unbalanced, particularly if it cannot do so in the critical littorals. Execution of Corbett's three areas can roughly be translated into three current mission areas: scouting, maritime-interception operations (MIO), and destruction. Enemy forces, and merchant ships, must be located through scouting. While ships and merchants could be simply swept from the sea, more often than not there is a need to be present to shape events and conduct visit, board, search, and seizure (VBSS) or MIO in support of sanctions, proliferation reduction, or other operations short of unrestricted warfare. VBSS/MIO is critical when there is a need to confirm the identity or contents of a vessel.

The characteristics of different platforms drive their strengths and weaknesses within these three mission areas. In the past, aircraft carriers were the best platforms to secure command of the sea. That role is being contested in anti-access/area-denial environments created by competitors. The air wing provided excellent scouting capabilities, but the U.S. Navy has determined land-based maritime-patrol aircraft (MPA) are best capable of searching large volumes of water, as long as the airspace is not being contested. The carrier is an inefficient vessel for VBSS. It is only used in the most extreme circumstances and limited in capacity. Further, because so many other mission capacities are tied up in one platform, using the carrier for VBSS (or humanitarian aid/disaster relief, for that matter) denies these capabilities to other missions during the duration of the operation. The carrier air wing is currently the best platform for destruction thanks to the volume of fire it can produce, and the mobility of the carrier as a home base, though it can be argued surface ships could be more cost-effective in this role. MPA can be effective in destruction but are limited by the fixed operating location of their airfield.

Submarines are poor scouting platforms with limited perception of the area around them, but they can enter anti-access areas often denied to surface ships and carriers. While they are poor VBSS/MIO platforms and have not been used in that role, submarines have an oversized impact on destruction. Their weapon of choice, as seen in the

Falklands War, can be extremely deadly, and the psychological shock of an unlocated submarine can neutralize an enemy fleet.

Surface ships are good scouting platforms, particularly if equipped with helicopters and/or unmanned aerial vehicles (UAVs). They are good platforms for destruction if armed with appropriate weapons. The U.S. Navy has long vacillated back and forth regarding arming them with Harpoon or other antiship cruise missiles (ASCMs) mostly because of target-identification challenges. Surface ships are the best platform for conducting VBSS/MIO, if there are sufficient numbers of ships. Today *Arleigh Burke*-class destroyers are conducting VBSS/MIO off the coast of Africa and other locations. Given the cost and other mission capabilities, does it really make sense for these air-defense destroyers or other large capital ships to conduct VBSS/MIO?

The U.S. Navy appears to be building a fleet to secure and dispute command of the sea, but not to exercise it. A fleet centered around aircraft carriers and submarines with few surface ships mostly defending the carrier will lack the ability to exercise command, and this can greatly limit strategy and policy. More important, such a force will find it difficult to be present to shape events in the future environment.

Tomorrow's Lethal Threat

The maritime arena is rapidly changing and in the near future will be quite deadly. ASCMs are rapidly proliferating as is the threat of mines.[4] While mines pose their own pernicious dangers, their area of effect is relatively limited. ASCMs on mobile launchers pose an ever-expanding threat. Hezbollah's 2006 surprise attack against an Israeli corvette was only the beginning. The weapon employed by Hezbollah was designed by the Chinese and exported by Iran.[5] We should expect those who wish to challenge the current power structure to proliferate such weapons to proxies, both government and nongoverning organizations. As the precision-strike regime (PSR), ironically created by the United States, propagates around the world, ASCMs and other threats to surface ships will expand. The speed of this proliferation may accelerate as new low-footprint manufacturing capabilities spread.[6]

This will greatly change the security environment, particularly in the littorals, as it will greatly increase the lethality of smaller vessels and shore batteries.[7] This will in turn profoundly alter the security landscape. The Tamil Sea Tigers tied the Sri Lankan navy in knots through the use of small attack boats and suicide explosive vessels.[8] Had they possessed ASCMs they could possibly have won. Similar challenges may arise in an ally's conflict with irregular forces such as Abu Sayyaf in the Philippines' archipelagic environment. Closer to home could be the arming of semisubmersible platforms with ASCMs or other PSR weapons. The greatest threat will be to amphibious operations into places with conditions like Lebanon's.[9]

In the face of these challenges, warships have poor staying power. They are not capable of taking hits in proportion to their size (and, by proxy, cost). Multiple studies show the ability of a ship to take damage grows only at the cube root of its displacement; ships with a displacement of around 2,000 metric tons (such as the LCS) only require a single hit from an ASCM to be rendered out of action.[10] Others are even more pessimistic about the ability of modern ships to take damage from modern weapons, particularly those with large internal volume such as a mission bay.[11]

A ship's vulnerability to ASCMs is disproportionate to her staying power. The probability of a ship being detected and hit by an ASCM is increased by her radar cross section (RCS). As a ship's designed displacement grows, her RCS grows much more rapidly than her staying power.[12] This can be ameliorated by the use of expensive stealth approaches in the shaping and coating of ships. The use of hardkill systems such as Aegis comes at the expense of creating a high profile with a unique signature giving away the ship's position. The greater efficiency of fitting such weapon systems into larger ships is part of how the U.S. Navy arrived where it is today, with a dwindling number of expensive ships.

Since it has spent the last several decades operating in an uncontested environment, the Navy has designed its fleet accordingly. However, the combination of an increasingly threatening world with fewer ships will have significant tactical, operational, and strategic implications.

The tactical implications of a PSR weapons-proliferated environment are significant. The 2012 conflict between Israel and Hamas demonstrated how critical scouting capabilities are in the face of such threats, and also that there is never enough to meet the challenge. In the cluttered littoral environment, even in the midst of an active conflict, reaction times are short, hard-kill missiles have not historically worked, and ships cannot constantly operate electronic warfare systems or deploy short-lived decoys. Ships *will be lost* in the confusing and confined littoral region.[13] The question is what proportion of the U.S. Navy's capabilities will be lost when those losses occur. Numbers matter, and having a large signature is a good way to get hit.

Wanted: A Balanced Fleet

The key is balance. Rather than continuing our current trend of an all-large-ship navy, or eliminating all the large ships for smaller ones, a balanced force and a ship designed to fight in the littorals are both required. This dangerous environment was foreseen, and alternatives (including the Streetfighter concept) were forwarded as a potential solution.[14] However, the LCS was delivered instead. In an effort to advance the Navy's future capabilities in the dangerous littorals, it is important to identify existing alternatives within the U.S. inventory for rapid alteration and experimentation. There are at least two existing platforms that could be employed to meet our needs: the U.S. Coast Guard's Sentinel-class fast-response cutter (FRC) and the Mk-VI patrol boat.

The FRC has a far smaller signature than an LCS. It has endurance and operating range slightly shorter than an LCS's, but sufficient to transit the Atlantic or Pacific Oceans on its own. While they would lose some of their adaptability, an up-armed FRC could carry four ASCMs, a SeaRAM self-defense system, and decoys in addition to its current complement of a 25-mm auto-cannon and small arms. These patrol craft can operate in large numbers and maintain littoral sea control with far greater fidelity than larger platforms. For the cost of owning and operating an LCS and two MH-60 helicopters, between 14 and 28 FRCs can be owned and operated, depending on how they are modified and armed.[15]

The new Navy Mk-VI patrol boat could be modified to carry two ASCMs and decoy systems. It has a very low profile and an operating range of 600 nautical miles, which would require a mother ship to transport and sustain it. For the total ownership cost of a single LCS and two helicopters, 14 Mk-VIs and one mother ship based on the T-AKE design can be acquired and operated.[16]

Ironically, smaller ships require the expenditure of more ASCMs to kill them than do larger vessels. While the smaller ships given as alternatives would be destroyed by a single hit, the probability of hitting them is much smaller due to their smaller signature. Thus an enemy commander must launch more missiles to have confidence in the destruction of one of these smaller platforms than the larger one. To gain an 80 percent confidence in destruction against the Mk-VI, the enemy commander would have to launch more than three ASCMs, while the FRC and the LCS would require more than two ASCMs.[17] But instead of just one LCS, the enemy commander would be faced with the prospect of at least 14 platforms to track and target. While he could employ smaller weapons effectively against each platform, it will require a significantly larger investment to achieve the same confidence (140 ASCMs for the FRC flotilla, more for the Mk-VIs) than the prospect of a single lucky hit against a single ship.

The LCS is not designed to fight in the littorals. It is too large and lacks offensive punch with any reach. Claims that it has a reduced signature are simply not supported by the evidence. Both LCS designs have large internal volumes above the waterline and lack any sign of low-observable shaping that would change the results of the RCS prediction models.[18] However, the LCS *is* an effective launch platform for other systems such as helicopters, unmanned air systems, and unmanned surface vessels, which are potentially effective for combat in the littorals.

The dangers posed by shore batteries can be used to our own advantage. By reviving the Marine Corps Defense Battalions (or revising the Marine expeditionary unit mission set to include this historic mission) combined with Navy Expeditionary Combat Command teams and/or supporting allies' employment of shore-based ASCMs, land-based UAVs, and flotillas of Mk-VIs or FRCs to seize and/or create littoral outposts, we can project our own anti-access/area-denial capabilities against enemy aggression.[19] (Reviving this mission would return the Marine Corps to its roots.) Shore batteries and support facilities can employ denial-and-deception techniques to hide in the clutter on land or employ hardened facilities. However, these littoral outposts, employing combined arms, require doctrine and diplomacy with our regional allies in advance; they cannot be effective in an ad hoc manner.

Big Ship = Big Risk

There are significant operational and strategic implications with a small number of large-signature ships in a PSR-proliferated environment. The situation creates a brittle fleet, raises the stakes in a crisis, and increases the need to use force in a blockade operation. All of these decrease the options available to commanders and national command authority. On the other hand, a fleet that can be reinforced rapidly in a conflict can be a significant deterrent to an enemy looking for a rapid win.

The foremost operational effect is a brittleness of the fleet. The tactical impact detailed earlier has influenced U.S. Navy operations today. The deployment of advanced ASCMs to Syria posed an increased threat to ships should they have been off the coast. Commanders will increasingly be reticent to deploy small numbers of large-signature ships in this deadly environment for fear of potentially losing a significant amount of firepower in the loss of a single ship.

From that follows a loss of influence. With smaller numbers of ships, the United States will lack the ability to simply be present to shape events. Faced with a growing hidden threat, commanders will be reluctant to place large-signature ships in the littorals for extended periods of time. However, this is the exact area where they will be the most needed if the United States wishes to shape events and prevent conflict.[20]

A fleet conducting embargo or blockade operations is more effective and less likely to use force if it has more ships. While some argue a blockade employing offshore control is an effective strategy because it decreases the pace of escalation, that is only true if force is not routinely required to enforce it. Any selective embargoes/blockades focused on particular commodities or "contraband" will be platform-intensive, requiring multiple VBSS missions per day.[21] Ships conducting interception and boarding on one ship are not available against another, particularly given the immense size of many cargo vessels plying the ocean trade today. If a fleet's numbers, and therefore boarding capacities, drop below an effective number, a general embargo/blockade will be required. This will be less intensive but still require numbers, particularly if we wish to retain the capacity to employ VBSS techniques to stop those who would attempt to run the blockade without general destruction. If a fleet's numbers drop below the ability to board sufficient ships willing to risk running a blockade, then force will be required. An example will need to be made. It will be necessary to sink some merchant ships to demonstrate to the rest the blockade is "real and effective." This will of course have significant impact on the social and maritime environment with the sight of sinking merchant ships, oil leaks, etc.

In the case of rising tensions with a near-peer competitor, we face the significant possibility of miscalculation. The offensive-dominant environment created by ASCMs presents opposing commanders with the "use-'em-or-lose-'em" dilemma when there is a potential of spending most, if not all, of his force in a preemptive strike. Distributing firepower among more numerous, lower-profile ships can shift this environment back into our favor and reduce the impact of miscalculation.

All three of these examples illustrate the narrowing of options to commanders and national command authority as the size of a surface fleet decreases and their capabilities become concentrated on fewer, but larger platforms.

Changing the fleet architecture to incorporate more numerous and smaller vessels can increase our strategic depth. In the event of a conflict with a near-peer competitor, there is a significant possibility of loss to the forces on both sides when combat begins. The current fleet design employs ships that take years to build. While this timeline could be accelerated in the event of war, it would still take months to construct limited numbers of ships in the finite shipyards we have capable of building them. A fleet that includes a greater proportion of smaller vessels at the ready would be able to make use of a wider array of shipyards, some nowhere near the coastline, to build large numbers of replacement ships. This capability would be a strong deterrent against an enemy looking for an "assassin's mace" or knockout blow in the opening of a conflict.

A New Fleet Architecture

The U.S. Navy must reexamine its fleet architecture to remain relevant. Sea control consists of more than scouting and destruction. Exercising it is manpower-intensive, requiring large numbers of surface ships. A fleet focused on aircraft carriers and submarines is not balanced and will be limited in its capability to scouting and destruction. Employing multibillion-dollar air-defense platforms to conduct VBSS/MIO operations is not a cost-effective strategy. For a relatively small price, a large number of small ships can be employed to balance the fleet and enhance its ability to operate in the dangerous littoral environment.

The age of uncontested seas is coming to an end, and ASCMs are sounding its death-knell. The proliferation of such PSR weapons will continue and accelerate either through the distribution of such weapons by those who wish to contest U.S. dominance or through the spreading of additive manufacturing techniques. The lethality and reach of smaller vessels and obscured shore batteries will continue to increase. This will have a significant impact on the effectiveness of the U.S. fleet and the options it can afford its commanders and national leadership. Concentration of capabilities within a few large-signature ships creates a brittle fleet and the increased potential of miscalculation in a crisis. The smaller the number of surface ships available to conduct presence and other missions, the fewer options will be available, resulting in an increase in the requirement to use force to conduct operations such as an embargo or blockade.

Fortunately, the U.S. Navy has access to ship designs that can easily be modified to be cost- and combat-effective in this deadly environment. Bolstered by the revival of the Marine Corps' historic missions and the development of littoral outposts, the Navy can gain the upper hand in the littorals. This will require embracing more numerous and smaller-profile surface ships and a review of doctrine within the Navy and with our allies. The U.S. Navy must adapt to this new reality—or face potential failure in a conflict for which it is not prepared.

The Fourth Fleet

Russell Newquist

Editor's Introduction

We're going. Exactly when and how isn't clear, but we're going. First the asteroids, then the outer planets. The language doesn't have to be English. It might be Russian. Perhaps more probably Chinese. Perhaps Hindi. And maybe, just maybe, all of the above and then some.

And there will be war.

You haven't felt fear until you've been left to die in a giant tin can, one point two billion kilometers from home. The last thing we heard from the pirates was their laughter as they slammed the hatch shut. Then we watched out the tiny windows in terror as they flew away.

We did a thorough inventory of everything they'd left us. It wasn't much. Our batteries would last us a day or two—and we could probably extend that to a week if we powered down everything non-essential. But they hadn't left us any fuel to get anywhere, and they'd taken most of the oxygen, too. We weren't sure yet how much they'd left us. Our harvest—hydrogen- and helium-rich gases we'd mined out of Neptune's upper atmosphere—was by far the most valuable thing we'd had on board. They'd taken it first.

They hadn't left much beyond that, either. Not that we'd had a whole lot to start with. Every ounce of weight was extra money. Lots of extra money, when you shipped it all the way out to Neptunian space. Our little gas mining vessel didn't have a lot of extra niceties. Just enough to keep me and my two brothers alive for our two year contract.

We had about a day's worth of food in the crew stores. My brother John had a handful of meal bars that he'd brought on at our last resupply. We'd mocked him at the time for spending most of his per diem trying to put back on all the weight that a tightly rationed space diet had finally helped him shed. Now we wished he'd bought more. A couple of flashlights, the clothes on our backs, two rolls of spacer tape, and a smattering of random tools that hadn't been properly put away fleshed out our meager belongings.

We did what we could anyway. We powered down most of our systems, instituted emergency food rationing, and limited our activity to preserve the little water and air we had left. We even deployed the solar panels for extra juice, although they wouldn't do us very much good this far into the outer solar system. We'd take anything we could get. But we didn't really have any hope. Without any propulsion, we weren't going anywhere.

Everything changed when Simon tried to power down the harvester.

—From "Stranded in Space" by Matthew Holt

The Fourth Fleet ceased its deceleration burn some distance away in order to facilitate maneuvering. Most of the fleet initiated a 180-degree rotation pass to reposition their main engines behind them, where they would safely face away from enemy vessels. But SCVN-26, the USS *Theodore Roosevelt*, didn't need to perform this little dance. The engineers who designed her had duplicated the five massive fusion rockets from her stern on her bow as well. Not only could she accelerate or decelerate in either direction, but her engines themselves doubled as the ship's most devastating weapon.

The giant rotating core made her one of only a dozen or so ships capable of generating her own gravity. Well, a gravity-like sensation. It wasn't true gravity and didn't quite feel the same—besides being only about one half of Earth's gravity. Something about it just wasn't quite the same. Even so, its crew members could make very long space voyages without the health issues that came with zero gravity.

Like all United States Space Navy carrier vessels, she'd been named after a former President. The former Rough Rider served as a particularly apt moniker for the latest generation of carriers. Ushering in a new wave of technology, the *Roosevelt* and her sister ships were the largest vessels ever built by humanity.

As she approached Ganymede, the *Roosevelt* unleashed a swarm of drones. Some were sensor drones, sent out to gather information and beam it back to both their sisters and the mothership. Others were fighter drones, loaded with chain guns, lasers and missiles. All were independently controlled by remote operators on board the *Roosevelt* herself, yet they were capable of a great deal of automation should they lose contact with their control signals.

The *Roosevelt* made an impressive sight all on her own. At fifteen hundred feet long and eighty thousand tons of displacement, she carried four hundred twenty-four drones, eight large and twelve smaller railguns, forty-two laser banks, two hundred ship-to-ship missiles, and eleven hundred crew members. If you pressed the ship's crew—pressed them really hard, you might just get them to admit that the newest ship in the *Roosevelt* class, the USS *Warren G. Harding*, with almost a decade worth of newer technology, actually carried more firepower. Maybe. But no ship in any other class could touch it.

The rest of the Fourth Fleet may not have been so modern or large but they were quite impressive on their own. Even the newest of the bunch, the USS *Atlanta*, dated back to the war. But like every other ship in the formation, save the *Roosevelt* herself, it had seen plenty of action against the Chinese fleet and carried an impressive combat pedigree. Even without the carrier it would have been an impressive fleet. With it, it was one of the three most destructive combat forces ever assembled by humanity, rivaled only by the First and Ninth carrier fleets.

And all of that power was useless. Commodore Seamus MacGregor, captain of the *Roosevelt* and commander of the Fourth Fleet, already knew that his quarry was not here. The pirates he chased had launched another attack five hours previously, near one of the moons of Saturn. Which, due to their respective orbital periods, was currently almost perfectly aligned on the other side of the sun from his fleet, almost fifteen astronomical units away as the light shines and probably four times that via the shortest orbital path he could take.

Nine months, he did the estimate in his head. *If we're lucky. Probably more like eleven or twelve. And by then they'll be long gone.* For the fifth time since he'd received the news he pounded his fist on his chair. It didn't accomplish any more than it had the first four times. It didn't even relieve any of his frustration.

He tuned out the bridge chatter as thoroughly as the crew tuned out his outburst. The mood was sullen, but crisp. Every bit as frustrated as their commander, they nevertheless carried out their duties professionally.

There was plenty of work to do, pirates or no pirates. They had just set a new record for the fastest trip from Mars to Jupiter. Now they set about performing orbital maneuvers and docking preparations as they approached Galileo Station. Built over a fifteen-year period from prefabricated components lugged in by deep-space haulers, the station was considerably smaller than the *Roosevelt* herself.

The once heavily armed station occupied a halo orbit around the Jupiter-Ganymede L2 position. Due to its key strategic position it had faced multiple attacks during the war, but fended them all off. These days, however, the station served more of a support role for the civilians living and working in the Jovian sector. Much of the space once dedicated to storing munitions had been converted to hydroponics and fuel processing.

The great fleets that had once been stationed here had long since been downsized to a handful of patrol craft that tended not to stray too far. Had there still been even a single battle cruiser patrolling Jovian space, it's unlikely the pirates would have attacked in the first place. But most of the smaller cruisers were occupied with controlling smaller-scale conflicts around Mars and the larger asteroids.

For the next few hours docking procedures and a stack of paperwork on his desk demanded his attention. Presently he found himself so busy that he completely missed the actual moment of docking altogether. He left his paperwork with his assistant and quickly changed into his dress uniform and left to join the docking ceremony.

Captain Edward Stevens was an academy classmate of his and an old friend. After the formalities were done, they greeted each other warmly and Stevens took the Commodore on a personal tour of the small station. Finally the ended up in Stevens' office, getting down to business.

"How long are you sticking around, Mac?"

"We're not." Stevens feigned surprise, but he couldn't quite pull it off. "Don't look so hurt. We've got some supplies to drop off for you—quite a bit, actually—and then we're going to make a loop or three around the planet to show the colors. And then we're off."

"Pirate hunting?"

"You know I can't say."

"We really need more to work with out here. These attacks are getting out of hand—and we don't have the resources to deal with it. With the *Roosevelt* around they wouldn't even dare to attack–"

"Fleet wouldn't keep the *Roosevelt* here and you know it, Ed. There are only three of her kind in service and the solar system is a big place. And piracy isn't the only threat out there, not by a long shot. The Russians are acting paranoid over something, but when aren't they? The lunar colonies are restless and threatening to secede. And some kook on Deimos just went and declared himself Caliph. The pirates matter—a lot—but..."

"Yeah, I know. They're not the only thing that matters. And we're not all that important all the way out here. I'm sure you have other things to get up to back in the inner system."

"We're not headed back to the inner system."

"Oh?" Stevens was genuinely surprised this time. "Where to?"

"Saturn—and that's highly classified. The crews don't even know yet, not even the officers. Only the captains have been told."

"You *are* going hunting."

"I didn't say that." MacGregor's poker face was considerably better than his friend's.

"Right."

"We're not leaving you empty-handed. I've got three dozen nav satellites to launch while we're here."

"Wait, three dozen? We only need a few to get good nav around Ganymede."

"Not Ganymede. Jupiter. We're jumpstarting a whole nav constellation here, for all of near-Jovian space. And there's more. We've got some upgrades for your defense systems, computers, and an entire new solar array to deploy. It'll triple your available power, which should give you plenty of room to grow—even after we attach the new module we brought for the station."

"You brought an entire module out here? And kept it secret?"

"Our cargo bays are a bit bigger than advertised." The commodore winked at his friend.

"I'll say. And your towing capacity, too!"

"Fully expanded and in place, it should increase your usable interior space by about twenty percent."

"Why's Tranquility Base so interested in Jupiter all of a sudden?"

"It's not Tranquility Base. These orders come straight from the President. The going theory is that coming into power over half of the Earth and two thirds of man's space colonies has only whet the appetite of his ambition."

"What, a man who killed his own father to get the job hasn't given up his ambition?" Stevens almost laughed.

"Be careful where you say that, Ed," MacGregor cautioned him. "Some people might take that as treason."

"Going to turn me in, are you Mac?" Stevens did laugh this time.

"No, of course not. But there are plenty of others out there looking to curry favor." Stevens paused, lost in thought for a moment.

"You've met this guy."

"Once or twice, yeah."

"Is he as hot-headed as they make him out to be?" This time the commodore paused before answering.

"No, I don't think he is at all. Between you and me, I think it's all an act." Stevens nodded.

"That's my take, too. But it's hard to be sure this far away from everything."

"Well, shrewd or not, he's got one more gift for you—and you'll like this one."

"Oh? Is it Christmas already?"

We process the harvested atmosphere right there on the ship. It's a hell of a lot cheaper than shipping a bunch of extra material all the way back to Earth, right? But even more importantly, it means we don't have to ship fuel all the way out there. And Neptune's atmosphere has really high concentrations of hydrogen, so it's just right there for the taking.

That's probably why we were their first target. Most individual ships like ours wouldn't have even been on their list. But we had enough processed already to refuel their entire fleet four or five times over. We helped set them up logistically for their future plans.

But they missed something. In fairness to them, we missed it too, at first. The harvesting system works in a multistage process. First, it collects the gasses into a gigantic holding tank. Then, once we have sufficient pressure, it pushes it through the refinement chambers that separate out the mixture into its component gasses, which go into multiple tank.

The thing is, in the middle—during the processing, that is—it has to be stored somewhere. They took everything from our main harvesting tank, and they took everything from the separated gasses tanks. But they didn't think to check the processing tank itself. We didn't either, at first. But then Simon was powering everything down and he got an alert. The computer was worried the chamber would lose integrity without power.

He almost shut it down anyway, "knowing" that it was empty. But then he checked it. And it was full to the brim. We'd topped off everything we could possibly carry before we pulled out of the atmosphere, to get maximum haul. And the pirates had left us that tank.

We powered the harvester back up and processed it. Nearly destroyed the pumps, because there was no pressure at all in the input tanks—and that came back to haunt us later. But it worked. And the stuff we'd harvested was eighty-percent hydrogen, see? So that one tank was ninety-percent fuel. And that's how we made it back to the Triton station.

—From "An Interview with John Holt" in *Mars Today*

The Fourth Fleet saluted the cruiser as they lit their engines and started the burn that would take them to Saturn. The USS *Pennsylvania* was staying behind to augment security in Jovian space. Stevens had been thrilled, and so had the civilians. Everyone seemed to think that the pirates would be less bold with a ship of the line nearby.

Even so, Commodore MacGregor had smiled when the new orders came in. If he'd been in his office instead of on the bridge he might have even cheered. But commodores don't do that in front of their crews. Instead he'd calmly given his helmsman and navigator new orders and watched as they were faithfully carried out. He could tell that his crew had wanted to cheer, too.

The number crunchers on Earth had traced the pirates' last known trajectory when they'd cloaked and predicted that they were making a push for the asteroid belt next—specifically, they thought the pirates were heading toward Neptune.

They'd barely broken orbit from Jupiter when the signal came, which meant that they hadn't lost too much time heading in the wrong direction. Even better, with Saturn on the far side of the sun and Neptune on the same side as Jupiter, there was no way for the pirates to beat the *Roosevelt* to their target.

MacGregor had given the orders and the entire crew had waited over three long months of anticipation. All except for one, that is—a young enlisted man who had scowled every time the conversation came up. Something about it struck the commodore as odd, so he'd tracked the man down.

The petty officer who had looked up at him couldn't have been more than twenty. His uniform insignia indicated that he was in sensors. Tall, lanky and bespectacled, he had certainly looked the part. He had looked alert but very nervous.

"Petty officer… Ramsden," the commodore read his name off of his uniform. "Mind telling me what's bothering you?"

"It's not my place, sir."

"I'm making it your place." The young man was visibly nervous.

"They're not going to Neptune, sir."

"You're telling me that all of the techs on Earth and Luna have got it wrong and you've got it right?"

"Yes sir. The orbit's wrong, sir. They couldn't have done it without a massive burn. Earth and Luna are assuming that their stealth system is hiding it. OK, fine… their stealth system is that good." He'd said it like he didn't truly believe it. "But where would they get the *fuel*? The numbers don't add up, sir."

MacGregor had frowned and noted it, but that was that. Tranquility

Base had sent them to Neptune so that's where they were headed. Besides, it was one kid against the entire analyst section at HQ. He couldn't possibly have been right.

Except that now they were halfway to Neptune and the pirates had struck again—at Ceres, in the asteroid belt, completely in the other direction. The commodore had fumed. For a moment he'd even lost his cool and shouted at the bridge crew, before he withdrew to his office to calm down.

They'd been played. Even worse, for the time being he was out of the game. The pirates *had* hit Neptune before, one of their first targets, and command wanted to beef up the system there. The Fourth Fleet was to continue out to Neptune and reinforce the station there with a similar constellation of nav satellites and defense upgrades—but no new station modules. There was nowhere to stop to pick up another one, and the *Roosevelt's* cargo bay wasn't *that* big.

It was important—MacGregor could see that. But he didn't have to like it.

It wasn't very much fuel. The processing tanks themselves aren't particularly big. They're meant for short-term storage. And we had to redo the piping so that we could use some of the spare oxygen for breathing to oxidize the fuel. They'd taken most of our tools, too, so we had to get pretty creative. But at the end of the day we got thrust. The nav computer worked out a course to get us back and we prayed that we wouldn't starve before we got there.

It was a close thing, too. I can't speak for my brothers, but I know that they were starting to look mighty tasty to me. Two weeks on about a day's worth of food is pretty brutal. We stretched those food bars about as far as you possibly can, you know? My brothers used to harass me about keeping so many around, but now all three of us stash them away everywhere we can hide them. Once you've known hunger like that, you never, ever want to do it again. Honestly, we didn't think we'd make it.

In those days, Neptunian space was a real frontier, you know? Supply and fuel stations and a science station orbiting Triton and a dozen or so mining ships like ours. Back then they didn't even have nav satellites yet. The fleet brought those in while they were hunting pirates. We were on the wrong side of the planet when the pirate caught us, and orbiting nearly in sync with Triton.

We knew right away that it wasn't enough fuel to get there. So we tried another plan, and set course for another orbit. And then we waited. We sat there in the dim light telling each other stories, reading, watching the vids, whatever we could do to pass the time and keep our spirits up. We read the bible a lot. Alone and together. It became our fallback, when we couldn't find anything else to do. And we prayed. Man oh man did we pray.

—Simon Holt, speaking to the US Space Navy Academy

Captain Nelson of the *Pennsylvania* stepped out of the airlock and boarded the *Roosevelt*. A small collection of officers stood at attention to greet him. He snapped a salute to Commodore MacGregor which was promptly returned. After a small boarding ceremony of the type that hadn't changed all that much since the days when a distant family member had fought a famous battle at Trafalgar, the pair made for MacGregor's office. Small talk filled their conversation during the walk but the topic turned deadly serious once they closed the door.

"What happened, Bill?" MacGregor asked the young captain.

"I don't know how they did it, Commodore. Even though Intel said they were headed to Saturn, we kept an eye out. But somehow they snuck in right underneath us. They hit a mining operation on Amalthea while we were on the other side of the planet—*and* in completely the wrong orbit. It took us eighteen hours to change orbit and get there, and by then they were already gone."

"Eighteen hours isn't a big head start. Why didn't you follow?"

"There was nothing *to* follow, Commodore. They disappeared."

"Where were they headed this time?"

"That's just the thing. None of our observation stations caught their burn, and by the time we got to Amalthea they'd activated that damned stealth tech of theirs. We have no idea where they went."

"Fleet couldn't give you a heading?"

"*Nobody* saw the burn, sir. Fleet had nothing."

"Nothing at all?" MacGregor was stunned.

"Not then, sir. I had all the techs comb through all of our data, down to the raw, unprocessed stuff. Looking for anything."

"You found something?" MacGregor's tone changed into excited anticipation.

"Well... we don't know. Maybe. There are a couple of blips in the data that don't make any sense. The software filtered it out as noise, but our techs don't think so. They think maybe it's some artifact caused by the pirates' stealth tech, but they can't make heads or tails out of it."

"Forward the data to Tranquility Base. Make sure their people are on it."

"Sent it months ago, sir, before the fleet started the trip back here. I talked to them this morning. They still have nothing—or at least that's what they're telling me."

MacGregor frowned and pursed his lips in thought for a moment. Then he hit the intercom on his desk.

"Bradley!" he barked.

"Sir?" came the response.

"Get Ramsden in here, now."

"Yes, s–" the Commodore released the button, cutting off his aide mid-word.

Nelson raised an eyebrow at him.

"I've got a real bright Petty Officer who's been looking at a lot of the sensor data. He says something's bugging him about it all, but he doesn't know what. Made himself real obnoxious. But his lieutenant says he's the brightest kid he's ever seen, and the other techs all say the same. They've been giving him everything on this, and he's got some giant simulation he's cooked up."

"Fleet has better people. And better computers and simulations."

"Better computers, for sure. Better simulations… maybe, but I'm not so sure. Better people? You haven't met this kid. Mark my words, as soon as they find out about him they're going to snatch him away from us."

"That sharp?"

He never got his answer. A rapping sound came from the door, followed momentarily by the creak of hinges as Lieutenant Bradley escorted Petty Officer Ramsden into the office. He stopped before the officers and snapped up a smart salute. They returned it.

"You wanted to see me, sir?"

"At ease, Mr. Ramsden." The young man relaxed. "This is Captain Nelson, from the *Pennsylvania.* His men have some raw data recordings from the last pirate attack, and they noticed some anomalies. I'd like you to put another pair of eyes on it. See what you can make of it."

"Aye aye, sir!" The response and the salute came out smart and quick as required, but the young Petty Officer couldn't hide his excitement—or suppress his giant grin.

We used up most of our fuel in that first burn, and all of the rest in the second. We knew this was our only chance, and if we screwed it up we were toast. That was it, we had nothing left. And then, when we finally got there, the timing. Oh, the timing. We had about an hour and a half to do everything perfectly and that was it. After that our orbit would decay too much and we wouldn't have the fuel to pull out of Neptune's gravity again. And the pumps weren't working at anything close to capacity after the stunt we'd pulled with them earlier, so we didn't even know if we could do it.

But we'd rehearsed everything about three dozen times in the days it took us to get into place. We'd written everything down into a perfectly choreographed schedule. We figured that if we did it all right we'd have about ten minutes to spare. But not much more.

Because our orbit was total crap. We didn't have enough fuel to set up for a proper mining orbit. Instead we were on a course that would take us far too deep into the atmosphere. The only way we were getting out of it was to get enough fuel processed before it was too late to fire off another burn and stabilize our orbit. But it was tight. Really, really tight.

Hell yeah, I was scared. I mean, no pressure, right? But here's the thing. I was there with my brothers. And we all knew what we were about. And we'd been through about ten rehearsals now where we'd done everything flawlessly. We'd scripted the whole thing down to who is pushing what button when and for how long and in what order.

We were waiting at our positions as we coasted into range. And as soon as we crossed the line, we all started at once. I'd like to tell you that we made some great quips. That guy who played me in the vid had some wonderful ones that I really wish I'd said. But the truth is, we were pretty quiet. We were all too afraid of screwing it up.

—From "An Interview with John Holt" in *Mars Today*

"Petty Officer Ramsden is here to see you, Commodore."

"After the briefing, Lieutenant Bradley."

"He says it can't wait, sir."

Commodore McGregor scowled at the younger officer.

"Fine, send him in." He waited impatiently at his desk as the sensor analyst marched in.

"What is this about, Ramsden? I have a conference with the fleet captains in ten minutes." He read the name off of the young man's chest.

"You'll want to see this first, Commodore, I promise." the petty officer assured him. "May I use your display, sir?" Ramsden carried a small computer in his hand. At McGregor's nod he connected it to the holodisplay in the middle of the briefing room. He worked the controls to pull up a three-dimensional map of the solar system. As it loaded, he talked.

"Sir, I've been examining the reports from the pirate attacks. Looking for patterns, trying to figure out how they're getting the drop on everybody."

"The best analysts in the fleet have been over this, Ramsden. They can't crack the stealth systems the pirates are using." He didn't even try to hide his annoyance.

"Exactly, sir. And they never will." The younger man tried hard to contain his excitement. He didn't quite succeed. Commodore McGregor frowned at him.

"Would you mind explaining to me why this is so exciting?" The young spaceman managed to calm down.

"Sorry, sir. Here, let me show you." He worked the controls and a series of points glowed within the map.

"This is every known attack by the pirate fleet." He worked the controls again and a series of lines connected them. "Here we have them all connected, in order, showing time between attacks." His hands moved and the display shifted one more time. "And here, I've computed the orbital mechanics necessary to move their fleet from target to target in the time allotted."

"Here." The commodore pointed. "Why is there a break in the pattern?"

"Because at this point, sir, they either didn't have enough fuel or didn't have enough time. Here, let me show you." His hands moved and the display refocused around the two points that didn't connect. Here," Ramsden pointed at the first point, "is where they attacked a mining vessel leaving Io. And here, this second point is where they attacked a convoy transferring orbits near Ceres, two hundred eleven days eight hours and seventeen minutes later. It's where they screwed up, sir."

"Screwed up? Screwed up how?" the Commodore was paying attention now.

"Yes, sir. They attacked thirty-four minutes early." The Commodore's brow furrowed as he brought his palms together and pressed his fingers to his lips.

"I don't understand, petty officer. Tranquility Base processed these numbers and said that the fleet could have made the trip in two hundred eleven days."

"Yes sir, I read the report. The original report. The official summary left off a detail. The quants who did the math came up with the same answer I did—two hundred eleven days, eight hours and *forty-one minutes*. But they assumed that their calculations were off, given such a small margin of error."

"That sounds like a safe assumption to me, son. That's off by... what? Zero point zero two percent?"

"Zero point one nine seven two percent, sir. And it would be a safe assumption on its own. They based their calculations off of the maximum fuel capacity of the ships in the pirate fleet, which at that point were all pretty standard models and well-known. But look at this." He moved the controls and an image came up.

"This is a Lockheed-Boeing 6748 freighter. The pirates commandeered it in their first attack, near Iapetus. This image was taken from footage found on one of the recovered ships in the Io attack." He moved again and a second, nearly identical image came up next to the first. "This is an image of the ship taken from the Ceres attack, two hundred eleven days later."

"Son of a bitch." McGregor shook his head and lifted the comm device from his desk. "Bradley, get Tranquility Base on the horn. Maximum encryption, level A priority." He put the phone down and turned back to Petty Officer Ramsden.

"Command is going to want more to go on than this. Do you have it?"

"Yes sir."

The Good Lord was with us that day, I have no question about that. My brothers and I have always been good at what we do. That's why we wanted to go out together in the first place. We trusted each other. But I'd never seen them move like that before. I'd never seen myself move like that before. It was like the most beautiful dance you'd ever seen. Or maybe it just felt that way because my life was on the line and everything was going perfectly. Whatever, I don't care. We pulled that maneuver off flawlessly and it was awesome. That part of the vid they nailed perfectly.

—From "Stranded in Space" by Matthew Holt

"You have more than just the one image, don't you?" Admiral Barnes was polite but pointed.

The video screens around the walls of his office showed several men, all clean-cut and wearing crisp uniforms. To civilians they might have all just looked like high-ranking naval officers. A trained eye, however, could easily pick out the seven captains of the Fourth Fleet from the Admiral back on Luna. The deference of the fleet captains was one clue. The way their uniforms hung—or rather, failed to hang—in microgravity was a bigger one.

"Yes sir. I've crossed-checked every image available from every attack." Petty Officer Ramsden keyed in a command and a series of images flashed up on the screen. "As best as I can tell, they started off with two groups. But they've been expanding as they captured ships on each run, and it looks like they're up to four individual fleets now."

"Damn. And the cloaking device?" asked Captain Morelli from the *Arizona*.

"Doesn't exist, sir. Never did. It was sleight of hand all along. One group attacks, conquers its target, squawks off a challenge loud and clear, and then maneuvers itself into one of the fleet's blind zones, and then disappears. Later on—barely enough time for their fleet to have maneuvered itself there—a second group attacks somewhere else."

"You'd need a lot of coordination to pull this off," chimed Captain Schafer from the *Farragut*.

"And patience," added Captain Clark from the *Dallas*.

"Not to mention money," Morelli finished. "Just getting the initial two fleets going would cost a fortune. Then you'd have to fuel it and prep it and ensure they had some kind of home base—two of them, actually. Somebody with considerable resources at their disposal set this up. It would take some serious doing for the USSF to pull this off, much less anybody else."

"You'd better believe we'll be chasing that down on our end," Barnes replied.

"What about our end, Admiral?" MacGregor cut to the point.

"I'm glad you asked, Commodore," a new voice cut in. MacGregor watched the general confusion on his screens, but he and Barnes, at least, recognized the voice and snapped to attention. A new vid feed joined the others on his screens and confirmed the identification.

President Harrison Trajan Covington no longer wore the uniform but he still carried himself like the general and war hero that he'd been. His dark hair was longer than typical military fashion, more in the style of the special operations forces he'd been a part of. But he was still in fighting shape, still stood ramrod-straight, and still possessed a stare that could make a drill sergeant cry. Rumor was that it had, and more than once.

"I've been monitoring this conversation. Good work, Petty Officer. Very good work indeed. If you're interested in a new challenge, I have another interesting problem you might be able to help me with."

"I'm always interested in a challenge, Mr. President."

President Covington nodded curtly.

"You'll be receiving your new orders shortly, then. My apologies, Commodore, for stealing one of your finest. I assure you he'll be well used."

"Of course, Mr. President."

"Now, about those pirates…"

Once we'd gotten our orbit straightened out, we had the time to mine as much fuel as our hearts desired. Well, all the time our stomachs desired. We were all pretty damn hungry at that point. But with a stable orbit and fuel coming on board, we had plenty of power. And although we were hungry, we didn't want to get stranded on Triton Station, either. So we brought on enough fuel to get us there, enough to get us back, and enough to sell for food and other supplies when we got there.

It took us the better part of two days to collect it all and process it and get it transferred to the ship's fuel tanks. Neptune's atmosphere is pretty thin at that altitude. But we did it, under protest from our bellies the whole time.

This time, though, we weren't worried about saving fuel. We'd done the math—it was a lot faster to collect more fuel and waste it than it was to save it on the way back. And we didn't care about the money at this point. We were too hungry.

When we got to Triton Station they hadn't even known what happened, but they broke out the quickest meal they could make us—black beans and rice. And then we just put our noses right back to the grindstone and went to work.

But I'll tell you what—I've never had a better meal in my life than those black beans and rice.

—Simon Holt, speaking to the Virginia Entrepreneur's Club

The press conference set off shock waves across Earth and the colonies. When asked where they had found the resources for their construction, President Covington evaded. When asked how they had kept the whole operation secret he flat-out refused to answer. After he wowed them with the presentation, the reporters weren't terribly interested in pressing the point anyway.

The massive colony ships dwarfed even the *Roosevelt*-class carriers that had been assembled to ensure their safety—all four ships assembled at once around the formerly secret construction facility in the asteroid belt. Together the fleet became both the largest colonization effort ever organized by man and the greatest gathering of destructive force in history.

Until, that is, the fleet began its mission. One by one the carrier ships escorted their larger sisters to Earth, Mars, and Luna. They met massive legions of volunteers, spurred by generous grants of land and government investments to start new lives in the outer systems. Each ship staffed up and crewed up, and then one by one the colony ships set off for their final destinations: Jupiter, Saturn, Uranus and Neptune. And one by one, as they passed out of easy reach of the Chinese, Indian and Caliphate fleets, their carrier escorts broke off, with great fanfare, headed for alternate destinations.

The departures were carefully choreographed for maximum publicity. The news outlets buzzed with the calculations that had been done so carefully to ensure that the ships all arrived at their destinations simultaneously. The entire effort was scripted to ensure that the publicity came back on as the colonists arrived, and the commentators spent some time talking about the President's gift for public relations.

The entire operation was highly publicized. The press was there every step of the way, the vid feeds on every channel. President Covington led the publicity campaign, even flying out to the asteroid belt himself to see the first batch of colonists off. It was the furthest from Earth a sitting president had ever journeyed, and the most watched video of all time.

Naturally, it was all a lie.

It's funny how much work it takes to be an "overnight success." Believe it or not, we still pulled a profit off the mission. And I'm not talking about book deals or speaking fees, either. That didn't come until later. We didn't even know we were famous until years later, when we finally came home.

No, we'd mined some extra fuel to ensure that Triton Station wasn't our final resting place instead of a low orbit over Neptune. We all wanted to make it back, but we knew the station didn't have enough fuel to send us home. And we weren't sure they had enough extra fuel to send us back out again. The worst part was, they relied on us for all of their spare. So if we came back completely empty-handed, they didn't have anything to help us with.

We over-estimated what we needed on purpose. As hungry as we were, we knew we could survive that. But we wouldn't make it if we didn't have enough fuel. So we toughed it out and mined a bit of extra, and then a bit of extra on top of that for a margin of error.

We didn't make a fortune—it was barely a profit. But we had enough to restock the ship without a loan, and just barely enough fuel to get back down to a mining orbit. Ordinarily we wouldn't have gone out again like that, with no room for error. But we knew we could do it this time. We pared our stocks down to a minimum, floated down there, and sucked up every bit of that exotic atmosphere that we could. And then we did it again.

A year or three later the colony ships arrived. And they all needed fuel—fuel for everything. Construction, maneuvering, transport, maintenance: you name it, they needed fuel for it. And for a while we were the only game in town. And that's when we got totally, obscenely rich.

—Matthew Holt, at the twentieth Holt Energy Industries annual shareholders meeting

The Chinese were the first to detect that something was amiss, sending ripples up and down their space command. Their space observation array was top notch, perhaps even the best there was. It certainly gave the Americans and the Indians a run for their money. Like the Americans, they tracked everything. And the numbers didn't add up.

It started with a technician explaining masses, burn ratios and thermodynamics to his Major. The American colonization ships simply hadn't put out enough thrust to accelerate the way they did. The Major explained it to his Colonel who explained it to his General. To nobody's surprise, the information was quickly given maximum security classification.

Chinese high command scrambled its engineers with one directive: figure out the new drive system that the Americans were using. Clearly they had a new thrust advantage, and that could not be allowed to stand. In the event of another space war, such an advantage would be devastating.

The Indian observers took longer to figure it out. Strangely, the Indian government learned about the discrepancy via a well-placed spy in the Chinese observation program several days before their own observation team made the connection. They already had spies in the Chinese research program, but they took steps to get better intelligence from the Americans. They, too, designated the information with a maximum security classification.

The Caliphate, operating with sub-standard observation systems and having recent difficulty with its intelligence departments, never made the connection at all. If they had, they very well might have leaked it to a certain group of freelance space scavengers that they sometimes leaked information to. Due to some dirty tricks of their own, that group would have very quickly figured out exactly what the Americans were up to and had months to prepare—plenty of time to flee the oncoming assault.

Even the amateurs noticed the unusual deceleration burns, but this came days after President Covington's very public announcement that the colony ships would each be taking a scenic approach to their destinations. The vessels were set to fly a wide sweep around, giving each of the colonists an expansive view of the planetary space they would soon be inhabiting. Some of the spectacular views as they passed moons, planets, and asteroids were livecast back to near-Earth space, and quickly became some of the most popular footage on the news nets.

Well aware that nearly all of humanity was watching, Commodore MacGregor ordered the *Roosevelt* to shed the camouflage shell it had hidden within on the route to Neptune. He could feel their eyes on him as he ordered the space-based bombardment of the hidden pirate moon base on the moon Thalassa. He knew that billions of people could see perfect, high-resolution video of his drone fighters blowing the pirates straight to hell.

Nearly four billion miles away the *Harding* instituted an almost identical assault in Uranian space. Almost simultaneously, their sister ships rained down death and destruction around Saturn and Jupiter. Four billion human beings watched as the United States Space Navy massacred the most notorious pirates in history down to the last man.

When the slaughter was over Commodore MacGregor retired to his quarters, where he retrieved a very special bottle of Scotch that had chilled in his personal storage for years. The small bottle had cost him a fortune, and he knew that he'd be back on the firing line soon. But it was the most satisfying drink he'd ever had.

My fellow Americans,

For years our citizens, and indeed all of humanity, have been dealing with vicious pirate attacks in deep space. These brutal outlaws have been murdering and ravaging their way through the outer solar system, taking what they want and leaving death and destruction in their wake. This band of pirates seemed to exhibit some unknown form of stealth transportation that allowed them to move undetected from target to target. They always appeared to be one step ahead of us.

However, we recently learned that this stealth propulsion system was nothing more than a clever ruse. There was not just one band of pirates, but rather four distinct groups. Using an elaborate series of maneuvers and a system of expertly hidden bases, they were able to convince us that they were constantly on the move. In fact, each band has been operating out of a specific area of the solar system.

Earlier this afternoon, the *USS Theodore Roosevelt, the USS William Howard Taft, the USS Woodrow Wilson* and the *USS Warren G. Harding,* utterly and completely demolished these operating bases. We have eliminated their forces entirely. There were no survivors, and we have taken no prisoners. The piracy threat to our citizens has been eliminated.

To carry out this unprecedented operation, we disguised the carriers as colony ships using inflatable hulls coated in a special reflecting paint to fool scans by radar, lidar and other active sensors. A similar ruse was used to portray derelict freighters as the elite carrier groups we sent into deep space…

—President Harrison Trajan Covington, video address to the American People

The monstrous vessel drifted through space on a Hohman transfer orbit, leaving Deimos to enter a light orbit around Mars. The ship still broadcast a bogus identification code erroneously identifying it as the USS *Theodore Roosevelt.* A well-armed Chinese strike group circled Mars as well, on an orbit that would soon bring it within attack range. The remainder of the Fourth Fleet escorted the misidentified ship, but without a carrier in the center the fleet would have little chance against the oncoming attack.

Onboard the vessel's bridge, Commodore Reynolds and his crew stood at rigid attention. President Covington's calm figure filled the large main forward display. The men listened, still and silent.

"Your crew has carried out the deception flawlessly, Commodore. Your secrecy, discipline and professionalism is well noted—and will serve you well in the next phase."

"Thank you, Mr. President."

"Are your men ready for the attack?"

"Yes, Mr. President. We are ready." He hesitated a moment. "Are we certain that it's coming?"

"We have the communications intercepts. The Chinese fleet received their attack orders several hours ago. We're expecting similar attacks against your sister ships. As expected, moving all of our carriers out to deep space proved too tempting a target for them."

"And the Indians, sir?"

"They appear to be sitting this one out, Commodore. But we'll see what happens over the next few hours."

"Yes, Mr. President."

"Then I will leave you to your battle, Commodore. Godspeed."

"Thank you, Mr. President."

"Oh, and one more thing." Covington paused. "I believe it's time to fix that little transponder issue. There's no reason to hide your true identity anymore."

Commodore Reynolds smiled.

"Yes, Mr. President." The screen went blank. Reynolds barked a few orders and his men immediately returned to stations. Frenetic activity commenced across the bridge.

Amateur trackers across Mars noticed the change immediately. Forums across the networks lit up, first with a trickle and then an explosion of activity. A Chinese fleet had launched an attack on the bogus carrier in orbit. The Chinese and the Americans were once again at war. But that was no surprise. Given the realities of orbital mechanics, the amateurs had known the battle was coming for hours. The real shock came when the Americans finally updated the transponder code on their carrier.

As the Chinese attack fleet came into range and began their assault,

Commodore Reynolds stood on the bridge of the USS *Harry Truman* and ordered his drone fighters launched. The newest of the *Roosevelt*-class carriers, it had been built in secret with its three sister ships in preparation for this exact moment. The most powerful warship ever built by man advanced into the oncoming storm and opened fire.

Canny

Brian J. Noggle

Editor's Introduction

Rudyard Kipling wrote a whole volume of barracks room ballads, all worth reading. One of the better known is "Tommy", about Tommy Atkins, the common British squaddie.

I went into a public-'ouse to get a pint o' beer,
The publican 'e up an' sez, "We serve no red-coats here."
The girls be'ind the bar they laughed an' giggled fit to die,
I outs into the street again an' to myself sez I:

O it's Tommy this, an' Tommy that, an' "Tommy, go away";
But it's "Thank you, Mister Atkins", when the band begins to play,
The band begins to play, my boys, the band begins to play,
O it's "Thank you, Mister Atkins", when the band begins to play.

I went into a theatre as sober as could be,
They gave a drunk civilian room, but 'adn't none for me;
They sent me to the gallery or round the music-'alls,
But when it comes to fightin', Lord! they'll shove me in the stalls!

For it's Tommy this, an' Tommy that, an' "Tommy, wait outside";
But it's "Special train for Atkins" when the trooper's on the tide,
The troopship's on the tide, my boys, the troopship's on the tide,
O it's "Special train for Atkins" when the trooper's on the tide.

Yes, makin' mock o' uniforms that guard you while you sleep
Is cheaper than them uniforms, an' they're starvation cheap;
An' hustlin' drunken soldiers when they're goin' large a bit
Is five times better business than paradin' in full kit.

Then it's Tommy this, an' Tommy that, an' "Tommy, 'ow's yer soul?"
But it's "Thin red line of 'eroes" when the drums begin to roll,
The drums begin to roll, my boys, the drums begin to roll,
O it's "Thin red line of 'eroes" when the drums begin to roll.

We aren't no thin red 'eroes, nor we aren't no blackguards too,
But single men in barricks, most remarkable like you;
An' if sometimes our conduck isn't all your fancy paints,
Why, single men in barricks don't grow into plaster saints;

While it's Tommy this, an' Tommy that, an' "Tommy, fall be'ind",
But it's "Please to walk in front, sir", when there's trouble in the wind,
There's trouble in the wind, my boys, there's trouble in the wind,
O it's "Please to walk in front, sir", when there's trouble in the wind.

You talk o' better food for us, an' schools, an' fires, an' all:
We'll wait for extry rations if you treat us rational.
Don't mess about the cook-room slops, but prove it to our face
The Widow's Uniform is not the soldier-man's disgrace.

For it's Tommy this, an' Tommy that, an' "Chuck him out, the brute!"
But it's "Saviour of 'is country" when the guns begin to shoot;
An' it's Tommy this, an' Tommy that, an' anything you please;
An' Tommy ain't a bloomin' fool—you bet that Tommy sees!

Brian Noggle gives us a grimmer version for the future. A nation that does not love her soldiers gets the soldiers she deserves.

On Darus IV, we cleared the countryside of Sauran tanks.
In Nask, the shopmen closed their commerce sites to us in thanks.

They watched with narrow eyes until we boarded outbound ships
And only then exhaled relieved through whitened purséd lips.

But it's "Get 'em, canny; stop 'em, canny; canny, get your gun."
Then it's back to sleep, the cryobunk, when battle's lost or won.
When battle's lost or won, my boys, when battle's lost or won.
Then it's back to sleep, the cyrobunk, when battle's lost or won.

On Kush, we watered jungle vines with rebel worker blood
But couldn't linger to observe the Goran flowers bud.
The trooper ships were system out before the day could close.
But when the Kushies call again, they'll beg us to impose.
But it's "Get 'em, canny; stop 'em, canny; canny, be our friend."
And when the violence arises, they waken us again.
They waken us again, my boys, they waken us again.
And when the violence arises, they waken us again.

They bottle breed us for our quickness, mold our minds to fight
To keep the civvies' hands all clean and keep their conscience light.
Unlike the Outer Worlders, cannies aren't the worst they find.
We're best beloved or least disliked when out of sight and out of mind.

But it's "Get 'em, canny; stop 'em, canny;" then packed away for years.
Forgotten and foresworn until another crisis nears.
Until another crisis nears, my boys, until another crisis nears.
Forgotten and foresworn until another crisis nears.

No children women born will serve as soldiers to defend
Without the praise or citizenship at the service end
They say the cannies lack all ethics, blood-warm heart, and head
Beyond the safety of the squad, the tactics, and the bed.

But it's "Get 'em, canny; stop 'em, canny; canny, you're the best."
But when the ceasefire silence falls, it's "Canny, take a rest."
It's "Canny, take a rest," my boys, it's "Canny take a rest."
But when the ceasefire silence falls, it's "Canny, take a rest."

We wouldn't mind a country or a planet of our own
A home to watch the seasons change, to reap what we have sown.
But corporate's got us patented, marked and titled like a herd.
Our souls are static noise; our fair concerns are never heard.

So it's "Get 'em, canny; stop 'em, canny; canny, nothing more."
Another bottle troop to die upon a distant shore.
For as it is and as it was, forever so it seems,
But know, and fear: when canny sleeps, the canny plots in dreams.

What Price Humanity?

David VanDyke

Editor's Introduction

David VanDyke is a former U.S. Army Airborne soldier and USAF officer who has rapidly become one of the leading military science fiction authors. Here is a tale of future space war that seems as if it's going to follow a familiar pattern. Be warned. It doesn't.

With their vast, intelligently designed living ships, the hostile aliens we call Meme employ superior strategic mobility in the outer Solar System. They are able to operate with few bases and no resupply more advanced than the nearest collection of asteroids and cometary nuclei. They lurk within the Kuiper Belt and Oort Cloud, losing themselves among millions of objects across incredible distances, consuming ices, metals and silicates to refuel, replenish and reproduce.

While gathering strength, they raid, attacking our outposts and asteroid acquisition operations, our transiting cargo ships and task forces, looking for easy victories, forcing us to expend more resources than they. In accordance with their conservative—the misinformed might say cowardly—nature, they hit and run, always with the aim of preserving themselves while damaging us.

In return, we employ heavy sweeps of areas where we suspect their presence. When we meet them, we defeat them if they stand; thus, they seldom give battle. Screened by clouds of living hypervelocity missiles, they flee faster than we can pursue until we retire again to the orbit of Jupiter, the true edge of human territory.

Thus, for a time, we fight the classic asymmetric war. Our machines, our discipline and our locally superior firepower are mismatched by the Meme ability to strike with little warning, inflict damage, and withdraw with impunity.

That is until, every decade or two, reinforcements arrive from beyond the Solar System.

Each time, the Meme gather to conduct a massive assault, hoping to penetrate our defenses and damage our single, fragile home planet. Each time, we have beaten them back with great losses, heroic sacrifices. Each time, their remnants withdraw to the outer reaches to continue their guerrilla warfare and await the next push.

And each time, they come closer to wiping us out.

We are losing this war, not because we are getting weaker, but because they grow stronger more rapidly than we are. And they can afford to lose, whereas we must win, every single time.

To continue to win, I believe humanity has no choice but to consider inhumane solutions to inhuman threats, to fight fire with fire.

And yet, if we ignite this conflagration, might we not burn down our own house?

—Excerpt from *A Personal Memoir: Survival Against the Meme*, by Xiaobo HUEN, Admiral, EarthFleet, Commanding; 2109 A.D.

* * *

"Do you know who you are?"

The woman's warm, professional voice soothed him. "Sure. I'm Vango Markis. Captain Vincent Markis, EarthFleet, Aerospace branch, I mean. What happened? Did I get hurt?"

"Nothing we can't fix. You'll be fine."

"I'm blind. Why can't I see?"

"You don't have use of your eyes."

"Why can't I feel anything? Will I fly again?"

"We'll explain all that soon, Captain Markis. For now, we need to re-baseline your cognitive profile while we work on your body."

"Call me Vango. It's my call sign. You're a doctor?"

"I am."

"How bad is it, doc?"

"You're not dead. You're thinking clearly enough to converse."

"But will I fly again?"

"Yes, Captain Markis. You'll fly."

Vango detected a false note behind her calm and wondered what she wasn't telling him. How bad could it be? Between the Eden Plague's healing and the reconstructive nanotech, if the brain made it back alive and undamaged, the body could eventually be regenerated, cell by cell, good as new.

That must be it. He couldn't remember, but he must have been hit bad, really bad, worse than he'd ever been. He wondered about the other fliers in his squadron. Did they make it back?

Make it back from what, though? He couldn't remember.

"Doc, what happened?"

"What's the last thing you recall? Tell me your last memory of anything at all."

"I'll rack my brain." He tried to laugh, but felt no muscles respond. How was he speaking? It must be a low-level neural link, audio only.

"Was that supposed to be humorous? Humor's a good sign. Now please answer the question, Captain Markis."

"You can call me Vango. Really. I remember… I remember heading back to Earth from Callisto, sealing into the coldsleep cocoon. Hate those things, the slime and everything. Don't trust captured Meme biotech."

"Do you remember waking up?"

"No."

"Do you remember anything after that? A mission, perhaps?"

Vango mulled this over, trying to strain out the most recent memory among the many sorties he'd flown against the Meme, but everything seemed to muddle together. "I'm not sure. I remember a lot of missions. Last one I'm sure of is when we beat the Destroyer."

"That's all right. Confusion is to be expected."

"Why aren't I in full VR link? Is my visual cortex damaged?"

"We're taking it slow, working from the ground up. We've already done as much as we could while you were unconscious. Now we have to ask you a battery of questions. Please bear with us."

"Yes, ma'am."

"Please let me know when you're ready."

"What's your name, doc?"

"My name's Sue, Captain Markis. What's yours?"

If he had eyes to roll, he would have, and didn't bother to insist a third time she call him Vango. "Humor's a good sign."

"Humor's a good sign."

"Okay, fire away."

"Is there a fire?"

"No… go ahead and ask, I mean."

Although the doctor's voice rang with tones of purest English, Vango couldn't precisely identify her accent. Still, he thought it sounded a bit unnatural. A translation program, then, for someone speaking another language. Software often stumbled over idioms or translated varying phrases exactly the same.

"Where are you from, doc?"

"Cambridge, Massachusetts. How about you?"

Interesting. His guess about Sue as a non-native speaker of English seemed to be wrong. "I'm from Carletonville, South Africa, as you should know."

"Why should I know?"

Awkwardly, Vango struggled for words as he always did when confronted with the fact that his father, Daniel Markis, was the Chairman of the Council of Earth, the man most people thought of as humanity's political leader. "Never mind. It's not important."

"We need to move on, Captain Markis. I have many patients to attend," Sue said. "We're going to start with maths. What's five plus eight?"

"Thirteen."

"Twelve times three?"

"Thirty-six."

"The value of pi?"

"To how many decimal places?"

The questions went on like this for hours, becoming rapidly more complex and covering language, history, science and more. Vango found himself happy to exercise his mind and felt little fatigue, experienced no difficulty.

"How'd I do?"

"Very well, Captain Markis. Tomorrow we'll run some more sophisticated tests."

"Tomorrow? What'll I do until then?"

"Sleep. Pleasant dreams, Captain Markis."

"Dammit, I'm not–"

Vango awoke with no sensation of drifting or lethargy, nor did he remember dreaming. It was as if someone threw a switch and he came whole unto consciousness.

"Good morning, Captain Markis. Did you sleep well?"

"I think so. Can I see something today?"

"Auditory tests will be conducted today."

"I can hear you just fine, Sue."

"We still have to run the tests."

Vango sighed mentally and compartmentalized, telling himself it was just another hurdle to be jumped, another step toward getting back into the cockpit.

The day dragged, and at the end of it he was almost glad to be put to sleep.

"Good morning, Captain Markis. Did you sleep well?"

"You can ditch the script, Sue. Just talk to me like a normal person. English isn't your first language, is it?"

"No, it's not."

"But you said you were from Massachusetts."

"That's true."

"It's true that you said it, or what you said is true?"

"Both are true."

"What's your first language, anyway?"

There came a perceptible pause. "Unfortunately, I'm not allowed to discuss anything further about myself at this time, Captain Markis."

"At this time? Why?"

"We don't want to skew the tests. You and I must remain emotionally detached."

"Who said?"

"That's another thing I can't discuss. You'll understand in time."

"Maybe I want to understand it now. Maybe I'm sick of your damn tests and won't take any more until I get some information." He wasn't fed up—not quite—but perhaps as a negotiating ploy…

"Your readings do not indicate sufficient agitation to refuse. Besides, you're a military man. You raised your hand and swore to uphold Earth's constitution and obey the lawful orders of the officers appointed over you."

"Are you an officer appointed over me?"

"No, but I'm relaying the instructions of those who are."

"Then I demand to know who's giving the orders."

"These orders come from Admiral Huen."

"Not from my father?"

"Chairman Markis and the Council of Earth have delegated authority to Admiral Huen in these matters. You know how the chain of command works."

"Does he know what's happened to me?"

"To which 'he' do you refer?"

"My father."

"Your father has been briefed."

"Why can't I talk to him?"

"You must complete the program first. Now, Captain Markis, we must proceed with the testing regimen."

Vango sighed, or tried to, though he felt no lungs, no air. "Sue, you're one hardass bitch."

"You're not the first to say so. We will now continue with the testing regimen."

"Then for the love of God, please tell me I get to *see* something today."

"Yes, a bit later. Touch and smell baselining will take a couple of hours. Afterward, you will see."

He steeled himself for more tedium. "Okay, let's get moving."

The first visual Vango received was of a blank plain, a whiteness broken only by the hint of a horizon at an indeterminate distance. He looked down and saw his feet, his legs and his torso, and when he moved them into view, his hands. They lacked the exquisite detail of the real thing, though, identifying this as a VR sim, a virtuality not so different from what he saw when he linked in to the computer network in a fighter, though of lower resolution.

"Is that better?" Sue said.

"Hugely. You have no idea what it's like to be stuck inside your own head with no one to talk to."

"You might be surprised." The horizon clarified, and the plain took on a texture like carpet. "Walk, please."

Vango walked. Shapes appeared, resolving themselves into three-dimensional geometric representations—cubes, pyramids, spheres—

then into more complex objects such as chairs and tables, houses and cars, airplanes and Fleet spacecraft. Each time he was asked to identify and interact with the items.

"Look, I'm acing these tests. Obviously I'm not impaired, right?"

"Not significantly. Your cognition is running above ninety-seven percent of normal."

"Then please, may I see something real? Link me into the grid. Give me full VR with people in here. I'm sick of playing your games."

"These are not games, Captain Markis. They are evaluations designed to identify flaws."

"Flaws in what?"

"Your ability to perform to specifications."

"You make me sound like a part in a machine."

"What is a pilot but the most important piece of his craft?"

"Like you're the most important piece of the mechanism of modern medicine?"

"Of course."

"Doc, are you even human?" Vango meant it as a joke, but the question had an unexpected effect, bringing on an extended pause, and then he felt himself losing consciousness.

When he came to, no Sue spoke in greeting. Instead, he woke up in a dimly lit, nondescript chamber bereft of windows.

Not his bed and not his room. Not a bunk in an officer's shipboard stateroom. Someplace dirtside, then. He felt about one G of pull, which meant he was likely on Earth in some kind of medical facility.

Swinging his legs out of bed, he stood in loose-fitting pajamas and bare feet on a warm, carpeted floor. The motion evidently triggered the lights, showing a small desk with a chair, a wall locker and nothing else.

All this confirmed his suspicions. He occupied a high-class simulation. His body must still be undergoing reconstruction in a nanotank. He'd never been injured badly enough to need one for more than a day, but a full rebuild would take months. He resigned himself to a stretch inside the virtuality, and afterward the inevitable VR-addiction detox, the bane of those who spent too much time in the link.

Opening the room's locker, he found a flight suit with his name and rank on it and pulled it on, along with socks and boots. Better to obey the rules of this virtuality than override them, if that was even allowed. As an experiment he tried to call a lit cigarette into being, and then a cup of coffee, but failed. So, no freebies.

Suitably attired, he squared his shoulders and opened the door, finding a hallway that could have come from any Aerospace-branch barracks, with the usual art on the walls showing fighters, bombers, attack and transport craft from eras stretching back to the Wright Brothers.

"Token!" Vango felt a greater flood of relief than he'd expected as he spotted his tall, ebony-skinned wingman stepping into the hall, similarly attired.

"Hey, Vango. You getting rebuilt too?"

"I guess. They haven't told me much for sure. Nothing since the tests."

"Yeah, me neither. And they didn't let me contact anyone."

"Maybe we're on slow time. That way it won't feel like months."

"All the more reason to let us talk to someone."

Vango looked up at the ceiling, a common habit when addressing a ship's computer or a sim's controller. "Sue, you there? Anyone?"

No answer came.

"Maybe this is more testing," Token said. "Maybe we're supposed to figure things out for ourselves as a way of keeping us occupied."

"I don't appreciate being played games with. I don't usually like to drop the Markis name, but I hope someone's listening when I say I doubt my father will be pleased when he hears we've been poorly treated."

Token waited a moment, eyes also lifted as if to see whether that declaration would bring a response, and then he shrugged. "You know how doctors are. Petty gods. They'll claim medical necessity."

"We'll see." Vango strode down the hall, banging on doors until more than two dozen people stood in the hallway, all of varying degrees of familiarity, but none unknown. He had the odd feeling that some of them were out of place, as if they didn't quite match with his recollections, or with each other.

That was it. He was certain they hadn't all served together at the same time. And one of them…

"Stevie?"

The short, blonde lieutenant as usual crackled with energy and filled out her flight suit in a way that made him ache with powerful nostalgia, though oddly, not the lust he expected. Before, when they'd been involved, she'd been his wildest fling, full of fiery chemistry.

"Hey, Vee." Her strong Southern-U.S. accent brought back a flood of memories. "Fancy meeting you here."

Vango seized her in a crushing hug, drawing catcalls and whistles from the others as he kissed her tentatively, she more enthusiastically. "Stevie, I don't understand," he said into her bobbed hair. "You're dead. I saw you die."

"Guess not, old son." She slapped him on the butt and pushed him to arm's length, continuing in a Mark Twain drawl, "It seems reports of my death have been greatly exaggerated."

Vivid memories flooded into him, of the medics carrying her cold, dead body out of her quarters on a stretcher, the rubber hose of her speedball addiction still wrapped around her arm. Nobody came back from that, Eden Plague or nanotech notwithstanding… right? "What's your last memory?"

Stevie's face turned cagey. "I remember dumping a plate of gumbo on your head in a restaurant in the Quarter."

"That's it? The very last memory? Come on, Stevie, this is important."

"I remember going to the infirmary."

"Why?"

She shrugged. "Bitch cut me on the street. It was pretty bad. Bad enough they stuck me in an autodoc tube all day."

Something made Vango ask, "Did they put you under? General anesthesia?"

"I guess. That's the last thing I remember."

Vango turned to Token. "What's your final memory before waking up here?"

"Getting on the transport back to Earth after we beat the Destroyer. Getting in the cocoon."

"Me too." He pointed at Lock, a slim, no-nonsense female senior transport pilot well known for getting out of extreme scrapes. "What about you?"

"The same. Coldsleep. After the Destroyer."

"Wild Bill?"

The calm, taciturn man said, "After. Coldsleep, too."

"Does anyone have a final memory of *anything* except going into coldsleep or an autodoc?"

All of those present shook their heads or muttered negatives.

Token said, "Is it possible we were all damaged in the cocoons? Maybe our bodies didn't come out of coldsleep properly, but they were able to salvage our brains."

"So," Stevie cocked a hip and raised a finger, "we're disembodied brains? Like in some old pulp movie?"

"Until they rebuild our bodies," Vango replied. "Nothing to worry about."

"But what about the autodoc?" Token asked.

Vango rubbed his jaw. "I think it's not about coldsleep, but getting put under. Something went wrong. Something new and unexpected."

Wild Bill sniffed. "Then why haven't they simply told us what's going on? We're not children. We can handle a little bad news. Hell, it's just a vacation in VR. We've all been here before. Where's the sun and the surf, the ski slopes, the mountain meadows? We should all be hang-gliding by day and clubbing by night. Instead, we're in this," he gestured, "this *institution.* Something's not right."

Vango growled deep in his throat and slammed the heel of his hand into the nearest wall, then again, and again. He could feel pain and a sensation of injury, so the virtuality was sophisticated and accurate, almost flawless. "Sue!" he yelled. "Someone talk to us, or we'll…"

Stevie turned, shrugged in apology and kicked Wild Bill in the crotch. "Sorry, dude," she said as he rolled in agony on the floor. "Try to remember it's just VR." She put a booted foot into his ribs with enthusiasm, and then reared back for a stomp, until three others grabbed her and pulled her back.

"What the hell are you doing?" Lock said, taking a fistful of Stevie's flight suit near the neckline and shaking the smaller woman.

"Trying to get the warden's attention."

Everyone paused for a moment, waiting, but nothing happened.

"It was worth a try," Vango said, standing over Wild Bill, "but no more of that. We might not be hurt physically, but with pain feedback enabled we can be mentally damaged."

"Psycho bitch!" Wild Bill gasped, holding his genitals.

"Pussy," Stevie replied. "I've taken worse beatings," She struggled in Lock's grip. "Now let go of me unless you want some too."

"Everybody throttle down," Vango said. "Is this all it takes to set us at each others' throats?"

They had the decency to look sheepish.

"So what's the plan, Vango?" Token asked.

Everyone was staring at him, even the others of similar rank. He wasn't sure who was technically senior. Apparently the Markis name was the tiebreaker. People expected him to lead. No big deal. He was used to it.

"First, no more brawling. We're EarthFleet officers, not a bunch of street punks." He glared at Stevie, who merely grinned at him.

"Second, it seems like we have two choices. We can wait, or we can do something. Anyone here the waiting type?"

Voices raised in denial until Vango waved them down. "Good. Half of you go that way with Token, the other half come with me this way." He pointed emphatically down the hall to match the directions as he spoke, and then took off.

When both Stevie and Wild Bill followed him, Vango stopped and said, "Bill, you better go with Token."

Wild Bill shot Stevie a poisonous glance and then sneered. "Fine. Keep thinking with your prick." He turned to stalk off.

Vango sighed. He'd sent Wild Bill off because he didn't trust anyone else to handle Stevie, not because he was lusting after her. Until the situation clarified, he would keep an eye on her, keep her under control.

Not that he'd done very well at that the last time around. She'd died, after all, because he hadn't been able to compete with a needle and a packet of white powder. Like every day since, he wondered what that said about him.

At the end of the hall in the direction he'd chosen, Vango found a room full of old Mark III flight simulators. Those with him crowded past and ran their hands over the machines, checking them for function and status. Stevie jumped into one and reached for the link wire, plugging it into her skull before he could object.

That made Vango reach up to touch the socket in his own skull. "Does anyone else think it's weird that we're inside a VR sim looking at flight simulators that have been obsolete for years?"

Lock nodded. "Yeah, and pointless. Why bother with representations of simulators anyway? Usually we just request a revision of the virtuality and suddenly we're flying. This seems… primitive."

"Walking before we run?" said Butler, a tall male warrant officer. "Still evaluating our responses?"

Vango frowned. "I suspect you're right. Stevie, can you hear me?

"Yeah."

"What do you see?"

Stevie had begun manipulating the manual controls, standard back-ups even though all functions on modern craft were handled via link. "Only one program, labeled XM-58. Extremely high maneuverability and acceleration. Whatever ship I'm flying, it's shit-hot, hotter than anything I've ever tried before. Can't find the weapons, though."

"Probably not available until later," Lock said.

Vango ran his hand over the simulator's shell. "Until later… why?"

Lock gave him a stare as if he were dense. "They obviously want us to use these things. Look at this room. No doors. Even the one we came in disappeared. Eleven of us, eleven simulators. We're in VR, remember? They can control our environment in detail and they're not telling us anything, so obviously they want us to play along. The others are probably experiencing the same thing."

Vango remembered Lock was always a thinker, even smarter and more driven than the usual elite pilot. "Fine. Let's play." He hopped into one of the chairs and reached for the link.

The others followed suit.

Like Stevie reported, the program put him inside the cockpit of the fastest, most maneuverable ship he'd ever driven. Sure, it might be an imaginary craft, something never built, but what point to simulate a phantom?

And the vehicle obeyed the laws of physics. It had limits, though those limits were extraordinary, and he felt nothing of the body—no G forces, no vibrations, no feedback.

Forgetting about his situation within the greater virtuality, he lost himself in the joy of flight, launching from and landing on moons and planets, ships small as frigates and large as carriers and everything in between, zooming within cruising fleets, buzzing his way past near-collisions in trajectories far too dangerous for reality.

At no time was he able to see the craft itself, though, neither interior nor exterior, even reflected in shiny surfaces. He had the impression it was cylindrical, like a fuselage, although that may have been an artifact of the sim.

After several subjective hours, just as he felt he had achieved basic mastery of the thing—building on his extensive experience with less capable craft, of course—a new section appeared on his avionics display: a standard sensor panel. It cued him to an incoming Meme hypervelocity missile.

He easily avoided the missile, and it vanished. Two came next, and then four, then more, doubling in number each wave. Eventually he was brought down by one of thirty-two, at which point the count stabilized until he passed that level. Then it doubled again until he couldn't dodge them all no matter how he improved.

This exercise presaged a run of combat scenarios of ever-increasing complexity. He encountered squadrons of Meme stingship fighters, corvettes, frigates and cruisers, all the way up to Destroyers, those massive, kilometers-wide living battleships, firing at him with missiles small and large, with fusors, even with the less-common biolasers and scatterguns.

Never was his ship provided with weapons, though he was allowed to self-destruct using his internal suicide fusion bomb, or ram when all hope of escape was lost, exploding that selfsame warhead on contact. Not an advisable tactic, usually, but something every pilot no doubt contemplated in his or her heart of hearts. Better to go out in a blaze of glory and take one of the hated enemy along.

Fatigue began to set in. A check of the sim chrono told him he'd been at it for ten hours straight, but he pushed himself for a couple more, hungry to complete whatever process this was, to see the end of it and, he hoped, regain the real world and his freedom.

He was still at it when he lost consciousness.

Once more Vango woke up in the featureless room with its nondescript furnishings. This time, when he stepped into the corridor, his comrades awaited him. Vango prevented his own door from closing. "Can you go back into your rooms?"

A couple of people opened doors. "Seems like it," one called. "Why?"

"I'm trying to find out how much they're going to push us to do what they want. So today, we're not playing in their sims."

"So what are we gonna do?" Stevie said, stepping up to him and grabbing him around the waist.

"Exactly," Vango replied with a slight blush. "We're going to do anything but play along. Have sex, talk, play word games, whatever you like. Just don't go to the simulators. Let's see what happens."

"Ooh, I like this plan already," Stevie said, grabbing his hand and pulling him into his room to the hoots and hollers of the others. Inside, his dead former girlfriend—or whoever she was—stripped out of her flight suit to stand naked in front of him, posing like a short, buxom pinup model. "Like what you see?"

"Of course," Vango said, his voice even. "Only one problem." He stepped out of his own flight suit and spread his arms. "Not working."

Stevie stared at Vango's lack of erection. "That never happened before."

"Oh, I know."

"Let's try a little harder, then." Stevie pushed him onto his bunk and soon both were doing their best to bring about the desired result.

"Damn," she said after a few minutes. "These bastards turned off the fun parts."

"I was afraid of that. They're not going to make it easy to entertain ourselves."

"I never heard of a sim like this. Even in training, there's rules, right, Vee? They're supposed to treat us the same in or out of the virtuality. That's the law."

Vango stroked Stevie's hair absently as they lay naked on the bed. "Yeah, that's the law. The fact that they're not following it means something."

"What if there was a coup? Somebody else took over when we were lying injured. Hell, it could be years later than we remember."

"If we'd all boarded the same ship and had the same last memories, I might believe that, but that doesn't seem to be the case. And you were dead, believe me."

"I'm not jonesing either." Stevie slapped the inside of her elbow as if to raise a vein. "I mean, I kinda want it, but mostly because I'm bored."

"Bored with me here?"

Stevie laughed and rolled onto an elbow. "It's that small-town insecurity that makes you so edible."

Vango sighed. "Not today, it seems. Speaking of edible, have you felt hungry or thirsty yet?

"Nope. Haven't even had to pee."

"That settles that, then."

"Why us, though?" Stevie asked. "Why these twenty-four people?"

"Well, I served with all of you one time or another."

"Really?" Stevie jumped out of bed and pulled on her flight suit. "I don't know most of these people, but you do? Maybe you're the nexus. Come on, let's go find out."

That possibility hadn't occurred to him. He dressed quickly and started pounding on doors, rousting everyone into the hallway again. "I presume you all got the same negative results we did?"

A few raunchy jokes floated his way, but all eventually agreed that sex simply hadn't been allowed to work.

"Stevie pointed out something I missed," Vango said. "I've served with every single one of you at some time, but she hasn't. Is there anyone here who knows everyone from before, like me?"

No one raised a hand.

"So for some reason, I'm the center of all this. It makes me wonder if you're all real, or just sims within the virtuality."

That started them buzzing. Wild Bill, now seemingly fully recovered, stepped forward. "I feel like myself. I remember my life. I can describe it in detail if you want."

"Proves nothing," Stevie retorted. "Vango says I died. I don't remember that. But from his point of view, we could be programmed to say or do anything."

"How can we be sure any of us are real?" Lock said.

"We can't," Vango replied. "But we seem to be consistent. If we had writing instruments, we could probably construct a time line and some matrixes showing when and where we served, what our last memories were, what all our relationships were. But we don't even have that. Our rights are being violated. Earth law and EarthFleet regs regarding VR says nothing can be done inside a virtuality without our consent, and that we can leave at any time."

"Except in case of medical necessity," Lock pointed out.

"That covers keeping us here, but not failing to provide information, forcing us to do all those tests, giving us nothing to do except what they want..."

Token spoke. "It might be operational necessity."

"How do you mean?" Vango said.

"What if what we're doing is vital to the war effort?"

"Then why not tell us that? We've all dedicated our lives to fighting the Meme. What's the point of keeping us in the dark?"

A hand went up in the crowd, attached to a big man called Canyon. "What if it's not friendlies that have us?"

"Come again?"

"What if we're not under EarthFleet control? What if we've been captured by the Meme and they're, I don't know, studying us?"

The pilots' faces all reflected varying expressions—shock, skepticism, disgust, thoughtfulness—as that idea percolated through their minds. Conversation began, turning to chatter and argument.

"I don't believe that," Vango said, raising his voice to cut through the noise. "Remember, the Meme can blend with prisoners. They can take over their bodies and suck all the knowledge out of them. Their biological and genetic sciences are far superior to ours. That's why we use reverse-engineered Meme tech in our coldsleep cocoons and other devices. So, there's absolutely no need to study us in VR. They already know all there is to know about the human race, and if the Meme had captured us, they'd already have blended with us against our wills."

"How do we know they haven't?" Lock said, looking around.

"I guess we don't," Vango replied. "Stuck in VR like this, we don't know a damn thing except what the controllers want to tell us. So I guess the question is, do we play along with what might be some unfair and extralegal crap on the assumption it's all necessary, or do we assume this is all bullshit and resist as best we can?"

"Is this a democracy?" said Lock, giving him a hard look.

Vango nodded to her in thanks for reminding those here of their military discipline. He realized she was probably the oldest, longest-serving among them. If she hadn't been happy to remain a chief warrant officer, she'd no doubt outrank everyone here.

"Yeah, what do you say, Markis?" Canyon said. "You're in charge."

"Everyone agree to that?" Vango asked. "Some of you O-3s might have dates of rank earlier than mine, so if you want the job, say so now. Otherwise, I'm it and you'll follow my orders from now on."

He looked around, searching for disagreement and finding none. "Then we're going to play their game for now. We haven't been abused, and this thing feels to me like some kind of extended psychological test combined with training. It might be meant to keep us occupied or it might genuinely be teaching us how to fly a new vehicle. And that's what we do, people. We fly. So follow me, and let's fly."

At the same end of the hall as yesterday, he opened the door to the simulator room and waved everyone in. Twenty-four modules awaited them in the room, and the chamber seemed larger, confirming Vango's suspicion that it didn't matter that they'd split up the first time. All roads led to these simulators.

Vango's first surprise came when the simulator activated an IFF-Blue Force module that kept track of friendlies. Even before he launched from the asteroid he found himself on, he saw twenty-three other contacts designated friendly, each with appropriate personal call sign.

Experimentally, he spoke. "This is Vango. Anyone read?"

Chaos immediately broke out in the audio link.

"Pipe down, people," he said. "Looks like they gave us a common net, so use standard protocols and keep the chatter to a minimum."

"Token here. What are we supposed to do?"

As if in response, a mission brief appeared in Vango's HUD window. It directed him to lead his formation along certain routes, avoid threats, and to come within fifty meters of the designated targets. Those targets turned out to be Meme Destroyers, the enemy's largest ship class, living spheres two to three thousand meters in diameter and massing billions of tons.

Fifty meters might as well be ramming.

"Do you all have the mission brief?" Vango asked.

Terse affirmatives told him they saw it. "What's the point?" asked Stevie. "Get close to Destroyers?"

"Obviously there's a program of increasingly difficult missions, like a tutorial. Since this is the first one where we can see and talk to each other in the VR field, let's cooperate and graduate to the next one and I'm sure we'll see. That's the point."

No one grumbled further, which heartened Vango. This might all be a game, but it felt like mission prep. As he'd taken the reins of leadership, he'd do the best he could.

He wondered briefly if this whole thing was a leadership test for him alone, using simulacra of people he'd known. If so, he resolved to pass with flying colors.

"All right, everyone report go for launch." When they'd done so, Vango gave a three-count and kicked his ship up off the asteroid. He swiveled his point of view backward and saw an ejection tube flush with the surface. All around him rose other craft like unadorned missiles.

Zooming his viewpoint in close, something that came naturally when fighting in VR space, he saw his comrades' ships still appeared as blank cylinders, tapered at the nose and blunt at the tail. No weapons, sensors or other fittings could be seen. A suggestion of fusion exhaust showed near their sterns, but when they adjusted course, no jets of any kind spurted. It was as if the sim controllers were deliberately suppressing any clue as to the real nature of these attack craft.

On the fly, Vango assigned each of his pilots roles and positions within a hierarchy, based on his memories of the people involved, dividing the twenty-four into six four-ships. He took Stevie, Token and Lock with him.

He told each flight to make its own way toward the objectives. They didn't get far. By halfway in, everyone had been destroyed. As the pilots died, they respawned back in the launch tubes, but were not allowed to begin again until everyone else had returned and Vango gave the word.

"How are we supposed to get there with no weapons to defend ourselves?" Stevie complained. "This is bullshit!"

"We have to figure out a way to at least get one ship into the objective zone," said Token. "We'll need to assign interceptors and decoys to sacrifice their ships. We have our suicide bombs."

"That's bullshit too," Stevie said. "That's not the way we'd really fight. Highly trained pilots don't throw themselves away."

Vango said, "They do if it's important enough. Besides, this is a low-grade sim. If they wanted us to treat it as real, they'd make it realistic in all aspects. Instead, this is like a kid's game where the goal is simply to beat the level and advance to the next. So we go with Token's idea. This next iteration, our objective is for one of us to complete the mission. After that, we can work on getting more there."

It took nine attempts, but with a series of wild maneuvers, eventually Vango made it through to break the fifty-meter range. Everyone else got knocked out, but they all still cheered. He felt as if he'd used them up as they decoyed and intercepted threats for him, but knowing it was a game, he was able to think like a football team captain rather than a flight leader. His only objective was to get the ball to the goal, and the ball was himself.

Vango said, "Great job, team. Now you see it can be beaten. This time let's get more people across the line."

His confidence quickly faded, however, as the next mission ramped up its difficulty. He abandoned all thought of multiple wins and settled for trying to get himself there again. This time it took five attempts, and he ended up ramming the Destroyer and killing his ship.

But he won, according to the simulator.

"This really is a game," Vango said to his people. "I didn't notice at first, but now I realize the success parameters didn't say anyone had to survive. We only have to cross the fifty-meter line, and that's a whole lot easier if we ram them at the end."

"Then I bet we can get several through," Token replied. The others agreed, and as it became clear there was no penalty for dying in the process, they waxed enthusiastic, proposing new and unconventional tactics to "win the game."

They won the game. In fact, three rammed the objective. Crossing the fifty-meter line seemed incidental.

"We're getting good at this," Stevie cried.

But hazards increased once more.

"They aren't letting us taste the fruits of our victory," Vango announced, "but we're improving by leaps and bounds. At some point there will be a new kind of challenge, not merely a harder one. Keep at it."

The day ended before the objective changed, though the difficulty increased four more levels. Every time Vango thought they had it licked and they got most of the ships across the goal line, it became tougher.

In what turned out to be the day's final run, Vango's consciousness faded as he alone crossed the fifty-meter mark.

This morning, Vango felt something had changed. As he opened his eyes, he noticed the ceiling seemed grainy, with much greater detail than before. He followed the join where it met the wall and noticed a smudge, and then a cobweb.

Rolling abruptly out of bed, he stared at the imperfection as if it were the world's most wonderful sight. Tearing his eyes away, he examined the room and found many such details, though the basic layout remained the same, with the addition of a door.

Opening it, he found a bathroom, with toilet, shower, soap and other supplies. He suddenly he realized he had to pee. The relief was nearly overwhelming, both psychological and physical. Had he finally been released from the virtuality?

He examined his hands, then the rest of his body, finding real, variable flesh, skin and hair, where before it had been minimalist and plastic, like a mannequin. Finding tweezers in a drawer, he stabbed himself in the forearm and drew blood from the tiny wound, blood which glistened for a moment before he smeared it to clotting. Then he sucked on his finger, smelling and tasting the iron.

Real. It was real.

Or a high-resolution sim, he told himself. *Don't get your hopes up too high. This may be simply one more test.*

Showering and dressing hurriedly, he found others in the hallway already talking earnestly. Some slapped back and spoke joyously, loudly. Others seemed intent on examining everything up close. He saw Token take down one of the pictures on the wall and look behind it, touching the hook that had held it there.

Arms grabbed his waist from behind and he turned to find Stevie wrapping herself around him. And this time, the missing desire surged inside him.

"Is that a pickle in your pocket, or are you glad to see me?" she said.

Vango grinned. "Very glad to see you." He leaned down to kiss her, hard.

"Break it up, you two," Lock said from behind them. "How do we know this is real?"

"Aren't you the buzz kill," Butler said, coming up to bump the tall woman with his shoulder. "Does it matter?"

"Of course it matters," she snapped.

"Why?"

"Because…" Lock trailed off. "It just does."

Vango disengaged from Stevie. "How can we know?"

Lock frowned. "We can test the limits of this virtuality, if there is one. If we find things that make no sense in the real world, we know we're still inside."

"And if not, we're still not sure." Vango shrugged and raised his voice. "Listen up, people. Spread out and try doors. Find windows or exits or… something, anything that proves we are—or aren't—still inside a simulation."

Five minutes of exploration were all it took to return the verdict: not real. No windows had appeared in their rooms. No exits could be found. And the room at the end of the hallway that had until now contained the flight simulators…

"Not what I expected," Vango said as the others ushered him into a room grown large, a hall now overflowing with the trappings of a feast. High ceilings supported chandeliers, and a banquet had appeared on one long heavy polished wooden table. Linen tablecloths and napkins set off silver flatware, crystal goblets and porcelain plates. Bottles of wine, beer and liquor vied for space with whole roast fowl, haunches of beef, pork and lamb, and mounds of side dishes. Off to the side he saw a dance floor outfitted with a music system. A robotic bar stood nearby.

"It's a party!" Stevie said. "And look what I found!"

Vango turned and saw that she was now dressed in a hot red number that showed a lot of skin and seemed to be supported by sheer willpower. Matching heels and clutch, plus a diamond necklace and bracelet combo, completed the outfit. "Very nice."

He noticed others had abruptly changed their clothing as well. Either they had found the unlikely civvies in their rooms, or…. Experimentally, he tried to conjure a lit cigar, a common VR trick for programs that allowed it.

The stogie appeared in his hand.

He willed it away, worried. "What the hell does this mean?" he said to Lock.

The tall woman surveyed the scene, and Vango followed suit. Many of the group were sampling food and drink. Canyon had taken a seat and begun eating as if he feared the banquet would disappear. Stevie had a highball glass in one hand and a bottle of Scotch in the other and had cranked up the music. Now she swayed, her eyes closed, dancing alone.

"It could be a graduation party… or our last meal," Lock said. "A transition of some kind."

Token stepped nearer with narrowed eyes. "Or a reward, like Pavlov's dogs. Maybe they decided to spare some processing power, give us a night of fun, and tomorrow we'll be back to the training regimen."

"No matter what, I suppose we should enjoy it. But it makes me uneasy," Vango said.

Lock and Token nodded.

"Go play along," Vango ordered. "Don't spoil it for the others. We're dancing to their tune in here, so let's make the best of it." With mixed emotions, he walked over to Stevie and took her in his arms.

Later, they lay in Vango's bed, entangled and exhausted.

"Not bad for a dead woman," Stevie said.

"Yeah, we've been ignoring that, but… how do we explain it?"

Stevie shrugged. "Who cares?"

"I care. It's an anomaly, and it must mean something. I feel as if I could only figure that out, I'd have a big piece of the puzzle."

"Oh, Vee, why can't you just live in the moment? Enjoy life as it comes and quit thinkin' so much."

"I'm not built that way, Stevie."

"Well, I am, and I'm not tired. Let's go back and get plastered."

"What if the sim is so good we're hung over in the morning?"

"All part of the fun."

"You're a lunatic."

"Like I ain't heard that before. Come on." She leaped up, tugging on his hand.

"No, you go on. I need to think for a while."

Later, Vango dressed and looked in on the party. He didn't see Stevie, only about half of his people in various states of debauchery, depending on their inclinations. Token was nowhere in evidence, which didn't surprise him. The man was happily married and Vango had never seen him drunk or out of control, despite the high-pressure lifestyle of an aerospace pilot.

Well, good on him.

Knocking on the door to Stevie's room brought no answer, but a memory and a premonition made him ease the door open—they had no locks—and let the light from the hallway spill onto her bunk. Though it didn't surprise him, he felt his heart clench anew as he saw the lighter, the spoon and the needle still clutched in her hand.

They—whoever they were—had allowed the full range of human vices, it seemed. Vango found it still hurt that he wasn't enough for her, but not as much as the first time around. And, at least in this incarnation, she wasn't being carried out on a stretcher.

Suddenly afraid, he stepped over to put a finger on her neck. Thankfully, her pulse beat strongly. Would they let her die? Probably not.

The limits of the virtuality dragged at him, frustrated him with his own helplessness. The only place he felt freedom and power was within the flight sim, which was undoubtedly what they wished. Already he felt a Pavlovian urge to find a simulator and lose himself in flight.

Instead, he shut the door and went to bed. For the first time in what seemed like days, sleep eluded him. Eventually, though, he caught it.

When he awoke, the lack of detail and the flatness of affect within him told Vango that they'd withdrawn the brief grant of near-normalcy, restoring the sensation of inhabiting a plastic simulacrum again. Well, at least now he didn't need to eat, drink, or pee. He sighed and rolled out of bed.

When he led his assembled comrades into the room full of simulators, it took him a moment to identify the difference in the room.

Then it hit him. The shield, Earth and orbiting warship of Earth-

Fleet hung on all four walls, along with the flags of the nations of all the pilots present. Vango's eyes teared up with the display, calling forth a surge of patriotic and martial pride that threatened to overwhelm him. The others seemed to be sharing the experience.

The cynical part of him wondered if they weren't being manipulated even beyond the obvious. Would the controllers insert such emotions into their minds, despite all law and regulation to the contrary?

But what could he do about it except try to maintain his bearing and dispassion, and to help the rest do the same?

"All right, people, snap out of it," he said with a voice like a whip. "Maybe the controllers thought we needed some extra motivation today, and that's all very nice, but none of us are cadets, saluting flags and singing songs. We're professionals, and we know why we fly. I have to believe what we're doing here is critical to our fight against the Meme. So let's play their games again, and by God we'll show them that no matter what they throw in our way, we'll win. Good luck, and good hunting."

With that, he climbed into the simulator and plugged in his link, feeling the expansion of the senses that came with it. His vision now extended millions of kilometers and encompassed thousands of objects—rocky asteroids, icy comet bodies, the moons of nearby Jupiter, Meme ships and the friendly task force from which he prepared to launch.

This time he was in a tube on a missile cruiser. The ship was composed of a spindle and an attached series of expendable box launchers, little more than a transport boat for the wingless cylinders. Was this a new way of deploying fighters? Vango searched his HUD for weapons, but still, the game gave him only a highly maneuverable fuselage, sensors and communications.

The comms linked him with his comrades, but no amount of trying would raise the Fleet net or any other entity. So, they were still on their own, except for the mission brief display, which changed with the objective.

This latest scenario showed a monstrous incoming Meme fleet, at least sixty Destroyers plus attendant smaller craft, speeding directly toward Earth, though still out beyond Saturn's orbit. The EarthFleet task force was already maneuvering to interpose itself.

"Everybody see that?" he said, marking the enemy with a caret. "That's what we'll be flying against."

A series of double clicks came back, shorthand for acknowledgement. "Looks ugly," Token said, no doubt voicing the thoughts of many.

"Ain't nothin' but a thang," Stevie chimed in, and her boundless confidence cheered him. "We score high enough and maybe we get another party tonight."

Vango couldn't fault her logic. "The primary objective's a little different this time," he pointed out. "Token, me, Lock and Stevie are directed to get within five thousand meters of Destroyers, separately. The rest of you get to run interference."

"Five thousand meters? Easy peasy," Stevie said.

"Don't get cocky," Lock said. "Nothing's been easy so far. There must be other factors that make it harder."

"Good thinking. Everyone stay on your toes."

"Hey," said Token, "You guys notice they upped the simulator resolution? Everything looks full standard now, like it's real."

Vango checked his. "Now I see. Maybe that's the point of this mission, to get us used to the real thing again."

A moment of quiet passed. "Any chance this is real?" Lock asked. "I mean, real real, as in happening IRL?"

"If it is," Vango said, "why wouldn't they give us any weapons? And there's no way our bodies could take the Gs these things pull, even with gravplate compensation. We can't be inside real ships."

"Could we be in remote control, and these are missiles? Maybe they're using our minds and skills while our bodies are in regen."

Token spoke up. "Nope. It's been tried. We're operating light-seconds away from the cruisers. The delay is too great for anything but close-in work. That's why all EarthFleet missiles have the best self-guiding algorithms possible, including true random evasion generators. Although… now that you mention it, these birds do seem more like missiles than anything."

Vango experimented with his time sense and found that he could control it. In fact, it appeared he was in charge of everyone's temporal speed, so he sped things up tenfold in order to make the inevitable maneuver-to-contact phase pass faster. When the cruiser carrying his squadron—that was how he thought of them now—entered the proper envelope, it kicked him out of the tube with a blast of fusion gases.

Lock spoke into the calm. "Look at your mission brief. Notice anything different about it?"

Vango did as she suggested. It took him a moment. "There's a date. August 11, 2109."

"Decades in the future," Token said. "Wonder why?"

"More head games," Stevie replied. "Just quit wonderin' and fly, boys and girls."

Vango said, "Good advice. Fly now, speculate later. We're coming up on the merge. Dropping to temp standard."

Now each pilot could control his or her own time sense, allowing for maximum effectiveness as they approached the engagement zone. Vango slowed the world by a factor of more than 100 as a flock of stingships closed in.

These were semi-intelligent sharks of the void whose sole purpose was to screen the larger ships against missiles and small craft. They used short-range biolasers and tiny countermissiles to thin out their enemies.

Normally the stingships died in droves when faced with sophisticated EarthFleet fighters, but they were cheap, they absorbed firepower, and now and then they killed something, especially missiles. And they never hesitated to collide with their targets, kamikaze fashion.

Faced with thousands of them in a broad cloud, Vango directed four of his twenty-four to sacrifice themselves, detonating their powerful suicide fusion bombs to clear a path through the mass.

The remaining twenty drove through, and the stingships couldn't follow fast enough, not with these new hot birds.

On the other side a picket wall of a dozen living frigates waited, each slim Zeppelin shape crewed by a trium of Meme. These ships launched sprays of tiny countermissiles. When the human craft dodged them easily, they opened up with their fusors, incandescent blasts of superheated plasma, like flamethrowers in space, reaching tens of kilometers before dissipating.

These caught two, and then they were eighteen.

"Not bad," Vango said over the net.

"We're kickin' ass!" cried Stevie.

Lock said, "They won't make it that easy. Something's going to spring."

"She's right. Stay frosty," Vango said.

Token marked ships ahead on their HUDs. "Cruisers coming up."

"Bypass them," Vango ordered. "The mission objective specifies only Destroyers get us the win, and only us four."

"Yeah, and I want to win," Stevie replied.

She wants to earn another rendezvous with her vices, Vango thought. *At least we're in VR, so she can't O.D.… and one of those vices is me. But what about when we're done? They'll have to put her in rehab or something. Obviously they know about her addiction. I don't want to lose her again.*

The cognitive dissonance of that thought, the nonsense of Stevie being alive when he *knew* she was dead, threatened to undo him.

"Vango, pay attention!" Lock snapped, and Vango threw his craft into a violent spiral to avoid an incoming trio of hypers. "Get your head in the game!"

"Thanks," Vango said. "Sorry."

He analyzed the cruiser pattern and decided to do something different this time, something he'd thought about but hadn't tried. "Canyon, you and Slapshot suicide on the center cruiser. We're punching straight through before he recovers. We'll lose fewer that way than everyone running the gaps."

"Right, boss," Canyon said, and led his wingman on a mad spiral path toward the midsized ship. He was picked off by a fusor ten klicks out, but Slapshot made it to impact.

The result was spectacular, far greater than Vango expected. The simulated suicide charge must be set to at least a hundred megatons, and the cruiser crumpled and died in a fusion fireball.

"Woohoo!" yelled Stevie. "Destroyers, here we come!"

Sixteen pilots and their suicide craft dove for the hole in the line, easily outracing the ships that tried to slide over and fill the gap. Beyond, the Destroyers came on in a compact mass, at least forty of them.

"That's insane," Vango muttered. "Too many in too small a space. They'll blanket each other with defensive fire. We can't dodge all those fusors."

"That's the twist," Lock said matter-of-factly. "Last I remember, it took everything we had to take down one Destroyer. How can anyone fight so many?"

"We don't have to fight so many," said Token. "This is a game, remember? All we have to do is get us each of us four to within five thousand meters of a Destroyer."

Vango grunted. "Token's right. We can do that."

"Still gonna be hard," said Wild Bill from up ahead. "We should perform a rolling detonation to white out their sensors. These uprated suicide charges should pump out a hell of a lot of interference, assuming the sim takes that into account."

"Good idea. Give me a minute and I'll set it up." Vango further slowed the world outside himself, yielding enough time to run 3D calculations and issue instructions to his twelve sacrificial lambs. "See you all back at the barracks," he said as he sent the data packets. "Drinks are on me."

Clouds of countermissiles issued forth from the Destroyer mass and closed in on the EarthFleet squadron. One by one, Vango's people detonated their ships to clear the way through and provide enormous electromagnetic pulses, blizzards of jamming that blinded the enemy.

They tended to blind his people as well, but all they had to do was fly their courses toward the huge targets.

Belatedly, those targets began to maneuver. If this were real, Vango would have laughed at the idea that ships two kilometers in diameter, with armor five hundred meters thick, would run from a few fighters, even armed with hundred-megaton fusion warheads. An explosion of that size would still need to be nearly in contact to do significant damage, because the vacuum of space provided no medium to carry a blast wave.

Good thing it wasn't real.

When the last of twelve detonations dissipated, Vango found himself and his remaining four-ship in superb position, spread fifteen klicks apart, each pointed at a frantically accelerating Destroyer. The big ships weren't nearly fast enough, though, even spreading out in all directions.

Fusors vomited into space, reaching for him, but with his accelerated time senses they seemed to move in slow motion, and he easily anticipated their paths. Maneuvering to avoid the white-hot zones, he closed toward his target like a gazelle in a dispersed herd of buffalo.

Stevie blasted at maximum and was the first to cross the five-thousand-meter line. Vango expected the usual notation to appear in the mission tracking module, but it didn't, this time. Closer and closer she flew, until a fusor blast seemed to reach for her. Vango wondered why the sim was waiting to record her score.

Then his sensors fuzzed and he lost all HUD cohesion for a long moment. When his viewing capability returned, he saw an expanding zone of annihilation ten kilometers wide. Stevie and the Destroyer were simply… gone. Another Destroyer on the edge of the sphere of death spun slowly, severely injured.

"Mother of God," he breathed. "What in hell was that?"

"Mother for sure," Lock replied. "The mother of all suicide bombs, a thousand times as big as anything I've ever seen."

"More like ten thousand times as large," Token said, ever the human calculator. "Remember the square-cube law. Double the blast radius needs eight-ish times the power."

Vango laughed, but grim. "Then let's go out in a blaze of glory. See you on the dance floor."

Token crossed his line, and then Lock. Vango felt no trepidation as he crossed the line and awaited detonation, only satisfaction at completing the mission combined with anticipation of another night with Stevie.

* * *

"These new semi-organic control modules are a pain in the ass," said Missile Tech First Class Pedro Weinauer as he fitted the half-meter black box into the last of the flight of twenty-four XM-58 capital missiles.

The cylindrical bodies, huge for weapons but small compared to even a one-man fighter, sat lined up on the flight deck of the assault carrier *Peterborough*. A line of cones kept the hustle and bustle of operations away from the delicate devices.

Warrant Officer Hudson stared flatly at Weinauer. "Shut up and finish. I'm initiating the integration program." She input a code into the Vango module—the master—and closed the access panel. "Network looks good. Everyone take an hour. Get some chow or some rack time. We start on the next set as soon as these are movable."

Weinauer nodded. "Thanks, boss," he said, leading the half-dozen missile techs waiting nearby toward the enlisted mess.

Hudson checked her secure control pad and stared at the hard cables snaking across the deck, connecting the brains into a network. After launch, they would go wireless, using microwave and laser comms.

But until then, would take that hour until the modules achieved full integration, more or less. Something about the variability in the

Meme-derived bioprocessors made the exact time uncertain. Then, the grabships would load the weapons into the cruisers' missile boxes and they'd be sent into battle together.

Hudson shrugged. Finicky or not, these things were taking down Meme warships. It didn't matter much what weird shit they put inside to make them work. In fact, she didn't really want to know.

She shivered. Sometimes she felt like the boxes were alive and looking at her.

* * *

Use of human engrams to guide missiles must be viewed as a mixed success. Their performance exceeded that of our best digital control systems, but the expense in time, resources, and particularly the moral cost to those who knew, the knowledge that our finest minds were being replicated, trained and deliberately sent to inevitable death, caused me to wonder whether it was worth it.

I must reluctantly conclude it was. During the Meme's most recent assault, use of our most skilled and dedicated officers' engrams brought us within a hair's breadth of victory. To quote Wellington, it was a damn near-run thing, and the fact that the Meme finally achieved their goal of smashing Earth with two kamikaze Destroyers in no way detracts from the efforts and heroic sacrifices of the virtual replicants.

Without them, we would have lost the entire Solar System. At least now we have a chance to rebuild. The Mars colony is robust, and Jupiter's moons contain the bulk of our spaceborne industry. While we hold those, hope remains.

—Excerpt from *A Personal Memoir: Survival Against the Meme*, by Xiaobo HUEN, Admiral, EarthFleet, Commanding; 2109 A.D.

FLUSH-AND-FFE

LtCol Guy R. Hooper, USAF, ret. and Michael L. McDaniel

Editor's Introduction

The nature of war changes. Sometimes it is a straightforward matter of winning large battles, of bringing everything you have to bear on the enemy's forces to win both the campaign and the war in a single engagement. Alexander effectively ended the Persian Empire at Arbela. Otto the Great ended nearly a century of Magyar raids into Europe at the Lechfeld. Sometimes wars seem to go on forever, with no decisive battles ever fought. The stronger side always looks for ways to bring the opponent to battle and defeat him once and for all. But sometimes that leads to disaster, as with the French at Dien Bien Phu.

Sun Tzu advises us to take what the enemy holds dear. The implication is that if you hold it strongly, the enemy will then break his teeth on your defenses, for defense always has the advantage; or if your defenses are too strong, he must negotiate and be amenable to your will. This principle has been long known, but like most principles of war, it is not always easy to put into practice. Clausewitz warns us that in war everything is very simple, but the simplest things are very difficult. And as von Moltke the Elder said, no battle plan survives contact with the enemy.

Guy Hooper and Michael McDaniel address the problem for modern powers in an age of asymmetric warfare, and illustrate the complexity of modern military operations planning, as we seek to bring irregular forces to decisive battle.

Modern precision firepower does not determine combat against either an entrenched enemy willing to accept losses or one skilled in camouflage, concealment, and deception. In Vietnam, the Persian Gulf, and Kosovo, liberal use of expensive precision weapons produced important results but still left the national leadership the unpalatable choice of accepting the terms of bombing alone or running up a butcher's bill by sending in troops to root out an enemy.

The time is right for a new operational concept that blends proven strategic principles of the past with the tactical revolution advanced by precision weapons and mobility. This idea involves forcing enemies from foxholes by seizing politically and materially vital areas, thus confronting them with a choice of their own—do nothing and lose, or engage superior precision firepower.

The time has come to fight with new combination tactics. This concept combines maneuver and fire warfare. Maneuver warfare puts boots on the ground to seize or threaten centers of gravity in the rear, then precision fires destroy enemy forces during the inevitable counterattack. The destabilizing effect of invasion acts as a forcing function. An enemy is compelled to react against an immediate threat to political control, yet it is exactly this reaction that exposes it to destruction from precisely targeted fire. Critical to strategists, the Flush-and-Fire-For-Effect (Flush-and-FFE) tactic answers the basic question of whose side time is on.

Harnessing the Revolution

Operational fires, attacking targets deep inside enemy territory with airpower, missiles, and long-range artillery to support theater-wide campaign objectives, have revolutionized modern war. A century ago, battlefields were a few acres in size, and forces not engaged eye-to-eye exerted little direct influence. Today the area can be thousands of square miles, and it is routine to attempt to win not just battles, but campaigns, by striking targets deep within an enemy's rear.

The revolution in operational fire has not led to a revolution in operational art. Operational fires have proven deadly against troops and vehicles in the open but have been nearly worthless against entrenched forces. Artillery barrages on the Somme, B-17 pickle-barrel bombing in World War II, B-52 strikes in Vietnam, and cruise missile attacks in Kosovo did not win the war against dug-in or concealed troops. Operational fires have only been slightly more effective against mobile or time-sensitive targets.

Somewhat paradoxically—and in the face of contrary evidence—operational art has raised the bar for precision firepower, expecting it to compel a political result by the efficient reduction of a carefully tuned not-too-hot, not-too-cold target list. Air strikes may cut off reinforcements, and rocket barrages may keep enemy heads down, but ultimately the United States counts on firepower to break the morale of enemy populations, who theoretically, and somewhat vaguely, are expected to spontaneously rise up and depose their own leadership to settle the conflict.

This has not occurred since World War I. Instead, populations tend to dig in and endure. Thus the Army believes, with justification, that ground forces ultimately settle conflicts by territorial battles. In its view, humble infantrymen are far from obsolete.

The proponents of landpower are generally correct, but unfortunately are afflicted by specific challenges. Ground forces have poor strategic mobility. Light infantry can be moved readily, but any sort of mechanized forces involve shipping large numbers of heavy armored vehicles, a sluggish process at best. More critically, ground assaults entail a high price because soldiers can't execute bloodless warfare.

Policymakers fearful of losses and the possible collapse of public support are unwilling to rely on ground attacks as their first option.

Future challengers to the United States will know how to counter its strength and exploit weaknesses inherent in large-scale deployment of heavy forces or precision weapons. Mobility, the humble spade, and the well-constructed decoy may have proven enough of a match for high-tech weapons to convince an enemy that it can hope to survive combat against the U.S. military.

Asymmetric Responses

The fleet-in-being principle has been adopted by small nations in confrontations with great powers. The idea of such a fleet is simple: keep a viable fighting force together and occupy enemy assets with the threat of a sortie. Since this force can choose the time and place of attack, its enemy must keep an equal or superior force in battle position continually as a counterweight. Considering the need to rest and refit this masking force, an enemy can tie up a force twice its size. This has made the fleet-in-being a favorite strategy of weak naval forces for centuries.

Recently this classic naval stratagem has been adapted to conflict on land. Enemies have learned that Americans are strong on bombing and weak in mobile logistics and the willingness to absorb casualties. They have come to realize that by avoiding bombs and preserving their assets, the United States will take months to transport strong ground forces to the theater and may never work up the will to commit that force to battle.

Countering this strategy is not easy, but it can be achieved. The weakness of the fleet-in-being is that minor fleets cannot control the seas. A nation that needs to use the seas must fight whenever it is challenged. And it is this fact, suitably transposed to the land environment, that is key. Flush-and-FFE is based on the simple proposition of taking control of a location the enemy can't afford to lose, then annihilating its forces with operational fires when it tries to reclaim it.

Naval strategists have long acknowledged that winning control of the seas and exercising day-to-day control demand different types of ships. Winning control involves either defeating or threatening to defeat an enemy in a pitched battle. This demands large, powerful vessels—ships of the line, battleships, and carriers. On the other hand, exercising control demands smaller, more numerous forces, such as frigates and cruisers—ships able to both stop enemy shipping and defeat opposing commerce raiders, but not intended to take part in a fleet action.

The same principles apply to warfare on land. Historically, heavy units such as infantry, cavalry, and artillery fight and win battles. But it is light, small units that exercise control over conquered territory: a troop of light cavalry on horseback, a regiment of light fighters, or even an infantry squad in a fighting vehicle. The *petit guerre* for exercising control remains the same.

Thus the concept of Flush-and-FFE calls for deploying a ground force powerful enough to exercise control over land that an enemy cannot concede, yet far enough way that an enemy cannot simply turn around in its foxholes and fight, but must instead redeploy its forces. When an enemy comes out and begins advancing toward the ground force, it is intercepted and defeated in detail.

Limits and Limitations

It is worth mentioning what Flush-and-FFE is not. First, it is not a recipe for dumping ground forces into the midst of an enemy army. The concept calls for inserting a force into an area with light defenses, with a good killing zone between the ground element and enemy main body.

Like frigates in the age of sail, the Flush-and-FFE ground force is not put in place to fight major battles. And like frigates, its primary job is taking the objective in a swift operation. It must be equipped to conduct a seizure operation, but it cannot be expected to fight an extended pitched battle in the process. But unlike frigates, the Flush force is the equivalent of a ship-of-the-line in formation. With adequate communications, precision fires can be targeted at a numerically superior enemy during an unexpected encounter.

Second, Flush-and-FFE is not close air support operating under a different name. The latter provides air strikes on the battlefield to support ground forces engaged in a pitched battle.

The aim of the Flush-and-FFE tactic is to wipe out an enemy before it closes with the land force with sufficient forces to dislodge it. This is a distinction that may be reduced in practice. The ground commander may be best placed to direct fires, so the result may use a concept similar to close air support. However, it is more likely that a covering force will protect inserted troops while massive fire is directed by the joint force air component commander against the main enemy responses.

Third, Flush-and-FFE is not an interdiction tactic. Classical interdiction strategy calls for taking out bridges and other transportation chokepoints to isolate the battlefield and prevent an enemy from bringing up reinforcements. Flush-and-FFE may use interdiction to channel the foe onto the killing ground, but the intent is to cut the enemy down, not to cut an enemy off. With this approach, chokepoints are places to find targets rather than targets in themselves. However, interdiction could be achieved as a byproduct of the main operation.

Concepts and Criteria

One key to Flush-and-FFE is selecting the correct ground targets. Most nations have a handful of major cities, each of which is a high-value political and industrial target. Over the centuries laying siege to capitals has proved one of the best ways to compel an enemy to fight or yield. Other potential targets for seizure are moderate-value, low-population areas, especially areas disaffected from central governments. Seizing high-traffic chokepoints is also useful. Blocking key mountain passes, stretches of rivers, or road networks might lead to economic collapse. Finally, there is the potential for flushing an enemy out into the open not by seizing any particular objective, but simply through placing a presence in his rear. It has long been acknowledged that movement creates doubt for one's enemies and opportunities for oneself.

No new operational art evolves without force structure implications. Several aspects of combined arms warfare for a Flush-and-FFE approach warrant consideration. The concept will not work without a ground element. A coalition approach offers one solution. Instead of using American troops, forces of local allies, or even an internal opposition movement can be employed to seize and hold ground while the United States provides the operational fires that destroy enemy combat forces, though for maximum flexibility the U.S. forces should maintain their own ground insertion capability.

Flush-and-FFE also has consequences for research, development, and procurement. Major requirements include:

Lighter ground forces. Some progress has been made in this arena over the last few years, but much of the focus has been on trying to equip rapidly deployed American troops to fight in urban environments. Opponents of lighter forces have noted that while light infantry equipped with light armored vehicles may be fine for peacekeeping or counterinsurgency, they will not last long against armored forces. The number one priority must be to find the right balance between organic firepower and mobility for ground forces.

All-weather operational fire capability. The United States can deliver operational fires at night or in poor weather. But the challenge is introducing this capability across the joint force.

Saturation reconnaissance capabilities. Flush-and-FFE requires that an enemy is detected and destroyed *before* it can engage friendly ground forces. This implies reconnaissance systems with a genuine saturation capability. Continuous support is essential. Systems like the RQ-4 Global Hawk UAV can provide such coverage and will be needed in future operations.

Fire management. Flush demands not only fast reconnaissance, but flexible operational firepower. And this depends on fire management, the ability to put ordnance on the right target at the precise moment that an attack will achieve maximum effect. The U.S. military has the capability to send mobile target locations to strike aircraft in flight, and tests show that imagery can be sent with target coordinates. Unmanned weapons such as Tactical Tomahawk will have a similar real-time update capability in the near future.

Target management. Solving this problem is the greatest need and hinges on eliminating intelligence stovepipes and ensuring real-time re-tasking of operational fire assets. Current procedures involve extensive imagery analysis to support strike planning cells for the joint force air component commander, which plugs targets into the air tasking order for the next day. Such a process is not sufficiently responsive for new operational concepts. A new system is needed in which imagery (by saturation reconnaissance) is fed to fire controllers, who can quickly call on ready operational fires. Future campaigns will demand artillery-like timelines for operational fire support.

High-speed logistics. Rapid insertion of a ground force will demand a lot of logistical support, preferably not shackled to airfields. This may require special transport. Perhaps the true answer is an amphibious transport aircraft, capable of exploiting rivers and lakes as runways to deliver equipment where it is most needed.

Overload suppression of enemy air defense and electronic warfare capability. Logistics are quite likely to be conducted over an air bridge. The supply effort must be resilient in the face of enemy air defenses. In Kosovo, the Serbs adopted a fleet-in-being strategy with an air defense net, never turning the whole thing on at one time and thus preserving their assets to fight another day. It worked, so the U.S. military is likely to see this approach again. As a counter, an air and electronic blockade capability is needed. Instead of launching a handful of planes to fly defense suppression and jamming missions for the few minutes of an air strike, a joint task force will need platforms that can loiter over the battlefield until enemy defenses either turn radars on or fire surface-to-air missiles—and then instantly reply with jamming, antiradiation weapons, and fire missions. Unmanned combat aerial vehicles are likely to be part of this solution.

Air supremacy. Logistic and firepower support must not be vulnerable to air intercept. The future airspace is going to be hostile with sensitive netted defenses and highly lethal fighters. Flush-and-FFE puts a premium on dominating the skies.

Non-lethal weapons. Various non-lethal capabilities will be required to minimize collateral damage and civilian casualties. This will allow commanders to focus on military forces and reduce concerns over the civilian populace.

Redundant secure communications. To the Flush-and-FFE force, physical encirclement is far less threatening than interdicting communication. Without communications, timings will be disrupted and operations will become extremely high-risk.

Extraction. The Flush-and-FFE force must be able to disengage and withdraw as effectively as it is inserted. Under no circumstances can the force be left behind and susceptible to enemy capture.

Joint concept of operations. Ground forces can come from the Army or Marine Corps, depending on the circumstances. Firepower can be delivered by any service. Communications, terminology, and fire procedures must be transparent. Jointness is essential. No single service can be expected to provide all the capabilities to ensure effective employment. Not only is a multiservice approach crucial, but the integration of systems will have to be fully operational from the opening moment of the campaign.

Precision warfare is an inadequate basis for the future. Simply dropping more bombs will not solve the problem. Flush-and-FFE provides a new operational dimension that can stymie potential asymmetric responses such as the adapted fleet-in-being strategy. But to realize this concept, the U.S. military must make investments to place a more agile and lethal force on the battlefield.

Among Thieves

Poul Anderson

Editor's Introduction

I first read Poul Anderson in *Astounding Science Fiction* when I was in my last year of high school. I was, and still am, enormously impressed, and I continued to read him until, in 1962, the annual World Science Fiction Convention—WorldCon—was held in Seattle. I had never been to a WorldCon, but Poul Anderson and Robert Heinlein, my two favorite SF authors in all this world, were going to be there, and I might have a chance to meet them. I was then in an aerospace engineer/system analyst with the Boeing Company and I was involved with the space program, so I thought I might have something to say that one or both of them might be interested in. In those days, WorldCons were much smaller—there were about 300 attending that year—and Poul was not attending as Guest of Honor, so it was comparatively easy to meet him, and I ended up at a party with him stretching long into the night.

We became fast friends, and were until his death. We went sailing in the Straits of Juan de Fuca and the California Channel Islands together, went to conferences and AAAS meetings, and sang the old songs at numerous SF Conventions. He was one of the best friends I have ever had.

Poul's stories hold up well despite the enormous changes in technology since they were written. The nature of war has not changed, and

Poul understood its essence very well indeed. I first read *Among Thieves* when it came out in 1957, and I have remembered it ever since.

His Excellency M'Katze Unduma, Ambassador of the Terrestrial Federation to the Double Kingdom, was not accustomed to being kept waiting. But as the minutes dragged into an hour, anger faded before a chill deduction.

In this bleakly clock-bound society a short delay was bad manners, even if it were unintentional. But if you kept a man of rank cooling his heels for an entire sixty minutes, you offered him an unforgivable insult. Rusch was a barbarian, but he was too canny to humiliate Earth's representative without reason.

Which bore out everything that Terrestrial Intelligence had discovered. From a drunken junior officer, weeping in his cups because Old Earth, Civilization, was going to be attacked and the campus where he had once learned and loved would be scorched to ruin by his fire guns—to the battle plans and annotations thereon, which six men had died to smuggle out of the Royal War College—and now, this degradation of the ambassador himself—everything fitted.

The Margrave of Drakenstane had sold out Civilization.

Unduma shuddered, beneath the iridescent cloak, embroidered robe, and ostrich-plume headdress of his rank. He swept the antechamber with the eyes of a trapped animal.

This castle was ancient, dating back some eight hundred years to the first settlement of Norstad. The grim square massiveness of it, fused stone piled into a turreted mountain, was not much relieved by modern fittings. Tableservs, loungers, drapes, jewel mosaics, and biomurals only clashed with those fortress walls and ringing flagstones; fluorosheets did not light up all the dark corners, there was perpetual dusk up among the rafters where the old battle banners hung.

A dozen guards were posted around the room, in breastplate and plumed helmet but with very modern blast rifles. They were identical seven-foot blonds, and none of them moved at all, you couldn't even see them breathe. It was an unnerving sight for a Civilized man.

Unduma snubbed out his cigar, swore miserably to himself, and wished he had at least brought along a book.

The inner door opened on noiseless hinges and a shavepate officer emerged. He clicked his heels and bowed at Unduma. "His Lordship will be honored to receive you now, Excellency."

The ambassador throttled his anger, nodded, and stood up. He was a tall thin man, the relatively light skin and sharp features of Bantu stock predominant in him. Earth's emissaries were normally chosen to approximate a local ideal of beauty—hard to do for some of those weird little cultures scattered through the galaxy—and Norstad-Ostarik had been settled by a rather extreme Caucasoid type which had almost entirely emigrated from the home planet.

The aide showed him through the door and disappeared. Hans von Thoma Rusch, Margrave of Drakenstane, Lawman of the Western Folkmote, Hereditary Guardian of the White River Gates, et cetera, et cetera, et cetera, sat waiting behind a desk at the end of an enormous black-and-red tile floor. He had a book in his hands, and didn't close it till Unduma, sandals whispering on the great chessboard squares, had come near. Then he stood up and made a short ironic bow.

"How do you do, your excellency," he said. "I am sorry to be so late. Please sit." Such curtness was no apology at all, and both of them knew it.

Unduma lowered himself to a chair in front of the desk. He would not show temper, he thought, he was here for a greater purpose. His teeth clamped together.

"Thank you, Your Lordship," he said tonelessly. "I hope you will have time to talk with me in some detail. I have come on a matter of grave importance."

Rusch's right eyebrow tilted up, so that the archaic monocle he affected beneath it seemed in danger of falling out. He was a big man, stiffly and solidly built, yellow hair cropped to a wiry brush around the long skull, a scar puckering his left cheek. He wore Army uniform, the gray high-collared tunic and old-fashioned breeches and shiny boots of his planet; the trident and suns of a primary general; a sidearm, its handle worn smooth from much use. If ever the iron barbarian with the iron brain had an epitome, thought Unduma, here he sat!

"Well, your excellency," murmured Rusch—though the harsh Norron language did not lend itself to murmurs—"of course I'll be glad to hear you out. But after all, I've no standing in the Ministry, except as unofficial advisor, and–"

"Please." Unduma lifted a hand. "Must we keep up the fable? You not only speak for all the landed warlords—and the Nor-Samurai are still the most powerful single class in the Double Kingdom—but you have the General Staff in your pouch and, ah, you are well thought of by the royal family. I think I can talk directly to you."

Rusch did not smile, but neither did he trouble to deny what everyone knew, that he was the leader of the fighting aristocracy, lover of the widowed Queen Regent, virtual step-father of her eight-year-old son King Hjalmar—in a word, that he was the dictator. If he preferred to keep a small title and not have his name unnecessarily before the public, what difference did that make?

"I'll be glad to pass on whatever you wish to say to the proper authorities," he answered slowly. "Pipe." That was an order to his chair, which produced a lit briar for him.

Unduma felt appalled. This series of informalities was like one savage blow after another. Till now, in the three-hundred-year history of relations between Earth and the Double Kingdom, the Terrestrial ambassador had ranked everyone but God and the royal family.

No human planet, no matter how long sundered from the mainstream, no matter what strange ways it had wandered, failed to remember that Earth was Earth, the home of man and the heart of Civilization. No human planet—had Norstad-Ostarik, then, gone the way of Kolresh?

Biologically, no, thought Unduma with an inward shudder. Nor culturally—yet. But it shrieked at him, from every insolent movement and twist of words, that Rusch had made a political deal.

"Well?" said the Margrave.

Unduma cleared his throat, desperately, and leaned forward. "Your Lordship," he said, "my embassy cannot help taking notice of certain public statements, as well as certain military preparations and other matters of common knowledge–"

"And items your spies have dug up," drawled Rusch.

Unduma started. "My lord!"

"My good ambassador," grinned Rusch, "it was you who suggested a straight-forward talk. I know Earth has spies here. In any event, it's impossible to hide so large a business as the mobilization of two planets for war."

Unduma felt sweat trickle down his ribs.

"There is... you... your Ministry has only announced it is a... a defense measure," he stammered. "I had hoped... frankly, yes, till the last minute I hoped you... your people might see fit to join us against Kolresh."

There was a moment's quiet. So quiet, thought Unduma. A redness crept up Rusch's cheeks, the scar stood livid and his pale eyes were the coldest thing Unduma had ever seen.

Then, slowly, the Margrave got it out through his teeth:

"For a number of centuries, your excellency, our people hoped Earth might join them."

"What do you mean?" Unduma forgot all polished inanities. Rusch didn't seem to notice. He stood up and went to the window.

"Come here," he said. "Let me show you something."

The window was a modern inset of clear, invisible plastic, a broad sheet high in the castle's infamous Witch Tower. It looked out on a black sky, the sun was down and the glacial forty-hour darkness of northern Norstad was crawling toward midnight.

Stars glittered mercilessly keen in an emptiness which seemed like crystal, which seemed about to ring thinly in contracting anguish under the cold. Ostarik, the companion planet, stood low to the south, a gibbous moon of steely blue; it never moved in that sky, the two worlds forever faced each other, the windy white peaks of one glaring at the warm lazy seas of the other. Northward, a great curtain of aurora flapped halfway around the cragged horizon.

From this dizzy height, Unduma could see little of the town Drakenstane: a few high-peaked roofs and small glowing windows, lamps lonesome above frozen streets. There wasn't much to see anyhow—no big cities on either planet, only the small towns which had grown from scattered thorps, each clustered humbly about the manor of its lord. Beyond lay winter fields, climbing up the valley walls to the hard green blink of glaciers. It must be blowing out there, he saw snow-devils chase ghostly across the blue-tinged desolation.

Rusch spoke roughly: "Not much of a planet we've got here, is it? Out on the far end of nowhere, a thousand light-years from your precious Earth, and right in the middle of a glacial epoch. Have you ever wondered why we don't set up weather-control stations and give this world a decent climate?"

"Well," began Unduma, "of course, the exigencies of–"

"Of war." Rusch sent his hand upward in a chopping motion, to sweep around the alien constellations. Among them burned Polaris, less than thirty parsecs away, huge and cruelly bright. "We never had a chance. Every time we thought we could begin, there would be war, usually with Kolresh, and the labor and materials would have to go for that. Once, about two centuries back, we did actually get stations established, it was even beginning to warm up a little. Kolresh blasted them off the map.

"Norstad was settled eight hundred years ago. For seven of those centuries, we've had Kolresh at our throats. Do you wonder if we've grown tired?"

"My lord, I… I can sympathize," said Unduma awkwardly. "I am not ignorant of your heroic history. But it would seem to me… after all, Earth has also fought–"

"At a range of a thousand light-years!" jeered Rusch. "The forgotten war. A few underpaid patrolmen in obsolete rustbucket ships to defend unimportant outposts from sporadic Kolreshite raids. We live on their borders!"

"It would certainly appear, Your Lordship, that Kolresh is your natural enemy," said Unduma. "As indeed it is of all Civilization, of Homo sapiens himself. What I cannot credit are the, ah, the rumors of an, er, alliance–"

"And why shouldn't we?" snarled Rusch. "For seven hundred years we've held them at bay, while your precious so-called Civilization grew fat behind a wall of our dead young men. The temptation to recoup some of our losses by helping Kolresh conquer Earth is very strong!"

"You don't mean it!" The breath rushed from Unduma's lungs.

The other man's face was like carved bone. "Don't jump to conclusions," he answered. "I merely point out that from our side there's a good deal to be said for such a policy. Now if Earth is prepared to make a different policy worth our while—do you understand? Nothing is going to happen in the immediate future. You have time to think about it."

"I would have to… communicate with my government," whispered Unduma.

"Of course," said Rusch. His bootheels clacked on the floor as he went back to his desk. "I've had a memorandum prepared for you, an unofficial informal sort of protocol, points which his majesty's government would like to make the basis of negotiations with the Terrestrial Federation. Ah, here!" He picked up a bulky folio. "I suggest you take a leave of absence, your excellency, go home and show your superiors this, ah–"

"Ultimatum," said Unduma in a sick voice.

Rusch shrugged. "Call it what you will." His tone was empty and remote, as if he had already cut himself and his people out of Civilization.

As he accepted the folio, Unduma noticed the book beside it, the one Rusch had been reading: a local edition of Schakspier, badly printed on sleazy paper, but in the original Old Anglic. Odd thing for a barbarian dictator to read. But then, Rusch was a bit of an historical scholar, as well as an enthusiastic kayak racer, meteor polo player, chess champion, mountain climber, and… an all-around scoundrel!

* * *

Norstad lay in the grip of a ten-thousand-year winter, while Ostarik was a heaven of blue seas breaking on warm island sands. Nevertheless, because Ostarik harbored a peculiarly nasty plague virus, it remained an unattainable paradise in the sky till a bare two hundred fifty years ago. Then a research team from Earth got to work, found an effective vaccine, and saw a mountain carved into their likeness by the Norron folk.

It was through such means—and the sheer weight of example, the liberty and wealth and happiness of its people—that the Civilization centered on Earth had been propagating itself among colonies isolated for centuries. There were none which lacked reverence for Earth the Mother, Earth the Wise, Earth the Kindly: none but Kolresh, which had long ceased to be human.

Rusch's private speedster whipped him from the icicle walls of Festning Drakenstane to the rose gardens of Sorgenlos in an hour of hellbat haste across vacuum. But it was several hours more until he and the queen could get away from their courtiers and be alone.

They walked through geometric beds of smoldering blooms, under songbirds and fronded trees, while the copper spires of the little palace reached up to the evening star and the hours-long sunset of Ostarik blazed gold across great quiet waters. The island was no more than a royal retreat, but lately it had known agonies.

Queen Ingra stooped over a mutant rose, tiger-striped and a foot across; she plucked the petals from it and said, close to weeping: "But I liked Unduma. I don't want him to hate us."

"He's not a bad sort," agreed Rusch. He stood behind her in a black dress uniform with silver insignia, like a formal version of death.

"He's more than that, Hans. He stands for decency—Norstad froze our souls, and Ostarik hasn't thawed them. I thought Earth might–" Her voice trailed off. She was slender and dark, still young, and her folk came from the rainy dales of Norstad's equator, a farm race with gentler ways than the miners and fishermen and hunters of the red-haired ice ape who had bred Rusch. In her throat, the Norron language softened to a burring music; the Drakenstane men spat their words out rough-edged.

"Earth might what?" Rusch turned a moody gaze to the west. "Lavish more gifts on us? We were always proud of paying our own way."

"Oh, no," said Ingra wearily. "After all, we could trade with them, furs and minerals and so on, if ninety per cent of our production didn't have to go into defense. I only thought they might teach us how to be human."

"I had assumed we were still classified Homo sapiens," said Rusch in a parched tone.

"Oh, you know what I mean!" She turned on him, violet eyes suddenly aflare. "Sometimes I wonder if you're human, Margrave Hans von Thoma Rusch. I mean free, free to be something more than a robot, free to raise children knowing they won't have their lungs shoved out their mouths when a Kolreshite cruiser hulls one of our spaceships. What is our whole culture, Hans? A layer of brutalized farmhands and factory workers—serfs! A top crust of heel-clattering aristocrats who live for nothing but war. A little folk art, folk music, folk saga, full of blood and treachery. Where are our symphonies, novels, cathedrals, research laboratories… where are people who can say what they wish and make what they will of their lives and be happy?"

Rusch didn't answer for a moment. He looked at her, unblinking behind his monocle, till she dropped her gaze and twisted her hands together. Then he said only: "You exaggerate."

"Perhaps. It's still the basic truth." Rebellion rode in her voice. "It's what all the other worlds think of us."

"Even if the democratic assumption—that the eternal verities can be discovered by counting enough noses—were true," said Rusch, "you cannot repeal eight hundred years of history by decree."

"No. But you could work toward it," she said. "I think you're wrong in despising the common man, Hans… when was he ever given a chance, in this kingdom? We could make a beginning now, and Earth could send psychotechnic advisors, and in two or three generations–"

"What would Kolresh be doing while we experimented with forms of government?" he laughed.

"Always Kolresh." Her shoulders, slim behind the burning-red cloak, slumped. "Kolresh turned a hundred hopeful towns into radioactive craters and left the gnawed bones of children in the fields. If Kolresh killed my husband, like a score of kings before him, Kolresh blasted your family to ash, Hans, and scarred your face and your soul–" She whirled back on him, fists aloft, and almost screamed: "Do you want to make an ally of Kolresh?"

The Margrave took out his pipe and began filling it. The saffron sundown, reflected off the ocean to his face, gave him a metallic look.

"Well," he said, "we've been at peace with them for all of ten years now. Almost a record."

"Can't we find allies? Real ones? I'm sick of being a figurehead! I'd befriend Ahuramazda, New Mars, Lagrange—We could raise a crusade against Kolresh, wipe every last filthy one of them out of the universe!"

"Now who's a heel-clattering aristocrat?" grinned Rusch.

He lit his pipe and strolled toward the beach. She stood for an angry moment, then sighed and followed him.

"Do you think it hasn't been tried?" he said patiently. "For generations we've tried to build up a permanent alliance directed at Kolresh. What temporary ones we achieved have always fallen apart. Nobody loves us enough—and, since we've always taken the heaviest blows, nobody hates Kolresh enough."

He found a bench on the glistening edge of the strand, and sat down and looked across a steady march of surf, turned to molten gold by the low sun and the incandescent western clouds. Ingra joined him.

"I can't really blame the others for not liking us," she said in a small voice. "We are overmechanized and undercultured, arrogant, tactless, undemocratic, hardboiled... oh, yes. But their own self-interest–"

"They don't imagine it can happen to them," replied Rusch contemptuously. "And there are even pro-Kolresh elements, here and there." He raised his voice an octave: "Oh, my dear sir, my dear Margrave, what are you saying? Why, of course Kolresh would never attack us! They made a treaty never to attack us!"

Ingra sighed, forlornly. Rusch laid an arm across her shoulders. They sat for a while without speaking.

"Anyway," said the man finally, "Kolresh is too strong for any combination of powers in this part of the galaxy. We and they are the only ones with a military strength worth mentioning. Even Earth would have a hard time defeating them, and Earth, of course, will lean backward before undertaking a major war. She has too much to lose; it's so much more comfortable to regard the Kolreshite raids as mere piracies, and the skirmishes as 'police actions.' She just plain will not pay the stiff price of an army and a navy able to whip Kolresh and occupy the Kolreshite planets."

"And so it is to be war again." Ingra looked out in desolation across the sea.

"Maybe not," said Rusch. "Maybe a different kind of war, at least—no more black ships coming out of our sky."

He blew smoke for a while, as if gathering courage, then spoke in a quick, impersonal manner: "Look here. We Norrons are not a naval power. It's not in our tradition. Our navy has always been inadequate and always will be. But we can breed the toughest soldiers in the known galaxy, in unlimited numbers; we can condition them into fighting machines, and equip them with the most lethal weapons living flesh can wield.

"Kolresh, of course, is just the opposite. Space nomads, small population; they are able to destroy anything their guns can reach, but they can't dig in and hold it against us. For seven hundred years, we and they have been the Elephant and the Whale. Neither could ever win a real victory over the other; war became the normal state of affairs, peace a breathing spell. Because of the mutation, there will always be war, as long as one single Kolreshite lives. We can't kill them, we can't befriend them—all we can do is be bled white to stop them."

A wind sighed over the slow thunder on the beach. A line of sea birds crossed the sky, thin and black against glowing bronze.

"I know," said Ingra. "I know the history, and I know what you're leading up to. Kolresh will furnish transportation and naval escort; Norstad-Ostarik will furnish men. Between us, we may be able to take Earth."

"We will," said Rusch flatly. "Earth has grown plump and lazy. She can't possibly rearm enough in a few months to stop such a combination."

"And the entire galaxy will spit on our name."

"All the galaxy will lie open to conquest, once Earth has fallen."

"How long do you think we would last, riding the Kolresh tiger?"

"I have no illusions about them, my dear. But neither can I see any way to break this eternal deadlock. In a fluid situation, such as the collapse of Earth would produce, we might be able to create a navy as good as theirs. They've never yet given us a chance to build one, but perhaps–"

"Perhaps not! I doubt very much it was a meteor which wrecked my husband's ship, five years ago. I think Kolresh knew of his hopes, of the shipyard he wanted to start, and murdered him."

"It's probable," said Rusch.

"And you would league us with them." Ingra turned a colorless face on him. "I'm still the queen. I forbid any further consideration of this… this obscene alliance!"

Rusch sighed. "I was afraid of that, your highness."

For a moment he looked gray, tired. "You have a veto power, of course. But I don't think the Ministry would continue in office a regent who used it against the best interests of–"

She leaped to her feet. "You wouldn't!"

"Oh, you'd not be harmed," said Rusch with a crooked smile. "Not even deposed. You'd be in protective custody, shall we say. Of course, his majesty, your son, would have to be educated elsewhere, but if you wish–"

Her palm cracked on his face; he did not move or respond. "I… won't veto–" Ingra shook her head. Then her back grew stiff. "Your ship will be ready to take you home, my lord. I do not think we shall require your presence here again."

"As you will, your highness," murmured the dictator of the Double Kingdom.

* * *

Though he returned with a bitter word in his mouth, Unduma felt the joy, the biological rightness of being home, rise warm within him. He sat on a terrace under the mild sky of Earth, with the dear bright flow of the Zambezi River at his feet and the slim towers of Capital City rearing as far as he could see, each gracious, in its own green park. The people on the clean quiet streets wore airy blouses and colorful kilts—not the trousers for men, ankle-length skirts for women, which muffled the sad folk of Norstad. And there was educated conversation in the gentle Tierrans language, music from an open window, laughter on the verandas and children playing in the parks: freedom, law, and leisure.

The thought that this might be rubbed out of history, that the robots of Norstad and the snake-souled monsters of Kolresh might tramp between broken spires where starved Earthmen hid, was a tearing in Unduma.

He managed to lift his drink and lean back with the proper casual elegance. "No, sir," he said, "they are not bluffing."

Ngu Chilongo, Premier of the Federation Parliament, blinked unhappy eyes. He was a small grizzled man, and a wise man, but this lay beyond everything he had known in a long lifetime and he was slow to grasp it.

"But surely..." he began. "Surely this... this Rusch person is not insane. He cannot think that his two planets, with a population of, what is it, perhaps one billion, can overcome four billion Terrestrials!"

"There would also be several million Kolreshites to help him," reminded Unduma. "However, they would handle the naval end of it entirely and their navy is considerably stronger than ours. The Norron forces would be the ones which actually landed, to fight the air and ground battles. And out of those paltry one billion, Rusch can raise approximately one hundred million soldiers."

Chilongo's glass crashed to the terrace. "What!"

"It's true, sir." The third man present, Mustafa Lefarge, Minister of Defense, spoke in a miserable tone. "It's a question of every able-bodied citizen, male and female, being a trained member of the armed forces. In time of war, virtually everyone not in actual combat is directly contributing to some phase of the effort—a civilian economy virtually ceases to exist. They're used to getting along for years at a stretch with no comforts and a bare minimum of necessities." His voice grew sardonic. "By necessities, they mean things like food and ammunition—not, say, entertainment or cultural activity, as we assume."

"A hundred million," whispered Chilongo. He stared at his hands. "Why, that's ten times our total forces!"

"Which are ill-trained, ill-equipped, and ill-regarded by our own civilians," pointed out Lefarge bitterly.

"In short, sir," said Unduma, "while we could defeat either Kolresh or Norstad-Ostarik in all-out war—though with considerable difficulty—between them they can defeat us."

Chilongo shivered. Unduma felt a certain pity for him.

You had to get used to it in small doses, this fact which Civilization screened from Earth: that the depths of hell are found in the human soul. That no law of nature guards the upright innocent from malice.

"But they wouldn't dare!" protested the Premier. "Our friends… everywhere–"

"All the human-colonized galaxy will wring its hands and send stiff notes of protest," said Lefarge. "Then they'll pull the blankets back over their heads and assure themselves that now the big bad aggressor has been sated."

"This note of Rusch's." Chilongo seemed to be grabbing out after support while the world dropped from beneath his feet. Sweat glistened on his wrinkled brown forehead. "Their terms… surely we can make some agreement?"

"Their terms are impossible, as you'll see for yourself when you read," said Unduma flatly. "They want us to declare war on Kolresh, accept a joint command under Norron leadership, foot the bill and—no!"

"But if we have to fight anyway," began Chilongo, "it would seem better to have at least one ally."

"Has Earth changed that much since I was gone?" asked Unduma in astonishment. "Would our people really consent to this… this extortion… letting those hairy barbarians write our foreign policy for us—why, jumping into war, making the first declaration ourselves, it's unconstitutional! It's un-Civilized!"

Chilongo seemed to shrink a little. "No," he said. "No, I don't mean that. Of course it's impossible; better to be honestly defeated in battle. I only thought, perhaps we could bargain–"

"We can try," said Unduma skeptically, "but I never heard of Hans Rusch yielding an ångström without a pistol at his head."

Lefarge struck a cigar, inhaled deeply, and took another sip from his glass. "I hardly imagine an alliance with Kolresh would please his own people," he mused.

"Scarcely!" said Unduma. "But they'll accept it if they must."

"Oh? No chance for us to have him overthrown—assassinated, even?"

"Not to speak of. Let me explain. He's only a petty aristocrat by birth, but during the last war with Kolresh he gained high rank and a personal following of fanatically loyal young officers. For the past few years, since the king died, he's been the dictator. He's filled the key posts with his men: hard, able, and unquestioning. Everyone else is either admiring or cowed. Give him credit, he's no megalomaniac—he shuns publicity—but that simply divorces his power all the more from any responsibility. You can measure it by pointing out that everyone knows he will probably ally with Kolresh, and everyone has a nearly physical loathing of the idea—but there is not a word of criticism for Rusch himself. When he orders it, they will embark on Kolreshite ships to ruin the Earth they love."

"It could almost make you believe in the old myths," whispered Chilongo. "About the Devil incarnate."

"Well," said Unduma, "this sort of thing has happened before, you know."

"Hm-m-m?" Lefarge sat up.

Unduma smiled sadly. "Historical examples," he said. "They're of no practical value today, except for giving the cold consolation that we're not uniquely betrayed."

"What do you mean?" asked Chilongo.

"Well," said Unduma, "consider the astropolitics of the situation. Around Polaris and beyond lies Kolresh territory, where for a long time they sharpened their teeth preying on backward autochthones. At last they started expanding toward the richer human-settled planets. Norstad happened to lie directly on their path, so Norstad took the first blow—and stopped them.

"Since then, it's been seven hundred years of stalemated war. Oh, naturally Kolresh outflanks Norstad from time to time, seizes this planet in the galactic west and raids that one to the north, fights a war with one to the south and makes an alliance with one to the east. But it has never amounted to anything important. It can't, with Norstad astride the most direct line between the heart of Kolresh and the heart of Civilization. If Kolresh made a serious effort to bypass Norstad, the Norrons could—and would—disrupt everything with an attack in the rear.

"In short, despite the fact that interstellar space is three-dimensional and enormous, Norstad guards the northern marches of Civilization."

He paused for another sip. It was cool and subtle on his tongue, a benediction after the outworld rotgut.

"Hmmm, I never thought of it just that way," said Lefarge. "I assumed it was just a matter of barbarians fighting each other for the usual barbarian reasons."

"Oh, it is, I imagine," said Unduma, "but the result is that Norstad acts as the shield of Earth.

"Now if you examine early Terrestrial history—and Rusch, who has a remarkable knowledge of it, stimulated me to do so—you'll find that this is a common thing. A small semi-civilized state, out on the marches, holds off the enemy while the true civilization prospers behind it. Assyria warded Mesopotamia, Rome defended Greece, the Welsh border lords kept England safe, the Transoxanian Tartars were the shield of Persia, Prussia blocked the approaches to western Europe… oh, I could add a good many examples. In every instance, a somewhat backward people on the distant frontier of a civilization, receive the worst hammer-blows of the really alien races beyond, the wild men who would leave nothing standing if they could get at the protected cities of the inner society."

He paused for breath. "And so?" asked Chilongo.

"Well, of course suffering isn't good for people," shrugged Unduma. "It tends to make them rather nasty. The marchmen react to incessant war by becoming a warrior race, uncouth peasants with an absolute government of ruthless militarists. Nobody loves them, neither the outer savages nor the inner polite nations.

"And in the end, they're all too apt to turn inward. Their military skill and vigor need a more promising outlet than this grim business of always fighting off an enemy who always comes back and who has even less to steal than the sentry culture.

"So Assyria sacks Babylon; Rome conquers Greece; Percy rises against King Henry; Tamerlane overthrows Bajazet; Prussia clanks into France–"

"And Norstad-Ostarik falls on Earth," finished Lefarge.

"Exactly," said Unduma. "It's not even unprecedented for the border state to join hands with the very tribes it fought so long. Percy and Owen Glendower, for instance… though in that case, I imagine both parties were considerably more attractive than Hans Rusch or Klerak Belug."

"What are we going to do?" Chilongo whispered it toward the blue sky of Earth, from which no bombs had fallen for a thousand years.

Then he shook himself, jumped to his feet, and faced the other two. "I'm sorry, gentlemen. This has taken me rather by surprise, and I'll naturally require time to look at this Norron protocol and evaluate the other data. But if it turns out you're right"—he bowed urbanely—"as I'm sure it will–"

"Yes?" said Unduma in a tautening voice.

"Why, then, we appear to have some months, at least, before anything drastic happens. We can try to gain more time by negotiation. We do have the largest industrial complex in the known universe, and four billion people who have surely not had all their courage bred out of them. We'll build up our armed forces, and if those barbarians attack, we'll whip them back into their own kennels and kick them through the rear walls thereof!"

"I hoped you'd say that," breathed Unduma.

"I hope we'll be granted time," Lefarge scowled. "I assume Rusch is not a fool. We cannot rearm in anything less than a glare of publicity. When he learns of it, what's to prevent him from cementing the Kolresh alliance and attacking at once, before we're ready?"

"Their mutual suspiciousness ought to help," said Unduma. "I'll go back there, of course, and do what I can to stir up trouble between them."

He sat still for a moment, then added as if to himself: "Until we finish preparing, we have no resource but hope."

* * *

The Kolreshite mutation was a subtle thing. It did not show on the surface: physically, they were a handsome people, running to white skin and orange hair. Over the centuries, thousands of Norron spies had infiltrated them, and frequently gotten back alive; what made such work unusually difficult was not the normal hazards of impersonation, but an ingrained reluctance to practice cannibalism and worse.

The mutation was a psychic twist, probably originating in some obscure gene related to the endocrine system. It was extraordinarily hard to describe—every categorical statement about it had the usual quota of exceptions and qualifications. But one might, to a first approximation, call it extreme xenophobia. It is normal for Homo sapiens to be somewhat wary of outsiders till he has established their bona fides; it was normal for Homo Kolreshi to hate all outsiders, from first glimpse to final destruction.

Naturally, such an instinct produced a tendency to inbreeding, which lowered fertility, but systematic execution of the unfit had so far kept the stock vigorous. The instinct also led to strongarm rule within the nation; to nomadism, where a planet was only a base like the oasis of the ancient Bedouin, essential to life but rarely seen; to a cult of secrecy and cruelty, a religion of abominations; to an ultimate goal of conquering the accessible universe and wiping out all other races.

Of course, it was not so simple, not so blatant. Among themselves, the Kolreshites doubtless found a degree of tenderness and fidelity. Visiting on neutral planets—planets which it was not yet expedient to attack—they were very courteous and presented an account of defending themselves against one unprovoked aggression after another, which some found plausible. Even their enemies stood in awe of their personal heroism.

Nevertheless, few in the galaxy would have wept if the Kolreshites all died one rainy night.

Hans von Thoma Rusch brought his speedster to the great whaleback of the battleship. It lay a light-year from his sun, hidden by cold emptiness; the co-ordinates had been given him secretly, together with an invitation which was more like a summons.

He glided into the landing cradle, under the turrets of guns that could pound a moon apart, and let the mechanism suck him down below decks. When he stepped out into the high, coldly lit debarkation chamber, an honor guard in red presented arms and pipes twittered for him.

He walked slowly forward, a big man in black and silver, to meet his counterpart, Klerak Belug, the Overman of Kolresh, who waited rigid in a blood-colored tunic. The cabin bristled around him with secret police and guns.

Rusch clicked heels. "Good day, Your Dominance," he said. A faint echo followed his voice. For some unknown reason, this folk liked echoes and always built walls to resonate.

Belug, an aging giant who topped him by a head, raised shaggy brows. "Are you alone, Your Lordship?" he asked in atrociously accented Norron. "It was understood that you could bring a personal bodyguard."

Rusch shrugged. "I would have needed a personal dreadnought to be quite safe," he replied in fluent Kolra, "so I decided to trust your safe conduct. I assume you realize that any harm done to me means instant war with my kingdom."

The broad, winkled lion-face before him split into a grin. "My representatives did not misjudge you, Your Lordship. I think we can indeed do business. Come."

The Overman turned and led the way down a ramp toward the guts of the ship. Rusch followed, enclosed by guards and bayonets. He kept a hand on his own sidearm—not that it would do him much good, if matters came to that.

Events were approaching their climax, he thought in a cold layer of his brain. For more than a year now, negotiations had dragged on, hemmed in by the requirement of secrecy, weighted down by mutual suspicion. There were only two points of disagreement remaining, but discussion had been so thoroughly snagged on those that the two absolute rulers must meet to settle it personally. It was Belug who had issued the contemptuous invitation.

And he, Rusch, had come. Tonight, the old kings of Norstad wept worms in their graves.

The party entered a small, luxuriously chaired room.

There were the usual robots, for transcription and reference purposes, and there were guards, but Overman and Margrave were essentially alone.

Belug wheezed his bulk into a seat. "Smoke? Drink?"

"I have my own, thank you." Rusch took out his pipe and a hip flask.

"That is scarcely diplomatic," rumbled Belug.

Rusch laughed. "I'd always understood that Your Dominance had no use for the mannerisms of Civilization. I daresay we'd both like to finish our business as quickly as possible."

The Overman snapped his fingers. Someone glided up with wine in a glass. He sipped for a while before answering: "Yes. By all means. Let us reach an executive agreement now and wait for our hirelings to draw up a formal treaty. But it seems odd, sir, that after all these months of delay, you are suddenly so eager to complete the work."

"Not odd," said Rusch. "Earth is rearming at a considerable rate. She's had almost a year now. We can still whip her, but in another six months we'll no longer be able to; give her automated factories half a year beyond that, and she'll destroy us!"

"It must have been clear to you, sir, that after the Earth Ambassador—what's his name, Unduma—after he returned to your planets last year, he was doing all he could to gain time."

"Oh, yes," said Rusch. "Making offers to me, and then haggling over them, brewing trouble elsewhere to divert our attention; it was a gallant effort. But it didn't work. Frankly, Your Dominance, you've only yourself to blame for the delays. For example, your insistence that Earth be administered as Kolreshite territory–"

"My dear sir!" exploded Belug. "It was a talking point. Only a talking point. Any diplomatist would have understood. But you took six weeks to study it, then offered that preposterous counter-proposal that everything should revert to you, loot and territory both—why, if you had been truly willing to cooperate, we could have settled the terms in a month!"

"As you like, Your Dominance," said Rusch carelessly.

"It's all past now. There are only these questions of troop transport and prisoners, then we're in total agreement."

Klerak Belug narrowed his eyes and rubbed his chin with one outsize hand. "I do not comprehend," he said, "and neither do my naval officers. We have regular transports for your men, nothing extraordinary in the way of comfort, to be sure, but infinitely more suitable for so long a voyage than… than the naval units you insist we use. Don't you understand? A transport is for carrying men or cargo; a ship of the line is to fight or convoy. You do not mix the functions!"

"I do, Your Dominance," said Rusch. "As many of my soldiers as possible are going to travel on regular warships furnished by Kolresh, and there are going to be Double Kingdom naval personnel with them for liaison."

"But–" Belug's fist closed on his wineglass as if to splinter it. "Why?" he roared.

"My representatives have explained it a hundred times," said Rusch wearily. "To put it bluntly, I don't trust you. If… oh, let us say there should be disagreement between us while the armada is en route… well, a transport ship is easily replaced, after its convoy vessels have blown it up. The fighting craft of Kolresh are a better hostage for your good behavior." He struck a light to his pipe. "Naturally, you can't take our whole fifty-million-man expeditionary force on your battle wagons; but I want soldiers on every warship as well as in the transports."

Belug shook his ginger head. "No."

"Come now," said Rusch. "Your spies have been active enough on Norstad and Ostarik. Have you found any reason to doubt my intentions? Bearing in mind that an army the size of ours cannot be mobilized for a given operation without a great many people knowing it."

"Yes, yes," grumbled Belug. "Granted." He smiled, a sharp flash of teeth. "But the upper hand is mine, Your Lordship. I can wait indefinitely to attack Earth. You can't."

"Eh?" Rusch drew hard on his pipe.

"In the last analysis, even dictators rely on popular support. My Intelligence tells me you are rapidly losing yours. The queen has not spoken to you for a year, has she? And there are many Norrons whose first loyalty is to the Crown. As the thought of war with Earth seeps in, as men have time to comprehend how little they like the idea, time to see through your present anti-Terrestrial propaganda—they grow angry. Already they mutter about you in the beer halls and the officers' clubs, they whisper in ministry cloakrooms. My agents have heard.

"Your personal cadre of young key officers are the only ones left with unquestioning loyalty to you. Let discontent grow just a little more, let open revolt break out, and your followers will be hanged from the lamp posts.

"You can't delay much longer."

Rusch made no reply for a while. Then he sat up, his monocle glittering like a cold round window on winter.

"I can always call off this plan and resume the normal state of affairs," he snapped.

Belug flushed red. "War with Kolresh again? It would take you too long to shift gears—to reorganize."

"It would not. Our war college has prepared war plans for all foreseeable combinations of circumstances. If I cannot come to terms with you, another war plan goes into effect. And obviously, it will have popular enthusiasm behind it!"

He fixed the Overman with a fish-pale eye and continued in icy tones: "After all, Your Dominance, I would prefer to fight you. The only thing I would enjoy more would be to hunt you with hounds. Seven hundred years have shown that to be impossible. I opened negotiations to make the best of an evil bargain—since you cannot be conquered, it will pay better to join with you on a course of mutually profitable imperialism.

"But if your stubbornness prevents an agreement, I will declare war on you in the usual manner and be no worse off than I was. The choice is, therefore, yours."

Belug swallowed. Even his guards lost some of their blankness. One does not speak in that fashion across the negotiators' table.

Finally, only his lips stirring, he said: "Your frankness is appreciated, my lord. Some day I would like to discuss that aspect further. As for now, though… yes, I can see your point. I am prepared to admit some of your troops to our ships of the line." After another moment, still sitting like a stone idol, he added: "But this question of returning prisoners of war. We have never done it. I do not propose to begin."

"I do not propose to let the poor devils of Norrons rot any longer in your camps," said Rusch. "I have a pretty good idea of what goes on there. If we're to be allies, I'll want back such of my countrymen as are still alive."

"Not many are still sane," Belug told him deliberately. Rusch puffed smoke and made no reply.

"If I give in on the one item," said Belug, "I have a right to test your sincerity by the other. We keep our prisoners."

Rusch's own face had gone quite pale. The room grew altogether silent.

"Very well," he said after a long time. "Let it be so."

* * *

Without a word, Major Othkar Graaborg led his company into the black cruiser. The words came from the spaceport, where police held off a hooting, hissing, rock-throwing mob. It was the first time in history that Norron folk had stoned their own soldiers.

His men tramped stolidly behind him, up the gangway and through the corridors. Among the helmets and packs and weapons, racketing boots and clashing body armor, their faces were lost, they were an army without faces.

Graaborg followed a Kolreshite ensign, who kept looking back nervously at these hereditary foes, till they reached the bunkroom. It had been hastily converted from a storage hold, and was scant cramped comfort for a thousand men.

"All right, boys," he said when the door had closed on his guide. "Make yourselves at home."

They got busy, opening packs, spreading bedrolls on bunks. Immediately thereafter, they started to assemble heavy machine guns, howitzers, even a nuclear blaster.

"You, there!" The accented voice squawked indignantly from a loudspeaker in the wall. "I see that. I got video. You not put guns together here."

Graaborg looked up from his inspection of a live fission shell. "Obscenity you," he said pleasantly. "Who are you, anyway?"

"I executive officer. I tell captain."

"Go right ahead. My orders say that according to treaty, as long as we stay in our assigned part of the ship, we're under our own discipline. If your captain doesn't like it, let him come down here and talk to us." Graaborg ran a thumb along the edge of his bayonet. A wolfish chorus from his men underlined the invitation.

No one pressed the point. The cruiser lumbered into space, rendezvoused with her task force, and went into nonspatial drive. For several days, the Norron army contingent remained in its den, more patient with such stinking quarters than the Kolreshites could imagine anyone being. Nevertheless, no spaceman ventured in there; meals were fetched at the galley by Norron squads.

Graaborg alone wandered freely about the ship. He was joined by Commander von Brecca of Ostarik, the head of the Double Kingdom's naval liaison on this ship: a small band of officers and ratings, housed elsewhere. They conferred with the Kolreshite officers as the necessity arose, on routine problems, rehearsal of various operations to be performed when Earth was reached a month hence—but they did not mingle socially. This suited their hosts.

The fact is, the Kolreshites were rather frightened of them. A spaceman does not lack courage, but he is a gentleman among warriors. His ship either functions well, keeping him clean and comfortable, or it does not function at all and he dies quickly and mercifully. He fights with machines, at enormous ranges.

The ground soldier, muscle in mud, whose ultimate weapon is whetted steel in bare hands, has a different kind of toughness.

Two weeks after departure, Graaborg's wrist chronometer showed a certain hour. He was drilling his men in full combat rig, as he had been doing every "day" in spite of the narrow quarters.

"Ten-SHUN!" The order flowed through captains, lieutenants, and sergeants; the bulky mass of men crashed to stillness.

Major Graaborg put a small pocket amplifier to his lips. "All right, lads," he said casually, "assume gas masks, radiation shields, all gun squads to weapons. Now let's clean up this ship."

He himself blew down the wall with a grenade.

Being perhaps the most thoroughly trained soldiers in the universe, the Norron men paused for only one amazed second. Then they cheered, with death and Hell in their voices, and crowded at his heels.

Little resistance was met until Graaborg picked up von Brecca's naval command, the crucial ones, who could sail and fight the ship. The Kolreshites were too dumfounded. Thereafter the nomads rallied and fought gamely. Graaborg was handicapped by not having been able to give his men a battle plan. He split up his forces and trusted to the intelligence of the noncoms.

His faith was not misplaced, though the ship was in poor condition by the time the last Kolreshite had been machine-gunned.

Graaborg himself had used a bayonet, with vast satisfaction.

* * *

M'Katze Unduma entered the office in the Witch Tower. "You sent for me, Your Lordship?" he asked. His voice was as cold and bitter as the gale outside.

"Yes. Please be seated." Margrave Hans von Thoma Rusch looked tired. "I have some news for you."

"What news? You declared war on Earth two weeks ago. Your army can't have reached her yet." Unduma leaned over the desk. "Is it that you've found transportation to send me home?"

"Somewhat better news, your excellency." Rusch leaned over and tuned a telescreen. A background of clattering robots and frantically busy junior officers came into view.

Then a face entered the screen, young, and with more life in it than Unduma had ever before seen on this sullen planet. "Central Data headquarters—oh, yes, Your Lordship." Boyishly, against all rules: "We've got her! The *Bheoka* just called in… she's ours!"

"Hmm-mm-mmm. Good." Rusch glanced at Unduma. "*Bheoka* is the super-dreadnought accompanying Task Force Two. Carry on with the news."

"Yes, sir. She's already reducing the units we failed to capture. Admiral Sorrens estimates he'll control Force Two entirely in another hour. Bulletin just came in from Force Three. Admiral Gundrup was killed in the fighting, but Vice Admiral Smitt has assumed command and reports three-fourths of the ships are in our hands. He's delaying fire until he sees how it goes aboard the rest. Also–"

"Never mind," said Rusch. "I'll get the comprehensive report later. Remind Staff that for the next few hours all command decisions had better be made by officers on the spot. After that, when we see what we've got, broader tactics can be prepared. If some extreme emergency doesn't arise, it'll be a few hours before I can get over to HQ."

"Yes, sir. Sir, I… may I say–" So might the young Norron have addressed a god.

"All right, son, you've said it." Rusch turned off the screen and looked at Unduma. "Do you realize what's happening?"

The ambassador sat down; his knees seemed all at once to have melted. "What have you done?" It was like a stranger speaking.

"What I planned quite a few years ago," said the Margrave.

He reached into his desk and brought forth a bottle. "Here, your excellency. I think we could both use a swig. Authentic Terrestrial Scotch. I've saved it for this day."

But there was no glory leaping in him. It is often thus: you reach a dream and you only feel how tired you are.

Unduma let the liquid fire slide down his throat.

"You understand, don't you?" said Rusch. "For seven centuries, the Elephant and the Whale fought, without being able to get at each other's vitals. I made this alliance against Earth solely to get our men aboard their ships. But a really large operation like that can't be faked. It has to be genuine—the agreements, the preparations, the propaganda, everything. Only a handful of officers, men who could be trusted to… to infinity"—his voice cracked, and Unduma thought of the war prisoners sacrificed, of the hideous casualties in the steel corridors of spaceships, of Norron gunners destroying Kolreshite vessels and the survivors of the Norron detachments that failed to capture them—"only a few could be told, and then only at the last instant. For the rest, I relied on the quality of our troops. They're good lads, every one of them, and therefore adaptable. They're especially adaptable when suddenly told to fall on the men they'd most like to kill."

He tilted the bottle afresh. "It's proving expensive," he said in a slurred, hurried tone. "It will cost us as many casualties, no doubt, as ten years of ordinary war. But if I hadn't done it, there could have easily been another seven hundred years of war. Couldn't there? Couldn't there have been? As it is, we've already broken the spine of the Kolreshite fleet. She has plenty of ships yet, to be sure, she is still a menace, but she's crippled. I hope Earth will see fit to join us. Between them, Earth and Norstad-Ostarik can finish off Kolresh in a hurry. And after all, Kolresh did declare war on you, had every intention of destroying you. If you won't help, well, we can end it by ourselves, now that the fleet is broken. But I hope you'll join us."

"I don't know," said Unduma. He was still wobbling in a new cosmos. "We're not a… a hard people."

"You ought to be," said Rusch. "Hard enough, anyway, to win a voice for yourselves in what's going to happen around Polaris. Important frontier, Polaris."

"Yes," said Unduma slowly. "There is that. It won't cause any hosannahs in our streets, but… yes, I think we will continue the war, as your allies, if only to prevent you from massacring the Kolreshites. They can be rehabilitated, you know."

"I doubt that," grunted Rusch. "But it's a detail. At the very least, they'll never be allowed weapons again." He raised a sardonic brow. "I suppose we, too, can be rehabilitated, once you get your peace groups and psychotechs out here. No doubt you'll manage to demilitarize us and turn us into good plump democrats. All right, Unduma, send your Civilizing missionaries. But permit me to give thanks that I won't live to see their work completed!"

The Earthman nodded, rather coldly. You couldn't blame Rusch for treachery, callousness, and arrogance—he was what his history had made him—but he remained unpleasant company for a Civilized man. "I shall communicate with my government at once, Your Lordship, and recommend a provisional alliance, the terms to be settled later," he said. "I will report back to you as soon as… ah, where will you be?"

"How should I know?" Rusch got out of his chair.

The winter night howled at his back. "I have to convene the Ministry, and make a public telecast, and get over to Staff, and—no. The devil with it! If you need me inside the next few hours, I'll be at Sorgenlos on Ostarik. But the matter had better be urgent!"

"Among Thieves" Backstory, by Karen Anderson

Poul was a fan as well as a pro in the early years. He had been active in the Minneapolis Fantasy Society for some years before 1947 and his first sale, and on moving to Berkeley in 1953 for our marriage he naturally followed me into the Elves', Gnomes', and Little Men's Science Fiction, Chowder and Marching Society. (I'd come a few months earlier from Maryland myself and was active in the Washington Science Fiction Association.) We both threw ourselves into everything they did, including committee membership for the 1954 Worldcon and 1956 Westercon.

Poul had been so popular in the MFS that several members followed him to Berkeley; notably the Larsons and the Rostomilys. Their games were what started me on poker. We were very broke and we played for match-sticks at a tenth of a cent: I remember one lucky night when I won all of fourteen cents. That was when a copy of ASF could be had for a quarter.

But it was luck. I hadn't developed the skills, especially while drinking, that came later in the Eastbay poker circle that included Rog and Honey Phillips, Mick McComas, Reg Bretnor, and notably Tony Boucher. And I certainly hadn't learned by the convention when Poul and I were in that game with Hans...

What convention? Since the story that arose ran in ASF in 1957, I'd guess it was the '56 Westercon, at the Leamington in Oakland. At any rate, one night we'd gone drinking late from one fan party to another until we reached one where a small group including Hans were playing penny-ante poker amongst a lot of talking. I don't know how we first met Hans. Poul may have known him from past days, they might have struck up a correspondence through a magazine, or we may have met him first at this convention.

Penny-ante... we could stand that. We sat in. Besides playing, Poul and Hans did a lot of talking. Eventually I ran out of change and didn't want to break into a dollar, and Poul thought it was time for bed. The other players, including Hans, wanted us to stay. He wanted to give me something to go on with, but Poul demurred. So Hans offered us an exchange. "Put my name in a story," he said, "and I'll stake Karen to a dollar's worth of pennies."

And so it was agreed:

Poul was to write a story with him as a lead character who was a thoroughgoing villain. Moreover, his name was to be given in full: Hans von Thoma Rusch.

Hence Poul's idea of a villainous character.

Fly-By-Night

Larry Niven

Editor's Introduction

Larry Niven has been building the Known Space universe for fifty years. He started when science fiction was in a phase known as New Wave, concentrating on character development over story. Niven wrote imaginative hard science fiction, and his stories restored that to favor, largely with stories of Known Space. When our friend, editor, and publisher Jim Baen suggested that Larry open up Known Space for others to write stories in, he initially declined, then thought it over and allowed contributions to one period—the Man/Kzin Wars.

The Kzinti were already known to readers, and in fact had inspired the tiger warrior Kilrathi in the *Wing Commander* universe; the series took off, and a number of well known writers contributed to it. The series continues to this day.

The first of the Man/Kzin wars took place in a universe in which neither race had learned faster than light travel, and continued long after both Kzinti and humanity learned how to travel faster than light. There were four wars, each deadly, and each of which threatened the existence of the human race. This story takes place after the wars ended in a complicated treaty called the Covenant, but could start again at any time.

Most Kzinti owe allegiance to the Patriarchy. They have many customs. One is that they must earn a name; otherwise they have only designations. Fly-By-Night belongs to a very unusual group of Kzinti with a different history, but he is Kzin.

Human customs have also changed, as we developed near immortality and star drives. The galaxy is a big place, and there may even be ways to get outside it. The universe is very large. The Covenant allows Man and Kzin to live in peace.

The Covenant may not last forever. Perhaps there will be war.

The windows in *Odysseus* had been skylights. The doors had become hatches. I ran down the corridor looking at numbers. Seven days we'd been waiting for aliens to appear in the ship's lobby, and nothing!

Nothing until now. I felt good. Excited. I ran full tilt, not from urgency but because I *could*. I'd expected to reach Home as frozen meat in one of these Ice Class cargo modules.

I reached 36, stooped and punched the steward's bell. Just as the door swung down, I remembered not to grin.

A nightmare answered.

It looked like an octopus underwater, except for the vest. At the roots of five eel's-tail segments each four feet long, eyes looked up at me. We never see Jotoki often enough to get used to them. The limbs clung to a ladder that would cross the cabin ceiling when the gravity generators were on.

I said, "Legal Entity Paradoxical, I have urgent business with Legal Entity Fly-By-Night."

The Jotok started to say, "Business with my master–" when its master appeared below it on the ladder.

This was the nightmare I'd been expecting: five to six hundred pounds of orange and sienna fur, sienna commas marking the face, needle teeth just showing points, looking up at me out of a pit. Fly-By-Night wore a kind of rope vest, pockets all over it, and buttons or corks on the points of all ten of its finger claws.

"–is easily conducted in virtual fashion," the Jotok concluded.

What I'd been about to say went clean out of my head. I asked, "Why the buttons?"

Lips pulled back over a forest of carnivore teeth, LE Fly-By-Night demanded, "Who are you to question me?"

"Martin Wallace Graynor," I said. Conditioned reflex.

The reading I'd done suggested that a killing snarl would leave a Kzin mute, able to express himself only by violence. Indeed, his lips wanted to retract, and it turned his Interworld speech mushy. "LE Graynor, by what authority do *you* interrogate *me?*"

My antic humor ran away with me. I patted my pockets elaborately. "Got it somewhere–"

"Shall we look for it?"

"I–"

"Written on your liver?"

"I have an idea. I could stop asking impertinent questions?"

"A neat solution." Silently the door swung up.

Ring.

The Jotok may well have been posing himself between me and his enraged master, who was still wearing buttons on his claws, and *smiling.* I said, "Don't kill me. The Captain has dire need of you and wishes that you will come to the main workstation in all haste."

The Kzin leapt straight up with a half turn to get past the Jotok and pulled himself into the corridor. I did a pretty good backward jump myself.

Fly-By-Night asked, "Do you know why the Captain might make such a request?"

"I can guess. Haste *is* appropriate."

"Had you considered using the intercom, or virtual mail?"

"Captain Preiss may be afraid they can listen to our electronics."

"*They?*"

"Kzinti spacecraft. The Captain hopes you can identify them and help negotiate."

He stripped off the corks and dropped them in a pocket. His lips were all right now. "This main workstation, would it be a control room or bridge?"

"I'll guide you."

* * *

The Kzin was twisted over by some old injury. His balance was just a bit off. His furless pink tail lashed back and forth, for balance or for rage. The tip knocked both walls, *toc toc toc.* I'd be whipped bloody if I tried to walk beside him. I stayed ahead.

The Jotok trailed us well back from the tail. It wore a five-armhole vest with pockets. It used four limbs as legs. One it held stiff. I pictured a crippled Kzin buying a crippled Jotok… but Paradoxical had been agile enough climbing the ladder. I must have missed something.

The file on Jotoki said to call it *they*, but that just felt wrong.

"Piracy," the Kzin said, "would explain why everything is on its side."

"Yah. They burned out our thruster. The Captain had to spin us up with attitude jets."

"I don't know that weapon. Speak of the ship," he said. "One? Kzinti?"

"One ship popped up behind us and fired on us as it went past. It's a little smaller than *Odysseus.* Then a Kzin called us. Act of war, he said. Get the Captain to play that for you. He spoke Interworld… not as well as you." Fly-By-Night talked like he'd grown up around humans. Maybe he was from Fafnir. "The ship stopped twenty million miles distant and sent a boat. That's on its way here now. Our telescopes pick up markings in the Heroes' Tongue. We can't read them."

He said, "If we were traveling faster than light, we could not be intercepted. Did your Captain consider that?"

"Better you should ask, why are we *out* of hyperdrive? LE Fly-By-Night, there is an extensive star-building region between Fafnir and Home. Going through the Tao Gap in Einstein space is easier than going around and gives us a *wonderful* view, but we're *in* it now. Stuck. We can't send a hyperwave help call, we can't jump to hyperdrive, because there's too much mass around us."

"*Odysseus* has no weapons," the Kzin said.

"I don't have actual rank aboard *Odysseus.* I don't know what weapons we have." And I wouldn't tell a Kzin.

He said, "I learned that before I boarded. *Odysseus* is a modular cargo ship. Some of the modules are passenger cabins. Outbound Enterprises could mount weapons modules, but they never have. None of their other commuter ships are any better. The other ship, how is it armed?"

"Looks like an archaic Kzinti warship, *dis*armed. Gun ports slagged and polished flat. We haven't had a close look, but ships like that are all over known space since before I was born. Armed Kzinti wouldn't be allowed to land. Whatever took out our gravity motors isn't showing. It must be on the boat."

"Why is this corridor so long?"

Odysseus was a fat disk with motors and tanks in the center, a corridor around the rim, slots outboard to moor staterooms and cargo modules. That shape makes it easy to spin up if something goes wrong with the motors… which was still common enough a century ago, when *Odysseus* was built.

In the ship's map display I'd seen stateroom modules widely separated, so I'd hacked the passenger manifest. That led me to read up on Kzinti and Jotoki. The first secret to tourism is, *read everything.*

I said, "Some LE may have decided not to put a Kzin too close to human passengers. They put you two in a four-passenger suite and mounted it all the way around clockwise. My single and two doubles and the crew quarters and an autodoc are all widdershins." That put the aliens' module right next to the lobby, not far apart at all, but the same fool must have sealed off access from the aliens' suite. Despite the Covenants, some people *don't like* giving civil rights to Kzinti.

I'd best not say *that.* "We're the only other live passengers. The modules between are cargo, so these," I stamped on a door, "don't currently open on anything."

"If you are not a ship's officer," the Kzin asked, "what is your place on the bridge?"

I said, "Outbound Enterprises was getting ready to freeze me. Shashter cops pulled me out. They had questions regarding a murder."

"Have you killed?" His ears flicked out like little pink fans. I had his interest.

"I didn't kill Ander Smittarasheed. He took some cops down with him, and he'd killed an ARM agent. ARMs are–"

"United Nations police and war arm, Sol system, but their influence spreads throughout human space."

"Well, they couldn't question Smittarasheed, and I'd eaten dinner with him a few days earlier. I told them we met in Pacifica City at a water war game… anyway, I satisfied the law, they let me loose. I was just in time to board, and *way* too late to get myself frozen and into a cargo module. Outbound Enterprises upgraded me. Very generous.

"So Milcenta and Jenna—my mate and child are frozen in one of these," I stamped on a door, "and I'm up here, flying First Class at Ice Class expense. My cabin's a closet, so we must be expected to spend most of our time in the lobby. In here." I pushed through.

* * *

This trip there were two human crew, five human passengers and the aliens. The lobby would have been roomy for thrice that. Whorls of couches and tables covered a floor with considerable space above it for free fall dancing. That feature didn't generally get much use.

An observation dome exposed half the sky. It opened now on a tremendous view of the Nursery Nebula.

Under spin gravity, several booths and the workstations had rolled up a wall. There was a big airlock. The workstations were two desk-and-couch modules in the middle.

Hans and Hilde Van Zild were in one of the booths. Homers coming back from Fafnir, they held hands tightly and didn't talk. Recent events had them extremely twitchy. They were both over two hundred years old. I've known people in whom that didn't show, but in these it did.

Their kids were hovering around the workstations watching the Captain and First Officer at work, asking questions that weren't being answered.

We'd been given vac packs. More were distributed around the lobby and along the corridor. Most ships carry them. You wear it as a bulky fanny pack. If you pull a tab, or if it's armed and pressure drops to zero, it blows up into a refuge. Then you hope you can get into it and zip it shut before your blood boils.

Heidi Van Zild looked around. "Oh, *good!* You brought them!" The little girl snatched up two more vac packs, ran two steps toward us and froze.

The listing said Heidi was near forty. Her brother Nicolaus was thirty; the trip was his birthday present. Their parents must have had their development arrested. They looked the same age, ten years old or younger, bright smiles and sparkling eyes, hair cut identically in a golden cockatoo crest.

It's an attitude, a lifestyle. You put off children until that second century is running out. Now they're precious. They'll live forever. Let them take their time growing up. Keep them awhile longer. Keep them *pure*. Give them a *real* education. Any mistake you make as a parent, there will be time to correct that too. When you reverse the procedure and allow them to reach puberty they'll be better at it.

I know people who do that to kittens.

Some of a child's rash courage is ignorance. By thirty it's gone. The little girl's smile was a rictus. Aliens were here for her entertainment; she would not willingly miss any part of the adventure; but she just couldn't make herself approach the Kzin or his octopus servant. The boy hadn't even tried.

First Officer Quickpony finished what she'd been doing. She stood in haste, took the vacuum packs from Heidi and handed them to the aliens. "Fly-By-Night, thank you for coming. Thank you, Mart. You'd be Paradoxical?"

The woman's body language invited a handshake, but the Jotok didn't. "Yes, we are Paradoxical, greatly pleased to meet you."

The Kzin snarled a question in the Heroes' Tongue. Everybody's translators murmured in chorus, "Is *this* the bridge?"

Quickpony said, "Bridge and lobby, they're the same space. You didn't know? We wondered why you never came around."

"I was not told of this option. There is merit in the posture that one species should not see another eat or mate or use the recycle port. But, LE Quickpony, your security is a joke! Bridge and passengers and no barrier? When did you begin building ships this way?"

Captain Preiss looked up. He said, "Software flies us. I can override, but I can disable the override. Hijackers can't affect that."

"What of your current problem? Did you record the Kzin's demand?"

The Captain spoke a command.

A ghostly head and shoulders popped up on the holostage, pale orange but for two narrow, lofty black eyebrows. "I am *Mee-rowreet*. Call me Envoy. I speak for the Longest War."

My translator murmured, "*Mee-rowreet*, profession, manages livestock in a hunting park. *Longest War*, Kzin term for evolution."

The recording spoke Interworld, but with a strong accent and flat grammar. "We seek a fugitive. We have destroyed your gravity motors. We will board you following the Covenants sworn at Shasht at twenty-five naught five your dating. Obey, never interfere," the ghost head and voice grew blurred, "give us what we demand. You will all survive."

"The signal was fuzzed out by distance," Captain Preiss said. "The ship came up from behind and passed us at two hundred KPS relative, twenty minutes after we dropped out of hyperdrive. It's ahead of us by two light minutes, decelerated to match our speed."

I said, speaking low, "Please madam," alerting my pocket computer, "seek interstellar law, document Covenants of Shasht date twenty-five-oh-five. Run it."

Fly-By-Night looked up into the dome. "Your intruder?"

We were deep into the Nursery Nebula. All around were walls of tenuous interstellar dust lit from within. In murky secrecy, intersecting shock waves from old supernovae were collapsing the interstellar murk into hot whirlpools that would one day be stars and solar systems. Out of view below us, light pressure from something bright was blowing columns and streams of dust past us. It all took place in an environment tens of light years across. Furious action seemed frozen in time.

We had played at viewing the red whorl overhead. In IR you saw only the suns, paired protostars lit by gravitational collapse and the tritium flash, that had barely begun to burn. UV and X-ray showed violent flashes and plumes where planetesimals impacted, building planets. Neutrino radar showed structure forming within the new solar system.

We could not yet make out the point mass that would bend our course into the Tao Gap and out into free space. Turnpoint Star was a neutron star a few miles across, the core left by a supernova. But stare long enough and you could make out an arc on the sky, the shock wave from that same stellar explosion, broken by dust clouds collapsing into stars.

My seek system chimed. I listened to my wrist computer:

At the end of the Fourth Man-Kzin War, the Human Space Trade Alliance annexed Shasht and renamed the planet Fafnir, though the long, rocky, barren continent kept its Heroes' Tongue name. The Covenants of Shasht were negotiated then. We were to refrain from booting Kzinti citizens off Fafnir. An easy choice: they prefer the continent, whereas humans prefer the coral islands. They were already expanding an interstellar seafood industry into Patriarchy space.

In return, and having little choice, the Patriarch barred himself, his clan and all habitats under his command, all others to be considered outlaw, from various acts. Eating of human meat… willful destruction of habitats… biological weapons of certain types… killing of Legal Entities, that word defined by a *long* list of exclusions, a narrower definition than in most human laws.

Futz, I wasn't a Legal Entity! Or I wouldn't be if they learned who I was.

***

Quickpony projected a virtual lens on the dome. I'd finish listening later. The Kzinti ship and its boat, vastly magnified, showed black with the red whorl behind them. There was enough incident light to pick out some detail.

For a bare instant we had seen the intruder coming up behind us, just as our drive juddered and died and left us floating. After it slowed to a relative stop, a boat had detached. The approaching boat blocked off part of the ship. Gamma rays impacting their magnetic shields made two arcs of soft white glow. Ship and boat bore the same glowing markings.

The ship was moving just as we were, its drive off, falling through luminous murk toward Turnpoint Star at a tenth of lightspeed.

First Officer Helm said, "*Odysseus*'s security systems can deal with hijackers, but they're just not much use against an armed warship. Is that what we're seeing?"

"I see a small warship designed for espionage and hunting. I don't know the make. My knowledge is too old. The name reads *Sraff-zisht.*" My translator said, "Stealthy mating."

Fly-By-Night continued, "Captain, I can't see, are there magnetic moorings on *Sraff-zisht*?"

"No need. Those big magnets on the boat would lock to the ship's gamma ray shielding."

"The boat is armed, the ship is not? There is no bay for the boat? Understood. Leave the boat in hiding among asteroids. Land an unarmed converted cargo ship on any civilized world. Yes?"

"Speculative," Preiss said.

"Do you recognize the weapon?"

"No. I assume it's what burned out our thrusters… our gravity motors."

I sat and dialed a cappuccino. The Kzin joined me, dwarfing the booth. I dialed another with double milk, thinking he ought to try it.

The other passengers shrank back a little and waited. Any human being knows how to fear a Kzin.

I said, speaking low, "Pleasemadam, seek Heroes' Tongue references, stealthy mating, literal, no reference to rape." There had to be a way to narrow that further. I guessed: "Seek biological references only. Run it."

Fly-By-Night tasted the cappuccino.

Captain Preiss said, "Why would they be interested in *us?*"

"In me. The boat is close." Fly-By-Night sipped again. "Do you know of the *Angel's Pencil?*"

The Kzin was speaking Interworld as smoothly as if he'd grown up with the language. Some of us gaped. But his first words to me had been Interworld, after I startled and angered him… and he liked cappuccino.

Fly-By-Night said, "*Angel's Pencil* was a slowboat, one of Sol system's slower-than-light colony craft. Four hundred years ago, *Angel's Pencil* sent word of our coming. Sol system was given years to prepare. My ancestor Shadow contrived to board *Pencil* after allying himself with a human captive, Selena Guthlac. He and she joined their crew."

"That must have been one futz of a makeup job," Nicolaus Van Zild said.

"He had to stoop and keep his ears folded, and depilate! Whose story is this, boy?" Nicolaus grinned. The Kzin said, "*Angel's Pencil's* crew had already destroyed *Tracker.* They later destroyed *Gutting Claw,* the first and second kills of the First War, not bad for a ship with no intended armaments.

"*Pencil* was forced to pass through Patriarchy space before they found a world to settle. None of those ramscoop ships were easy to turn, and none were built for more than one voyage. We were ninety light years from Earth. One hundred and six years had passed on Earth."

I asked, "We?"

"*Gutting Claw's* Telepath, later named Shadow, is our first sire. *Pencil* rescued six females from the Admiral's harem. Our species have lived together on Sheathclaws for three hundred years. We remained cut off. Any message laser aimed at human space would pass through the Patriarchy. We spoke with no sapient species, we did not even know of faster-than-light travel, until...." Fly-By-Night looked up.

Stealthy-Mating's boat had arrived. We were looking directly into an obtrusively large electromagnetic weapon.

Nicolaus asked, "Can you read minds?"

"No, child. Some of us are good at guessing, but we don't have the drug. Where was I?" Fly-By-Night said, "They told me in the hospital after my first failed name quest. The universe had opened up–" He cut himself off as a furry face popped into hologram space in the workstation.

"I am Envoy. I speak for the Longest War. Terminate your spin. Open the airlock."

Captain Preiss nodded to Quickpony. Reaction motors whispered, slowing us.

Fly-By-Night spoke more rapidly. "Boarding seems imminent. You cannot protect me. Give me to them. If you live long enough to speak to your people, tell them that three grown males left Sheathclaws on our name quests. Half our genes derive from Shadow, from a telepath. The Patriarch needs telepaths. Now he will learn of a world peopled by *Gutting Claw's* telepath, none of whom has felt the addiction to sthondat lymph in three hundred years."

Gravity eased away until sideways thrust was all there was, and then that was gone too. *Odysseus's* outer airlock door opened.

The boat thumped into place against our hull. The older Van Zilds and I had our seat webs in place. The children floated, clinging to the arms of couches.

"They will have *my* genes. They will find Sheathclaws," Fly-By-Night concluded. "You will face my children in the next war, if they have their way."

Two big pressure-suit shapes left the boat on jet packs. One entered the lock. We heard it cycle. The other waited on the hull, to shoot the dome out if he saw resistance.

The inner door opened. The armored Kzin entered in a leap, up and into the dome where his companions could see him, a half turn to keep us in view. In his hand was a light that he aimed like a weapon. He was graceful as a fish.

I squinted to save my vision. The light played over every part of the lobby and workstation. What he saw must have been reassuring.

Envoy said, "We have demands. The Covenants will be followed where possible. All losses will be paid. Give us your passenger. He is in violation of our law. Fly-By-Night, is this Jotok your slave?"

"Yes."

"Fly-By-Night, Jotok, you must enter your vacuum packs. Fly-By-Night, give your w'tsai to Packer."

"W'tsai?" Fly-By-Night asked. "This? My *knife?*"

"Carefully."

Giving up his w'tsai was the ultimate surrender. If *I* knew that from my reading, surely a *Kzin* knew it. Three hundred years among humans.... Had they lost the tradition?

But Fly-By-Night was offering a silver knife-prong-spoon ten inches long and dark with tarnish.

A spoony? We ate with those! They matched several shapes of digits and were oversized for human hands. *Odysseus's* kitchen melted the silver to kill bacteria, then squirted it into molds for the next meal.

Packer took it, stared at it, then showed it to Envoy's hologram. Envoy snarled in the Heroes' Tongue. He wasn't buying it.

Our passenger answered in Interworld. "Yes, mine! See, here is my symbol," the sign of Outbound Enterprises, a winged craft black against a crescent world. "Fly by night!"

A laugh would be bad. I looked at the children. They looked solemn.

Of Packer's weapon I saw only a glare of light. But he held it on Fly-By-Night as if it *had* to fire something deadly, and he snarled a command and lashed out with his tail. Under the minor impact Fly-By-Night spun slowly so that Packer could examine him for more weapons.

He snarled again. Fly-By-Night and Paradoxical pulled tabs on vacuum packs. The packs popped into double-walled spheres. Held open by higher pressure, the collar on each refuge inflated like a pair of fat lips.

Fly-By-Night had trouble wriggling through the collar. Once inside he had room. These vacuum refuges would have held the whole Van Zild family. Paradoxical looked quite lost in his.

Envoy spoke. "Captain, you carry human passengers frozen in three cargo modules. Release these modules."

The world went gray.

I began to breath deep and hard, to hyperoxygenate, because I dared not faint.

Captain Preiss's hands hadn't moved. That was brave, but it wouldn't save anyone.

The elder Van Zilds buried their faces in each other's shoulders. The children were horrified and fascinated. They watched everything. Once I caught them looking at their parents in utter contempt.

Like them, I had been half enjoying the situation.

This would have been my last interstellar flight. Chance had me riding not as frozen cargo, but as a passenger, aware and entertained.

Flying the ship would have been more fun, of course.

Quickpony had suggested joining our cabins, as we were the obvious unpaired pair. I showed Quickpony videos displayed by the circuitry in my ring. Our lockstep ceremony. Jenna/Jeena just a year old. Sharrol/Milcenta not yet pregnant again; I should have updated while I could. *We are lockstepped, see, here is our ring.* Quickpony admired and dropped the subject.

And that left *what* for entertainment?

Kzinti hijackers!

I'd treated it like a game until *Stealthy-Mating* claimed my family. Bound into my couch by a crash web, I let my hand rest on the release while I considered what weapons I might have at hand.

Lips drawn back, fangs showing, Envoy's speech was turning mushy. "Examine the Covenants, Captain Preiss. They were never altered. We take only hostages. They will be returned unharmed when our needs are satisfied. Compensation will be paid for every cost incurred."

"What crime do you claim against Fly-By-Night?" Quickpony asked.

"His ancestor committed treason against his officers and the Patriarch. Penalties hold against his blood line forever. We may claim his life, but we will not. We value his blood line."

"Has *Fly-By-Night* committed a crime?"

"False identity. Purchase of a Jotok without entitlement. Trivia."

Dumb and happy Mart Graynor wasn't the type to carry weapons aboard a spacecraft. The recorded Covenant of 2505 might be the only weapon I had. I let it play in one ear. The old diplomatic language was murky....

Here it was. Hostages are to be returned in health if all conditions met, conditions not to be altered... costs to be assessed in time of peace at earliest....

Was I supposed to bet *lives* on *this?*

Heidi asked, "Do you eat human meat?"

Packer and the hologram both turned to the girl. Envoy said, "Hostages. I have *said.* The Covenants *say.* Kitten, we consider human meat to be... *whasht-meery*... unsafe. Captain Preiss, the modules we want are all addressed to Outbound on Home, yes? We will deliver them. Else we would face all the navies of human space."

Preiss said, "I have no such confidence."

Packer kicked down from the dome. He set his huge hands on the girl's waist and looked into her face. He still hadn't spoken.

Nicolaus screamed and leapt. As he came at the armored Kzin, Packer reached out and wrapped both children against his armored chest. They looked up through the bubble helmet into a Kzin's smile.

Nicolaus bared his teeth.

Envoy said, "Pause, Packer! Captain Preiss, think! Without gravity generators you must still fall around Turnpoint Star and into flat space. Hyperdrive will take you to the edge of Home system. Call for help to tow you the rest of the way. What other path have we? We might smash your hyperdrive and hyperwave and leave you to die here, silenced, but your absence at Home will set the law seeking us.

"This is the better risk, to violate no law unless we must. We take hostages. You must not call your authorities until you arrive near Home. We will transport our prisoner, then deliver your passengers."

Packer's arms were full of children: hampered. Preiss and Quickpony were on a hair trigger. I was unarmed, but if they moved, I would.

"Wait," Envoy said. Preiss still hadn't moved. "You carry stock from Shasht? Sea life?"

"Yes."

"I must speak with my leader. Lightspeed gap is two minutes each way. Do nothing threatening."

We heard Envoy yowling into his communicator. Then nothing.

My pocket computer *dinged*.

Everyone twitched, yelped or looked around. Heidi floated to the rim of my booth and listened over my shoulder.

Sea lions around the Earth's poles live in large communities built around one alpha male, many females and their pups, and several beta males that live around the edges of the herd. When the alpha male is otherwise occupied, an exile may rush in and mate hurriedly with a female and escape. Several species of Earth's mammals have adapted such a breeding strategy, as have life forms on Kzin and even many Kzinti clans. Biologists, particularly reproductive biologists, call them *sneaky-fuckers.*

I said, "Maybe there's a more polite term for the journals. Anyway, good name for a spy ship. Pleasemadam, seek Longest War plus Kzinti plus piracy, run it."

We waited.

When Hans Van Hild couldn't stand the silence any more, he said, "Heidi, Nicolaus, I'm sorry. We should have let you grow up."

"Hans!"

"*Yes*, Hilde, there was all the time in the world. Hilde, there's *never* time. Never a way to know."

Envoy spoke. "Release one of the modules for Outbound Enterprises and two addressed to Neptune's Empire. The passengers will be returned. Neptune's Empire will be recompensed for their stock."

Fish?

Captain Preiss's fingertips danced. Three cargo modules slowly rose out of the rim. I felt utterly helpless.

Packer left the children floating. He pushed Fly-By-Night's balloon toward the airlock.

I said, "Wait."

The armored Kzin turned. I squinted against the glare of his weapon. "We do not permit slavery aboard *Odysseus*," I said. "*Odysseus* belongs to the Human Space Trade Alliance. The Jotok stays."

"Who are you? Where derives your authority?" Envoy demanded.

"Martin Wallace Graynor. No authority, but the law–"

"Fly-By-Night purchased a Jotok and holds him as property. We hold Fly-By-Night as property. Local law crawls before interspecies covenants. The Jotok comes. Are you concerned for the well-being of the Jotok?"

I said, "Yes."

"You shall observe if he is mistreated. Enter a vacuum refuge now."

I caught Quickpony's horror. She spun around to search her screen display of the Covenants for some way to stop this. Packer pulled Fly-By-Night toward the airlock. He wasn't waiting.

Neither did I. I launched myself gently toward the refuge that held the Jotok.

It would not have occurred to me to hug the only available little girl before I disappeared into the Nursery Nebula. I launched, Heidi launched, and she was in my path, arms spread, bawling. I hugged her, let our momentum turn us, whispered something reassuring and let go. She drifted toward a wall, I toward the Jotok's bubble.

She'd put something bulky in my zip pocket.

I crawled through the collar into the Jotok's vacuum refuge and zipped the lips closed.

Packer pushed Fly-By-Night into the airlock, closed it, cycled it. His armored companion on the hull pulled the bubble into space. Packer came back for us and cycled us through.

***

Two bubbles floated outside *Odysseus*, slowly rotating, slowly diverging. Packer was still in *Odysseus.*

The boat jerked into motion. We watched as it maneuvered above one of the brick-shaped cargo modules attached to *Odysseus.* A pressure-armored Kzin stood below, guiding.

Nobody was coming after us.

The Jotok asked, "Martin, was that sane? What were you thinking?"

I said, "Pleasemadam, seek interspecies diplomacy plus Kzinti plus Longest War. Run it. Paradoxical, I was thinking of a rescue. I tried to bust you loose. You know more about Fly-By-Night than I could ever learn. I need what you can tell me."

"You have no authority to question us," the Jotok said, "unless you hold ARM authority."

I laughed harder than he would have expected. "I'm not an ARM. No authority at all. Do you want Fly-By-Night freed? Do you want your own freedom?"

"We had that! LE Graynor, when Fly-By-Night bought us from the orange underground market on Shasht, he swore to free us. On Sheathclaws chains of lakes run from mountains to sea. We would have bred in their lakes. All of the Jotoki populace of Sheathclaws would be our descendants. We have been robbed of our destiny!"

I asked, "Did Fly-By-Night take more slaves than just you?"

"No."

"Then who did you expect to mate with?"

"We are five! Jotoki grow like your eels, not sapient. Reach first maturity, seek each other, cluster in fives. Brains grow links. Reach second maturity, seek a lake, divide, breed and die, like your salmon. LE Mart, you yourselves are two minds joined by a structure called *corpus callosum*. Join is denser in Kzinti, that species has less redundancy, but still brain is two lobes. We are five lobes, narrow joins. Almost individuals cooperate, *Par-Rad-Doc-Sic-Cal, Doc* talks, *Par* walks, *Cal* for fine scale coordination. Almost five-lobe mind, sometimes lock in indecision. In trauma or in fresh water we may divide again. May join again to cluster differently, different person. You perceive?"

Futz, it was an interesting picture, but I'd never grasp what it was like to *be* Jotok. The point was that Paradoxical was a breeding population.

I asked, "Are you hungry? What do you eat?"

"Privately."

"Didn't Fly-By-Night see you eat?"

"Only once."

I'd put a handmeal in my pocket, but I wouldn't eat in front of Paradoxical after that. "Orange market?"

"An extensive market exists among the Shasht Kzinti. They trade intelligence, electronics, stolen goods and slaves. Shasht the continent is nearly lifeless. They seeded several lakes for our breeding and confinement, but without maintenance they die off. The trade could be stopped. Our lakes must show a different color from orbit. I surmise the law has no interest."

"You once held an interstellar empire–"

"My master tells me so. The slavers don't teach us. Properly speaking, they do not hold slaves at all. They hold fish ponds. When a purchaser wants a Jotok, five swimming forms are allowed to assemble. Our master is the first thing we see."

"Who chose your name?"

"My master. I am free and slave, many and one, land and sea dweller, a paradox."

"He really does think in Interworld, doesn't he? They must teach kzinti as a second language."

A magnetic grapple locked in place, and the first module came free.

My pocket computer *ding*ed. We listened:

Longest War, a political entity never named until after the Second War With Men, has since been claimed by many Kzinti groups. It may appear in connection with piracy, disappearing LEs or disappearing ships, but never an action against planets or a major offensive. Claim has been made, never proved, that Longest War are any Patriarch's servants whom the Patriarch must disclaim. We surmise also that the Longest War names any group who hope for the eye of the Patriarch. Events include 2399 Serpent Swarm, 2410 Kdat—

* * *

Fly-By-Night had drifted so far that he was hard to find, just a twinkle of lensed light as starfog glow passed behind his vac refuge. Why didn't they retrieve him? Was it really Fly-By-Night they wanted, or something else?

I watched *Stealthy-Mating*'s boat retrieve a second cargo module. They weren't being careful. Two of those boxes held only Fafnir's thousand varieties of fish, but the other... was in a quantum state. It held and did not hold Sharrol/Milcenta and Jenna/Jeena, until some observer could open the module.

In all the years I'd flown for Nakamura Lines, I had never seen a vac pack used. Light years from any world, miles from any ship, with nothing but clear plastic skin between me and the ravenous vacuum... it seemed a good time to look it over.

This wasn't the brand we'd carried. It was newer, or else a more expensive model.

Loops of tough ribbon hung everywhere: handholds. Air tank. A tube two liters in volume had popped out. Inner zip, outer zip: an airlock. We could be fed through that, or get rid of wastes... a matter I would not raise with Paradoxical just yet.

A light. A sleeve and glove taped against the wall, placed to reach the outer zip. Here was a valve... hmm... a valve ending in a little cone outside. Inside, a handle to aim it.

To any refugee there might come a moment when a jet is more important than breathing-air.

Not yet.

"Why would you want to rescue my master?" Paradoxical asked.

"They have my wife and daughter and unborn, one chance out of three. Two out of three they're still safe aboard *Odysseus*. Would you bet?"

"No Jotok knows his parent. Might you find another mate and generate more children?"

I didn't answer.

"How do you like your battle plan so far?"

I couldn't hear sarcasm, but I inferred it. I said, "I have a spare vac pack. So does Fly-By-Night. Did you see what he did? He triggered a pack on the wall. Kept his own. And Heidi passed me something."

"What did the girl give you?"

"Might be some kind of toy."

The Jotok said, "*Mee-rowreet* means make slaves and beasts go where can be killed. Not *Envoy. Whasht-meery* means infested or diseased, too rotted or parasitical for even a starving predator. Prey that dies too easily, opponent who exposes belly too soon, is suspect *whasht-meery*."

I waited for our spin to hide me from *Stealthy-Mating's* telescopes before I pulled Heidi's gift free.

It was foam plastic, light and bulky. A toy needle gun. If this was real, her parents.... Wait, now, Heidi was almost forty years old!

They wouldn't think quite like human adults, these children, but their brains were as big as they were going to get. Their parents *might* want them able to protect themselves... and if not, she and her brother had spent decades learning how to manipulate their parents.

I couldn't test it.

"Needle gun. Anaesthetic crystals," I told Paradoxical. "They won't get through armor. One wouldn't knock out a Kzin anyway. Better than nothing, though. Where is Fly-By-Night's w'tsai?"

"You saw."

"Paradoxical, we are in too much trouble to be playing children's games."

Paradoxical said nothing.

Stealthy-Mating's boat locked on to the third cargo module.

I said, "That was fun to watch, though. Giving Packer silverware!"

Paradoxical rotated to show me his mouth.

I saw a star of tentacles around a circle of lip enclosing five circles of tiny teeth in a pentagon. Something emerged from one circle of teeth. Paradoxical vomited up a long, narrow, padded mailing bag. I pulled it free, unzipped it, and had a yard of blade and handle.

The blade looked like dark steel. The light caught a minute ripple effect... but it was all wrong. To my fingertip's touch the ripple was just a picture. The blade weighed almost nothing. The weight was all in the handle.

In the end of the hilt was a small black enamel bat. Bats exist only on Earth and in the zoo on Jinx, but that ancient *Batman* symbol has gone to every human world. *Fly by night.*

Futz, I had to try it on *something.*

My lockstep ring had a silver case. That's a soft metal, but the blade only scratched it. I tested my thumb on the edge, gingerly. Blunt.

Customs change. A weapon can be purely ceremonial… but why make the handle so heavy? Why was Paradoxical watching me?

Because it was a puzzle.

Push the enamel bat. Nothing.

Wiggle the blade. Push it in, risk my fingers, feel it give. A Kzin could push *harder.* Nothing? Pull *out,* and my fingertips felt a hum. The look of the blade didn't change. Carefully now, don't touch the edge—

It sliced neatly through my lockstep ring, with a moment's white sputter as circuitry burned out. The cut edges of the classic silver band shone like little mirrors. There should have been *some* resistance.

A variable-knife is violently illegal: hair-fine wire in a magnetic field, all edge and no blade, thin enough to slice through walls and machinery. Often enough it hurts the wielder. When it's off it's all handle, and the handle is heavy: it holds the coiled wire and the mag generator.

This toy was similar, but with a blade of fixed length, harder to hide. More sporting. A groove around the edge housed the wire until magnets raised it for action.

The onyx bat was recessed now. I pushed and it popped out. The vibration stopped.

We had a weapon.

What was keeping Packer? They had the telepath, they had hostages, they had two modules of Fafnir seafood. What was left to do in there? Get on with it. I had a weapon!

"Wait before you use it. I know my master," the Jotok said. "He will take command of the boat. The larger ship is weaponless against it."

"Paradoxical, he'd be fighting at least three warriors trained in free fall. Don't forget the pilots. Four if we get as far as the ship."

"*Whasht-meery* may currently be on autopilot or remote. Possession of armor does not imply training. Fly-By-Night was a champion wrestler before he was injured. We fear you're right. But we must try!"

"Wrestler?"

"He tells me they fight with capped claws on Sheathclaws."

Somehow I was not reassured.

* * *

Packer emerged.

He and his companion jetted toward Fly-By-Night's bubble. They pulled Fly-By-Night toward the boat. Clamshell doors opened around the snout of the solenoid weapon. The three disappeared inside.

I safed and wrapped the w'tsai and gave it to the Jotok. He swallowed it, and the needler after it. He must have a straight gut… five straight guts, I thought, like fish or worms all merged at the head.

The two armored Kzinti came for us. They towed us toward the boat.

The boat was a thick lens, like *Odysseus* but smaller. The modules were anchored against one side. The other side was two transparent clamshell doors with the hollow solenoid sticking out between them.

The doors closed over us.

The interior had been arrayed around the solenoid weapon. There were lockers. Hatch in the floor, a smaller airlock. A kitchen wall big enough for a cruise ship, with a gaping intake hopper. A big box, detachable, with a door in it. I took that for a shower/washroom. I didn't see a hologram stage or a mass pointer.

Mechanisms fed into the base of the main weapon. A feed for projectiles? The thing didn't just burn out electronics, it was a linear accelerator too, a cannon.

Fly-By-Night's vacuum refuge had been wedged between the cannon and the wall. He watched us.

The doors came down and now our balloon was wedged next to his. Gravity came on. *Stealthy-Mating's* crew anchored us with a spray of glue, while a third Kzin watched from the horseshoe of a workstation. The two took their places beside him.

Four chairs; three Kzinti all in pressure suit armor. There was no separate cabin because they might have to work the cannon. It could have been worse.

They talked for a bit, mobile mouths snarling at each other inside fishbowl helmets. They fiddled with the controls. A sound of tigers fighting blasted from Paradoxical's backpack vest. My translator murmured, "So, Telepath! Welcome back to the Patriarch's service."

Two or three seconds of silence followed. In that moment *Odysseus* abruptly shrank to a toy and was gone. Disturbing eddies played through our bodies. The boat must be making twenty or thirty gravities, but it had good shielding. This was a warcraft.

Their prisoner decided to answer. "You honor me. You may call me LE Fly-By-Night."

"Honored you should be, Telepath, but your credit as a Legal Entity is forged, a telepath has no name, and Fly-By-Night is only a description, and in Interworld, too! Still you will command a harem before we do. We should envy you." That voice was Envoy's.

"Call me Fly-By-Night if I am expected to answer. Does the Patriarch still make addicts of any who show the talent?"

"You have hibernated for three centuries? We use advanced medical techniques in this age. Chemical mimic of sthondat lymph, six syllable name, more powerful, few side effects, diet additives to minimize those."

A second Kzin voice said, "You need not taste the drug yourself, Telepath, by my alpha officer's word."

"Only my poor kits, then. But how well do Kzinti keep each other's promises? I know that *Odysseus* was disabled despite all reassurance."

What? Fly-By-Night had *no way* to know that. *I* was only guessing, and his vac refuge had floated further from *Odysseus* than our own.

But Envoy said, "All follows the Covenants sworn with men at Shasht. That was my assurance, and it is good."

"Do those allow you to maroon a Legal Entity ship in deep space?"

"Summon them. Read them."

"My servant carries my computer and disk library."

The pilot tapped; we heard a *click*, then silence.

Paradoxical turned off his talker. "We can use this to speak to my master, but they may listen. What can you say that those oversized intestinal parasites may hear too?"

"Right now, nothing. Thrusters were yours first, weren't they? Called the *gravity planer*?"

"Jotoki created gravity planers, yes. Kzinti enslaved us and stole the design. Your folk stole it from Kzinti invaders."

"Is there anything you know about thrusters that they don't? Something that might help?"

"No. Idiot. What *we* learned of gravity motors, we learned from Kzinti!"

"Futz—"

"I had thought," Paradoxical said carefully, "that they would not keep their control room in vacuum."

"Their hostages are all frozen. Can't fight. Can't escape. Maybe they like that? Anything we try now would leave us dying in vacuum. How long can a Jotok stand vacuum?"

"A few seconds, then death."

"Humans can take a few minutes." Humans had, and survived. It was rare. "I might go blind first. Do you mind if I think out loud for a bit?"

"Do you talk to yourself to move messages across that narrow structure in your brain, the *corpus callosum?*"

"I have no idea." So I talked across my corpus callosum. "This is bad, but it could be worse. We might have been in a separate cargo hold, *still* in vacuum and locked out of a flight cabin."

"Rejoice."

"I thought I wouldn't have to worry about *Odysseus.* The ship's on a free fall course around Turnpoint Star, through the Gap and into free space. They still had hyperdrive and hyperwave and the attitude jets, last I saw. Attitude jets are just fusion reaction motors. That won't *take* them anywhere. Hyperdrive only works in flat space, so it won't get them *into* a solar system. They could still cross to Home system, call for help and get a tow. Two weeks?"

"Envoy said all of that to Captain Preiss. Wait—but—stop—didn't Envoy confess otherwise?"

"I heard. Futz." Fly-By-Night had done that very cleverly. But Envoy hadn't confessed; he had only insisted that he had not violated the Covenants.

"We'd better assume Packer shot up the control board. That would leave *Odysseus* as an inert box of hostages. Leave them falling. Retrieve them later."

Paradoxical said nothing.

"Next problem. Fly-By-Night can't get out of his refuge."

"Surely–"

"No, look, he can't *slash* his way out. He's got only his claws. He can *zip* it open. All the air spews out, and now he can try to get through the opening. He's too big. He'd die in vacuum while he was trying to wiggle free with those three laughing at him."

"Yes. Less than flexible, human and Kzinti. Are you small enough to get through the collar?"

"Yes." I was pretty sure. "Now, we can't warn Fly-By-Night. Any fighting, I'll have to start it. You're dead if I slash the refuge open, so I don't. I unzip it. Air pressure blows me out, *poof.* You zip it behind me *quick* so the refuge re-inflates. I'm in vacuum. I slash Fly-By-Night's refuge wide open and hand him the w'tsai. We're *both* fighting in vacuum against three Kzinti in pressure armor. How does it sound?"

"Beyond madness."

"There's no point anyway. If we could take the boat, we still couldn't break lightspeed, because the hyperdrive motor is on the ship. We'd die of old age here in the Nursery Nebula."

"You don't have a plan?"

I was still feeling it out. "The only way out has us waiting for these bandits to berth the boat to *Stealthy-Mating*. Maybe it's a good thing Fly-By-Night doesn't have his w'tsai. Kzinti self control is… there's a word—"

"Oxymoron. But my master integrates selves well."

"They'll have to move the cargo modules inside the ship. Can't leave them where they are, they're blocking the magnets, the docking points. Where does that leave us? Whatever we do, we want the ship *and* the boat. After they berth the boat, likely enough they'll *still* leave the cabin in vacuum and us in these bubbles."

"My kind can survive six days without food. Two without water."

* * *

Two of the Kzinti crew might have been asleep. The third wasn't doing much.

One presently stirred—Envoy, by his suit markings—got up and disappeared into the big box with a door in it. Fifteen minutes later he was back.

Wouldn't a shower or a toilet *have* to be under pressure?

I watched my alien companions and my alien enemies. I watched the magnificent pageant of stars being born. I thought and I read.

Read everything.

Covenants of 2505. Commentary, then and recent. Kzinti sociology. Revisions: what constitutes torture… loss of limbs and organs…

sensory deprivation. Violations. The right to a speedy trial, to speedy execution, not to be evaded. What is a Legal Entity....

Male Kzinti were LEs. A computer program was not. Heidi and Nicolaus were not, poor kids, but Kzin kittens weren't either; it was a matter of maturity as an evolved being. Jotoki and Kdat were LEs unless legitimately enslaved. Entities with forged identities were not. Ice Class passengers were LEs. Good! Was there a rule against lying to hostages? Of course not, but I looked.

Paradoxical produced a computer from his backpack and went to work. I didn't ask what he might be learning.

I did *not* see Fly-By-Night tearing at his prison. When I caught his eye, I clawed at my own bubble. Our captors might be reassured if they saw some sign of hysterics, of despair.

He didn't take the hint.

Maybe I had him all wrong.

A telepath born among the Kzinti will be found as a kzitten, conscripted, and addicted to chemicals to bring out his ability. Telepaths detect spies and traitors; they assist in jurisprudence; they gradually go crazy. Alien minds drive them crazy much faster.

If a telepath feels an opponent's pain, he can't easily fight for mates. For generations the Patriarchy discouraged their telepaths from breeding. Then, battling an alien enemy during the Man-Kzin Wars, they burned them out.

Probably Envoy had spoken truth: what the Kzinti wanted from Fly-By-Night was more telepaths.

They'd get the location of Sheathclaws out of him. After they had what they wanted, they'd give him a harem. They'd imprison him in luxury. Envoy had said they wouldn't force the drug on him; it might be true.

A Kzin might settle for that.

I could come blasting out of my plastic bottle, screaming my air away, w'tsai swinging... cut him loose, and find myself fighting alone while he blew up another bubble for himself.

Fly-By-Night floated quite still, very relaxed, ears folded. He might have been asleep. He might have been watching his three captors guide the boat toward *Stealthy-Mating.*

I watched their ears. Ears must make it hard for a Kzin to lie. Lying to a hologram might be easier… and they wouldn't have called him *Envoy* for nothing.

Flick-flick of ears, bass meeping, a touch on the controls. We were flying through a lethal intensity of gamma rays.

The Jotok's armtips rippled over his keyboard. His computer was a narrow strip of something stiff; he'd glued or velcroed it to the bubble wall. The keyboard and holoscreen were projections. I knew the make—"Paradoxical? Isn't that a Gates Quintillian?"

"Yes. Human-built computers are superior to Patriarchy makes."

"Oh, that explains the corks! Fly-By-Night's fingers are too big for the keyboard, so he puts corks on his nails!"

The Jotok said, "You are Beowulf Shaeffer."

I spasmed like an electrocuted frog, then turned to gawk at him. "How can you possibly…?"

How can you possibly think that a seven-foot-tall albino has lost fourteen inches of height and got himself curly black hair and a tan?

Hair dye and tannin secretion pills, and futz that, we had *real* trouble. I asked, "Have you spent three hours researching *me?*"

"You are the only ally at hand. I need to understand you better. You are wanted by the ARM for conspiracy abduction, four counts."

"Four?"

"Sharrol Janss, Carlos Wu, and two children. Feather Filip is your suspect co-conspirator. ARM interest seems to lie in the lost genes of Carlos Wu, but Sharrol Janss is alleged to be a flat phobe, hence would never have left Earth willingly."

"We all ran away together."

"My interest lies in your abilities, not your crimes. You were a civilian spacecraft pilot. Were you trained for agility in free fall?"

"Yes. Any emergency in a spacecraft, gravity is the first thing that goes."

"You're agile if you've escaped the ARM thus far. What has your reading gained you?"

"We have to live. We have to *win*."

"These would be good ideas–"

"No, you don't get it." The Jotok *had* to understand. "The Covenants of 2505 permit taking of hostages. They only put restrictions on their treatment. I've played those futzy documents three times through. *Odysseus* is hostages-in-a-box, live and frozen. They won't starve. Envoy can take Fly-By-Night anywhere he likes, however long it takes, then come back and release *Odysseus*. It's all in the Covenants."

"If anything goes wrong," Paradoxical said, "they would never come."

"No, it's worse than that! If everything goes *right* for them, there's *no good reason* to go back unless it's to fill the food lockers! The Covenants only apply when you're caught. My family is one hundred percent dead if we can't change that."

"Envoy's word may be good. No! Bad gamble. We should study the pot odds. Beowulf, have you evolved a plan?"

"I don't know enough."

The three crew were awake now, watching us as we watched them, though mostly they watched Fly-By-Night.

Paradoxical's talker burst to life. My translator said, "Tell us of the fight that injured you."

Fly-By-Night was slow to answer. "Sheathclaws folk are fond of hang gliding. We make much bigger hang gliders for Kzinti, and not so many of us fly. I was near grown, seeking a name. My intent was to fly from Blood Park to Touchdown, three hundred klicks along rocky shore and then inland, at night. Land in Offcentral Park. Startle humans into fits."

Packer snarled, "Startling humans is no fit way to earn a name!"

and the unnamed Kzin asked, "Wouldn't the thermals be different at night?"

Fly-By-Night said, "Very different."

"Your second naming quest brought you here," Envoy stated.

"Yes. I hoped that a scarred Kzin might pass among other Kzinti. Challenge would be less likely. Any lapse in knowledge might be due to head injury. I might pass more easily on a world part Kzin and part human, like Shasht-Fafnir."

"You dance lightly over an important matter. Who lifted you from your world?"

"Where would be my honor if I told you that?"

"Smugglers? Bandits? What species? You will give us that too, Nameless." We heard the click: communication severed.

One of the Kzinti stood up. Another slashed the vacuum, a mere wrist gesture, but the first sat down again. The stars wheeled… and something that was not a star came into view, brilliant in pure laser colors: *Stealthy-Mating's* riding lights.

I said, "We're about to dock. If anything happens, you keep the needle sprayer, I want the blade. Closing the zipper turns on the air, so don't lose *that*."

"No fear," said Paradoxical.

Gravity went away. We floated. The ships danced about each other. I would have docked less recklessly. I'm not a Kzin.

"*They* know too much about *us*," I said.

Paradoxical asked, "In what context?"

"They knew our manifest. They knew our position–"

"Finding another ship in interstellar space is not a thing they could plan, Beowulf."

"LE Graynor to you. Look at it this way," I said. "The only way to get here, falling through the Tao Gap in Einstein space, is to be going from Fafnir to Home. *Stealthy-Mating* got our route somehow. They started later with a faster ship. They might catch us approaching Home during deceleration… track our graviton wake… or snatch you and

Fly-By-Night after you got through Customs. They *could not possibly* have expected to find *Odysseus* here. Catching us here was a fluke, an opportunity. They grabbed it."

"As you say."

"I *like* it."

Paradoxical stared. "Do you? Why?"

"Clients, overlords, allies, any kind of support would have to be told that *Stealthy-Mating* is on route to Home. Any rendezvous with *Stealthy-Mating* is *at Home*. When could they change that? They're still headed for Home!"

"Very speculative."

"I know."

* * *

Stealthy-Mating's cargo bay was bigger than the boat's, under doors that opened like wings.

The boat released the cargo modules. Two Kzinti went out and began moving them. Envoy stayed behind. He watched the action in space, ignoring us.

"Not yet," Paradoxical said. I nodded. Fly-By-Night floated half curled up. He seemed to be asleep, but his ears kept flicking open like little fans.

I ate my handmeal. Paradoxical averted its eyes.

Packer and the nameless third crewperson set the modules moving one by one, and juggled them as they approached *Stealthy-Mating*. Waldo arms reached up to pull them into the bay and lock them. It seemed to take forever, but I'd have moved those masses one at a time. They were in a hurry. Rounding a point mass would scatter this loose stuff all across the sky.

Turnpoint Star must be near.

The cargo doors closed. *Stealthy-Mating* rotated, and the boat was pulled down against the hull. Now we were all one mass.

The hatch in the floor opened. Three Kzinti came through in pressure suits to join Envoy. The newcomer's chest and back showed a Kzinti snarl done in gaudy orange dots-and-commas. He spared a glance for me and Paradoxical, then turned to Fly-By-Night.

My translator said, "I am Meebrlee-Ritt."

"Futz!" Fly-By-Night exclaimed in Interworld.

"Your concern is noted. Yes, I am of the Patriarch's line. Your First Sire was *Gutting Claw's* Telepath, who betrayed the Patriarch Rrowrreet-Ritt and showed prey how to destroy his own ship!"

"And he never even went back for the ears. Then again, they were inside a hot plasma," Fly-By-Night said.

To Envoy Meebrlee-Ritt said, "This one was to be tamed."

Envoy cringed, ears flat. Even I could hear the change in his voice, the whine. "Dominant One, this fool crippled himself for a failed joke, and that joke was his name quest! A lesser male he must be, never mated. His arrogance is bluff or insanity, or else life among humans has made him quite alien! But let Tech give us air pressure, release the telepath, and the stench of your rage will cow him soon enough!"

"Let us expend less effort than that." Meebrlee-Ritt turned back to Fly-By-Night. "Telepath, your life may be taken by any who happen upon you."

"Did you need my consent for this?"

"No!"

"Or my First Sire's confession? *That* may be summoned by any Sheathclaws school program. Then what shall we discuss? Tell us how you gained your name."

"I was born to it, of course. Let us discuss your future."

"I have a future?"

"Your blood line may be forgiven. You may keep your slaves, such as they are, and a harem of my choosing–"

"*Yours?* Dominant One, forgive my interruption, please continue."

Even if he was familiar with human sarcasm, it wasn't likely Meebrlee-Ritt had been getting it from Kzinti! I'd read that Kzinti telepaths were flighty, not terribly bright. Meebrlee-Ritt spoke more slowly. "Yes, *my* choosing! You may live your life in honor and luxury, or you may die shredded by my hands."

"Meebrlee-Ritt, you would not expect me to leap into so difficult a decision. Will you bargain for the lives of your hostages?"

"Submissive and unarmed Humans." Meebrlee-Ritt sneezed his contempt. "But what would you bargain *with?* Your world?"

"Only my genes. Consider," said Fly-By-Night. In the Heroes' Tongue his speech was a long snarl, but the translation sounded placid enough. "He who is obeyed, who fights best, who *mates* is the alpha, the dominant one. You command that I mate? How will you persuade me that I am dominant? Submit to this one easy demand. Rescue my erstwhile hosts. Release them at Home."

"Why would I want you in rut? There are no females aboard *Sraff-zisht.* Packer, Envoy, you remain. Leave the gravity off. Tech, with me. Turnpoint Star is near."

Two Kzinti went through the hatch. Two took their seats. Their hands were idle. Now the boat rode *Stealthy-Mating* like a parasite.

I asked, "Can you see Turnpoint Star?"

"At point six kilometers across? You flatter me. I surmise it may be centered in that curdle," said Paradoxical.

Curdle? The tight little knot of glowing gas? I watched, watched... A red point blew up into a blue-white sun and I fell into it. The stars wheeled. The balloons that housed us rippled as if batted by invisible children. My body rippled too.

I'd been through this once, but much worse. I clutched the ribbon handholds in a death grip. I howled.

It only lasted seconds, but the terror remained. One of the Kzinti pointed at me and both laughed with their teeth showing.

Packer made his way to the shower/toilet. The other, Envoy, stayed at the board to look for tidal damage.

Fly-By-Night took handholds, subtly braced, ears spread wide. His eye caught mine. I said, "Paradoxical, *now.*"

Paradoxical splayed itself like a starfish across the wall of the refuge, just next to the opening. It disgorged the handle of the w'tsai.

I pulled the wrapped blade from its gullet and stripped off the casing. Clutched the blade against me, exhaled hard, opened the zipper all in one sweep, smooth as silk. Pressure popped me out into the cabin, straight toward Envoy's back, screaming to empty my lungs before they exploded.

Push the blade in, pull out, feel the vibration.

I had thought to recoil off a wall and slice Fly-By-Night free. That wasn't going to work. The Kzin diplomat saw my shadow and spun around. I slashed, aiming to behead him, and shifted the blade to catch the cat-quick sweep of his arm.

He swept his arm through the blade and whacked me under the jaw.

That was a powerful blow. I spun dizzily away. His arm spun too, cut along a diagonal plane, spraying blood. Attached, it would have ripped my head off.

I caught myself against a wall and leapt.

The seat web still held Envoy. His right arm and sleeve sprayed blood and air. Envoy smashed left-handed at the controls, then hit the seat web and leapt out of my path. I got his foot! The knife was hellishly sharp. My ears were roaring, my sight was going, but vacuum tore at him too as his arm and ankle jetted blood and air. His balance was all off as he recoiled from the dome and came at me. He kicked. My angle was wrong and he grazed me.

Spinning, spinning, I starfished out so that the wall caught my momentum and killed my spin. I tried to find him.

The roar continued. My sight was foggy… no. The *cabin* was thick with fog. Fly-By-Night clawed his refuge wall, which had gone slack. We had air!

I *still* didn't have time to free Fly-By-Night because—*there* he was! Envoy was back at the controls. I was braced to leap when a white glare blazed from his hand.

He had the gun.

I changed my jump. It took me behind the cannon. Two projectiles punched into the wall behind me. I swiped the w'tsai in a wide slash across Fly-By-Night's vacuum refuge, and continued falling toward the shower/toilet. Packer couldn't ignore Ragnarok forever.

The door opened in my face and I chopped vertically. Packer was naked. His left hand was on the doorlock so I changed the cut, right to catch his free hand, his claws and the iron w'tsai he'd been holding. He whacked me hard but the blow was blunt. I spun once and crashed into Envoy and slashed.

Glimpsed Paradoxical behind him, braced myself and slashed. Paradoxical was firing anaesthetic needles. The Kzin wasn't fighting back. I didn't see the implication so I kept slashing.

"Mart! LE Mart! *Beowulf!*"

I screamed, "*What?*" Disturbing me now could… what? Before me was a drifting cloud of blood and butchered meat. Paradoxical had stopped firing needles into it. Behind me, Fly-By-Night was on Packer's back, gnawing Packer's ear and fending off the hand that still had claws. Packer beat him with the blunted hand. They both looked trapped. Packer couldn't reach Fly-By-Night, but Fly-By-Night dared not let go.

I approached with care. Packer's arms were busy so he kicked to disembowel me. I chopped off what I could reach. Kick/slash, kick/slash. When he slowed down I killed him.

* * *

The air was thick with blood globules and red fog. We were *breathing* that futz. I got a cloth across my face. Fly-By-Night was snorting and sneezing. Paradoxical had placed meteor patches where Envoy had fired at me, but now he floated limp, maybe dying. I put him into the refuge and got him to zip it.

Fly-By-Night went to the controls. Minutes later we had gravity. All the scarlet goo settled to the floor and we could breathe.

I had gone berserk. Never happened before. My mind was slow coming back. Why was there air?

Air. Think now: I slashed Envoy's suit open. He pressurized the cabin to save his life. Paradoxical must have come out then. The Jotok's needles knocked Envoy out despite pressure armor… why? Because Paradoxical was putting needles into flesh wherever I'd slashed away the Kzin's armor. And of course I hadn't got around to releasing Fly-By-Night until late—

I safed the blade. "Fly-By-Night? I believe this is yours."

He took it gingerly. "No witness would have guessed *that*," he said, and handed it back. "Clean it in the waterfall."

Kzinti custom: *never* borrow a w'tsai. If you do, return it clean. Waterfall?

He meant the big box. The word was a joke. I found a big blanket made of sponge, a tube attached. When I wrapped it around the w'tsai, it left the blade clean. I tried it on myself. The blanket flooded me with soapy water, then clean water, then sucked me dry. Weird sensation, but I came out clean.

The toilet looked like an oval box of sand with foot- and handholds around it, though the sand stayed put. *Later.*

A pressure suit was splayed like a pelt against the wall for easy access.

There was a status display. I couldn't read the glowing dots-and-commas, but the display must have told Packer there was air outside, and he'd come charging out—

I was starting to shake.

I emerged from the waterfall box into a howling gale. The blood was all gone. I couldn't even smell it. Fly-By-Night and Paradoxical were at the kitchen wall feeding butchered meat into the hopper.

"This kind of thing must be normal on Patriarchy spacecraft," Fly-By-Night said cheerfully. "Holes in walls and machinery, blood and corpses everywhere, no problem. This hopper would hold a Great Dane… a big dog, Mart. The cleanup subsystem is running smooth as a human's arse." He saw my shivering. "You have killed. You should feed. Must your meat be cooked? I don't know that we have a heat source."

"Don't worry about it."

"I must. I'm *hungry!*" Fly-By-Night smiled widely. "You wouldn't like me *hungry*, would you?"

"Futz, no!" A Sheathclaws local joke? I tried to laugh. Shivering.

Paradoxical was crawling over one of the control panels. "This kitchen was mounted separately. It is of Shashter manufacture, perhaps connected to the orange underground. It will feed slaves." It tapped at a surface, and foamy green stuff spilled into a plastic bag. Pond scum? It tapped again and the wall generated a joint of bloody meat. Again: it hummed and disgorged a layered brick.

A handmeal. While Paradoxical sucked at his bag of pond scum and Fly-By-Night devoured hot raw meat, I ate *three* handmeal bricks. They never tasted that good again.

Fly-By-Night had kept Packer's ears, one intact and one chewed to a nub, and Envoy's, both intact. These last he offered to me. "Your kill. Mart, I can dispose of–"

I took them. *My* kill.

* * *

We had taken the boat. Now what?

Fly-By-Night said, "The hard part will be persuading Meebrlee-Ritt that all is well here." His voice changed. "*Dominant One, all runs as planned but for the Telepath's behavior. Cowed by fear, he has soiled his refuge. Shall we clean him? It might be a trick—*"

Funny stuff. I was still shivering. "That's *very* good, *I* can't tell the difference, but Meebrlee-Ritt or Tech might."

"Guide me."

"I can't find the hologram stage."

Fly-By-Night touched something. This whole side of the main weapon became a window, floor to dome, a gaudy panorama across orange veldt into a city of massive towers. We'd been prisoned on the other side of it.

I said, "Tanj! He'll see every hair follicle. All right, I'm still thrashing around here. We've got Packer's pressure suit. The orders were to leave the, ah, prisoners in vacuum and falling. Try this—

"Whenever Meebrlee-Ritt calls, Packer is in the waterfall room." We hadn't heard enough of Packer's speech to imitate Packer. "LE Fly-By-Night, you're Envoy. You're in the pressure suit, we're in the vac refuges. We'll have to change the markings on the suit. I'd say Envoy's move is to wait patiently for his Alpha Officer to call." I didn't like the taste of this. "He could catch us by surprise."

"I should find an excuse to call *him*."

"Anything goes wrong, you give us air *instantly*. Paradoxical, have you found an emergency air switch?"

"Here, then here."

"Stet. Envoy, what's wrong with your voice?"

"Nothing," said Fly-By-Night.

"Well, there had better be."

"Stet," the Kzin said. "And we don't really want vacuum, do we? Let's try this instead. I'm calling because we're *not* in vacuum, and my voice–"

And his tale was better than mine, so we worked on that.

We spent some time looking those controls over, trying a few things. We found air pressure, air mix, emergency pressure, cabin gravity, thrust. Weapons would be harder to test. There were controls you could hit by accident without killing anyone, and that was done with virtual control panels. Weapons and defenses were hard-wired buttons and switches, a few of them under locked cages, all stiff enough but big enough that I could turn them on or off by jabbing with the heel of my hand. Paradoxical couldn't move those at all.

The hologram wall was the telescope screen too. Paradoxical got us a magnificent view back into the Nursery Nebula, all curdles and whorls of colored light. It found *Odysseus* a light hour behind us, under spin and falling free with no sign of motive power, only a chain of corridor lights and the brighter glow of the lobby. That didn't tell us if they still had hyperdrive. They couldn't use it yet.

Ahead was nothing but distant stars. We had to be approaching flat space, where *Stealthy-Mating* could jump to hyperdrive.

Fly-By-Night was wearing Envoy's pressure suit. The markings were right. He would keep the right sleeve hidden. We had cut off part of the helmet, raggedly, to obscure his features. Now Fly-By-Night tapped at the kitchen wall. It disgorged a soft, squishy dark red organ that might have been a misshapen human liver. He smeared blood over his face and chest, then into the exposed ear.

My shivering became a violent shudder. Fly-By-Night looked at me in consternation. "LE Mart? What's wrong?"

"Too much killing."

"*Two* enemies is too much? Get out of camera view, then. Are we ready?"

"Go."

* * *

Meebrlee-Ritt snarled, "Envoy, this had best be of great interest. We prepare for hyperdrive."

"Dominant One, the timing was not of my choosing," Fly-By-Night bellowed into the oversized face. "The human attacked while Packer was visiting the waterfall. I have killed the telepath's slave–"

"The Jotok is dead?"

Fly-By-Night cringed. "No, Dominant One, no! Only the man. The Jotok lives. Telepath lives."

"The man is nothing. Telepath did not purchase the man! Is Packer functional, and are you?"

"Packer is well. I have nosebleeds, lost lung function, lost hearing. The man had a projectile weapon, a toy, but he damaged my helmet. I managed to put the cabin under pressure. Packer keeps watch on Telepath. Shall I return the cabin to vacuum? One of us would have to remain in the waterfall."

"Set Packer at the controls. What can he ruin while there is nothing to fly? Maintain free fall. You and Packer trained for free fall, our prisoner did not. You, Envoy, talk to Telepath. Learn what he desires, what he fears."

Cringe. "Dominant One, I shall."

Again we faced an electromagnetic cannon. I said, "Good. Really good."

Space around me winked like an eye. I caught it happening and looked at the floor. Fly-By-Night looked up, and blinked at the distortion. "Mart, I don't think… Mart? I'm blind."

Paradoxical was in a knot, his arms covering all of his eyes. I said, "Maybe you'd better take Paradoxical into the waterfall and stay there."

"Lost! Confused! Blind! How do you survive this?" the Jotok demanded. "How does any LE?"

"They'll close off the windows on *Stealthy-Mating*. I don't see how to do that in here. I guess they leave the boat empty if they can. Fly-By-Night, lower your head. Look at the floor. See the floor? Hold that pose."

"Stet."

I got under Paradoxical and he wrapped himself around me, sixty pounds of dry-skinned octopus. I eased him onto Fly-By-Night's shoulders until he clung. "Gravity's on, right? Just crawl on around to the waterfall. Don't look up."

* * *

In hyperdrive something unmeasurable happens to electromagnetic phenomena, or else to organs that perceive them: eyes, optic nerves, brains. A view of hyperspace is like being born sightless. The Blind Spot, we call it.

In the waterfall room we straightened up and stretched. Fly-By-Night said, "None of us can fly–"

"No. We're passengers. Stowaways. Relax and let them do the flying."

Paradoxical asked, "How can any mind guide a ship through this?"

I said, "There are species that can't tolerate it. Jotoki can't. Maybe puppeteers can't; most of them never leave their home system. Humans can use a mass pointer, a psionics device to find our way through hyperspace, as long as we don't look into the Blind Spot directly. But that's… well, part of a psionics device is the operator's mind. Computers don't see anything. Kzinti don't either. There are just a few freaky Kzinti who can steer through the Blind Spot directly."

"It is the Patriarch's blood line," Paradoxical said. "After the first War with Men, when Kzinti acquired hyperdrive, they learned that most cannot astrogate through hyperspace. Some few can. The Patriarch paid with names and worlds to add their sisters and daughters to his harem. Today the -Ritts can fly hyperspace."

Fly-By-Night said, "Really?"

"It happened long after your folk were cut off. LE Graynor, I did research on more than just you. Of course you see the implications? Meebrlee-Ritt must fly *Stealthy-Mating*. He will be under some strain, possibly at the edge of his sanity. Tech must see him in that embarrassing state. Envoy and Packer need not, and no prisoner should."

"He won't call?" I made it a question.

"He would not expect answer. Packer and Envoy would be hiding in the Waterfall," Paradoxical said.

That satisfied us. We were tired.

* * *

For three days we lived in the waterfall room.

One Kzin would have crowded the waterfall. With a man and a Jotok it was just that much more crowded. The smell of an angry Kzin made me jumpy. I couldn't sleep that way, so a high wind was kept blowing at all times.

We used the sandpatch in full view of each other. There were ribald comments. The Jotok was very neat. Fly-By-Night covered his dung using gloved feet and expected me to do the same, but it wasn't needed. The magnetized "sand" churned and swallowed it to the recycler.

Somebody had to come out for food. It developed that nobody could do that but me.

Our talk ranged widely.

Fly-By-Night never told us how he had reached Fafnir, nor even how he had passed through Customs. He did tell us something about the two who had come with him on their name quests. "I left Nazi Killer still collecting computer games and I set out to buy a Jotok–"

"What kind of name is 'Nazi Killer'?"

"It's an illicit game. Our First Sires' children found it among exercise programs in *Angel's Pencil.* Nazi Killer is very good at it. On Shasht he bought improved games and modern computers and waldo gloves for Kzinti hands, thinking these would earn his name."

"Go on."

"Maybe he's already home. Maybe the Longest War caught him. He would not have survived that. As for me, I wasted time searching out medical techniques to heal my broken bones. Such practice has only evolved for Humans! Kzinti still keep their scars. Customs differ.

"But Grass Burner got what *he* wanted. Kittens!"

"Kittens?"

"Yes, six unrelated, a breeding set. On Sheathclaws there are only photos and holos of cats, and a library of tales of fantasy cats, and children who offer a Kzin kit a ball of yarn just because it makes their parents angry, nobody remembers why. Cats will get Grass Burner his name. But we remember Jotoks too. Paradoxical, if two species are smarter than one, three should be smarter yet. You will earn my name, if we can reach Sheathclaws."

* * *

I snapped out of a nightmare calling, "What was its name? *Stealthy-Mating?*"

"We were asleep," Paradoxical complained. "We love sleeping in free fall. Back in the lake. But we wake and are still a self."

"Sorry." I almost remembered the dream. A lake of boiling blood, Kzinti patrolling the shores, wonderfully desirable human women in the shadows beyond. I was trying to swim. The pain was stunning, but I was afraid to come out.

Broken blood vessels were everywhere on my body. It hurt enough to ruin my sleep.

It was our fourth morning in hyperdrive.

"*Sraff-zisht,*" said Paradoxical.

"Pleasemadam, seek interstellar spacecraft local to Fafnir, Kzinti crew, Heroes' Tongue name *Sraff-zisht*. Run it."

Fly-By-Night woke. He said, "Make a meat run, Mart."

When I went out for food, we detached the shower blanket so I could use it as a shield. Meebrlee-Ritt had ordered us to keep the boat in free fall. No way could we be *really* sure he wouldn't call. I had to use handholds. I'd made a net for the food.

My computer dinged while we were eating. We listened:

Sraff-zisht was known to the Shasht markets, and to Wunderland too. The ship carried red meat to Fafnir and lifted seafood. At Wunderland, the reverse. Crew turnover was high. They usually stayed awhile. This trip they'd lifted light and early.

"*Sraff-zisht* is not armed," I said. I'd hoped it was true, but now I knew it. "Wunderland customs is careful. If they never found weapons or mounts for weapons, they're not there. We have the only gun!"

"*Yes!*" Fly-By-Night's fully extended claws could stop a man's heart without touching him.

"I've been thinking," I said. "There *has* to be a way to close that window strip. A Kzinti crew couldn't hide out in here! They'd tear each other to pieces!"

"I knew that. It's too small," Fly-By-Night said. "I just didn't want to go out there. Must we?"

* * *

We three crawled out with the shower blanket over us, Paradoxical riding the Kzin's shoulders. We stayed under the blanket while we worked the controls. I felt like a child working my flatscreen under the covers after being sent to bed.

There was a physical switch under a little cage with a code lock. None of us had the code. The switch wasn't a self-destruct. We *knew* where *that* was. When we ran out of options I sliced the cage away with the w'tsai, and flipped the switch.

From under the blanket we saw the shadows changing. I peeked out. Lost my vision, lost even my memory of vision… saw the edge of a shield crawling across the last edge of window.

If Meebrlee-Ritt had called earlier, he would have seen us flying hyperspace with windows open. Some mistakes you don't pay for.

"I think you'd better spend a lot of time in disguise and out here," I told Fly-By-Night. I saw his look: better not push that. "The next few days should be safe, but we should practice getting a disguise *on* you. Meebrlee-Ritt *will* call when he drops us out, and he *will* expect an answer, and he *will not* expect you to be still covered with blood and half hidden in ripped-up armor. Home is an eighteen-to-twenty-day trip, they said. Ten to go, call it three in hyperspace."

The Kzin was tearing into a joint of something big. "Keep talking."

"We need to paint you. Envoy had a smooth face, no markings except for what looked like black eyebrows swept *way* up."

"What would you use for paint?"

"The kitchens on some of the Nakamura Lines ships offered dyes for Easter eggs. Then again, they went bankrupt. What have we got? Let's check out the kitchen wall."

* * *

Choices aboard *Sraff-Zisht*'s boat were sparse. One variety of handmeal. Paradoxical's green sludge. Twenty settings for meat… "Fly-By-Night, what *are* these?"

"Ersatz prey for Kzin, I expect. Not bad, just strange."

They weren't all meat. We had two flavors of blood, and a milky fluid. "Artificial milk with diet supplements," Fly-By-Night told us, "to treat injuries and disease. Adults wouldn't normally use it."

Three kinds of fluids. Hot blood—"Is one of these human?"

"I wouldn't know, and that's one damn rude question to ask someone you have to live with–"

"I'm sorry. What I–"

"–for the next nine to ten days. If I get through this they'll *have* to give me a name."

"I just want to know if it coagulates."

Silence. Then, "Intelligent question. I've been on edge, Mart."

I didn't say that Kzinti are born that way. "Ease up on the cappuccino."

"We should thicken this. Mix it with something floury. Mush up a handmeal?"

The handmeals would pull apart. We worked with the layers: a meatlike pâté, a vegetable pâté, something cheesy, shells of hard bread. The bread stayed too lumpy: no good. Cheese thickened the blood. One kind of blood did coagulate. We got a thick fluid that could be spread into a Kzin's fur, then would get thicker. Milk lightened it enough, but then it stayed too liquid. More cheese?

We covered Fly-By-Night in patches everywhere, except his face, which we didn't want to mess up yet. This latest batch looked good where we'd spread it on his belly. I gave him a crossed fingers sign and worked it into his face.

Not bad.

We tried undiluted blood for the eyebrows. Too pale. Work on that later. I stood back and asked, "Paradoxical?"

"The marks weren't symmetrical," Paradoxical said. "You tend to want him to look too human. They're not eyebrows. Trail that right one almost straight up–"

"You'd better do it."

He worked. Presently he asked, "Mart?"

"Good!"

That was all Fly-By-Night needed. He set us spinning as he jumped for the waterfall room. We gave him an hour to dry off, because the shower blanket didn't suck up all the water, and another to calm down. Then we started over.

We couldn't get the eyebrows dark enough.

Finally we opened up a heating element in the kitchen wall, hoping we wouldn't ruin anything, and used it to char one of Envoy's ears. We used the carbon black to darken Fly-By-Night's "eyebrows". We bandaged one ear ("exploded by vacuum").

Then we made him wait, and talk.

"*Sraff-Zisht* drops back into Einstein space. There's an alarm. Do we get a few minutes? Does Meebrlee-Ritt clean himself up before he shows himself? Does he want a nap?"

"I was not raised among the children of the Patriarch."

"He's dropped us out in the inner comets. That's a huge volume. He's not worried about any stray ship that happens along, but he might want to check on *us*. He still has to worry that the big bad telepath has murdered his crew. Fly-By-Night? Massacres are routine?"

"Duels, I think, and riots. Mart, the cleanup routines are very simple. Any surviving crew with a surviving fingertip could set them going."

"Meebrlee-Ritt calls. Right away?"

"He will set a course into Home system. Then he will make himself gorgeous. Let the lesser Kzinti wait. Count on forty minutes after we enter Einstein space."

"Stet. He calls. Envoy's all cleaned up. Big bandage on his ear. What is Envoy's attitude?"

Fly-By-Night let his claws show. Kzinti do sweat, but we'd cooled the cabin. His makeup was holding. "Half mad from sensory deprivation, still he must cringe before his alpha officer. Repress rage. Meebrlee-Ritt might enjoy that. Change orders just to shake up Envoy."

"Cringe," I said.

Fly-By-Night pulled himself lower in his chair. His ear flattened, his lips were tight together.

"Good. Envoy wouldn't *eat* in front of Meebrlee-Ritt—?"

"No!"

"Our makeup wouldn't stand up to that."

"No, and I promise not to eat the makeup!"

We kept him talking. I wanted to see how long the makeup would last. I wanted to see if he'd go berserk. A little berserk wouldn't hurt, in a Kzin who had been trapped in sensory deprivation for many days, but *he had to remember his lines.*

Three hours later… *he* didn't crack, but the makeup started to. We sent him off to get clean.

* * *

Morning of the ninth day. I couldn't stop chattering.

"We'll drop out of hyperspace at the edge of Home system. We almost know when. There is only one speed in hyperdrive—" though Quantum Two hyperdrive is hugely faster and belongs to another species. "If *Sraff-Zisht* has been traveling straight toward Home at three days to the light year, we'll drop out in…."

"Four hours and ten minutes," Paradoxical said.

"The jigger factor is, *where* does Meebrlee-Ritt drop us out? Hyperdrive takes "flat" space. If there are masses around to distort space, the ship's gone. Pilots are *very* careful not to get too close to their target sun. *Really* cautious types aim *past* a target system. Just what kind of pilot is Meebrlee-Ritt?"

"Your pronunciation is terrible," said Fly-By-Night.

"Yah?"

"Crazy Kzin. Dive straight in. Cut the hyperdrive ten ce'meters short of death. Let our intrinsic velocity carry us straight into the system. Mart, that is the only decent bet."

"Where is Packer? *Still* in the waterfall?"

"I will think of something."

"I want you in makeup two hours early."

"No."

"H–"

"*Yes*, he might drop out short! But he might circle! He might enter Home system at an angle. Our window of opportunity has to slop over on either side." Fly-By-Night's speech was turning mushy again, lips pulling far back, *lots* of gleaming white teeth. Even Envoy didn't look like that. Sheathclaws must have good dental hygiene.

"We *know* that he will not show himself to Envoy and Packer after nine days of letting the Blind Spot drive him crazy and ruin his hairdo. You'll have forty minutes to make me beautiful."

"Stet. What next? Decelerate for a week. Drop the boat somewhere, maybe in the asteroids, without changing course. The Home asteroid belt is fairly narrow. Still plenty of room to hide.

"They'll bring you aboard ship just before they drop the boat. Because you're dangerous. Thanks." He'd dialed me up a handmeal. "You're dangerous, so they'll keep you in free fall until the last minute. If we're wrong about that, we could get caught by surprise."

"Bring me aboard? How does that work? Order Envoy and Packer to stun me and pull me through the small lock? We can't *do* that. They're dead!"

"Lure the technology officer in here."

"How?"

"Don't know. Make up a story. Let's just get through dropout without getting caught."

* * *

A recording spoke. A computer whined, "Dominant Ones, we have returned to the universe. Be patient for star positions."

Paradoxical started the curtain retracting. Stars emerged. I went to the kitchen wall and dialed up what we needed.

The recording reeled off a location based on some easy-to-find stars and clusters. Paradoxical listened intently. "Home system," he said. "We will use the telescope to find better data. Can you do that alone?"

"Yah." We'd practiced. In free fall we were still a bit awkward, but I mixed the basic makeup, then added char to a smaller batch. A bit more? *All?* Ready. "You do the eyebrows, Doc."

"First I will finish this task."

Fly-By-Night held still while I rubbed the food mixture into his facial fur.

Paradoxical said, "Graviton wake indicates a second ship."

"Damn!" Fly-By-Night snarled. I flung myself backward; my seat web caught me.

Paradoxical said, "We find nothing in visible light."

"Don't move your mouth. Aw, Fly-By-Night!" He was in an all-out snarl, trying to talk and failing. Drool made a darker runnel. "If Meebrlee-Ritt saw *that* he wouldn't care *who* you are. Lose the teeth!"

Fly-By-Night relaxed his mouth. "Your extra week is down the toilet, Mart. They're making pickup here and now."

The makeup had stayed liquid. "Paradoxical, give him eyebrows." I brushed out the drool, then settled myself out of camera range. They'd given me the flight controls. Paradoxical on astrogation, Fly-By-Night on weapons.

Paradoxical finished his makeup work and moved out of camera range, fifteen minutes ahead of schedule. I asked, "Shall we talk? Is this second ship just an escort?"

"No. Why make *Sraff-Zisht* conspicuous? Transfer the telepath, then move on to Home. This new ship runs to some outer world, or to Kzin itself–"

Meebrlee-Ritt popped up bigger than life and fourteen minutes early. He demanded, "Envoy, is the telepath well?"

Fly-By-Night flinched, then cringed. "The telepath is healthy, Dominant One. I judge that he is not in his right mind."

"The Jotok? Yourself? Where is Packer?"

"The Jotok amuses themself with a computer. I will welcome medical attention. Packer... Dominant One... Packer looked on hyperspace."

"He knew better!"

"Envoy" recoiled, then visibly pulled himself together. "Soon or late, Dominant One, every Hero looks. Wealth and a name and the infinite future, if he has sisters and daughters, if he can stay sane. Packer did not. He hides in the waterfall when I let him. Set him in a hunting park soon or he will die."

"That will not be our task. *Leap For Life* will be here soon. Transfer the boat to *Leap For Life*. Haste! No need to take Telepath out of his vacuum refuge. You will be relieved aboard *Leap For Life*."

"Yes, Dominant One!"

"Packer must guard the telepath. The telepath will attack now if ever."

"Yes–"

Meebrlee-Ritt was gone.

"We have it!" Paradoxical projected what he was seeing against the cannon casing.

Still distant, backlit by Apollo, Home's sun, a sphere nestled in a glowing arc of gamma ray shield, its black skin broken by holes and projections and tiny windows. Dots-and-commas script glowed brilliant orange. "We find heavy graviton wake. That ship is decelerating hard."

"Built in this century," Fly-By-Night said.

Sraff-Zisht dropped us free.

This was not much of a puzzle. I spun the boat, aimed at *Leap For Life* and said, "Shoot."

My hair stirred. Fly-By-Night's fur stood up and rippled. He said, "Done. Doc?"

"The graviton wake is gone. You burned out its thrusters."

I boosted us to put *Sraff-Zisht* between us and*Leap For Life*. *Leap For Life* had the weapons, after all. I set our gun on *Sraff-Zisht* and said, "Again."

"Done. I burned out something."

"Graviton flare," Paradoxical said, just as *Sraff-Zisht* vanished.

"Meebrlee-Ritt must have tried to return to hyperspace," Fly-By-Night said. "We burned out the hyperdrive. But he still has thrusters!"

I rotated the boat to focus the gun on the immobilized *Leap For Life*. "Projectiles. Shoot it to bits."

Fly-By-Night punched something. We heard the weapon adjusting, but he didn't shoot. "Why?"

I screamed, "They've got all the weapons, our *shield* has flown away–"

"Stet." The boat's lone weapon roared. It was right in the middle of the cabin/cargo hold. The noise was amazing. The boat recoiled; cabin gravity lurched to compensate. *Leap For Life* jittered and came apart in shreds.

"–And *they* don't have the hostages! And now it's one less tanj thing to worry about."

"Stet, stet, I understand!"

Paradoxical said, "We win."

We looked at the Jotok. He said, "We may report all that has happened, now, via laser broadcast to Home. We fly the boat to Home with our proofs. The law of Home can arrange to retrieve *Odysseus*. With his hyperdrive burned out, Meebrlee-Ritt is trapped in Home system. In the full glare of publicity he must follow the Covenants. He may trade his hostages for some other consideration such as amnesty, but they must be returned. Stet?"

"He's still got my family! But I think we can turn on the cabin futzy gravity now, *if* you don't mind–" I stopped because Meebrlee-Ritt, greatly magnified, was facing Fly-By-Night.

"Some such consideration," he mimicked us. "You look stupid, Telepath, covered with food. Only one consideration can capture my interest! Read my mind if you doubt me. Release my entourage and surrender! The hostages for yourself!"

Fly-By-Night's claw moved. No result showed except for Meebrlee-Ritt's widening eyes, but Fly-By-Night had given him a contracted view. He was seeing all of us.

"Lies! You killed my Heroes? Eeeeerg!" A hair-lifting snarl as Fly-By-Night lifted Packer's ear into view.

It seemed the right moment. I showed Envoy's surviving ear. "We had to use the other."

"Martin Wallace Graynor, you may buy back your hostages and your *life* by putting the telepath into my hands!"

It began to seem that Meebrlee-Ritt was mad. I asked, "Must I subdue him first?"

A killing gape was my answer. I asked, "And where would you take him then, with no hyperdrive?"

"Not your concern."

"We're going to call for help now. Over the next few hours all of Home system is going to know you're here. A civilized solar system *seethes* with telescopes. If you have allies in the asteroids, you can't go to them. You'd only point them out to the Home Rule."

"What if you never make that broadcast, LE Graynor? And I can…

thaw... sss." He'd had a notion. He stepped out of range. Ducked back and fisheyed the view to show his whole cabin. The other Kzin, Tech, was at his workstation, watching.

A wall slid away. Through an aperture ten yards wide I could see a much bigger cargo hold and all of *Odysseus'* cargo modules. Meebrlee-Ritt moved to one of them, opened a small panel and worked.

Back he came. "I can reset the temperature on these machines. I thought you might wonder, but soon I will show you thawed fish. You cannot do to me what you did to *Leap For Life* without killing my hostages too. If you broadcast any message at all, I will set the third module thawing, and then I will show you thawed dead hostages."

I was sweating.

The Kzin aristocrat said, "Telepath... Fly-By-Night. I will give you a better name. Your prowess has earned a name even as an enemy. What is it we ask of you? Take a harem. Raise your sons. See your daughters grow up in the Patriarch's household. A life in luxury buys survival for sixty-four Human citizens.

"Think, then. I can wait. A boat's life support is not the match for an interstellar spacecraft. Or else–"

The mass of an interstellar spacecraft jumped into our faces. Meebrlee-Ritt was tiny in its window, huge in the hologram stage. He threw his head back, a prolonged screech, mouth gaping as wide as my head. Forced his mouth to close so he could ask, "Graynor, have you ever flown a spacecraft? Do you think you have the skill to keep me from ramming you?"

I said, "Yes. Space is roomy, and the telepath is *our* hostage. Doc, can you give me a deep-radar view of yon privateer?"

Paradoxical guessed what I meant. The mass outside our dome went transparent.

I looked it over. Fuel... more fuel... a bulky hyperdrive design from the last century. Gravity and reaction motors were also big and bulky. Skimpy cargo space, smaller cabin, and that tiny box shape must be a waterfall room just like ours.

I spun the boat. "You say I can't shoot?"

Meebrlee-Ritt looked up. He must have been looking right into our gun. "Pitiful! Are all Humans natural liars?"

Fine-tuning my aim, I said, "There *is* a thing you should know about us. If you eat prey that is infested… *whasht-meery*… you may be very sick, but it doesn't kill off your whole blood line. Shoot," I said to Fly-By-Night.

The gun roared. Meebrlee-Ritt's image whirled around. The boat recoiled: gravity imbalances swirled through my belly. In our deep-radar view the waterfall room became a smudge.

Then *Sraff-Zisht* was gone.

"We track him," Paradoxical said. "Gravitons, heavily accelerating, *there*."

A green circle on the sky marked nothing but stars, but I spun the boat to put cross hairs on it. "Electromagnetic," I shouted.

"Am I a fool?" The gun grumbled, shifting from projectile mode.

"Graviton wake has stopped."

Fly-By-Night cried, "I have not fired!"

I said, "He's got no hyperdrive–"

Paradoxical said, "Gravitons again. He will ram."

The room wobbled, my hair stood on end, Fly-By-Night fluffed out into a great orange puffball. "Graviton wake is gone," Paradoxical said.

I moved us, thirty gee lateral, in case his aim was good.

Sraff-Zisht, falling free, shot past us by two miles. I chased it down. Whim made me zip in alongside the ship's main window. Grinning like a Kzin, I screamed, "*Now* wait us out!"

In the hologram stage Meebrlee-Ritt hugged a stack of meteor patches while he pulled on the waterfall door. Vacuum inside would be holding the door shut. We could see Tech working his way into a pressure suit, but Meebrlee-Ritt hadn't thought of that yet. He turned to look at the camera, at us.

He cringed. Down on his belly, face against the floor.

* * *

Paradoxical set our com laser on Home. The lightspeed lag was several hours, so I just recorded a help call and sent it. Then, as we'd have to anyway, we three began recording the whole story. That too would arrive before we could—

Tech stood above Meebrlee-Ritt, watching us. When Fly-By-Night looked at him he cringed, a formal crouch. "Dominant One, what must we do?"

Fly-By-Night said, "Tend your cargo until you can be towed to Home. Meebrlee-Ritt also I place in your charge. Set your screamer and riding lights so you can be found. You may dream of betrayal but do not act on it. You know what I am. I know *who* you are. Your hostages' lives will buy back your blood line."

He'd said he couldn't read minds. I still think he was bluffing.

* * *

A century ago the new settlers had towed a moonlet from elsewhere into geosynchronous orbit around Home. Home Base was where incoming ships arrived, and where they thawed incoming Ice Class passengers.

The law had business with hijackers and kidnappers; we were their witnesses. We were the system's ongoing news item. Media and the law were waiting.

I rapidly judged that anchorpersons and lawyers were my fate. The only way to hide myself was to sign with Home Information Megacorp and talk my head off until my public grew bored.

If Carlos Wu tried to call me they'd be all over him too. I hoped he'd wait it out.

Sraff-Zisht we had left falling free through Home system. Home Rule had to round up ships to bring it back. It took two of their own, four Belters acting for the bounty, and one shared by a media consortium, all added to the several they sent after *Odysseus*. It took them ten days to fetch *Sraff-Zisht.*

For eight days I was questioned by Home and ARM law and by LE Wilyama Warbelow, the anchor from Home Information Megacorp. Wilyama was wired for multisensory recording. What she experienced became immortal.

They'd wanted to do that to me too.

The last two days were a lull: I was able to more or less relax, and even see a bit of the captured asteroid. Then *Sraff-Zisht* descended on tethers to Home Base, and everybody wanted Mart Graynor.

The Covenant against sensory deprivation as torture has long since been interpreted as the right to immediate trial, not just for Kzinti but throughout human space, a right not to be evaded. I was to submit to questioning by Meebrlee-Ritt and Tech, by their lawyer and everyone else's, while two hundred Ice Class passengers were being thawed elsewhere.

I screamed my head off. Cameras were on me. The law bent. When they thawed the hostages from *Sraff-Zisht*, I was there to watch.

My wife and child weren't there.

And we all trooped off to use the holo wall in the Outbound Enterprises Boardroom.

* * *

The prisoners watched us from an unknown site. It didn't seem likely they'd burst through the holo wall and rip us apart. Meebrlee-Ritt's eyes glittered. Tech only watched.

The court had restricted the factions to one advocate each. All I had for company was Sirhan, a police commissioner from Home Rule; Judge Anita Dee; Handel, an ARM lawyer; Barrister, a runty Kzin assigned as advocate to the prisoners; a hugely impressive peach-colored Kzin, Rasht-Myowr, representing the Patriarch; and anchor-person Wilyama Warbelow.

Judge Dee told the prisoners, "You are each and together accused of violations of local law in two systems, and of the Covenants of 2505 at Fafnir. A jury will observe and decide your fate."

LE Barrister spoke quickly. "You may not be compelled to speak nor to answer questions, and I advise against it. I am to speak for you. Your trial will take at least two days, as we must wait for other witnesses, but no more than four."

Meebrlee-Ritt spoke in Interworld. "We have followed the Covenants. Where are my accusers?"

They all looked at me. I said, "Gone."

"*Gone?*"

"Fly-By-Night and Paradoxical and I signed an exclusive contract with Home Information Megacorp for our stories. I got a room here at Home Base. They'll thaw my family here, after all." If they lived. "We gave LE Warbelow," I nodded; the anchor bowed, "an hour's interview, presumed to be the first of many. Fly-By-Night and Paradoxical transferred to a shuttle. The Patriarch's representative missed them by just under two hours. They disappeared on the way down."

I've never doubted their destination. Fly-By-Night had come to Home for a reason, and he never told anyone *who* had arranged their transport to Fafnir.

The law raised hell, as if it were my fault they were gone. Warbelow was more sensible. She paid for my room, a major expense that wasn't in our contract. With the aliens gone, I had become the only game in town.

They got their money's worth. Mart Graynor emerged as a braggart with a Fafnir accent I'd practiced for two years. I played the same tune while various lawyers and law programs questioned me. I hoped nobody would see a resemblance to documentaries once made by Beowulf Shaeffer.

Barrister reacted theatrically. "Gone! Then who is witness against my clients?"

"We have LE Graynor, Your Honor," Sirhan said, speaking for Home Rule, "and the crew and passengers of *Odysseus* will be called. *Odysseus* had to be chased down in the Kuiper belt, the inner comets, and towed in. They'll be arriving tomorrow. Any of the passengers might press claims against the defendants."

The judge said, "LE Handel?"

The ARM rep said, "The Longest War threatens all of human space. We need what these Kzinti can tell us. They've violated the Covenants. There was clear intent to store humans as reserves of meat–"

"This was a local act against Homer citizens!" Sirhan said.

Judge Dee gestured at the big peach-colored Kzin, who said, "The Patriarch's claim is that Meebrlee-Ritt is no relative of his and has no claim to his name. I am to take possession–"

Meebrlee-Ritt leapt at us, bounced back from the wall—or from a projection screen—and screamed something prolonged. "I flew outside the universe!" said my translator. "Who can do that? Only the -Ritt! In cowardice does the Patriarch disclaim my part in the Long War!" He changed to Interworld: "LE Graynor knows! Nine days through hyperspace, accurately to my rendezvous!"

"I am to take possession and return him for trial, and his Heroes too. I must have Envoy's ear, Graynor, unless you can establish a kill. Nameless One, Kzinti elsewhere can fly hyperspace. Females of your line may have reached the -Ritt harem. What of it?"

"My line descends from the Patriarch! I violated no Covenants!"

The runty Kzin who was his advocate caught the judge's eye. He too spoke Interworld. "To properly represent the prisoners I must speak with them alone and encrypted to learn their wishes. I expect we will fight extradition. Rasht-Myowr," a prolonged howl in the Heroes' Tongue. The Patriarch's designate was trying to loom over him. My translator buzzed static. The runty Kzin waited, staring him down, until the big one stepped back and sheathed his claws.

Barrister said, "Violation of the Covenants would hold my clients here in any case, but none of these claims has any force until we can interview the victims. *Odysseus*'s crew and passengers will reach Home Base tomorrow. We have only LE Graynor's word for any of this."

"He's telling the truth, though," I said.

Meebrlee-Ritt barked his triumph. The ARM man said, "Futz, Graynor!"

Judge Dee asked, "LE Graynor, are you familiar with the Covenants of 2505?"

"As much as any law program. I've examined them half to death."

"Did you see violations?"

"No. I thought I had. I thought Packer must have shot out *Odysseus*'s hyperdrive and hyperwave, putting *Odysseus* at unacceptable risk, but it's clear he didn't. Hyperdrive got *Odysseus* into the Home comets, and they called ahead via hyperwave as soon as they were out of the Nursery Nebula."

Rasht-Myowr's tail slashed across and back. "Your other claims fail! The false lord is mine, and his remaining Hero too!"

I said, "Whatever these two learned about Fly-By-Night and his companions, taking them back to Kzin for trial gives that to the Patriarch. On that basis I'd keep them, if I was an ARM."

"But you're testifying," the ARM said bitterly, "that they didn't violate the Covenants."

"Yah."

"Mine! And Envoy's ear," Rasht-Myowr said. "His *one* ear. Did you kill him?"

"I killed them both. Do you need details? Fly-By-Night was trapped in his vac refuge. We'd just rounded Turnpoint Star and Envoy was flying the ship. Difficult work, took his full attention. Back turned, free fall, crash web holding him in his chair. I had Fly-By-Night's w'tsai." The police had already confiscated that. "He would have killed me if he'd released his crash web in time."

"He would have killed you anyway! Why would you keep only one ear?"

For an instant I couldn't speak at all. Then I barely remembered my accent. "I h-heated one for charcoal to paint Fly-By-Night. Packer was wrestling Fly-By-Night when I chopped *him* up, so Fly-By-Night got the ear. He chewed off the other one. They stole, *you* stole my wife and child and unborn, my *harem*, you *whasht-meery* son of a stray cat! I still haven't seen them alive. I memorized those *whasht-meery* Covenants. They only forbid my killing your relatives!"

"Duel me then!" Meebrlee-Ritt shouted. "Back turned, crash web locked, free fall, my claws only, *blunt* them if you like–"

"Barrister, you will silence your client or I will," the judge said.

"–And you armed! Prove you can do this!"

Meebrlee-Ritt, I decided, was trying to commit suicide. He didn't want to go with Rasht-Myowr. Let the Patriarch have him, I owed him nothing.

Almost nothing.

I said, "Judge Dee, if you'll let me ask a few questions, I may solve some problems here."

"You came to *be* questioned, LE Graynor. What did you have in mind?"

"Rasht-Myowr, if a violation of the Covenants can't be proved, then I take it these prisoners are yours–"

Judge Dee interposed. "They may be assessed for *substantial* property violations, Graynor. Rescue costs. A passenger ship turned to junk!"

"I will pay the costs," Rasht-Myowr said.

I asked, "You'll take them back to your Patriarch?"

"Yah."

"They'll be tried publicly, of course."

The peach-colored Kzin considered, then said, "Of course."

"The court will have a telepath to question him? They always do."

"Rrr. Your point?"

"Would you let a telepath find out what Meebrlee-Ritt saw of the telepaths of Sheathclaws? And learn how they live? *Really?*"

He didn't get it. I said, "Three hundred years living alongside Humans. Sharing their culture. Their schooling programs. Instead of theft and killing, hang gliding! Meebrlee-Ritt, tell him about Fly-By-Night."

The prisoner looked at the Patriarch's voice. He said, "I crawled on my belly for him."

Rasht-Myowr yowled. "With the -Ritt name on you? How dare you?"

"I meant it."

"Meant–"

"Do you think I was born with no pride, to take and defend a name like mine? I found I could fly the Outsider hyperdrive! I knew that I must be a -Ritt. Then fortune favored me again. A telepath lost on Shasht, healthy and arrogant, the genetic line that will give us the Longest War!

"Even after questioning, crippled, Nazi Killer tore up one of my unwary Heroes so that we had to leave him. He *knew* things about me… but Nazi Killer was no threat. Frustrating that we had to kill him, but he'd told us how to retrieve another. It was Fly-By-Night and his slaves who stripped me of everything I am! He killed my Heroes. He *became* Envoy! Reduced my ship to a falling prison."

Rasht-Myowr demanded, "Technical Officer, is your alpha officer mad?"

Tech spoke simply; his dignity was still with him. "I followed the telepath's commands exactly. What he had done to us, to him I followed, how could *I* face him? With what weapons? But Fly-By-Night was not alone. Kzin and 'man and Jotok, *they* took our ears."

I hoped then that there were unseen defenses, that nobody would have set fragile humans undefended among these Kzinti. Rasht-Myowr turned on me a gaping grin that would not let him speak. His alien stench was not that of any creature of Earth, but I knew it was his rage.

"You can't take them back to the Patriarchy," I said to Rasht-Myowr. Because they had kept faith.

* * *

Quickpony and the Van Zild children were with me when Outbound Enterprises thawed two modules of passengers taken from *Odysseus*. The way they were wrapped, I couldn't tell who was who until Jeena was wheeled out of the cooker. We clung to each other and waited. If Jeena was alive, so was her mother.

We waited, ice in our veins, and she came.

NOTES

The Deadly Future of Littoral Sea Control

1. *British Maritime Doctrine*, 3rd ed. (London: Ministry of Defence, 2004), 289.

2. Julian S. Corbett, *Some Principles of Maritime Strategy* (Annapolis, MD: Naval Institute Press, 1988 repub. of 1911 ed.).

3. CAPT Wayne P. Hughes Jr., USN (Ret.), *Fleet Tactics and Coastal Combat* (Annapolis, MD: Naval Institute Press, 2000).

4. Thomas G. Mahnken, "Weapons: The Growth & Spread of the Precision-Strike Regime," Daedalus, vol. 140, no. 3 (June 2011), 45–57. Scott C. Truver, "Taking Mines Seriously: Mine Warfare in China's Near Seas," *Naval War College Review*, vol. 65, no. 2 (Spring 2012), 30–66.

5. Randy Huiss, *Proliferation of Precision Strike: Issues for Congress* (Washington, DC: Congressional Research Service, 2012).

   Frank Gardner, "Hezbollah Missile Threat Assessed," BBC, 3 August 2006, news.bbc.co.uk/2/hi/middle_east/5242566.stm.

6. "New 3D Printing Center Aims to Boost US Manufacturing" LiveScience.com, 16 August 2012, www.livescience.com/22443-3d-printing-boost-manufacturing.html.

7. CAPT Wayne Hughes, USN (Ret.), "Take the Small Boat Threat Seriously," U.S. Naval Institute *Proceedings*, vol. 126, no. 10 (October 2000), 104–6.

8. Molly Dunigan et al., *Characterizing and Exploring the Implications of Maritime Irregular Warfare* (Arlington, VA: RAND, 2012).

9. *The Proliferation of Precision-Guided Weapons and the Future of Naval Irregular Warfare: Assessment and Implications* (Washington, DC: Center for Strategic and Budgetary Assessments, 2010).

10. Richard L. Humphrey, "Warship Damage Rules for Naval Wargaming," presentation to the TIMS/ORSA Joint National Meeting, Naval Warfare Center, Silver Spring, MD, May 1990. Hughes, *Fleet Tactics*, Figure 6-1.

11. John C. Schulte, "An Analysis of the Historical Effectiveness of Anti-ship Cruise Missiles in Littoral Warfare" (Monterey, CA: Naval Postgraduate School paper, September 1994).

    K. W. Brzozowsky and R. M. Memmesheimer, "The Application of the Sochard Ship Damage Model to World War II Ship Damage" (unpublished Naval Surface Warfare Center monograph, 1988).

12. "Ship RCS Table," www.mar-it.de/Radar/RCS/Ship_RCS_Table.pdf.

13. Sandy Woodward, *One Hundred Days: The Memoirs of the Falklands Battle Group Commander* (Annapolis, MD: Naval Institute Press, 1997). Schulte, "Analysis."

14. VADM A. K. Cebrowski, USN, and CAPT Wayne P. Hughes Jr., USN (Ret.), "Rebalancing the Fleet," U.S. Naval Institute *Proceedings*, vol. 125, no. 11 (November 1999), 31–34.

15. Richard C. Arthur, "Patrol Craft Can Maintain Littoral Sea Control," U.S. Naval Institute *Proceedings*, vol. 125, no. 8 (August 1999), 70–71.

16. "Defense Acquisition Management Information Retrieval," DAMIR website, www.acq.osd.mil/damir/.

17. Larry Bond and Chris Carlson, *Harpoon 4: Modern Tactical Naval Warfare* (Sassamansville, PA: Clash of Arms Games, 1996).

18. "Ship RCS Table."

19. Maj. Charles D. Melson, USMC (Ret.), *Condition Red: Marine Defense Battalions in World War II* (Washington, DC: Marine Corps Historical Center, 1996). CAPT Wayne P. Hughes Jr., USN (Ret.) and Jeffrey Kline, "A Flotilla to Support a Strategy of Offshore Control" (Monterey, CA: Naval Postgraduate School paper, January 2013).

20. CDR Henry J. Hendrix, USN, "More Henderson, Less Bonds," U.S. Naval Institute *Proceedings*, vol. 136, no. 4 (April 2010), 60–65.

21. Col. T. X. Hammes, USMC (Ret.), "Offshore Control is the Answer," U.S. Naval Institute *Proceedings*, vol. 138, no. 12 (December 2012), 22–25.

CPSIA information can be obtained
at www.ICGtesting.com
Printed in the USA
BVHW031724161219
566839BV00001B/7/P

9 789527 303245